To the thousands upon thousands
of women, men, and children –over
the centuries—whose entrapment in
the sugarcane fields of the Caribbean
has accounted for untold riches ---
for others!

   . . . and especially to the sacred memories
of *mi mamá* and *mi abuelita,* two formidable
women whose lives were shaped by the rigors
of working in these cane fields.

Gracias de nuevo, Julio, por tu más fiel apoyo.

. . . *y por supuesto, a tí, Carmen, que en paz descanses.*

What Critics In The Caribbean Have Said About *AZÚCAR!*

"A reading experience that is truly unique; one that conveys with intimate honesty and magical artistry the complex drama, the burdensome past, the pride and the passion of the Caribbean." *France-Antille* (Pointe-à-Pitre, Guadeloupe)

" Flight, exile, return, questions of colour, and very central to the region's literature—the quest for a sense of identity and wholeness are some of the most insistent realities in our Caribbean: Cambeira captures masterfully this reality; his narrative is spell-bounding in every sense."
Sept Magazine (Baie-Mahault, Guadeloupe)

". . . A beautiful rendering of classic Caribbean syncretism; a microcosm of the Caribbean melting pot, peopled with an entire cross-section of exciting types . . . "
Trinidad Express (Port of Spain, Trinidad/Tobago)

"A rich blending of cultural threads that produces the quintessential Caribbean hybrid; Alan Cambeira's treatment is immediately reminiscent of Luis Rafael Sánchez in his *Voyage to Caribbean Identity*."
Primera Hora (San Juan, Puerto Rico)

". . . A brilliant first novel which reveals the visionary history of a Caribbean island with an intensity and originality that dares place it alongside Lovelace, Danticat, Marshall, and Alvarez." *The Nation* (Bridgetown, Barbados)

"His (Cambeira's) writing is boldly lyrical, reflecting Caribbean sensuousness, rhythms and mysticism; this is an energetic, very unusual, and above all, enlightening novel; readers will eagerly await its inevitable sequel."
The Observer (Kingston, Jamaica)

The Antilles, The Caribbean, the West Indies . ... totally different names for just one geo-cultural region? The legendary gold-rich "Indies" of the 16th century quickly became known as the "Sugar Islands" during the 18th century. The different names for this single area reflect the extent to which the region has been defined and shaped by a succession of powerful influences from "the outside."

Azúcar (ă – zōō′ kăr): sugar

There is convincing evidence of various botanical factors that places sugarcane's site of origin in the lush valleys of northeastern India. Sometime between 1800 and 1700 B.C. sugarcane cultivation spread to China, then to the region of the Philippines, Java, and Hawaii. By the time Spanish adventurers arrived in the Pacific hundreds of years later, cane was already growing wild on many Pacific islands. The Arab conquest introduced sugar cultivation throughout the Mediterranean zone –becoming extremely profitable in the eastern end by the 15th century. As the Ottoman Turks and the Islamic rulers of North Africa encroached and eventually occupied the entire region, the sugar industry (heavily financed by Venetian and Genoese capital) moved from here altogether. The Christian Crusades initiated sugar cultivation in the conquered territories of Syria and Palestine (using Arab methods and slave labor). By the 12th century, the Crusaders were expelled from these regions and sugar operations again moved . . . now towards the western Mediterranean islands of Crete, Cyprus, and Sicily. The advancing Turks prompted the industry to continue moving westward--first to the Iberia Peninsula—where some cultivation had already been introduced earlier by the Muslim occupation, then to newly conquered islands in the Atlantic, (Madeira, the Canaries) and off the African coast (Cape Verde, Fernando Po and São Tomé). On his second voyage to the Caribbean (1493) Christopher Columbus brought sugarcane to Hispaniola (today the Island shared by Haiti and the Dominican Republic). Sugar cultivation, with the parallel development and expansion of the

African Slave Trade, began on the Island in 1506. By 1521, the first sugar exports back to Spain were well underway. By about 1527 productive *ingenios* (sugar mills) were in high gear.

batey (bă-tāy'): a word of pre-Columbian Amerindian (Taíno) origin that referred to the area in the indigenous settlement used alternately as a ceremonial ball-court and open market space. In the Spanish–speaking Caribbean the word came to mean the area of a large sugarcane plantation occupied by living accommodations for workers, grocery stores or *bodegas*, as well as the sugar factory operations and related buildings. Today. the *batey* is now widely synonymous with the squalid, often substandard living quarters of the contract sugarcane workers regularly recruited from around the Caribbean.

*****

ALAN CAMBEIRA was born in Samaná, República Dominicana. He emigrated with his family first to Barbados, then to Pennsylvania. He holds a Bachelor's Degree in Spanish, a Master's Degree in Latin American and Caribbean Literatures, and a Doctorate in Latin American and Caribbean Cultures. In addition to numerous published articles in both Spanish and English about various aspects of Caribbean and Latin American culture, he has published *La fobia antihaitiana en la cultura dominicana* (1987). *Quisqueya La Bella: The Dominican Republic in Historical and Cultural Perspective* (1997). *¿Quiénes son los dominicanos? Caleidoscopio turbulento* (2002).He has been the recipient of a National Endowment for the Humanities Award, as well as a Presidential Scholars - Distinguished Teachers Award.

UNO

It was as though the gods were engaged in some sadistic competition among themselves to see who could create the hottest day for all living creatures. The tropical sun was oppressive; the heat was relentless, with no gentle breezes to temper its fury. Although the incessant chorus of the many different species of birds could be heard in every direction, the feathered chorus members themselves were nowhere to be seen since, as if on cue, they knew precisely when to seek relief from the afternoon heat deep within the thick, luxuriant foliage of the expansive flamboyán trees, with their readily accessible and welcomed camouflage of huge crimson-colored blossoms. There was also a sanctuary of coolness to be found under the abundant cover of the tamarind, the macaw, the guanábana, the guayába groves with their flowery fragrances, or beneath the huge umbrella-like jackfruit and breadfruit trees with their large, lustrous leaves.

The afternoon heat was no match for any mortals on the compound of the century-old sugarcane plantation that had been named *Esperanza Dulce*, "Sweet Hope," by its original owners. Slave labor, in 1839, had constructed the massive plantation, extending some 11,000 *tareas*, which was equivalent to about 754 square yards per *tarea*. At one time the plantation boasted of having a railroad network of almost five miles, so extensive were the sugarcane fields. The owners were an aristocratic family of Creole descent, having formed part of the early planter élite that had fled the ravages and excesses of Dessalines and Christophe following the triumph of the slave uprising on the other side of the Island. One of the Island's oldest and largest plantations, this had been the classic *ingenio* of the long-gone colonial era: magnificent *Casa Grande*, "Big House" or manor, an infirmary, a chapel, acres and acres of

1

sugarcane fields— the legendary *cañaverales* visible from all directions and stretching to the horizon, grinding mill, warehouses, housing for the plantation managers, ample quarters for the slaves— often numbering in the hundreds on the larger estates.

Nowadays the sugarcane workers at *Esperanza Dulce* lived in the *batey*, an ignominious site of substandard dwellings whose actual structural condition could only be described as squalid and miserable. The easily victorious heat at this hottest point of the day played unexaggerated havoc with the open sewage trough that meandered through the entire length of the decrepit housing compound of some seventy-five or so separated, single-room, wooden cabins with zinc roofs. Some observers might be readily inclined to define the dwellings as shacks or huts; in some instances there were larger barrack-like structures provided for housing work crews made up of single men, mainly the contracted migrant laborers, *braceros*, from neighboring islands.

Living conditions in the *batey* were precarious at best. Despite being provided free to the workers, such housing was sorely inadequate. There was neither electricity nor disposal for waste; no drinking water; no indoor plumbing of any kind; no sewage or draining system; no medical dispensary. Dysentery, malaria, and tuberculosis were common among residents. Many children easily displayed symptoms of malnutrition and the majority of school-aged youngsters simply did not attend school because of the urgency to contribute to the household income by themselves working in the fields. Besides, in most cases there was no school whatsoever in the *batey*. Nothing much had changed here since the era of plantation slavery.

Heat vapors rose from the fowl-smelling, slow-flowing sludge as it oozed along the narrow, shallow trough. The unforgiving malice of the sun's rays seemed to be baking the repugnant conglomerate of ingredients that made up the discarded garbage of each cabin along both sides of the route of the trough. One could discern floating lazily in the sludge intermingling animal and human dung; stale urine; castoff, rotting food (what little there was to throw away); infants' diapers dirtied by dried excrement; heavily soiled feminine napkins encrusted with putrid blood; the decomposed carcass of somebody's cat smothered in maggots; emptied sardine tins; broken bottles; empty, crushed beer cans — a genuinely eclectic collection of trash. The stench was beyond any odor imaginable . . . and so the heat certainly didn't help matters.

The afternoon's uncontested heat was the bitter enemy of everything delicate and prone to speedy dehydration. But of course, though, none of these observations applied to the men, women, and children who worked the sugarcane fields everyday except Sundays. They all had a job to perform and they were expected to do it. Damn the sun's ominous rays! While Nature's other creatures were routinely fortunate enough to obtain refuge under the protective awning of the trees, the mortal souls of the *batey* were condemned like shackled prisoners to anywhere from twelve to fourteen hours of unremitting toil, eight in the fields and up to six indoors in the oven-hot mill. Assignment in the fields, working row upon row of sugarcane stalks was particularly hard. There, under the brutal afternoon sun, bent low in the traditional stooped position of sugarcane cutters, with trusted, but lethal machete in the right hand, the workers whacked! whacked! whacked! at the thick, tough 12-foot high stalks. The cutter held the cane stalk in the left hand, then first hacked off the leaves with one swift, downward stroke of the machete. Moving quickly along the long rows, the worker then cut the cane as near as possible to the ground with a second swift stroke of the razor-sharp machete and just as quickly, threw the stalk aside, out of the way. Frequently an exhausted *bracero* would accidentally whack his own lower legs, shins, ankles, feet, toes; one careless, misplaced stroke of the machete could do serious damage to a worker's extremities, leaving the wretched soul permanently scared or maimed. The work was treacherous and the sun seemed to derive some kind of sinister glee from this grotesque spectacle of human suffering beneath the torture of its rays.

So, the *batey* was rendered completely still by the angry sun. Except for the chirping of what seemed to be the entire aviary and the steady, slow ripple of the offensive trough, there were absolutely no other discernible sounds or movement of any kind. Even the air was still during this time of day. Then without warning, the torrid afternoon stillness was pierced by the sudden sharpness of a bone-crushing shriek ... one loud, horrifying cry of a human creature in the throes of some unrecognizable terror. The cry was long and painful, disrupted intermittently by short, uncontrollable screams and desperate gasps for breath.

"*No! No me mate! Suélteme*! No! Don't kill me! Let me go!" Then the equally dreadful, steady cry, "Help! Por favor! *Alguien, socórreme, por favor*! Please, somebody help me!" These were the frightening cries of a young child in agonizing pain. The shrill cry rang out again . . . . then was smothered. All the anguish within that child erupted violently; the voice became a single, terrifying scream . . . believing that death was imminent. Didn't anyone hear her?

Trouble was certainly nothing new or out of the ordinary in the batey. Sadly, just the opposite was true. The *batey* regularly witnessed more than the norm for trouble, in addition to its shameful misery and despicable squalor. Traditionally, the *batey* exemplified trouble. Violent physical altercations were common: inhabitants of the *batey* would fight upon the most trivial of provocation and it need not be sparked necessarily by drunkenness. False accusations of theft; cheating at an otherwise amicable game of dominos; a seemingly harmless, however truthful remark about a neighbor's ill-behaved children; dancing too closely with someone else's paramour, especially when the two unmatched partners should not have been dancing together in the first place.

But the startling nature of this incessant cry for help ... in the blazing heat of the afternoon when every living being residing in the *batey* was supposed to be in the fields whacking sugarcane stalks and routinely engaging in the arduous tasks associated with this plantation crop... evoked particular doom. No one among the work crew had been privileged to remain behind for any reason, however plausibly humane.

The screams grew louder and louder, shriller than before and seemingly more heavily laced with extreme pain, seemingly more torturous. The screams were definitely those of a young female in trouble--- not a very young child, but also not a fully adult woman. The young girl's voice, quivering with an unidentifiable fright, then let forth ponderously abandoned shrieks. Shock waves ripped through the thickness of the flamboyán trees, the colorful blossoms and leafy foliage of which had earlier served as a respite from the unmerciful heat for the many birds lodged there. The sudden flurry of commotion by the birds in the trees easily shook loose the delicate petals of crimson, causing them to fall hopelessly to the ground below.

The screams were coming from the far end of the *batey*, one of the last rows of cabins that lined the central sewage trough. Almost all of the residents disliked this section of the quarters

5

because it was the most isolated . . . even though the few cabins here offered more interior space, had a side window and had been built with a back door. Besides being situated next to the widest part of the open trough, where the trough itself eventually flowed into the nearby channel bed, this section of dwellings was far removed from the hub of social activity for the community. The residents didn't congregate aimlessly in this section of the quarters as they did at what was called "up at the gate," which was the main entrance into the quarters. Also, the walking distance from this far end to the cane fields was a considerably lengthy walk. A few of the cabins here were unoccupied at the time; but they would soon house more families (always exceeding the occupancy maximum for each dwelling) as harvest time approached and many more contract laborers would be arriving from many other islands around the Caribbean where unemployment remained acute.

The screams, now wilder and more relentless than before, poured out of old Doña Felicidad's cabin. This was the very last one on the row, separated from the two unoccupied shacks by an ample *conuco*, the old woman's modest vegetable garden that she herself had planted some time ago and maintained regularly. But the old widow Doña Felicidad wasn't inside. Despite her undisclosed age (she truthfully didn't know her own age, only that she was born long ago one Easter Sunday at the nearby *Santa Flor ingenio*), she was alongside the other sugarcane workers . . . laboring still in the afternoon sun.

Doña Felicidad, or Doña Fela, as just about everybody inside the batey affectionately called her, occupied the cabin with her granddaughter Azúcar, her only known blood relative. Azúcar was a timid and recalcitrant, but sweetly beautiful 13-year old waif whose birth mother had been the only child of Doña Felicidad. Absolutely no one could recall having heard anything about the actual particulars of Doña Fela's life. When or where

6

was she born? (Someone once speculated on the neighboring plantation). Who were her parents? Did she have any brothers or sisters?

Exactly when did she herself arrive at *Esperanza Dulce*? "She just seemed to always have been here," most people said. Practically everyone else living in the batey arrived a long time after Doña Fela. At any rate, Azúcar's mother had died while delivering the child. The child's suspected father (whose real identify was never quite certain) had been hacked to death by machete during a drunken brawl involving several fellow sugarcane workers when Azúcar was almost a year old; the father had been accused of stealing a piglet from a neighbor's sty. It was learned a few days following the burial of Azúcar's father that the piglet had somehow escaped from the sty and was found in the nearby woods. The little boy who witnessed the animal's escape never told anyone what he had seen that day. "Nobody asked me," was all he could reply fearfully when his father, upon overhearing him tell his younger brothers, wondered why the boy had never spoken up to possibly save an innocent man's life. Thus, Azúcar grew up without ever knowing her birth parents, only Doña Fela.

Young Azúcar was not a sickly soul, even given the fact of her scraggy body frame ... some would describe her as delicate like the flamboyán petals; she was certainly just as beautiful and frail. Since all able-bodied youngsters in the batey were expected to work alongside the adult members of the labor crew in the sugarcane fields, Azúcar was therefore no exception. But for some unknown reason, she was there in the cabin that hot afternoon. Perhaps she had become dehydrated or had fallen ill because of the intense heat. Maybe she had not eaten enough earlier that morning to sustain her throughout the day. Nevertheless, the maddening screams coming from inside Doña Fela's house were unmistakably those of little Azúcar.

As it happened, Azúcar was not alone. She was there ... being viciously attacked by Mario, the oldest of the three sons of the *capataz*, the plantation foreman, a position that during the colonial period was that of slave overseer. Mario was considered handsome with his deep-set, large dark eyes that were constantly darting about his surroundings; his eyelashes were thick and black, like the heavy stock of black, shiny, curly hair that hung low into his lively eyes; his complexion was a rich tropical *trigueño*, a kind of perpetually dark-colored wheat, with dramatically contrasting large white teeth that sparkled under his thick black mustache. His features were broad and rough: the nose, cheeks and chin; fleshy, sensuous lips encasing a wide mouth. But Mario was a monster of a man; his back and muscularly framed, six-foot, three-inches-tall body was like the mammoth ceiba tree; his forearms bulged like giant iron hammers; there was thickly-matted and profusely sweaty surface hair on seemingly every inch of that massive, malodorous frame.

Mario was crude in behavior, boisterous in tone, always ill-tempered and ready to fight; he was overly confident of his physical prowess, deliberately stalking his prey simply to provoke the combat in which he knew he would be the undisputed victor. Mario was a predator of the worst sort. Women of the *batey* ... or more precisely, only those women who weren't the least bit sexually attracted to or perversely curious about him...were fearful of him; men, however much the pugilist themselves, avoided arguments with him. Despite the fact that Mario was married to the beautiful daughter of one of the most prominent families in the region, he could be spotted sniffing around the quarters like any unleashed animal in heat, on the prowl any given late night, but most especially on weekends.

Now, in the middle of that scorching afternoon while everyone else was out in the fields cutting sugarcane stalks,

8

Mario was inside Doña Fela's cabin; the beast was raping the defenseless Azúcar. She was screaming desperately for her life.

"Please stop! No! Don't! You hurtin' me!" the little girl was screaming at the top of her tender lungs . . . struggling with all her earthly might against the crippling power of the beast. Although she fought with every ounce of strength that she was able to summon up, she was hardly a match for the monster.

"*Cállate, dulcecita.* Shut up, you sweet little thing! Let me taste some of that sweet sugar!" he growled menacingly and quickly smothered her tiny mouth with his fleshy lips. This frightened the young virgin even more. The animal was managing a forcible entry inside her with his huge penis, plunging deep and hard. At the same time he was snatching clumsy, wet and soggy kisses from her face and neck. He had the child pinned against the wall before roughly tossing her onto the only cot in the cabin; this was where Doña Fela slept.

"*Caña dulce.* Sweet sugarcane! So sweet!" he said as he drove his beastly pipe deeper. "*Te gusta*? Do you like it? Don't you wanna give just a little piece to *papi* ? I know you like it. Just shut up and enjoy it," the monster roared this time. "You'll be a real woman when I finish with you."

With that, a terrible blow crashed suddenly and hard across Azúcar's tiny face. The child thought that her head would burst open . . . the pain was so shattering. He continued striking her repeatedly with his giant, hairy paw. . . the blows landing across her upper body. She tried in vain to protect herself from the torrent of blows by using her hands and arms as shields; at the same time she was trying to prevent the painful, unwelcome thrusts of the nightmarish penis. She kicked, scratched, cried. . . in this strangely new terror that engulfed her.

"*Por favor.* Please stop. You hurtin' me. Don't," she begged for mercy between painful cries. But the beast wouldn't stop. He

9

kept up his vile thrusts, delighting in each deeper plunge. She was growing weaker with every thrust. Her virgin blood was everywhere about her and on Doña Fela's cot. The scene was grotesquely horrifying, one that would be indelibly engraved upon her memory. It would haunt her for a long time to come. It seemed as if the brutal assault continued for hours without an end in sight; repeatedly the hairy monster went deeper inside the timid, previously unspoiled young flesh. Repeatedly the frightened girl screamed with all her quickly disappearing energy . . . but no one heard the screams.

"*Ay, Espíritu Santo, en el nombre de mi madre ya fallecida, déjeme morir!*" she prayed to herself in sorrow. "In the name of my dead mother, let me die and join her!"

Azúcar was in sheer agony beyond anything her tender years could ever possibly conjure up. But she refused to faint ; she somehow sustained the blows as well as the forceful, uninvited thrusts that were tearing at her insides.

"Please, somebody, make him stop!" But the beast would not stop until he was thoroughly satisfied that he had become the victor of yet another of his shameless quests. "Oh, Sacred Spirit, let me die!" The child was enduring insufferable pain.

Her grandmother had made the smock-like dress that Azúcar wore that day. It was now hideously bloodstained and ripped to near shreds, hanging unattractively on her damaged frame. Doña Fela's customarily neatly kept cabin looked as if the routinely arriving hurricane had burst through in all its fury well ahead of season. Now satisfied, Mario at last finished his savage torture and casually slipped out the back door of the cabin without muttering any parting words —just the normally ravenous smirk of triumph registering across his face. Under the watchful glare of the afternoon sun, he disappeared into the nearby woods, much like that neighbor's piglet had done some years ago and occasioned the death of Azúcar's father. The damaged angel felt like she too had died this blisteringly hot, sunny afternoon in the batey.

"What did I do wrong to receive this punishment?" Azúcar continued to cry a mournful, loud cry. Not a single living soul heard her.

DOS

From the side of the nearby hill there appeared a dull redness as the sun began to sink behind the woods and the sugarcane fields. Before too long, night would shroud the entire compound in a different world, masked in an unrevealing costume far removed from the toils of the fields. Misery would be drowned in the shadows of delirious revelry and sleep. Then dawn would rise again with the crowing of cocks and the day would be resurrected ... but a resurrection without joy since the new day would be just as miserable as the one before. It was early evening; the batey would now get its much-deserved reprieve from the unmerciful torture of the afternoon heat. All the laborers, drenched in pure, hard-earned sweat, would be returning to the compound, having finished a full day in the fields or inside the mill.

Despite the backbreaking chores associated with working in sugarcane production, the compound was immediately enlivened with a new burst of energy from its overworked and exploited residents. This was their time on their own terms. The end of each day's grueling work was sufficient cause for the most minor of festivities . . . thus permitting the deserving workers to forget however briefly that day's ordeal. The traditional "three *D*s" of the *batey* --dominos, dancing, and drinking-- succeeded in anesthetizing the laborers, sweeping them away to drown in those deeper zones of unreal euphoria and peril where powerful forces reigned supreme. Heard from a short distance away from the front entrance to the compound was the returning crew of exhausted workers, literally including the entire congregation of *batey* residents. They were readily betrayed by their unrestrained rowdiness, raucous laughter, playful banter and spontaneous ribaldry.

Their paradoxically good-humored spirit announced that the day of toil was done. The *batey* was indeed a non-hypocritical entity, totally unlike the twisted, deceitful world of the mill owners, wherein the laborers were well aware of circumstances around them. Here in the *batey*, in all its characteristic quagmire of unattractiveness, deprivation, and abject misery, where children frequently could be heard crying from hunger, where anger and frustration were never repressed, and where a mere spark could instantly ignite into a blaze of violence . . . things were quite predicable and real.

Moreover, life here was extremely regimented. The inhabitants recognized this and therefore found themselves circumscribed by the regimented patterns and requirements of the Island's plantation agriculture that had reigned supreme for centuries. So all in all, the returning laborers were relieved to be ending their day within this kind of waiting predictability. The slightest breath of wind began to glide down over the flamboyán and macaw trees, landing in a sustained, rustling whisper, and the trek homeward was made all the more delightful to the laborers. Sunset had not yet come, but as the workers neared the compound, everybody anticipated the night's activities. Through the rising dust on the road leading to the compound, men, women, and children moved in an almost uninterrupted file...much like the historical African slave gangs that had been corralled for waiting slave ships and forced at gun-point to march through miles of forest.

Behind them were the immense sugarcane fields, the individual stalks registering bitter anger that they were being left abandoned for the night; the ox carts used to take away the green *bagasse* (crushed cane stalks) were now idle; the grinders and boilers at the sugar mill were silent. Ahead of them were the fowl-smelling trough and the adjacent cabins where, with the approach of evening after an undeniably torturous day, the *braceros* would nevertheless be able to rest their tired souls, surrounded by their comrades in shared misery. One man in the line directed a double-entendre question to a female cutter.

"*Oye*, Serafina, wha' you be sellin' tonight?" he asked, flashing a raunchy grin as he held up both his hands to his chest and began juggling an imaginary pair of sizeable melons in a manner of unmistakable sensuality. Other workers in the line laughed with relish at the exchange between Serafina and the man . . . certain to spark an ongoing, spirited retort equally as risqué.

"*Ay, m'hijo*, depend on what you wanna' be buyin'," the irreverent, quick-witted woman teased him. "I sure as hell ain't givin' nothin' away free."

Sarafina's bawdy laughter was contagious, since everybody understood quite clearly her coded remarks and thus laughed along with her.

"That's right, Sarafina," chimed in one of Sarafina's companions. "Tell that *papi chulo* that ain't nothin' free 'round here." At this, the entire work crew line erupted into hysterics.

"What time we startin' the dance tonight?" somebody wanted to know.

"See everybody back at The Pit 'round nine o'clock?" volunteered another person. There was no disagreement; the matter was settled just as arbitrarily.

'The Pit' was the open-air, sunken spot, caused from years of steady erosion of an earlier outdoor cooking pit or "*fogón*" that had long since been covered with mounds of dirt and debris from the old sugar mill house grinding stone, located near the front gates. This was the designated spot where impromptu dances took place most evenings when it didn't rain. A live combo of drummers and other percussionists, a guitarist and perhaps a singer usually provided the music. More elaborate dances were held on national holidays and harvest festivals, and of course, during the annual Carnival. Then, traditionally, the administration officials or mill owners would be responsible for bringing in professional musicians. Everybody returning from the fields was anxious to get out of their sweaty, rank work clothes, head for the shallow spring located in the woods where some residents bathed, or from which many other individuals preferred hauling buckets of water to their cabins for less public bathing. Then they would sit down to whatever subsistence meal could be scraped together, before heading up to The Pit.

By some magically orchestrated design, the family of occupants of each cabin lining both sides of the central trough would wave their good-byes, step out from the file of workers, and then vanish into the darkness of their hovel.

"See you later," a departing member would yell out. "*Hasta luego.*"

Doña Fela was always among the last group of persons to depart from the returning crew along the passage route because her cabin was one of those isolated ones at the far end of the trough. Because she knew practically everyone in the *batey* — being one of the longest residing members there and one of the oldest, she especially enjoyed the eager stroll back from the fields. Even though she too had labored all day in the hot sun and was tired and spent of all human energy, she nevertheless took extra delight in being able to chat and gossip with everybody along the way. Doña Fela actually held a very special position in the *batey*. She was the undisputed matriarch of this close-knot community and everybody dutifully revered her senior status. This daily return trek from the cane fields therefore afforded most individuals the opportunity to express their sense of respect for their saintly mother, which is how they regarded Doña Fela. She herself took special pleasure in being able to socialize freely and regularly with her "children" ...as she regarded her comrades and neighbors, often dispensing advice or picking up news of various sorts.

"You heard about the new load of all them Haitians and St. Lucians that's comin' in for the *zafra*?" Doña Fela asked her neighbor Clementina, a much younger woman with just one eye; there was a nondescript blank socket left in place where the other eye should have been.

When she was about five or six years old, Azúcar had asked her grandmother about the puzzling socket, which at first frightened the child. Doña Fela explained that Clementina had lost her eye as a child while working alongside her mother, a cutter in the sugarcane fields. The accident occurred one afternoon long ago when the child's mother was cutting stalks and didn't see her small child sitting beneath the stalks, worn out from working and trying to escape the unbearable heat. One swift stroke of her mother's machete took the child's eye. One-eyed Clementina lived with her husband and six children in one of the cabins also located at the far end.

"They say this will be one of the biggest loads yet. I don't doubt it."

Clementina, like everyone else, of course, knew that many more laborers from around the Caribbean would be contracted as always for the rapidly approaching *zafra*, those particularly hectic months of harvest normally between late December and early May, when everybody worked for extremely long hours each day. It was predicted that this season would produce a usually abundant crop; it was thought that there wouldn't be enough manual labor available for harvesting the crop. So, the estate management would naturally have to contract an exceptionally large work force. As long as sugar production remained basically dependent on large numbers of unskilled or semi-skilled laborers, the producers needed a continuous labor supply.

Clementina wasn't aware that workers from as far away as the eastern island of St. Lucia, part of the Windward group, would be arriving as well.

"*No me digas*! You don't say," another neighbor replied in curiosity. "I got my problems with those damn "*Ou konpran*" from Haiti, but those Black Caribs from St. Lucia can be worse.

"*Eh verda'*," added Clementina's husband Tomás, a jovial, tall, well-built, dark chocolate-hued man. "I once worked alongside some of 'um in Barbados. Expect some real trouble with this new mix. They got no shame... they just like wild dogs, I'm tellin' you."

"Where they goin' to put all them folks?" Clementina wondered aloud.

"The two empty cabins next to mine," Doña Fela said, gesturing toward the unoccupied cabins just ahead. "I heard the capataz gonna build a few more before the hurricanes come."

It was true that the foreman had indeed been ordered by central administration to construct additional barracks for the expected new arrivals that would be needed for the arriving cane harvest. The *batey* was already terribly overcrowded and there simply was nowhere to house an expected influx of more workers. Clementina and her family had reached their cabin and so they too bid their "*buenas noches*" and "*hasta mañanas*."

"*Buenas noches*," Doña Fela," both Clementina and Tomás said, gesturing a kindly kiss to the old woman, whom they genuinely loved and regarded as the community's Mother.

"Want me to come over later to see about Azúcar?" Clementina quickly remembered to ask Doña Fela. "She did make us all kind of nervous this afternoon with that awful sun beatin' down. I thought the capataz wasn't gone to let her leave the field; that old slave driver can be such a mean ol' bastard." Since her own childhood misfortune, Clementina was extremely sensitive to unattended children.

"No, child, you go and get a good night's rest for tomorrow. The day starts so early and you need to sleep," Doña Fela said. "I'm sure Azúcar just fine, *gracias*. Too much heat, that's all. She left on a empty stomach this mornin'. Couldn't get her to eat a thin'. Well, *buena' noche', mih niñoh.*"

Just a few more workers remained among those individuals living at this end of the central trough. A short walk further along and the line of workers grew thinner still. Doña Fela would soon be the last member of the returning crew. Normally, Doña Fela and Azúcar walked together— having done so since the child was about eight years of age. That was when she started working alongside her grandmother in the fields. There were many other young girls and boys the same age who had begun working then. Since the early days of the huge sugarcane plantations and slave labor all around the Caribbean, sugar production had always demanded a great number of workers who had to accomplish their tasks in a very important and specific period of time. So, planters pressed into service every physically able body to perform the grueling tasks of production.

Doña Fela finally neared where she lived. She was almost broken down under the weight of an immense fatigue for someone her age, especially this particular day under the boiling hot sun. Even so, she never failed to enjoy the personal and private delights of her existence, which she shared with her granddaughter on their return from the fields. These were things in her surroundings that had long buttressed her soul against the cruel harshness and unwarranted ugliness of life in the batey: the banana trees swaying seductively under the silky caress of the evening breezes, the bit of silvery evening light shimmering over the curtain of thorn acacias unfolding along the road; the seductive fragrance of the multicolored lilacs growing wild in the woods; the sound of the guinea fowl in those same woods, uttering their fervid call; decorative mass of rocks along the road, spurting long, elegant stems of amaryllis with necklaces of yellow blossoms; the spider ferns overrunning the banks of the shallow spring; her precious little *conuco* of tubers like ñames, yuca, and yautía, providing a constant supply of basic foodstuffs for her table. This, together with her sweet Azúcar, was the magical anesthesia for Doña Fela.

TRES

Doña Fela's cabin was tucked back under the quiet shade of a few calabash trees, in the tiny yard in front, distanced several feet from the sewage trough with its foul, decomposed odor. Since the trough was wide at this end of the passageway, she was always mindful to walk along the side on which her cabin was situated so that she would not have to try jumping across the trough. Her advanced years wouldn't have permitted this feat. The *conuco* at the side of the house added an ironic token of permanency to the place. Located as it was just at the edge of the woods, the spot was actually lovely and Doña Fela was duly proud of her home. She had worked in earnest to make it a place of serenity and modest comfort.

She was suddenly perplexed as to why Azúcar was not outside in front to greet her. After all, the child had been sent home earlier in the day because of visible fatigue; for whatever strange reason, the *capataz* had been uncharacteristically generous that day. Most times, laborers who fell ill— as determined by the overseer or crew leader-- during work are allowed to rest for a very brief period before being ordered back at the task. Time is always such a vital issue in sugar production. Not that the old woman was worried; she wasn't. Doña Fela was confident that her granddaughter would regain her stamina once she had eaten something. But there was a foreboding in the atmosphere. Something was not right. Doña Fela felt a cold chill. She clenched her fist.

"Azúcar! Azúcar!" she heard herself yelling loudly. There was no answer from inside the cabin. A continuous flow of mournful sobs could be heard over the uneasy cackling of the few guinea hens and chickens in the yard; they had not been fed all day. They were pecking aimlessly at the naked ground. The sobs increased in volume before changing to loud cries. Azúcar was still crying when her grandmother burst into the cabin to gaze upon an otherwise consistently tidy interior that was now in a state of unexplainable disarray. The blood-stained bed covering was in a tumbled heap on the floor; the rickety little kitchen table, normally made stable by a cinder block supporting one of the legs, now lay on its side; one of the two wicker chairs was ripped apart; the few treasured dishes were broken rubble scattered across the floor. The back door was wide open; one of the guinea hens had found its way inside.

"*Ay, Espíritu santo; en nombre de to' loh santo,*" was the only thing that the old woman could manage to yell, calling upon all the saints. "May the sacred ancestors help me. I call upon Manayèt!

Both grandmother and granddaughter connected with their teary eyes. Doña Fela rushed toward her distraught granddaughter, and in one giant swoop grabbed her up to her bosom. She pressed Azúcar to her. Both her strong, ancient arms engulfed the crying child. With her eyes closed, and in a voice weaker than a baby's breath, Doña Fela murmured, "*Mi azúcar morenita.* My little brown sugar lump! What they done to you? Who done this to you?"

Through the grandmother's tired eyelids, copious tears continued to flow. She refused to surrender to all the weariness of the long day's toil in the fields under the scorching sun. She was stoic in her grief as the wounded child curled up against the old woman's bosom. Doña Fela drew her traumatized granddaughter tighter and tighter to her old, tired bosom. Azúcar buried her swollen, bruised and wet face in her grandmother's supportive chest.

"*Por favor, abuelita!* Please don't let him hurt me! Please make him stop!" the child cried out in near delirium.

The grandmother looked down at her wounded angel, whose eyes were swollen from much crying and were dimmed, whose garment was torn beyond mending and was blood-soaked. Doña Fela immediately felt the strain of her many years of slave-like confinement to the sugarcane fields, biting her lip in order to maintain a muted, but bitter acceptance of the constant indignation and abuses of the planter, the planter's wife and family, *the capataz*, the crew leaders and everybody else connected with "*la maldita caña*," the cursed sugarcane. Her anger began to boil to the point that she felt her own hot blood running rapidly through the canals of her old tired body like a network of veins transporting renewed life to the depths of her being.

"Tell me what happened, child," the grandmother insisted, rolling her head back, her eyes turning upward to the ceiling of the cabin. Then she closed her eyes in silent anger.

The only word the child could manage was, "*Señor* Mario!" and again, "*Señor* Mario!"

The old woman understood, biting down so hard on her lip that it was bleeding slightly. At that, the child broke into a long, agonizing cry. She didn't need to say anything more. Doña Fela understood perfectly. She spoke with a slow, very deliberate and bitter vehemence, but in a low voice, as if the night itself were listening.

"That shameless bastard from hell. He'll be sorry for what he did to my innocent *azúcar morenita*. I swear on everything that is sacred. May the thunder turn me to ashes and the spirit of Mayanèt herself put out my old eyes if I don't get my revenge before I leave this miserable earth. They all will pay. *Todo' lo' malvados ban a pagá.*"

In the darkness of the ransacked room, Azúcar could only imagine how twisted with rage her grandmother's face was. Ironically, a strange, new kind of fear gripped the child's heart. She, of course, had never known her grandmother to become so infuriated. Upon thinking about it, in fact, the child had never before now seen her grandmother cry even a single tear. Doña Fela released the girl gently and hurried out into the tiny front yard.

She called as loudly as she could, "Clementina. Tomás. Clementina. Come quick. I need you! Clementina!" Controlled rage was evident in the tone of her voice. *"Vengan rápido. Leh necesito."*

The light of the distant stars in the night sky by now twinkled playfully and dizzily. Lanterns and fires from the small, outdoor fogón, where the residents cooked their meals over firewood, provided the only lighting at night throughout the *batey*. Shadows danced across the grounds of the compound like jagged streams in the moonlight. Silhouettes along the walls of the cabins suggested the activities of the occupants inside.

Not only Clementina and Tomás heard Doña Fela's cries for help, but also practically everyone else living in close proximity did. The anticipated night's festivities at The Pit had not begun as yet; it was still too early for the crowds to congregate. So, even though Doña Fela's calls were meant for her neighbors immediately next to her, there was an automatic, general response to the old woman's clearly recognized peril. Doña Fela didn't have to call again. Clementina, Tomás and the two oldest of their six children came running toward the calls; so did another neighboring couple, Lolita and her Haitian-born husband Estimé; also the couple that lived across from them, Cirilo and Teresa, along with her brother Ramón.

Within a few minutes a small crowd of people who had been on their way up to The Pit for the evening were now standing in Doña Fela's front yard. Then it seemed as though all attention turned immediately to an even larger group of people rushing in the direction of the far end of the trough.

"Somethin's happened down at Doña Fela's," someone shouted.

"She all right?" questioned anonymously another voice rushing to the scene of the commotion.

By now there seemed to be a convocation representing every corner of the *batey* gathered in Doña Fela's tiny front yard. The crowd was rapidly overflowing across the trough. Because of everybody's total and unconditional respect for this village elder, there was more than just idle curiosity on their part.

"She hurt?" asked one woman anxiously, standing toward the rear of the assembly and unable to see for herself because of the thickness of people huddled together.

"It's not Doña Fela," replied someone also unable to see, so was passing the word back to all the others at the rear of the crowd. "It 's her young granddaughter."

The crowd was made aware of exactly what had happened to Doña Fela's innocent granddaughter during the afternoon while everybody else was in the cane fields or in the mill. Mario, the mean-spirited eldest son of the *capataz*, Don Diego, found out that young Azúcar had been sent back to the camp because of extreme fatigue and near dehydration. Mario had secretly followed her there and brazenly forced his way into the cabin. The *capataz*'s son then brutally raped her and left her nearly bleeding to death.

"So, what's gonna happened to him?" one worker wanted to know. "Anybody tell Don Diego what his son did?"

There was instant silence. Both questions went unanswered because nobody wanted to venture an answer and possibly be misquoted later. Dispensing inaccurate or often exaggerated information or circulating rumors, however trivial-- especially about the *capataz* or his family, or any of the estate managers-- could prove dangerous and even lead to a worker's immediate dismissal. No one, whether island local or contracted *bracero*, wanted to risk eviction. Without exaggeration, this undoubtedly was the most damnable fate possible for a worker. So, nobody dared offer an answer.

But one person did dare to speak up. He was an old man, not as old as Doña Fela, but nevertheless quite old. His voice did not hesitate or quiver, but was very resolute, direct, and strong.

"*Coño*! When you folks goin' to let some sense into your head?" as he began his admonition to the attentive crowd. "This bunch of swine, cowards all of 'um, is the same they always been. *Carajo*! Damn it to hell! Used to be when the *capataz* would tear the skin off your back with his whip if we wasn't movin' fast enough . . . didn't matter none if it was woman or man, or even a child! But, all that changed. All this *vaina* gotta eventually change!"

The daring old man, his small, leathery black face covered with narrow gorges and deep crevices worn by the rays of the mean tropical sun, now moved almost center stage to position himself before the congregation. He lifted his noble, old head higher in order to allow his voice to cascade down upon the respectful crowd. His was a surprisingly powerful boom of a voice for a man his age. His strong voice roared on.

"Tellin' the *capataz* or even the plantation managers wouldn't help nothin' or nobody. Defilin' our virgin sweetness ain't nothin' new. *Ay, sí*, it's evil ... but those swine is evil. They always been evil; they always will be evil 'til change come. They do whatever they want to. Who we to them? We nothin' but poor, black slaves they brung here to cut their damn sugarcane and make them rich! We all the same to them. Don't make no difference. Dominicans, Haitians, Jamaicans, St. Lucians, Bajans, Anguillans, Trinidadians. All the same— just plain nothing! But without our black asses, wouldn't be no sugarcane, no sugar ... and without sugar, where would this shit-ass eatin' island be? I'm tellin' you, the situation gonna stay the way it is 'til you change it. Goddammit!"

The old cane cutter haranguing his fellow workers was the enigmatic old Don Anselmo, the "wise old man of the *batey, el sabio del batey*," with his indomitable, warrior spirit passed down to him from the ancestors. The old man was characterized by his pinpoint accuracy in always disregarding the trivia in life's circumstances. Old Anselmo himself didn't know if he was sixty or sixty-five or sixty-eight; there were no available documents to prove the date of his birth. He was ageless; his skin glistened with a penetrating blackness that he wore with ancestral pride. The coarse hair, what little was left around the temples, still had not turned white, neither had his short, unruly beard. He was short and thin, but the veins running the length of both arms were clearly visible and thick. His eyes were small, sharp and set close together; these were the eyes of wisdom, of pain, of pride...all mixed together. But deceptively so. Don Anselmo, despite the inexactness of his advanced years, was a wiry, agile, and strong little man with strong hands and back and an even stronger spirit. He had worked at various jobs on the estate, but preferred working in the fields mostly because he had more of an opportunity here than elsewhere to talk freely with his fellow workers. There was very little idle talk allowed inside the mill, so precision-oriented were the tasks there.

He was part of the large group of "permanent old hands," as they were called --laborers who had lived and worked on this plantation longer than most people could remember. They had been "contracted" long ago to "come n' work the sugar," as the expression goes. Only Doña Fela held the distinction of having lived here in this misery longer. Don Anselmo, together with his three brothers and their father and mother, had come with one of the first large gangs of contracted *braceros*, when ownership of the estate passed into the hands of a private Canadian investment corporation.

It was never quite clear whether Anselmo's father was Haitian or Dominican; all the members of the father's side of the family had been born somewhere in what was called *la zona fronteriza*, "the frontier zone." Most people always referred to this region as *la tierra de nadie*, "no man's land," because neither government on either side of the river ever reconciled the issue regarding exactly who owned this territory. Traditionally, much harmonious social and cultural interchange, along with intermarriage, occurred between both groups, Haitians and Dominicans. About Anselmo's father, most folks simply said that the old man was what was called a *prèt savann*, or "country priest" of sorts --- the respected religious elder who always read the Catholic prayers before traditional folk ceremonies.

At any rate, much mystery surrounded old Anselmo's origins. Don Anselmo's mother and father, along with two uncles, had been killed by soldiers a long time ago during "some kind of government raid " for some unknown reason; Anselmo never seemed to want to talk much about it. People said it was a campaign against Haitians living in the country at the time ... the details were fuzzy. It was rumored that two of Anselmo's brothers were killed somehow; the third brother escaped from the *batey*, leaving young Anselmo orphaned. So, from very early personal experiences, Anselmo knew intimately the abuse, violence and misery of life on a sugarcane plantation. Now an old man, Anselmo has long been bitter, angry, and tormented by the injustices he witnessed over time . . . injustices committed in the name of sugar. This latest horror in a long pattern of reprehensible abuses against the illiterate, helpless, miserable sugarcane workers simply angered him more. But this anger served to strengthen his resolve.

"That's the honest truth ... he's right," said one young man encouraged by the strength of the older man's conviction.

27

"Yeah, they piss on us and tell us it's rainin'," barked another worker defiantly.

Then it was Doña Fela's turn to speak to the crowd; she was measured and characteristically straightforward with what she had to say. First, she agreed with Don Anselmo that the deflowering of her preciously innocent Azúcar was an absolute vilification against everything held sacred to her mortal soul and to her ancestors; it was an unforgivable act of criminality. And yes, she was angry beyond words. She was also immediate in telling all her neighbors and fellow workers that her granddaughter had regained consciousness from her delirium, had managed to eat something and was trying to rest as best she could.

"*Mi Azúcar morenita* she gonna live through this," she reminded them with resolve. "She been hurt real bad; no doubt about that. But like Don Anselmo say, goin' to the *capataz* ain't goin' to change nothin'. Ain't never been no law or justice for us here, except what they say is the law. They ain't gonna do nothin' to that piece of vomit-shit of a son of the *capataz* ... that maldito Mario. *Es un malvado.* He is evil." Her voice still had not risen even as she referred to Mario as evil; it remained balanced and deliberate. But each word dripping from her mouth was easily tinged with deadly acid.

"Go back to your cabins, now, before they send the guards down here with their dogs and rifles. We don't want no more trouble tonight."

"We better go up to The Pit," said one-eyed Clementina. "All right, everybody, let's go."

She walked over to Doña Fela; the two women hugged each other tightly for a long time without saying anything. The orderly crowd was slowly beginning to disperse. There were no overheard complaints of any kind . . . only secret, muffled tones lingering in the air as people moved away from the yard and toward the trough. The crowd, however, was angry.

"When all this gonna end, Doña Fela?" Clementina whispered to her friend before the two broke apart from their embrace. Clementina left silently with her family. She, too, was angry. Watching them move off, Doña Fela shook her head solemnly; at the same time, her anger remained firmly intact. She picked up a piece of charcoal to light her pipe, which she took from her dress pocket. After everyone had gone away, she herself went into the house and closed the door. "*Por loh santo,* like Don Anselmo say . . . this gotta change."

CUATRO

It seemed more like a few years rather than a mere few weeks had passed since Mario had forced his way into Doña Fela's cabin and brutally snatched from Azúcar her sweet and angelic innocence. A world away from the wretchedness of the batey and the unending despair of the residents there, the night air was delicious with the harmonious blend of fragrances of the tropical vegetation decorating the large veranda of the sumptuous two-story house belonging to Blanchette and Mario Montalvo. The night, in stark contrast to the scorching afternoon, turned refreshingly cool. The moon was high; its silvery and cool beams produced seductive profiles of the clusters of pale-purple blossoms of the jacaranda trees.

From the veranda there was a spectacular panorama of the front yard with the dark, lush green leaves of the banana trees, the flowery tamarind and guayába trees standing guard alongside the mango trees that bent whimsically downward. Beauty prevailed from every angle. The broad shadows of the rustling giant macaw palms made the house seem even more palatial than it really was. The house had been a wedding present to Blanchette and her new husband from the bride's parents. Both of Blanchette's parents, Maurice Desgraves and Yvette Origène-Desgraves, were descendants from a long line of prosperous sugarcane plantation owners that had made their fortune prior to Toussaint's slave-led revolt in what was called Saint-Domingue centuries ago.

Like all the other members of the colonial planter class at the time who were lucky enough to escape the vengeful wrath of Toussaint's unforgiving successors, the prominent families of Desgraves and Origène abandoned their profitable estates in the war-ravished colony only to reestablish themselves in more favorable locales--- the territory on the other side of the river Artibonito, for instance, or in Puerto Rico, Cuba, Venezuela, or

Louisiana. Their sugar production success followed them. Thus, Blanchette Origène-Desgraves had never known the strains of deprivation or work— not so much because she was the sole female offspring of Yvette and Maurice, but more because hers and her brother Pierre-Raymón's heritage reflected that of the traditional Caribbean elitist plantation society. This was a society intricately subdivided into castes and classes. Following the rigid pattern of the region's slave society of the past, the present caste to which the Origène-Desgraves belonged still corresponded to the historical racial divisions in which membership was hereditary and defined by strict practice.

So, the announced marriage between Blanchette and Mario came as a total surprise, perhaps even a jolt to the entire membership roll of her social group. Opposed to this miscast union immediately from the outset, most assuredly, were the young girl's outraged parents.

"*Alors, qui c'est? Qui sont les parents?* Who is he, anyway? Who are his family?" Madame Yvette Origène-Desgraves had insisted. "How can we be certain that his family is entirely White? *Nous allons à la catastrophe!* "

Breaking the otherwise uninterrupted lineage of the traditional island Creole pedigree was no small matter. There was neither ambivalence nor ambiguity that characterized the solidly fixed attitudes of this elite group of self-styled agrarian aristocrats who dominated the society by virtue of their considerable wealth and political influence. Indeed, Blanchette's family expressed great consternation, even disappointment regarding their young, inexperienced daughter's choice of romantic interest.

"*Mon bel ange de Dieu!* She is but a foolish child," exclaimed Madame Origène-Desgraves.

"She has no idea of the ruin she will bring upon our family. *Qu'est-ce que nous allons faire?*"

Yvette's scandalously libertine sister, Nanette, ventured the bold remark, "He's so handsome and quite a giant of a man!" Long without a husband (only because she did not desire one), Nanette and her erotic thoughts led her to fantasize about specific parts of this giant's physical anatomy.

"*Mais oui*. Yes, but he's also terribly crude and without lineage," Yvette countered angrily to her decadent sister. "*C'est tout un bête*. He's an absolute beast!"

"He's nothing! He comes from nothing. *Ah! feu de Dieu!*" one of the cousins added.

"*Le bon Dieu* created those two, but the devil in all his wickedness united them," someone whispered at the lavish wedding shortly afterwards.

Blanchette's father, Maurice Desgraves, had openly threatened to kill Mario when it became known--- but only to the Origène-Desgraves clan--- that the young heiress was carrying Mario's child of three months when the lovely bride knelt solemnly at the altar in Santa Altagracia Cathedral on her lavishly-planned wedding day.

On the other hand, Mario's father, Don Diego Montalvo, had exhibited wide-eyed amazement that his first-born son had been lucky enough to win such a prize.

"*Coño*. My son Mario has got a solid foot in the door, Goddammit! He's already there, being taken in by society," was how the proud father-of-the groom boasted to his peers about his son's fate. "This match was preordained. *Dios es bueno*."

Diego Montalvo truly believed that he had become the lucky recipient of a pot of gold upon Mario's marrying into what everyone perceived as "proper society." Shortly before Diego and his wife became parents, the young bride had been told by an old *santería* priestess to name each of her male offspring with the same first initial. By doing so, according to the priestess, the young family would remain prosperous. That is how the four Montalvo brothers, beginning with the first born, Mario, received the names Miguel, Manolo, and Marcelo. Their mother almost died while delivering her last baby, Marcelo; it had been an extremely difficult and ominous delivery. Everybody at *Esperanza Dulce* whispered that the newborn exited the mother's womb feet first. And although Cristiana Montalvo wanted desperately to have a girl child, she was doomed not to be able to bear more children. After that, her behavior began to change noticeably.

As far as Diego Montalvo knew, or so he had been told by the older men in the family, all the Montalvo men in this line -- although evidence seemed to suggest that more than a few women as well-- have worked on sugar plantations. These men worked in a wide range of capacities and had held varying degrees of responsibility over the generations of engagement in sugar production. At one time or another, Montalvo men have served as estate managers for absentee owners; *mayorale* and *capatazes* (supervisors and overseers, respectively); *boyeros* or supervisors of the plantation livestock; *mayordomo*, or chief bookkeeper; and perhaps one of the most important positions of all -- *maestro de azúcar* ("master of sugar" or boiling-house chief). Thus was there a long Montalvo tradition of extreme pride in having held such positions of considerable strategic responsibility on the Island's sugar plantations.

While still a boy, Diego had heard about the instances whereupon members of the Montalvo clan suffered severely from the sudden displacement of many small, poor farmers like themselves due to the greed of the sugar barons. An entire social class of landless Whites and many mulattos would later form the bulk the administrative and managerial positions of the plantation. This was the embittered class to which, increasingly, more and more of the Montalvos would inherit membership. It was within this group that there developed a deep-seated racial hatred that took the form of inhumane treatment and sadistic punishments for African slaves ... later, for their descendants -- the contracted *braceros* from around the Antilles. Diego's grandfather had regularly participated in the vicious hunting expeditions after *cimarrónes,* run-away slaves who eluded capture by seeking refuge in those impenetrable, vibrant settlements that were concealed deep within the mountainous regions of the Island -- the historical and truly awesome *manieles* whose resolute occupants fought fierce and ongoing resistance battles for decades against their determined exterminators.

But hidden deep in the shadowy memory of Montalvo family history was also another story, and with equal potency. It was always said, although never too loudly, that the Montalvos dared not "scratch too deeply" . . . *detrás la oreja,* "behind the ear." This profound socio-psychological expression readily uttered throughout the Spanish-speaking islands referred to the perceived shame (but only according to some people of European ancestry) of having a mere trace of African blood buried within one's family lineage. If an individual therefore "scratched deeply enough behind the ear," then the previously undetected Blackness would be exposed for the whole world to see! Young Diego Montalvo had also heard older members of the family whisper this dreaded, carefully guarded secret.

So, it was no surprise when so many years later, the older Diego felt triumphant as he stood in the chapel that afternoon of his son's fortuitous marriage to the lovely daughter of one of the Island's wealthiest sugarcane planters. People everywhere talked about the great social event. As the wedding day neared, the excitement grew more intense, with discussions becoming even more divided.

"*Ay, Santa Virgen María.* Who do you suppose they are

going to invite? Who will come? Did you get an invitation yet? Where will the newly-wed couple live?"

Some people expressed delight, while others scoffed at the very idea of marriage between these two unlikely individuals representing opposing castes and classes. The gossip even on the appointed wedding day turned into a kind of crude contest between two opposing camps, predicting good and bad consequences . . . winners and losers.

The bride's exasperated mother was overheard saying, "*Mon Dieu!* May heaven protect our innocent little angel from this disgusting brute."

Madame Origène-Desgraves's more tolerant sister Nanette was overheard to have murmured in a most risqué fashion, without raising her eyes, "*Ay!* Such a giant could make my blood boil until it turned to cane molasses!"

Such were the random thoughts floating lazily through Mario's head as he lay stretched out in one of the hammocks on the veranda. A half-empty rum bottle was at the side of the hammock, an empty glass about to fall from his hand. He was half awake, dozing off now and then into an almost drunken slumber. This was his nightly routine after the usually late supper and heavy consumption of rum on the front veranda. It wasn't because of the troublesome night-flying insects and gnats that Blanchette never joined Mario on the veranda. Besides, she preferred staying up with the twin girls, Cécile and Chelaine, now five years old. Blanchette would read to them until they too nodded off to sleep. Rather than be with Mario, the twins and their mother were in the comfort of their locked bedroom on the second floor of the sprawling house.

Since the birth of Cécile and Chelaine, Blanchette had lost all sexual desires of any kind for Mario. Whatever intimacies there might have been between the two had waned long ago, before finally becoming altogether non-existent. She, in all probability, no longer loved Mario. Theirs had ceased being a marriage between husband and wife; they merely occupied the same house, under different terms. Moreover, once Blanchette discovered her husband's penchant for late-night prowls down to the batey – and most certainly not to play dominos with the men there, she decided she would not assume the legendary role of the stoic plantation mistresses of a bygone , romanticized era when plantation owners, their sons, their slave overseers and any other White man on the estate, even if they were house guests, would saunter at will through the slave quarters and simply pluck out his sexual playmate or bed-warmer for the night. Blanchette was vehement in her stance on the issue. She was determined not to remain silent.

"Mario, you shameless swine. I will not turn a blind eye to your monstrous immorality," she had directed at him on one occasion. "You will not climb back under my sheets after being with those filthy black whores from the *batey*. You even dare come back into my house after your whoring!"

"Those black whores, as you call them, give me what my own fuckin'wife won't!" Mario roared back. "You treat me like swamp scum … like you can't stand the sight of me or don't want me to touch you. *Carajo*, woman. I'll do what the hell ever I please."

"Oh, dear God, what kind of heartless, depraved beast did I marry?" she stammered nervously. The humiliated young wife continued sobbing throughout that entire night, alone and abandoned. "When will this nightmare end for me?"

That was a long time ago. Blanchette eventually grew completed uninterested in disclosing to Mario her thoughts about anything. The two were never again to share the same conjugal bed or bedroom. Every night for years after that painful incident, however, the family --- Mario, Blanchette and the twin girls, would sit down together at the huge, handcrafted and aged ceiba wood, heirloom dining table, and eat their meal in a deadening silence; they would then excuse themselves from the table . . . but at least not before saying good-night to one another with the utmost civility. The twins, however, did routinely and genuinely kiss their father goodnight.

"*Te amo, papá,*" they always said in unison, each planting her little kiss on either side of their father's cheeks.

Then everyone would all take immediate refuge in their separate spaces: Blanchette and the twins heading up to the girls' bedroom where their mother would read to them until they fell asleep; Mario, always with a full bottle of locally-brewed rum in hand, a lighted cigar hanging from one corner of his wide mouth, heading for the coolness of the veranda and plopping down in the hammock to drink himself to sleep; Blanchette finally roaming in and out of the dark, empty rooms before finally going off into her own bedroom, habitually locking the door once inside.

"*Por Dios.* Were we ever happy together?" she heard herself ask the mirror, while tears poured sadly down her cheeks. "Oh Dear God, for the sake of the twins, please change all this madness, " Blanchette pleaded in anguish. Below, on the veranda outside, Mario continued sleeping soundly with his private thoughts.

CINCO

The next morning life stirred again, early and routinely. The first signs of daylight reddened the horizon, and the residents of the *batey* . . . sleepy, still exhausted from the previous day... in their miserable cabins, were beginning to come to life. It was as if nothing was different from the day before--- and the day before that. Life followed the same pattern, the same misery-worn path as before, with the same cruel and wretched indifference ... or so it seemed. Such was life on the sugarcane plantation, very much as it had always been down through the years. Everybody in the batey was up before dawn. Smoke was rising behind the cabins; the aroma of morning coffee drifted through the air. The *batey* was officially awake. Most of the households had already sent someone, usually the oldest boy child, to the nearby ravine for buckets of water. Most everybody had used their outhouse, which was normally situated in a shed located at the rear of their cabins.

Through the narrow cracks in the dim sky, the first flickers of light slipped through and quickly dispersed. Soon the silhouette of the impatiently waiting sugarcane stalks became visible, fringed in all their dread. As soon as the sun tinged the woods just barely enough to lift its intersecting paths through the protective foliage, the workers would be on their way again to complete another day of the seemingly perpetual sentence in the fields. It was once again time to get ready for the day's toil.

"The sun's risin', *m'hita*," Doña Fela said to Azúcar, who was still drowsy from the previous night's unexplained restlessness. "We'll be startin' out soon."

"I'll be ready, *abuelita*," was all that Azúcar managed to murmur.

Grandmother and granddaughter customarily greeted each other every morning with a tender embrace, not needing to say anything more.

"*Mi azúcar morenita* seem to be getting weaker each day," the old woman mused. But even if this were so, the child showed no signs of physical exhaustion; she continued working alongside the adult women in the fields as though she possessed the same stamina as they. Since that terrifying afternoon with Mario, not only Doña Fela and Azúcar, but also every other female living in the batey took extra precautions to safeguard the young girls from savage predators like Mario. It was understood by everybody that none of the girls were to be left alone for any reason since the incident in Doña Fela's cabin.

In the corner of the cabin, Doña Fela kept drinking water in a big earthen jar, a *jarra*. She placed a small basin of fresh water on the stool in front of her granddaughter's cot. Azúcar rinsed her mouth and washed the sleep from her still-tired, puffy eyes. The old woman broke off two sizable portions of the wrapped-up cassava, shared one piece with her granddaughter, and dipped her own piece into her hot coffee. Azúcar did the same. While Doña Fela was gingerly sipping her freshly made coffee, trying to avoid burning her lips, she asked her granddaughter if the child truly had slept well because the vigilant old woman had heard the constant and agitated stirrings of restlessness (for what reason?) from her granddaughter, whose nightly bedding mat on the floor was placed quite close to hers.

"No, *abuelita*, I didn't sleep well at all. I don't know why," Azúcar replied. "I woke up in the middle of the night and kept turnin' over and over the rest of the night."

Doña Fela looked at her granddaughter with anxious warmth, but remained silent. The girl began to smile, less concerned now about sleepless nights ... of these, there had been several lately.

Somehow, though, her grandmother always made everything all right.

The impatient sugarcane fields were beckoning. Throughout the community, the morning smoke from the charcoal burner's fogón was diminishing. It was time for everybody to be heading for the fields or to the mill. Their meager breakfast finished, Doña Fela and Azúcar prepared to leave for another long day's labor. Azúcar went to another corner of the cabin and, ever since being tall enough to do so, she grabbed both machetes that were leaning against the wall. One after another, the occupants all poured begrudgingly out of their dark cabins. The morning trudge to the fields was contrasted from the evening's return trip by the almost dead silence of the work crew at the start of each new day. There were normally just whispered tones, as if not wishing to disturb the serenity of Nature so early in the morning. Iridescent-colored hummingbirds were already darting from one patch of fragrant blooms to another.

But things had changed these past few weeks ... slightly, but changed nevertheless. The trek now was more animated, softer and more guarded, but still noticeably more spirited than previously. Even after a few weeks, there were still rumors, conjecture and speculation that persisted. Supposedly, there were even alleged eyewitness accounts of what had happened to Azúcar. The fact remained, however, that no one had actually seen what had happened that ill-fated, hot afternoon in Doña Fela's cabin; but everybody offered an opinion.

"Doña Fela's neighbors say the child not eatin' much these days. No appetite," said one woman to her companion.

"Or just no will to eat, if you ask me," quickly interrupted the companion. "But that girl has the strength of any of us full grown women."

"Sí, eh verda'. Yes, it's true," added one woman who herself

40

had actually witnessed the recently surfacing, impressive stamina of young Azúcar.

While it wasn't at all out of the ordinary for youngsters Azúcar's age to be working in the fields or in the mill house, their chores were limited largely to a variety of non-strenuous menial tasks like sweeping the mill floor clear of the dry pulp remaining from the extracted cane juice, or hauling the water buckets and dippers for the cutters among the stalks, perhaps herding the ox teams used to carry the cut stalks to the mill. But relatively few young girls were engaged in actually using the treacherous machete; boys, yes, but the swift and strong wrist action essential in whacking away at the tough cane stalks required seasoned practice. Traditionally, few girls ever mastered the skill. Doña Fela had tutored her granddaughter in the technique when the child was about nine or ten years old.

The on-hand witness continued her account.

"I think that girl deliberately drive herself like that out of pure anger. Don't expect the poor thin' to forget any time soon what the capataz's son Mario done to her. *Qué monstruo!* What a monster!"

Don Anselmo had overheard everything that the chatty old women had said. Because he admitted having known Doña Fela over a longer period of time and more closely than anyone else among the workers of the batey, he naturally felt confident in offering his ominous commentary with a respected air of authority.

"Don't none of you make no mistake," he warned. "Doña Fela is in the pit of her anger. At the same time, she carryin' on her old shoulders the unsaddled weight of all our sacred ancestors who themselves are grievin' in silence for our continued misery and sufferin' at the greedy paws of the sugar producers. Believe me, my sisters and brothers, the old woman's

41

pain run deep." Don Anselmo ended his harsh comments, "Even the devil hisself would be foolish not to regret havin' crossed the path of Doña Fela."

At this boldness on the part of Don Anselmo, the little group of well-meaning womenfolk in an instant became silent, all the while not missing a single beat in the strident rhythm of their pace as they were nearing the entrance to the cane field. The mill house was a short distance away, on the other side of the fields. Even though the early morning sun was on its way to becoming sweltering, each of the women could readily feel Don Anselmo's own piercing glaze on their face, forcing its way into the deepest recesses of their true thoughts. What did he mean by that last remark? Was this old soothsayer of the batey, in some cryptic fashion, warning of present or future calamities? Exchanging no further comments, the little group hurried into the open corral to await the day's assignments from the capataz.

These past few weeks had also witnessed certain restlessness with Don Diego. Several nights now had been sleepless for the seemingly inexhaustible capataz – but this sleeplessness was not because of his tastelessly dull, traditionally unattractive job of managing the work crew during the long, hot, days. There had always been the usual emotional and physical strains associated with the job: making sure every laborer had been assigned the precise task in the endless chain of routine operations; then seeing to it that the task was being performed correctly and efficiently; constantly maintaining the desired production pace in an effort to assure quality control; monitoring worker morale; in a word, keeping things running smoothly and on schedule. But lately, Don Diego found himself unable to sleep soundly through an entire night.

"How it pains me that you didn't sleep well again last night, *querido*. Your body must be crying for decent rest. Are you troubled?" Cristiana would lament the following morning.

"*Coño*. It's that damn mattress! Woman, how many times do I have to remind you to just order a new one?" Tossing an admonishing glance at his wife, Diego, as usual, would manage rather casually to lie. He normally barked at his always passive, submissive wife in the same crude manner that he unnecessarily yelled commands at the contract *braceros* he supervised all day in the cane fields.

Of course, the old sagging mattress was not the annoying culprit that, night after night, was robbing the *capataz* of his much-needed sleep. Throughout the night filled with endless tosses and turns as he lay next to his sound-asleep Cristiana, Diego was worried about their eldest son. The old man felt dispirited and deeply troubled ever since that hot afternoon whereupon he had inadvertently overheard the tragically ugly rumors about Mario and the little granddaughter of the old woman Fela. Diego was keenly aware of the enviable reverence the old woman commanded among all the cane workers at *Esperanza Dulce.*

"*Es nuestra Santa Madre,*" everybody agreed. She was the very symbol of hope, radiating it magically. Doña Fela had a way of bringing life itself into proper focus for all those around her.

"She is our Saint."

Diego had overheard some workers testify to the saintliness of this old woman. Any scintilla of suspicion of illicit behavior involving the son of any estate manager and a minor from the *batey* — totally off-limits for them – was especially scandalous, potently disruptive to production. Routine hurricanes paled in comparison to the traditional force of scandal that could seriously jeopardize sugar profits.

SEIS

Diego Montalvo was far from being naïve about the long and frequently turbulent history of his Island's sugar industry and the implications of scandal or any other obstacle to lucrative sugar earnings for the planters. Not unlike the sugar plantations of the nineteenth-century Caribbean, present-day operations were all too often characterized by certain omnipresence, but dormant fear that seemed to permeate the delicate membrane of containment on the estate. Although men like Diego were completely immune to its occurrence, the constant abuse, the ruthless exploitation, and the rigid derogation of the labor force living in the *batey* were really what triggered this fear. It always has since the first *trapiche*, the primitive, manual wooden grinders operated by oxen traction on the *ingenios* of the island-colony during the early to mid-fifteen hundreds.

So, in the closed, feudalistic society of the sugar estates like *Esperanza Dulce*, where traditionally there has been a total lack of any degree of variety or flexibility, it was not the more serious matter of blatant criminality or any obvious breach of human decency that perturbed the *capataz*'s sleep. Rather, Diego Montalvo was genuinely unnerved about personal scandal that would cause any measurable disruption of an otherwise smooth operation and continuous flow of profits. This, in turn, could easily result in his personal ruin. On more than a few occasions, Diego had been uncompromisingly harsh in his warnings to his entire family, "*Coño!* Don't ever do anything to damage my reputation or threaten my position here. *Entendido?*" He wanted to make certain they all understood.

And to his four sons, especially, he minced absolutely no words whatsoever in reminding them regularly, "Hear me well! Never forget that your stupid bullshit actions around here could spell doom for all of us. You've got it good here. *Entendido?* The best of everything. Your fuckin' future is here in sugar! *Azúcar!* It's sugar, damn it! Don't ever risk it to bullshit!" Diego as *capataz* was charged with the strategic task and responsibility of assuring and maintaining quality control, one might say ... and the labor force itself was pivotal in the scheme of this assurance.

"You good-for-nothin' niggers had damn well better know that one slip and your black asses are sent straight back to where we found you. And believe me, you'll go back without one fuckin' *cheli.*"

He habitually issued such a warning at the motley crews of intimidated, unskilled laborers who had been contracted from a mosaic of the Antillean islandscapes in order to provide the never-ending supply of fodder for the sugar industry. In contemporary times, the laborers were part of officially drawn contracts between island governments, the receiving one and the sending one, in addition to the private, absentee corporations. Actual amounts of money would be stipulated in these contracts, but most of the workers themselves knew nothing about nor received no money as part of the exchange. Thus, these workers arrived with not one penny and almost daily were threatened with expulsion, leaving as they had come: "broke as hell, without one penny. *Pelao, sin ni un cheli.*"

But Diego, too, could be speedily dismissed from his coveted post should he be found even marginally undermining the estate's primary objective and very reason for existing. All members of his family would suffer the same fate –that of being evicted from the company-owned premises, including the operation of the company stores, or *bodegas*, where the sugarcane workers were required to buy all their oppressively overpriced provisions of every sort.

So, Mario's "bullshit actions" had the clear potential of total disruption because, even if the crews seemed intimidated by the constant warnings, these workers in all their human capacity still harbored sizable dosages of repressed anger and bitterness that was sealed all too loosely by an insecure, superficial lid. Any conceivable mutiny, as in the remote colonial past of the stone grinding presses, the entire *batey*, along with the cane fields, the mill house, the warehouses, the administrative building, the *bodegas* –all would be easy incendiary targets of boundless revenge for a thoroughly disgruntled mob, or even just one deranged individual with nothing to lose. Such was truly a nightmarish thought, conjuring up safely buried memories of legendary figures like Lemba, Boukman, Macandal, Dessalines, and others from the Island's blood-drenched and scarred history.

The resolute, yet signifying old cutter Anselmo was constantly reminding his downtrodden fellow workers, whether Haitian, Domínico-Haitian, Jamaican, Bahamian or St. Lucian; it didn't matter since they were all the same to Anselmo.

"The sugar barons sit around on their fat asses and treat us like shit. They know for sure that we're the ones that keep this stinkin' country's economy pumped up. *Coño*! We keep their ugly bellies full while ours always stay empty. And it's all about that maldito azúcar! Goddamn Sugar!"

Over the course of the past few weeks, then, the capataz without question did exhibit a troubling restlessness. His nights were painfully sleepless. He was becoming increasingly irascible. But the first time that he had overheard the tale about … "the son of one of the bosses," he gave little, if any concern whatsoever. This bit of salacious "field-gossip," as it was called, was a major diversion among male and female workers alike during their lunch break. Perhaps with the exception of the spontaneous bursts of uninhibited excitement provided by a group of makeshift musicians and jubilant dancers up at The Pit, a general monotony and lifelessness ruled amidst the depressing and squalid ambiance of the batey. Much the same described the rather limited and dull avenues of human discourse. As a result, cane workers were infamous for their reckless banter that did little else than fan rumors about the exaggerated or fantasized sexual exploits and easily-satisfied appetites of the many nameless young, inexperienced and rowdy, but terribly inept sons of so many of the plantation managers and administrators.

"Those young *blanquitos* get their sexual initiation with our young flowers and older women from the *batey*," one man remarked bitterly.

It was true enough. What these untamed, yet virgin young White boys could not dare do with the over-protected and repressed maiden daughters of the same class as their male counterparts, they were impudent enough to attempt with many of the more experienced unmarried females of the batey. And quite frequently these lusty, "easy" women never had to be forced; it was an open secret that an extremely popular, efficient and well-organized prostitution ring had been operating for years in the batey. The only real mystery was the precise identity of the person (or perhaps persons) who secretly controlled this flourishing moneymaking operation.

Routinely after supper was over and the early night began under what seemed like millions of fireflies, but was actually the shimmering light of a multitude of oil lamps, another life came alive in the *batey*. Various small groups of individuals, sitting in their separate circles with some people still munching on roasted corn, would remain outside their cabin until bedtime or until the smaller children had exhausted their imagination for creating additional fun things to do. Playing dominos or cards, arm wrestling, telling stories and rhymes from their respective islands --- those prolific Haitians must have a thousand and one tales about *loups-garous*, "were-wolves " and two friends called Bouki and Malice scuffling with machetes in mock battle--dominated nearly every evening.

"*Cric?*" said the Haitian Estimé, initiating the traditional riddle with his wife Lolita.

"*Crac!*" she answered with a ready smile, eager to solve the anticipated riddle.

"You go around this way, while I go around the other way and the two of us will meet," Estimé said next, confident that Lolita would be perplexed.

"*Pero, hombre eso eh muy fácil.* But, man, that's real easy! A belt," Lolita blurted out the answer after a few laughs. "*Mi amor,* how many times you tell me that same tired riddle?"

She laughed playfully again, so did the couple's two older youngsters who were listening and thoroughly enjoyed watching their parents in the contest of wits; the infant had already fallen asleep with his little head in his mother's lap. Lolita was ready to begin the second round.

"*Cric?*"

"*Crac!*" quickly answered her Haitian.

"*Redondo, redondo; barríl sin fondo.* It's round and round; it's a barrel without a bottom," offered Lolita this time, wearing a clear smirk because she knew that Estimé was stumped with the riddle. After closing his eyes and hesitating several seconds before repeating the riddle aloud, he was finally forced to make a reluctant confession.

"I don't know it," surrendered Estimé in frustration. "*Merde!* Shit!"

"*Un anillo.* A ring," Lolita announced triumphantly and playfully teasing her Haitian Estimé because it had been he who first taught his non-Haitian wife the traditional oral form of beginning a story or riddle in his native Kreyòl culture well before the two were married. They continued with their good-natured battle until quite late. This playfulness between the parents thoroughly amused their watchful children.

At another assembled group that same evening, other concerns were the focus of conversation.

"I hear that big-titty Nadine will spend the night with you for a plate of food that got a nice piece of meat in it," Ramón, one of the workers from Panamá, casually remarked without looking away from his shielded hand of dominos.

"Yeah, mon," replied one of the domino players from St. Kitts, "but she too black. I prefer the light brown skin, silky-haired Dominican bitches."

Imagine! The absurdity of a color hierarchy had clearly made its way into the already-sinister pathology of the batey, even when it came to the matter of the prostitution trade.

Ramón shot back, "*Pendejo.* Don't you know that those Dominican putas charge us too damn much? They sellin' their color, not their *chochas*!"

One of the other domino players at the table that night thought hard about what the other men had been arguing about before interjecting, "*Eh el ruido del chavo lo que reconoce bien la vagina, no eh jasi, mi 'ermano?*" Maybe it was true after all that "it's the sound of money alone that the vagina really recognizes." The game continued in all its intensity, with the sharp eyes of the players fixed solidly on each of his spotted dominos.

The next day when the *capataz* happened upon the work crew during their much-awaited relief in the way of a lunch break that afternoon, he had no idea whatsoever that the gossipy little group was talking about anyone he knew personally. Normally, in the insular world of the capataz, the incoherent exchange of chopped and abbreviated snatches of a mixed patois and jargon that more literate, élite classes would

49

describe as unintelligible, the capataz would hardly give a thought about what the workers were so animated about. But on this particular occasion he was literally jolted to his senses by the unobtrusive clarity of the words, "that nasty bastard Mario, the old pig's son." Deciphering this bit of conversation could not have been easier if someone had said, "Mario, the capataz's son." The words could not have dripped with more eager crispness from the lips of the lunch-break gossipmongers.

But strangely, the chatter this time – mused Diego– was not accompanied by the customary vengeful guffaws or unbridled snickers of the participants. There was an absence of hearty thigh slapping or rib-poking with the elbow this time. Something was decidedly different with the exchange this particular afternoon. The lunch-break group was solemn. Their tones were deliberate, but hushed — almost muted. There was intensity in the eyes of the speakers and listeners alike, not unlike the intense gaze of domino players around the table or mourners seated around the packed room during a *velorio*, or wake.

"They say the dirty *hijueputa* almost suffocated the little girl with his weight, " someone volunteered. There was no dissent among the speakers. Mario was a filthy son-of-a-bitch!

"I heard she almost bled to death," said one of Doña Fela's closest neighbors, Lolita with the extraordinarily huge ass —an ass so abundantly fluffy that it actually bounced up and down when she walked.

"What a horrible thing to happened to someone so sweet." Lolita's Haitian-born husband, displaying open anger in his normally tranquil voice, added, "That wild hairy hog Mario snatched the innocence from that harmless little flower. *Mwin ginyin la pèn.* I myself feel the pain." Estimé expressed the pain of his outrage.

Another of Doña Fela's neighbors, Teresa with the longneck,

grew agitated with a mixture of sadness and anger as she uttered, "Those savage dogs! When all this gonna end?"

An anxious silence assailed the group but not before Don Anselmo, sharing the same intensity and outrage of everyone else huddled over their meager lunches that torturous afternoon, issued a stinging rebuke.

"A long line of Mario's kind have committed many unmentionable horrors against our people over the generations. The horrors don't seem to be stoppin' no time some. Our bodies, our sweat, our souls have never been safe from the greedy beasts. Our mothers, our sisters, our daughters have been easy prey to their beastly appetites. It's time, goddamn it, we all realized that we're the only ones who got to stop these horrors."

"*Sé pa vouazin ka va ranjé sa pou nou,*" the Haitian Estimé agreed.

The Panamanian Ramón translated for his lunch companions, "*No es el vecino el que va a arreglar esto po nosotros!*" The feeling seemed to be generally accepted that . . . "it wasn't going to be one's neighbor who would straighten out this problem for us, but rather the folks themselves had to do this."

Luckily for the entire work crew, the capataz had not lingered long enough in his stupor to have over-heard what was clearly beyond the mere suggestion of insurrection. Luckily too that Diego had left the scene well before Don Anselmo's bitter remarks to the small group of agitated workers. The old cutter had begun a virtual tirade about the random liberties, abuses of authority, inhuman cruelty and overall decadence of men like Diego.

"The whole class of them is morally corrupt and infirm; their wickedness is of the sickest kind," bellowed old Anselmo.

As bold as he was, however, it was highly doubtful that Don Anselmo would have dared make such seditious pronouncements within earshot of any of the estate managers. During the days of slavery and for a time thereafter, such talk from a Blackman would have met the consequence of death by the vilest means. Neither did Diego overhear one of the workers announce the special event that was to take place later that night.

"You heard about tonight?" The companion inquired hastily, as if there might be some urgency in the question.

"No, mon. What be goin' on I don't know 'bout?"

It was Lolita's usually subdued husband Estimé who was the bearer of the message; he continued, "Won't be no singin' and dancin' at The Pit tonight. Everybody expected to be down at Doña Fela's by ten o'clock. Pass the word. No dancin' ... just be down at Doña Fela's by ten." Estimé made sure that everybody understood clearly when he repeated his message in Kreyòl.

"*Se non ki pou mété lod lan sa!*" It was Ramón who again passed on the message in Spanish. "*Somos nosotros quienes pondremos el orden allí!* We the ones who will straighten things out!"

But Don Diego Montalvo, who was never without his loaded pistol strapped to his side nor the intimidating frown he wore constantly on his crusty face as he rode his stallion through the cane field, had most certainly never overheard any of this.

SIETE

In the ominous stillness of the late afternoon, now that the sun had taken welcomed refuge, the coconut grooves atop the slight rise of the nearby hills turned into metallic shadows. The crimson sunset had begun to redden even the blackest sweaty faces of the exhausted laborers as they plowed their way routinely back to their cabins. They were completely worn out, but nevertheless greeted the end of yet another torturous jail sentence in the hellish cane fields and the unsympathetic mill house. Soon the tropical purple sky of evening would be alive with flickering fireflies. Almost every adult soul quickly prepared for the anticipated gathering later that night.

But there was not the usual eagerness of another night of dancing and uninhibited merrymaking at The Pit... as had been announced earlier in the day. Everybody was fully aware of the planned deviation from tonight's routine. Word had reached everybody about what lay ahead. The anxiety arose from the fact of simply not knowing what was going to happen at Doña Fela's.

Night finally arrived; the sun, having lost its prior strength, had disappeared behind the hills. The sky now shimmered like the top of a fogón. Unlike the usually cool night, this particular night was sticky and humid. From a quagmire nearby, the deep, resonant croaking of over-stuffed bullfrogs throbbed as steadily as a clock. In dramatic contrast, the delicate clicking of the invisible, tiny tree frogs of the Caribbean, the coquí, was non-stop in its repetitive, loud chirping. The prolonged and piercing shrills of the tropical cuckoo provided more elusive night sounds.

Azúcar, excited as she was, felt the frantic urge to ask her grandmother about the night's pending event, but did not dare. Her trepidation resulted from being able to see that her grandmother was deeply preoccupied with the meticulous preparations that had consumed her these past three days.

"How different everything seems," the imaginative young girl thought to herself.

So, Azúcar roamed about in silence, not being able to ask any of her many nagging questions. Everything remained a mystery to her. That silence was shattered when Doña Fela, in a burst of zeal, ordered, *"Mi azúcar morenita,* go light all the candles." Azúcar quickly obeyed, but still in puzzled silence. Never before had she seen so many candles, so many different and pretty colors, so many varying sizes and shapes . . . and all in just one room. The girl also wondered where and how her grandmother had gotten them. And why so many? And why they hadn't been lit before tonight? These particular mysteries and more would be unraveled before the next morning's light of dawn.

One-eyed Clementina and her husband Tomás were the first ones to arrive, living as close to Doña Fela as they did. All six of their children were in tow. The youngsters naturally regarded this evening's outing a genuine treat since particularly the youngest ones were never permitted to roam about the batey after sunset. But as anxious and fidgety as they were, all the children had been properly instructed to remain silent as they entered into the old woman's tiny front courtyard. Even the smallest toddler of the brood, as if on signal, had quieted his weeping.

"Tomás, what this all about? Why Doña Fela gathering everybody down here tonight? Why folks not up at The Pit singin' and dancin'? What you know 'bout all this?"

Impatiently and without allowing for an answer to one question before spitting out another one, Clementina pestered her usually taciturn husband. Because of her one eye, she always made a deliberate point of turning her head completely to face her husband or anybody else directly whenever she insisted upon an answer to a question of hers.

"Shhhhh! *Mi querida,* you talking too loud and askin' me too many questions," whispered Tomás softly, not at all in anger or with any sign of annoyance. It was not in his nature to be so. "Soon enough, Cleme," he calmly assured his wife. "Everythin' in time. Just be patient. When I got those candles for Doña Fela, she told me not to ask her no questions; so, I didn't. We all gonna' know everythin' when it's time."

They both then fell silent as they entered the front door. Next to arrive, again perhaps because they lived so close to Doña Fela's cabin, were Lolita and her Haitian Estimé. She always referred to her husband in that manner, "My Haitian." And like almost everybody else expected to show up this particular evening, Lolita and Estimé were also puzzled about the nature of the special gathering.

"*Bon Dié bon.* To the Good Lord and all the Saints of His court. Will somebody please to tell me what is goin' on here tonight," the Haitian wanted desperately to know. He had received the news by way of "*Radio Djol,*" that is, in the traditional fashion common of his Haitian countryside, by "mouth-to-ear," or as they say on that side of the river, "*chita tandé.*"

Lolita, much to her personal satisfaction and pride, usually kept herself well informed of just about everything that stirred in the cesspool that was the *batey,* day or night. She was deliberately withholding something from her Haitian; this was part of her playful tease.

"I do know for sure that Doña Fela has all kinds of pretty candles all 'round the place," she volunteered to her attentive husband. "At least that's what Clementina told me; Tomás got the candles for Doña Fela."

Lolita felt privileged with this piece of information, which she decided to share with her husband.

Before long, other neighbors began arriving. There was Cirilo, accompanied by his long-neck wife Teresa and Teresa's very talkative brother Ramón, who chatted incessantly like the little green, caged cotica parrots that regularly adorned the verandas of manor homes. Serafina came with a few other big-bosomed women like herself. Destine, a very pretty, very black, Domínico-Haitian woman with uncommonly high cheekbones, came with her equally black, velvety smooth-skinned husband Noél and two other women in the company of their male companions who seemed all to be of the same family. There was coffee-colored Milagros with her bulky Jamaican husband Keith. There was Damian from St. Kitts, along with several other men who shared the barracks with him-- Césair, Millien, Vincent, Pierre, and Nelson. Everybody greeted one another in genuinely cheerful, but hushed tones, as though they were entering a sanctuary, and then moved inside the rapidly filling-up room.

Perhaps some forty to sixty curious, but obedient souls -- most having arrived between ten and eleven o'clock -- were directed inside Doña Fela's now-crowded cabin where the "meeting" was to take place. Almost miraculously, the single room, overflowing with more human bodies than Azúcar had imagined could possibly squeeze inside, seemed quite spacious. The tiny kitchen table was now covered in white cloth . . . "Truly pretty," Azúcar thought. More white cloth artfully draped the walls and ceiling as if a kind of niche had been created for perhaps an altar. Tacked on the inner side of the white drapery were scores of dainty little yellow and white paper ribbon curls, the sort easily made by pulling ridged paper strips sharply, but very gently over the edge of a machete blade . . . without cutting the strips, of course.

When Azúcar saw not one, but three elaborately decorated cakes placed in the center of the table, still balanced on one side by a cinder block, the girl was at the same time overcome with joy and further confusion.

"It's not my birthday yet," she affirmed out loud. "Whose birthday party is this?"

The largest of the cakes featured an extravaganza of yellow and white sugar roses. There was a heart-shaped cake almost smothered in frothy blue cross-hatching. The third cake, to the young girl's total delight, was iced in delicate yellow, blue, and green flowers. There were two tastefully arranged bouquets of yellow flowers placed on either side of the cakes. Two large yellow candles burned on opposite ends of the little table; in front of this center display was a small statue of the Catholic saint St. Joseph.

To confuse matters even more for Azúcar were the three geometric markings on the cabin floor, which she simply thought were strange drawings of some kind, meticulously executed in what seemed to be cornmeal. One drawing looked like a scalloped heart with cross-hatching, while the other had a prominent letter "L." To the girl's amazement, however, the focal point of this beautifully arranged ritual display was the large mound of yams and dried fish at the foot of the table altar.

Soon, more than a few of the guests were certain of the purpose of this display on the table and in front of the two floor drawings. There must have been at least twelve hefty yams, about a dozen dried and salted fish, each one at least fifteen inches in length from dramatically gaping mouth to rigid tail fin. The yams and fish were piled up like cordwood on a royal cushion of dried palm branches; fresh green frangipani leaves, adding an aromatic showiness to the entire room, covered the top of the ceremonial stack. The room had become transformed, as if by magic, into an intoxicating atmosphere far beyond Azúcar's expectations.

Once the drums sounded, everybody in the room suddenly

57

stood practically motionless. They all seemed to know that it was time to begin the evening's event. The moment turned almost solemn and devotional. There was a muted excitement as the drumming pulsated, not necessarily louder, just more steady and controlled with the hypnotic effect that a certain kind of percussive rhythm can readily produce, especially under the lush tropical night skies.

"What does all this mean?" Azúcar continued to wonder. "Why didn't *abuelita* explain any of this to me?" More puzzlement and mystery.

Then, there appeared an ensemble of four old women, none of whom Azúcar recognized, dancing slowly and deliberately in a tight ring to the rhythm of the drumming; in the middle of the small circle there was a thin Black man — already old, but still visibly powerful. Only during these kinds of special ceremonies did people refer to this old man as *prèt savann*. He was carrying a long, crooked, very ornate wooden stick that he thumped rhythmically against the floor of Doña Fela's cabin. The drumming, as well as the dancers, paused as if to signal the formal entrance of the old man into the activity. It was Don Anselmo, pounding his stick again on the floor . . . more firmly this time, began to chant in a language that an alert Azúcar vaguely remembered hearing as a young child and frequently while at work in the sugarcane field.

"*Lafamni sanble, sanble nan. Se kreyòl nouye, Pa genyen Ginen ankò.*"

Estimé, Lolita's Haitian, moved closer to his wife and whispered the translation into her eager ears: "The family is assembled, gathered in. We are Creoles who have Africa no longer."

Doña Fela's manje yam ritual had officially begun, as all Vodou "parties" do with a series of juxtaposed, intermingled

Catholic prayers and traditional Creole chants. Don Anselmo had announced the occasion of the evening's special ceremony. Mamá Lola, the long-time cook and nanny in the elder Montalvo's household, had made possible all the preparations for such an elaborate ritual. Mamá Lola, who a very long time ago was an extremely captivating and very beautiful young woman, was now a noticeably handsome older mulatto woman, had served faithfully for many years in the plantation household of Yvette Origène's family, the mother of Mario Montalvo's wife, Blanchette. It was said with extreme caution . . . almost whispered, that much mystery surrounded the long relationship between old Mamá Lola and Yvette Origène.

It was Mamá Lola, also an excellent cook of local fame, who had personally provided the elaborately decorated homemade cakes for the evening's ceremony, also the white drapery and yellow and white ribbon curls adorning the walls of Doña Fela's cabin. Azúcar's eyes magnified with curiosity and even more excitement. She clutched the arm of one-eyed Clementina, who was standing next to the young girl.

"Are those birthday cakes on the table?" she asked Clementina.

"Ay, no, child," was the woman's reply. "The largest one with the yellow and white sugar roses on it is dedicated to the ancestral spirit Loko, a patron of priestly authority. The heart-shaped one is for Ezili Dantò, the fierce mother-warrior spirit. That other one covered in the yellow, blue, and green flowers is dedicated to all the spirits together."

At that point, Destine quietly slipped more information to the eager Azúcar.

"That drawing on the floor is what we call a *vèvè* for Legba, guardian of the gates to the spirit world. We draw the *vèvè* as a symbol of the spirit or loa we wish to call forth."

Azúcar was fascinated by what she was learning; she learned

further that one of the other ground drawings done in cornmeal was Ezili's scalloped heart; the other was a *vèvè* for Papa Loko, patron of temples, with the large letter "*L*" to identify the spirit. The watchful young girl consumed everything.

One by one, members of the assembled group moved closer and more protectively toward little Azúcar. There was an embracing air of familial warmth that had penetrated this secret spiritual world so far removed from the oppressive stench of the open trough that ran down the length of the *batey*, and also secluded from the daily torture of the sugarcane fields and grinding mills.

Much as with Doña Fela or Don Anselmo, people were not readily able to discern Mamá Lola's age; detection was difficult. Everyone simply guessed. Was she sixty of sixty-eight? Mamá Lola had a small, keen-featured face; and although her skin was wrinkled in a hundred different spots and was especially glistening around the eyes and mouth, that same mulatto cutis was drawn tight over her prominent cheekbones and pointed chin. Her large, round, wide-awake eyes were constantly vigilant and clear. She spied Azúcar listening with jubilant intensity as the old wrinkled-faced woman spoke. Mamá Lola's large eyes danced gleefully as she spoke instructively to the young girl.

"In our view of things, the living, the dead, and the spirits are all dependent on one another," she began her lesson. "We the living need advice, warning and protection provided by ancestors and spirits. They must be fed and honored if they are to possess the strength and will to protect us, the living."

As if a sudden reflection of bright light flashed across the face of a diligent pupil, Azúcar's eyes registered immediate comprehension. She thought to herself how true it was that she and all the others in the world of the batey really did need protection in this different life. The young girl, thinking grown up thoughts, had lately begun reflecting upon just how difficult merely living had become.

The drumming started up again, this time with a quickened drumming; those individuals who were able to do so, began chanting in full-voice unison, using the same language Azúcar had heard Don Anselmo speak earlier.

"Lafanmi sanble, Sanble nan. Se kreyòl nonye, Voye pwomès a lwa Ginen."

The last line of the chant was repeated several times more and much more stridently than the other lines: "I serve the African spirits pure and simple."

The drumming continued without any hint of stopping. The congregation clapped and swayed with the pulsating beats. The room was bathed in hypnotic euphoria. Everyone felt it, even the young children present. Together, everyone began swaying with the rhythm of the drums. One dominant voice would lead while the chorus repeated:

"Voye pwomès a lwa Ginen. Voye pwomès a lwa Ginen."

Perhaps to the uninitiated, the outsider, the stranger totally unfamiliar with the milieu of cultural diversity that characterized life in the *batey*, the mixed gathering might have seemed a rather bizarre portrait of humanity. After all, the faces and sounds registered a culturally diverse assemblage of destitute souls from all across the wide the Caribbean: there was Spanish, English, pidgin English, St. Lucian, Guadeloupean and Martiniquean patois, Haitian Kreyòl, Domínico-Haitian nagô; beliefs like Catholic, Protestant, Haitian Vodou, Santería, Regla de Ocha, Obeah, Changó. But not one was vying for dominance . . . not here. No. They were collectively searching how best to define *"Lafanmi"* --- "Family" under the most difficult conditions of trying to survive their shared misery.

The series of Catholic prayers and creole songs, especially some of the traditional opening songs of anonymous origin and authorship, often heard across superficial language and national

61

barriers, provided considerable insight into the complexity of family-building in African Diaspora communities. This was made all the more poignant in the contradictions, adversities, and ironies of the *batey*. The deceptively simple "*Lafanmi sanble*" chant, announcing "Family" as the occasion for gathering at Doña Fela's cabin and immediately acknowledging that this same Family had become beset with a "problem," served to remind the assembled group of individuals, despite their point of origin or language, that returning home was no simple matter and neither was locating and defining "Family." Little Azúcar was rapidly absorbing this important lesson; she had excellent and committed teachers.

OCHO

Mamá Lola smiled a broad, confident smile. She was assured ten-fold and moreso that she had been successful in impressing upon her apt pupil that the youngster was comfortably among "Family" gathered here in the cabin. Azúcar, in turn, had much to wonder about still. This special evening was to be a lesson to remind her of exactly who she was; where she had come from; how much she was loved; what were the forces of collective spiritual power. Throughout the fervor of the earlier part of the evening, Doña Fela had not been seen anywhere. A few individuals had remarked that maybe the old woman was simply exhausted from the rigors of preparing for this elaborate celebration.

"You seen Doña Fela tonight? Teresa asked nervously of her husband Cirilo. "Everybody been wonderin' where she was."

Like a circus contortionist, Teresa stretched her giraffe-like neck in almost humanly impossible angles trying to spot the evening's elusive hostess. But before Cirilo could venture a guess, the drums stopped abruptly for a second time that evening. Then from out of fading and distant shadows stepped Doña Fela herself, dressed completely in blazing white, with a white head wrap wound abundantly around her small head. She approached the decorated table and knocked on its edge several times; "rousing the spirits and announcing her arrival" was how she later explained this part of the ritual to her granddaughter.

Doña Fela took from the deep pocket of her white apron a small bottle of *kleren*, the pure cane liquor that is often the preferred rum of the batey, and proceeded to pour a few drops onto the floor. This gesture symbolized the act of honoring the ancestors. While the libation was spilled, Doña Fela chanted in a strong, deep voice and in the same language that Don Anselmo had used:

"Lova mwen, aprè Gran Mèt, m' se sou kont on."
Damian's comrades from the barracks, Césaire, Millien, Vincent, and Pierre, who had felt among family the moment they set foot inside the "party" and had recognized all the signs and symbols of the intricate and carefully executed ritual, were eager to translate for their friend from St. Kitts, who did not understand the strange-sounding language used throughout the evening.

"My spirits, after the Lord God, I am in your hands," Césaire translated what Doña Fela had chanted.

"The *kleren* is for Papa Gede," added Vincent. "She speakin' with the spirit Papa Gede for all of us; she askin' him for protection. *Ou ka konprann nwen*? You can understand me?"

Damian nodded a "Yes." Like everyone else assembled inside the cabin, Damian was fully aware that there was a "problem" in the Family. . . a serious one that weighed heavily upon all the members of the Family. Doña Fela had called the special gathering precisely because "the problem" was growing increasingly oppressive upon her spirit. Ever since that mournfully hideous, sultry afternoon when the *capataz*'s eldest son entered her cabin and forced his wicked bestiality inside the defenseless, innocent child. With each day that passed since then, Doña Fela had been driven into emotional maelstroms of sorrow and anger. But tonight was her night; tonight the old woman would receive the signs of the solution to "the problem." She would have that heavy weight lifted from her.

As the ceremony continued, the quartet of dancers, now with Doña Fela incorporated among their ranks, began to swirl gracefully in a kind of counterclockwise circular motion. Each of the women, including the hostess, seemed completely entranced. Their eyes were closed; their body movements now appeared effortless, as though these bulky old women were actually floating across a mystical lake in a dream; their old wrinkled and calloused hands formed subtle, delicately beautiful gestures seemingly associated with some manner of intricate sign language decipherable only among a privileged few of the spiritual pantheon. No one was quite certain.

The drummers were beating a slow rhythm, much like that heard earlier in the evening; then the drumming picked up tempo, becoming faster, which seemed to urge the dancers to spin even more rapidly, despite their aged, work-worn, bulky bodies. But clearly the dancers, including Doña Fela, exhibited a nimbleness that immediately belied their old age. Mamá Lola, who was still standing next to her young pupil, holding her hand, leaned over to whisper in the girl's waiting ear.

"*Escúchame*. Listen to me; when they come up to you, that's good; reach out to receive their blessing. Give them your hand, child, when they reach for you. The spirits of the ancestors have been summoned here to protect you from now on." The child was transfixed by the spectacle.

All five of the old, but agile women, in their rhythmic and synchronized paces, found their way to where Azúcar and Mamá Lola were standing solemnly. The women stretched out their hands in Azúcar's direction. As she had been ordered, Azúcar grabbed for the outstretched hands, one by one. The girl could not help wonder how the women had found her since their eyes seemed still to be closed tightly. Little did Azúcar know as well that night just how and to what extent she would be solidly protected henceforth.

Azúcar's eyes shone with an increased, but relaxed curiosity and excitement. She clutched more tightly Mamá Lola's strong arm. The dancing and drumming simultaneously slowed down before gradually coming to a halt. At last the circle broke apart and the dancers, all except Doña Fela, paraded past the attentive spectators, who respectfully saluted the tireless dancers as they made their way out of the cabin altogether and into the front courtyard. Doña Fela was left alone, standing in the center of the congregation. She was regal. All eyes were upon her majesty. The congregation was solemn.

The shadows became more and more dense with each passing hour. The late night was now heavy with silence. Somewhere far away a dog barked sadly and, from time to time, echoes of distant forest toads that were still awake could be heard. A tranquil night breeze slipped in and passed through the faithful gathering. There were minor signs of anxiety, even slight weariness among the crowd. It had been a long night and the hour was advancing. It was now past one o'clock and within a few hours more everybody would be rising from slumber to start another day with the impatiently awaiting sugarcane. This time, Doña Fela spoke to her friends and neighbors with an unmasked and bitter vehemence, but in a low voice, much as if the night itself were listening.

"*Mis amigos y vecinos*. My friends and neighbors," she began, "You all been called here tonight to witness as Family our sacred offerin' in the name of Mayanèt. Know that Mayanèt we do not see very often. She come in and out once in a while, maybe once every five years or so." The old woman, altering her already lowered voice to a more sinister tone, continued. "If you have somethin' in your family, somethin' very ugly and horrible that has happened . . . somethin' especially foul, Mayanèt must come. She will come and change things."

Doña Fela muttered as if each syllable of each word were being ripped from her mouth with a fisherman's knife prying open an oyster. "*Sí, mis hermanos y hermanas*. Yes, my brothers and sisters, I am angry — very angry and hurt, too. I ask Mayanèt to come protect *mi azúcar morenita* even now after the ugly deed been done against her. I ask Mayanèt to protect all of us gathered here tonight. That protection will come to us by way of Mayanèt's powerful vengeance, for Mayanèt is not sweet.

No, *señores*. Our sacred Mayanèt ain't sweet none. Don't be fooled by her easy smile that she wear on her lovely face. Just the opposite. Mayanèt is a very tough an' fearless lady. Always been so. An' know one thing for sure about our lady. Vengeance is hers alone! She never fail. Her powers of vengeance are to be feared. You'll see!"

Doña Fela had finished. Azúcar, with eyes open as wide as they could possibly be, moved even closer to Mamá Lola's side, as if Mamá Lola's small body served as the protective shield alluded to by the words of the girl's majestic grandmother. Mamá Lola clenched the girl's tiny hands tighter. One-eyed Clementina turned her entire head toward her husband Tomás, only this time holding back any questions. She just stared blankly from her one eye. Tomás, as if in a mysterious and pleading tone, almost reprimanded his otherwise irksome wife.

"*Cállate*! Quiet," he wanted to say to her, but found it unnecessary.

Lolita and her Haitian Estimé both looked at each other, but like the other couples, exchanged no words until they reached their own house afterwards. Longneck Teresa gently poked her husband Cirilo in the ribs with her elbow and said with hardly a whisper in his ear.

"Now, *yo konprann*."

Huddled against the same wall of the cabin as the others were big-bosomed Sarafina, Destine, her Domínico-Haitian friend with the prominent cheekbones, coffee-colored Milagros and her bulky Jamaican husband Keith, also Damian from St. Kitts and his barracks companions. Not at all strangely, everyone in one form or another was quite familiar with the summoned powers of Mayanèt. Everyone — no matter from what corner of the Caribbean he or she was from -- was also certain of the wrathful vengeance always associated with Mayanèt. They all became completely silent.

But it was old Don Anselmo who broke the silence, almost as expected, in a kind of collective attempt to respond directly to his long-time and trusted comrade of the *batey*. With ease, the old man made his way from the rear of the dense, sweaty and smoke-filled crowd, to the front where Doña Fela had positioned herself. He stood proudly facing her, their keen eyes indicating a profound mutual acknowledgment, respect and understanding. It was the son of that old *prèt savann* of a long time ago who spoke first, in a gentle, yet firm greeting.

"Oh, Mother of all the Saints."

Doña Fela, with both hands out-stretched, as a queen would do, summoned Anselmo into her regal embrace. She nodded her approbation of Anselmo's salutation. Looking first at the old woman, then at the gathering, Anselmo made his remarks plain and direct, but also with the continued and unmistakable vehemence that had been initiated by Doña Fela.

"My Sister, my Family. How I been waitin' a long, long time for this night to come! For twice as long here in this soil we all been enslaved and abused, humiliated and raped by plantation masters. Their unquenched greed and lust have been their weapons of torture against us. It didn't matter if we were Dominican, Haitian, Jamaican, Bahamian, Grenadian or Panamanian. Whether we come from St. Kitts or from St. Lucia. To the corporations, we ain't even human beings; we ain't nothin' but a lump of shit brought here from one shit-hole to a worse one, lured by a few tin cans of sardines and a handful of saltine crackers to work in their cane fields until we ain't no more use to nobody. We are lumps of shit to even our own governments who sell us off year after year to the highest bidder; an' that 'sposed to be a contract. When we arrive here in this miserable Island, we get a goddamn number to identify us to the plantation managers; a number, I remind you. Our own names bein' of no use to them once we in the system. Once inside the plantation, we chained to it forever. There ain't no escapin', no returnin' to our homes in our own native soils. We die here in this filthy shit-hole . . . What a twist of fate that we die here for the sweetness of sugar! *La maldita caña*." Anselmo let out a sardonic chuckle cut short by his dead seriousness.

He wasn't finished. "And how do we live? *Coño*. We live in shitty barracks and rundown shacks not fit for stray dogs because we regarded as less than dogs. The plantation owners' livestock live in better conditions than us . . . and you can believe even their own dogs do, too." Anselmo was churning with fire as he went on with his impassioned denunciation.

"But who keeps the sugar barons fat and their pockets full of pesos? Who keeps this *maldito* Island rich? The lumps of shit they search the whole fuckin' Caribbean for to do the meanest work on the face of the earth, that's who, *carajo*! And our pay? What fuckin' pay? The few *pesos* we get for bein' worked to death go straight back into the pockets of the plantation managers. The lousy shit they make us buy from their own miserable *bodegas* in the *bateys* we know is overpriced. So, we end up owin' them what little we do earn!"

The old man's words were leaping and lashing out like projectiles from an over-heated canon to the mesmerized group of listeners. Don Anselmo finally reached the keynote of his delivery, with all its volcanic explosiveness.

"Then the filthy bush hogs boldly and shamelessly rob us of our loveliest of gifts of all — the only pure symbol of our collective worth here in this perpetual cesspool of life as we been knowin' it on these murderous plantations. The greedy, overstuffed hogs keep stealin' from us our most tender young flowers that ain't even bloomed yet. Either we been unwillin' or we been incapable' of protectin' our most precious gifts. I say to you that this violation must end. So, we gather this night as Family to seek the protection and strength of our common ancestors. In the name of all that is sacred to our ancestors, may the spirits hear our collective petition and send forth the powers of Mayanèt."

The old man suddenly and very loudly pounded his stick on the floor of the cabin --- as if summoning Mayanèt to present herself before the assembly. But actually, he was announcing that he had finished. Don Anselmo had said all that he had intended to say. There was no mistake or misunderstanding in the message delivered that evening. As if on signal, Mamá Lola then cut into the elaborately decorated cakes that were on the table, one at a time until all three cakes had been properly sliced and served to the congregation. The mothers who had brought along their infants and toddlers woke them up and started approaching Doña Fela so that the spirits might bless the children on this almost sacred occasion. Weariness, sleepiness, and spiritual intoxication had exacted a heavy toll on the participants. But everybody felt that, unlike the exhaustion that regularly accompanies having to deal with the cane fields, this evening's fatigue was well earned.

The events of the evening concluded as abruptly as they had begun. Folks began leaving hurriedly, many still eating the thin slices of decorated cake with yellow and white sugar roses as they poured out of Doña Fela's front courtyard and onto the outer edges of the batey's central trough that lead individuals in the direction of their respective homes. There was not a single soul who had come to Doña Fela's that evening who was not thinking long and hard about what Don Anselmo had said, or about, of course, Doña Fela's plea to Mayanèt. Moreover, the departing souls, without exception, somehow felt confident that "the problem" would be resolved.

70

NUEVE

The numbers were far more than most people had expected or would even have imagined. There was both excitement and uncertainty about all the new workers arriving for the annual *zafra* at *Esperanza Dulce*.

"*Ay, por todo' loh santo'*. Where all these folks come from?" asked one-eyed Clementina.

"*Por mi madre, coño*. I wasn't 'spectin' so many neither," longneck Teresa joined in, with quick jerks of her long neck as if possibly to determine for her personal satisfaction the exact points of origin of what seemed to be an endless line of new arrivals being herded through the front entrance of the batey. They had been transported in a caravan of six trucks that disgorged their human cargo just outside the high stockade-like, iron entrance gate that was usually padlocked at night. From that point the contracted newcomers were led on foot into what would be their living quarters for the duration of the *zafra*.

"There must be at least two dozen people livin' in one of those cabins down next to Doña Fela," speculated Lolita. "I don't know how many in the other one."

The two cabins situated along one side of where Doña Fela and Azúcar lived had remained unoccupied until the anxiously awaited arrival of the additional braceros for the zafra. It was also true that management had hurriedly constructed a number of large barracks for the multitude of single men arriving among the contracted laborers.

"A hellava lot of *pesos* gonna be made here real soon; that's for sure. All those '*Ou konprann*' Haitians comin' without their womenfolk," was big-bosomed Serafina's coded remark to the group of equally curious and vulturous females (at least, of course, those without husbands) gathered early that Sunday morning by the front gates of the *batey* like a flock of ravenous predators. All the eager-eyed women cackled with delight to

71

register their agreement with Serafina's always expected and raunchy, yet truthful remarks.

"You just make sure you leave 'um a few *pesos* to send back home," another voice rang out, decidedly more sympathetic than Serafina's prediction. "*Pero, chica,* what kind of heart you got left inside you? *La maldita caña* take all the sweetness out of you, too?"

"*Mi hita,* everybody know all I got is sugar in me," Serafina responded sharply.

At that jokingly sarcastic reminder, the crowd of watchful females held back no remaining explosions of laughter. There really had been much speculation about the new people coming in for the sugarcane harvest, all of which resembled in nearly every regard the already-established socio-ethnic demographics of the *batey.*

Meanwhile, continuing to pass two-abreast through the front entrance into the compound were the new faces of young and middle-aged men, easily comprising the bulk of the new arrivals; a considerably number of healthy-looking young women, a few with their small children in tow; a noticeable number of baby-faced boys who appeared to be no more than perhaps nine or ten years old. Armed guards mounted on horseback accompanied this rag-tag multitude. Some of the weaponry was unmistakably of the semi-automatic variety . . . and very menacing. There was no guessing as to whether these guards actually knew how to use their sophisticated weapons.

The scene looked like a bizarre daguerreotype that had been made in the last century, showing African captives shackled together, fresh from the slave auction, being marched into the plantation compound by their triumphant new owners.

72

"We'll see how many of 'um make it through the end of the *zafra*," one of the onlookers smirked to his companion standing alongside.

"Fool, you made it, didn't you? Year after year an' you ain't gone yet," was the wry comment from the more optimistic companion.

The arriving entourage was ordered to stop in front of the small, box-like administration building that housed the offices of the estate accounting clerks and general management staff. It was from these offices that all record keeping, production tallies, supply orders, labor assignments, equipment maintenance records, and all other vital administrative matters emanated. In other words, this small, unobtrusive, unadorned building was the hub of strategic planning for plantation operations.

So many times as he passed this particular building, Don Anselmo has harbored one secret thought . . . one thought so burning with rage that there was the accompanying certainty of the severest consequences should this thought be revealed. The number of times he has dreamed of torching this wretched symbol of oppression and exploitation only he alone would ever know. He has also dreamed himself the reincarnation of the legendary maroon chieftain Boukman, officiating at that prophetic ceremony in the Bois Caïman. The old warrior saw himself leading the devastating assaults against the planters and --- like Boukman, who burned nearly a thousand plantations in the northern part of the Island--- saw himself indiscriminately slaughtering all his oppressors in order to free his enslaved comrades. These were sweet and very secret dreams to old Don Anselmo . . . as he dreamt of sugar!

Two pudgy White men, both North Americans--- one wearing thick eyeglasses, and both protected from the blazing early morning sun by broad-brimmed khaki hats, and both holding

73

those authoritative-looking clipboards that people in charge always seem to carry and from which their eyes never seem to become unglued— were waiting with an obvious display of contemptuous impatience.

"Can't they move it along more quickly? This sun is fuckin' burning my ass out here," the pudgy man with the thick eyeglasses said to his equally impatient companion.

A heavy and cold sweat was already pouring down his fat face even at this early hour in the day. His pudgy companion, also without looking up from his clipboard and seriously flipping through sheets of paper attached to the board, replied, "I'm double-checking to see precisely how many family units we have in this batch of new contract recruits; the vouchers go only to the men and I don't think the central office sent over enough initial vouchers." His observation did not have a tone of urgency, only a cursory indifference.

These two men, pivotal spokes in the local management machinery, represented the regional authority of the multinational corporation that now owned the bulk of the Island's sugarcane operations, once the exclusive domain of a handful of wealthy Island families. Such families had originally owned these *ingenios* since the establishment of the colony. Diego Montalvo, along with other locals placed in the coveted position of estate *capataz*, reported directly to men such as these two pudgy, seemingly always irritated bureaucrats.

Accompanying these two was an imposing armed guard, a non-smiling military type, very tense looking. He was a deeply tanned mulatto — the kind who quickly reminded everybody (perhaps himself?) of what he regarded as a very essential fact.

"*Yo no soy negro.* I'm not black and I'm certainly not Haitian. After all, only Haitians are Black." He had his semi-automatic rifle slung casually, but proudly across his broad shoulder.

The fourth individual making up the reception team for the new arrivals was an overly zealous Domínico-Haitian— the classic sycophant in island societies; the obnoxious type that constantly attempts to win favor or advance himself by "flattering the masters." He was so immediately transparent in his unctuous flattery and flashy exhibition (so totally unnecessary) of his finely honed multilingual skills, especially in the presence of company administrators. This was the sadly self-deceived type who earnestly believed there was a meritorious promotion within the company hierarchy awaiting him. He has been waiting year after year —-eight years now— for such a promotion that would never come.

This member of the team served as translator of anything that the pudgy White men needed to say to the group, but mostly to contracted braceros from Kreyòl-speaking Haiti. The Domínico-Haitian multilinguist, however, was available and found highly indispensable only at this very instance of introduction and orientation to the rules, procedures, and conditions of living and working on the plantation. After this Sunday morning, services for any kind of official translations would become a remote and fleeting memory for those lost souls disadvantaged by a language barrier.

The servile self-seeker, but unappreciated and under-utilized, very talented Domínico-Haitian translator repeatedly would find himself drifting from one town after another, often on both sides of the river, offering his highly prized skills to interested takers. Sometimes, he would manage to find temporary employment giving language lessons— French, Spanish, or English to the children or bored matrons of upper class households in the various towns he passed through.

By now many idly curious residents had gathered to form a small crowd of onlookers who positioned themselves a few yards away from the administration building. From there they commanded an almost perfect view of the entire scene. Since it was Sunday and thus a day of more-than-deserved rest from the fields, the spectators grew rapidly in number. The scene was nothing new, however; it was immediately and solidly recognizable. Each witness in attendance had a personal recollection of exactly the same procedures and routines that these new arrivals were experiencing now. The sun was beginning to beat down ferociously upon the scene.

"I remember my first day here in this hell-hole of the devil himself," said one woman onlooker. "Seein' these poor souls make me realize that ain't nothin changed."

"We just ain't nothin' in this miserable world," sighed one thin woman blinking her eyes from the intense glaze of the sun above. She also remembered with sadness arriving to the batey for the first time.

"*Sé pa vouazin ka va ranjé sa pou nou!*" quickly disagreed another woman standing immobile and firm among the spectators. "It ain't our neighbor who gonna' arrange things for us," she offered in translation.

What she meant was that obeying the laws of the spirit world and one's protective loas would be the answer to things. With immediate ease, everyone in attendance held points of personal remembrance and connection with the new arrivals.

One of the pudgy little White men, the one without the thick eyeglasses, began distributing two slips of paper to the adult males among the new arrivals. One slip of paper, white, had a large number, one through whatever, printed on it. This number indicated the cabin assignment: family units were housed together, single men were assigned to the men's barracks, single women – who were never given the white slip of paper— were assigned to the women's barracks. The other slip of paper, this one yellow, was the voucher or *vale*. The residents of the batey in lieu of actual currency used this all-important *vale*. These *vales* could not be used anywhere at all outside the physical limits of the *batey*— or at least not officially. This was the exclusive means by which the workers could purchase a variety of unscrupulously over-priced provisions at the local *bodegas* that were scattered around the *batey*. In fact, a person used the *vale* to buy whatever was needed; it was no secret that some men even used the *vale* to pay for the services of prostitutes.

"Another manner of very efficient control and exploitation," old Don Anselmo always reminded everybody. Because nearly all new arrivals were without money when they entered the front gate, these *vales* were customarily issued upon the day of arrival in order that workers might begin supplying their cabins with needed provisions, anything from kerosene lamps and kerosene oil, American cigarettes, *kleren*, canned food stuffs, dry goods, even vegetable seeds and basic planting tools for cultivating individual conucos. The maximum irony, of course, was that the workers had to use the *vale* to purchase even the one-pound bags of unbleached brown sugar for household consumption — on the very site where the product was cultivated, of course, from stalk to grinding mill.

"Nothing here in the *batey* is free; *Ni la chocha*; *hay que pagá la*. Not even pussy; you gotta pay for it." It was again the acerbic tongue of Don Anselmo that regularly reminded his comrades that the system of the *vale* was so corrupt that most often than not, the workers found themselves perpetually indebted to the *bodegueros*, "grocery store operators," who were in fact the paid employees of the plantation itself.

"The few pesos we make go straight back into the already over-stuffed pockets of the plantation owners," the old man growled.

Although he didn't know it at the time, Don Anselmo was never quite alone in his constant rebukes and denouncements of the very industry that paradoxically and simultaneously exploited and sustained him. He watched in bitter anger the thousands of Haitians and other Antillean nationals, all unwitting victims of fraud and exploitation, who are lured to the Island each year to come work in the sugarcane harvest. The *"Consejo Estatal del Azúcar,"* the State Sugar Council, contracts legitimately these physically robust workers, men as well as women. The contracts are then negotiated with the company representatives.

Don Anselmo was always ready to dispense meaningful lessons for the youngsters of the batey.

"The workers are called *braceros,* a Spanish word comin' from the word that really mean 'arm' or *'brazo'.* An' that's the only real reason the plantation need us --- for the naked force of muscle," he explained somberly to his attentive pupils, while smacking firmly the muscle of his own seasoned arm. "Cuttin' sugarcane take a lot of solid arms, or *brazos."*

He had been convinced long, long ago that the only desired attribute of the *bracero* is indeed the raw force of solid brawn, the well-tempered muscle so absolutely essential for the brutal task of cutting acres upon acres of sugarcane. Over a period of time and growing awareness, the subhuman living conditions and the appalling mistreatment of the *braceros* had begun to prompt attention and strident protests from a number of national and international human rights organizations.

But Don Anselmo, quite understandably, had absolutely no way of knowing that his cries of outrage ---while echoing in silence locally--- were nevertheless resonating loudly in the form of denouncements from non-governmental human rights groups that assailed the role of the Island's police and military units in the annual recruitment of desperately needed laborers. The reprehensible behavior, even the authorities of the State Sugar Council, whether within or beyond the dreaded period of the zafra, was being well documented. Many years would pass before he learned the name of one very surprising and formidable ally —and coming from an equally surprising corner— in his cries against the ghastly horrors of the sugar industry.

"*Pero coño.* Not a damned soul is listenin'," he would simply say. "But one day they'll pay for all this they done to us."

Among the many abuses underscoring daily life on the Island's sugar plantations and surfacing most prominently during the harvest, perhaps the one abuse that caused especially vociferous denouncement was the unconscionable plight of Haitian female laborers. While indeed all female braceras were vulnerable, Haitian women systematically were more cruelly victimized than other Caribbean women who arrived because their presence was not officially recognized in either the bateys or in the cane fields.

As a consequence, for example, Haitian women did not possess the fundamental right to housing for themselves—other than being assigned to the female barracks; nor were they entitled to the benefits of health services, meager as they were in the *batey*— but more often non-existent. No one ever ventured a specific reason, justification, or minimal explanation for this singularly targeted injustice.

"That's just the way it is," most people usually said. "*Así es.*"

" I don't know, but it always been so," others said.

Also, women laborers from the other side of the river were traditionally paid about half of what men received, and they rarely were issued vales. So then, the Haitian *bracera*, given her status of "non-person," could not hope to obtain official documentation of any kind nor any other types of benefits. She was thus condemned to a circumstance of "illegality" and as a consequence, to permanent exploitation. If she were lucky enough to be a married woman when she arrived, prayed constantly to her protective loas that her husband would not leave her a widow or would not be deported —for however minor an infraction of the local laws, especially those of the plantation. Thus, most women laborers had their fate cast to the whims of random assault from every possible angle.

Although Lolita was not Haitian and had a husband by way of an official marriage ceremony with a bona fide certificate to prove it, she nevertheless found herself constantly murmuring to herself in her secret moments. The prayer had become a regular part of her daily ritual.

"*Que Dio' me teng misericordia y no me quite mi marido, dejándome sin ná.* May God have mercy upon me and not take my husband away from me, leaving me abandoned and with nothing."

Standing alone in a resolute anger early that Sunday morning, Don Anselmo pondered heavy thoughts. How well he recognized the bewildered and lonely stares on the black and brown faces that directed the attached bodies toward the pudgy White estate managers holding on tightly to their clipboards. Don Anselmo watched in silence as the new arrivals, with outstretched, open hands— like beggars hoping anxiously for the charitable act of alms giving from their more fortunate brethren, waiting to be issued one white slip of paper for the cabin assignment and one yellow slip for the vales. The act was completed swiftly and perfunctorily; there was neither the humanly exchange of words nor the slightest of glances.

"The bastards don't even call out names," the old man grumbled angrily to himself. "We may as well be invisible to them."

80

The fact was that the plantation administrators rarely, if ever, bothered to utter the proper name of a *bracero* mainly because they never saw the need to do so. Managers simply never took the time to learn the different names of the workers, coming as they did from various places around the Caribbean and representing merely "a bunch of foreign workers" to the managers. Besides, and perhaps more importantly, to call the individual by his or her proper name realistically would be to acknowledge the individual's personhood, thus positioning the bracero on equal human footing with the administrators. And naturally, this could never happen according to the traditional social codes of the plantation . . . codes that had been in place since the remote *encomienda* system under which the Spain monarchy allotted specific numbers of indigenous people and their communal lands to "deserving" Spaniards as rewards for the soldiers' s indispensable role in the campaign of territorial and cultural conquest during the fifteenth century. The bottom line was that these masses were faceless *braceros* contracted to work the *zafra*. Period.

The two pairs of cobalt blue eyes of the managers remained fixed like cold magnets upon columns of contract "numbers" — true enough, not the names of actual persons. Each number represented a single contract unit that would be working this year's *zafra*. The clipboards held page after page after yet another page of cumbersome administrative lists; as a laborer passed before one of the managers, the self-seeking Domínico-Haitian assistant carefully read the identification number printed on the conspicuous tag that was pinned to the shirt pocket of each worker. As each number was called out, one or the other of the sweaty managers would check off that number appearing in the column.

"Goddamn this fuckin' oppressive heat," said one of the pudgy little bureaucrats, looking angrily at the noonday sky that was now baking him.

Although indeed tedious and quite time consuming, this task had been made easy for the managers because the Domínico-Haitian had previously and painstakingly — and not to say most eagerly, naturally, --- positioned the tag-bearing individuals in the proper number sequence . . . all six truckloads comprising that day's cargo of newly recruited workers. For this reason the truck convoys always arrived on Sunday mornings in order not to disrupt the production schedule during the workweek. The super efficient Domínico-Haitian assistant truly respected the importance of his job even if no one else did.

"Why doesn't the company recognize the value of my work?" he reflected pathetically. "Do they even see me?"

Pure humiliation was written on the man's face and registered unmistakably in his voice. Sadly, he never had the courage to utter these thoughts aloud for anyone to hear.

An early Sunday morning grew into mid-afternoon. It was already past two o'clock by the time the ritual of arrival, the tedium of calling out numbers and checking them off, the distribution of different colored slips of paper, the monitoring of newcomers to their new quarters, together with any other processing routines, all finally came to a halt. With the same air of impatient contempt that marked their unceremonious presence, the two pudgy White estate managers, now completely soaked in their own miserable sweat, their shirts clinging to their pudgy bodies, concluded their task with visible disdain and left. They were still accompanied by the stoic, armed, self-important mulatto guard. The four-man reception and official intake processing team departed in a company jeep chauffeured by one of them . . . the ever-faithful Domínico-Haitian. He hadn't heard his name mentioned by anybody throughout the entire morning . . . nobody called it.

"This took much longer than expected; I'm fuckin' glad it's over," growled the pudgy manager wearing the thick eyeglasses. "I hate being down here with these fuckin' shit eaters this long."

His companion agreed. "Yeah. The worst part of all this is over for us. Let's get the hell outta this stinking shit-hole."

Neither one hesitated in expressing eagerness to return to more comfortable surroundings and to be around their own kind, all the while ignoring completely the other two employees sharing the company jeep. The sun above by now was sizzling hot and spared no one below the vengeance of its rays. A skillet of fat readied for frying fish could not have been hotter.

Once the new arrivals were more or less settled in and their new neighbors had assisted them in adjusting to the way things generally run in the *batey*, and then explained who was who, there was little else to be done. Even for the long-time residents, it was now a matter of just waiting for the frantic work routines of the *zafra* scheduled to begin early the following morning. And now that the novelty of watching the processing of new arrivals had ended — although the "event" was routine and quite familiar to everybody who had witnessed it, things resumed to normal. It was merely another hot, uneventful, late Sunday afternoon in the *batey*. Everybody was just waiting . . . The *batey* lay blanketed under the violent weight of the afternoon heat; the air was breezeless like always at this time of day; it didn't matter if it was Sunday, Tuesday or Friday. Even though Sunday afternoons were normally days of rest, an entirely different sort of lassitude nevertheless hung low and heavy over the compound.

At that moment Doña Fela and her Azúcar were sitting together under the comforting shade of the flamboyán tree located a few yards from their cabin. The old woman was there patiently braiding her granddaughter's hair.

"*Ayiii, abuelita*, that's too tight," Azúcar pleaded with her grandmother even though the old woman was applying only loving touches to each twist of the girl's long, coarse hair. The hanging braids had been executed so perfectly that the girl registered a painful sensation where patches of her hair seemed to have been pulled from her scalp.

"*Mi   dulcecita*. My sweet little thing, now   how   many times I gotta tell you that women with their hair loose in the cane fields burn up quicker under the hot sun than if you braid it up?" Doña Fela thoughtfully reminded the girl.

The afternoon heat showed no mercy still. Grandmother and granddaughter were also waiting for the next day's franticness to begin . . . if only as an escape from the unyielding heat. Meanwhile, Don Anselmo was conducting his own version of an orientation session with a small group of new arrivals, many of whom had worked on sugarcane plantations located elsewhere on the Island or on other sugar producing islands scattered around the Caribbean. Unlike the long-time residents of the batey, many of the new arrivals contracted solely for the *zafra* formed part of a seemingly unbroken traditional migratory pattern of being shifted from island to island with the staggered periods of the *zafra*. Such was the nature of sugarcane production. But none of these *braceros* had worked a plantation as grand as *Esperanza Dulce*, which easily dwarfed most others where these laborers had worked previously. Anselmo was serious in his admonitions to the new recruits. Estimé served as translator for Don Anselmo.

"My brothers and sisters," he was saying, "I want you to remember well what I tell you. Be up an' ready as soon as the first rays of the sun be dryin' up the humidity of the night before. Don't dally about in your cabin as you take your mornin' coffee, *cassabe* an' corn porridge. Be quick!"

All eyes and ears were focused on the wise elder and his trusted translator Estimé. A hushed and studied anxiety dominated the air, thick as the listlessness of that blistering Sunday afternoon. But the new arrivals were attentive to Don Anselmo.

"Most important of all is to listen and follow exactly the orders of the *capataz*. The old bastard won't tell you twice to do somethin'. An' be especially careful of his son, Mario. He a meaner snake than his father."

Don Anselmo never referred to the capataz in the Island's traditional master-slave context, using the title "Don" before Diego Montalvo's name— certainly outside the presence of the capataz himself. Almost no one failed to address the capataz with this traditional title of unquestioned respect even when referring to him in conversation with comrades. But for Anselmo it was far more than being obstinate; this was Anselmo's Boukman reincarnation. Old Anselmo, the rebel chieftain, was fully aware of his actions and thoughts. He continued his admonitory remarks to the newcomers with the aid of Estimé, who proved invaluable since more than half of the new braceros were Haitian like their translator. In fact, their attention was gleefully directed toward Estimé, whose words in the recognizable tongue conveyed an open compassion and ready understanding. At one point, he departed from Don Anselmo's delivery, as earnest as it was, in order to underscore the existing bond among compatriots together on alien soil.

"*Mwin ginyin la pèn. Sé oun lavi' ki rèd.*"

Estimé felt compelled to remind his comrades.

"Life is difficult. I share so much of your pain."

Lolita, standing among the listeners, was exceedingly proud of her Haitian that hot Sunday afternoon. She could feel the tears of joy rolling freely down her cheeks as she smiled a wife's joyful smile for her hero and father of her three children.

"My beautiful Haitian," she whispered between muted sobs.

DIEZ

Azúcar, it seemed, was much like one of those new arrivals that old Don Anselmo had admonished about not dallying after their morning coffee . . . about being quick to start the impending labor associated with the frantic sugarcane harvest. But rather, she awoke in a strangely joyous and anxiety-filled spirit, having had a sound and complete sleep the previous night. Even before dawn broke, Azúcar was already up and moving about the cabin. As always, she was eager to begin her day chatting nonstop with her grandmother until it was time to depart for the fields. But Doña Fela had been up hours ahead of her granddaughter; the old woman had even been to the ravine with two large gourds in which to fetch drinking water. She had also fed the guinea hens and chickens that were pecking impatiently for starved attention in the patio yard.

The *zafra* had begun in earnest. Azúcar was much too young to remember every detail about past cane harvests. However, several things about this very special phase of sugarcane production did leave memorable impressions with the young girl. There were the canes in a variety of colors: ribbon cane, black cane, white cane, sukee cane.

"*Esperanza Dulce* has always been fine sugarcane land ever since the place was first built, with its dark, loamy earth," was what all the neighboring estate managers said with a certain degree of undisguised envy.

"God has truly blessed this sweet land with his kindness and bounty," a succession of owners since the initial founders of *Esperanza Dulce* has said.

Azúcar also held fond memories of tasting for the first time a piece of delectable black cane ---- really soft and full of rich juice which felt good against her tender young gums. Growing up on the plantation, how could she not forget the exciting week of sugar making? The tantalizing smell of the white cane liquor bubbling into hot brown sugar in the huge boilers! These smells were sweeter to her nostrils than the sweetest of forest blossoms. It was a sweetness so powerful that it blocked out all the foul, malodorous fumes rising from the shit, vomit, and rotting garbage floating in the open trough in the middle of the *batey*.

But the *zafra* also brought for young Azúcar many moments of despair. She recalled, for example, that everybody was always so extremely busy that they didn't have time for her: no morning chats, no early evenings spent looking for shiny amber stones in the nearby ravine, and particularly hurtful, no time for her grandmother to braid her hair as the child listened excitedly to a variety of stories or the two of them engaged in the playful *cric-crac* riddles. Doña Fela had gained a certain local fame for being the best storyteller in the *batey* — although little Azúcar always fell asleep in her grandmother's lap, hardly ever hearing the end of any of the old griot's tales.

Now that the young girl herself was part of the labor force at *Esperanza Dulce*, she was fully aware of what was expected of every resident of the *batey* during *zafra*. And of course, the invaluable experiences of her grandmother had served as unforgettable lessons as well for the girl. But it was essentially what her grandmother had told the child about the annual frenzy that Azúcar remembered with greatest accuracy.

"*Zafra* ain't no carnival, *m'hijita*; never been."

Doña Fela spat out the words to her granddaughter, not bitterly, just very emphatically in order to make the point clear.

"Everybody was expected to work to the bone... from dawn to dusk. It's hard work. *Por mi madre*, they work us like mules."

The girl just stared, allowing the words to penetrate deeply into her conscious. The old woman's accounts were painted with the focused meticulousness of a trained artist, gingerly dabbling her mental paint brush onto the multicolored palette to find all the necessary words that would describe faithfully the unrelenting torture of the dreaded *zafra*. Remembering her grandmother's factual accounts was, for Azúcar, like vital lessons of history about which she would later be tested. *Zafra* was an experience not very easily forgotten.

Doña Fela had told her about how she remembered listening to tales of her own mother and her mother's mother— tales that took place during the long, dark period of slavery in the Island. The old storyteller had heard about how the plantation slaves had their lives divided into two essential segments: zafra and what was called *tiempo muerto*, "dead season" when all activity associated with sugar production came to a halt. These two distinct segments basically described the cycle of yearly activities and in large measure determined the daily engagement for slaves everywhere throughout the sugar-producing Caribbean.

The old woman's crisp memory recalled how the distribution of basic clothing, for instance, always marked the start of zafra: all the slaves were regularly issued the first of two annual changes of clothes, once at the beginning of the harvest and again when it ended.

"*Y eh fácil?* And you say it's easy?" Doña Fela asked in understood irony . . . the local manner of speaking, whereupon a person often asks rhetorically the exact opposite of what is really intended. "The only reason I don't never wear stripes to this very day is 'cause of how they would give all us women folk that *maldito* cotton dress at the beginnin' of every *zafra*. When I was a girl your age, I swore that I long as I lived I would never again drape myself in those damn stripes," she confessed openly to her granddaughter. And indeed she meant it; nobody in the

89

community could recall ever seeing the old woman wearing dresses with stripes. She had resurrected every possible ounce of long-buried dread as she related this experience.

Much to Azúcar's surprise, the more she listened to her grandmother's account of what life was like on the plantation during the *zafra* of many years ago, the more the young girl realized how the pattern of monstrous toil had not changed significantly. As her grandmother related each phase of the harvest in dramatic detail, Azúcar — even at such a young age— was sufficiently aware of how, except for major mechanization in overall operations, the routines had remained fundamentally the same. As certainly was the case on today's mechanized corporate estates, the sugar plantations of past eras — as Doña Fela had pointed out to the attentive Azúcar—

"*Se andaba con la suavida' de un reló'.*" And it was true that these plantations "operated as smoothly as a clock." *Esperanza Dulce* was the perfect example of clock-like precision. Then as now, observed the young listener, well before the work routines actually got underway, it was absolutely imperative that all the workers know exactly the task he or she was assigned and where. The precise order of rotation of these forced laborers during slavery was important as well, according to Doña Fela's account. At the start of each *zafra* the plantation's entire labor force would be assembled and then the overseer — in the same fashion that Diego Montalvo did— began assigning specific routines.

Summoned before anyone else, the men for the strategic boiler house always received their assignment first. These men usually were physically the strongest men among the work crew and were placed under the direct charge of what was called the *maestro de azúcar*. Doña Fela's father and grandfather had been painstakingly trained to assume this key responsibility of being "sugar master," the individual specially trained to perfection of actually "making the sugar." For quite some time only Europeans held this prestigious job, among the highest paid on the plantation --for *los blancos*, the Whites, of course. But once these Europeans moved on to the higher-level administrative posts, the task fell to skilled slave labor. Normally, the number of boilers operating would determine the number of men needed in this assignment. Each boiler needed perhaps eight or nine strong attendants with an additional six for related odd jobs in the boiler house. A well-financed plantation of six boilers like *Esperanza Dulce* easily had forty men assigned here alone.

Called next were the *transportistas*, or the "carts men" who transported the cane stalks. When the later plantations lacked their own private railway network, the number of carts men equaled the number of men assigned to the boiler house. This was a management strategy that placed these two teams of men on rotating night shifts: the carts men took over the first night shift from the men in the boiler house after the former team completed their own day's work in the fields

Then came the *cortadores*, the "cutters," usually consisting of equal numbers of both men and women, and often children of a certain age if they looked robust enough — unlike the two previous teams. Cutters could number about fifty or sixty individuals for a medium-sized estate, but easily near two or three hundred for the much larger plantations like *Esperanza Dulce*. Azúcar remembered being taught at the age of ten the proper way of cutting the tough sugarcane stalks to assure maximum safety and maximum output at the same time. In former times all the male cane cutters usually relieved the men working in the purging house and those carrying the *bagasse* on the compound.

One non-negotiable rule about *zafra* was that it was most

definitely not a scene of idle hands or wasted time, about which Azúcar was constantly being reminded. Speed was everything during *zafra*. All the varied, but closely interlocking tasks were performed at breakneck speed by specifically designated *braceros* who knew perfectly their individual jobs.

"Cane gotta be groun' soon as if git cut; 'else the juice gonna shrink an' ferment," Don Anselmo, without fail, routinely drilled in the new, younger cutters, some of whom were just slightly taller than the ominous machete they carried. "*Carajo.* It only take a few days for the cut cane to begin to ferment an' rot."

There wasn't a minute to be wasted. The cutting, hauling, grinding, chemical clarification, filtration, evaporation, and final crystallization has to be executed, without pause, in successive steps, one after the other . . . but at such great speed that it seemed as if all the operations were unfolding miraculously at the same time. Any observer was completely transfixed by the seemingly supernatural rapidity with which the assorted operations took place in the complicated sugar cycle.

"*M' hija*," Doña Fela, quite worried, would constantly say to her granddaughter, "Don't never let the *capataz* see you just standin' 'round doin' nothin'. You gotta keep cuttin' till the whistle blow. Then you know it's time to take a break."

"*Ay, por favor, abuelita*, I am so tired. I just need to sit down and rest," the child would plead. She was about ten or eleven years old then, working alongside her grandmother and other adult women, trying with all her might to maintain the same amazing speed and stamina as they.

"No, *dulcecita.* You don't get tired 'til the *capataz* say it's time to be tired," was all Doña Fela would say firmly in order to reinforce to her granddaughter the brutal reality of sugarcane. Nothing else would be said ... or needed to be said.

Another certain rule about *zafra* was that it was the one period of total work for every living soul on the plantation. Even before she moved on to the more mature task of cutting cane at the skirt-hem of her seasoned grandmother, the child found herself among the many women, young boys and girls collecting the cane, stacking it, and helping to load it onto the ox-drawn carts standing waiting. Additionally, there were young boys changing the teams of oxen used to pull the big, heavily-laden carts; a number of older men and women were quickly gathering the cane which fell from the overloaded carts or railway wagons along the way; several men were carrying away the crushed canes (the green *bagasse*) from the mills; about a dozen or more men were carrying the dry *bagasse* and stoking the continuously burning fires in the gigantic boilers. There must have been at least forty or fifty more females, old and young, who were assigned the awesome responsibility of cooking enormous quantities of food and serving water to the workers in the fields.

Doña Fela told her granddaughter how, during the difficult months of *zafra*, laborers averaged a full workday of almost twenty hours, even on the smaller, but efficiently run plantations like *Santa Flor*, where the old woman was born.

"Even as a child 'bout the same age as you right now," Doña Fela recalled vividly, "I was workin' 'bout sixteen hours daily with three for restin' durin' daylight hours, and five at night for sleepin'. This was normal for practically everybody durin' *zafra*. As I said, *mi azúcar morenita, zafra* ain't never been no carnival for nobody."

Before abolition, according to the stories that Doña Fela had heard from her own mother, it was common practice everywhere to use the infamous *látigo*, the "whip," as the primary stimulus to work. As the most feared instrument of the

93

capataz on nearly all the plantations, the *látigo* was faithfully depended on for providing discipline . . . especially during the critical period of the *zafra*. Generally speaking, the incessant flogging — and not simply administered by sadistic or psychotic overseers ---was supposedly the one certain means by which the slaves could be kept focused on the job. It was also thought that the application of the feared *látigo* prevented slaves from falling asleep or even dallying on the job.

But the always eager listener Azúcar had already heard Lolita's Haitian husband Estimé tell some rather frightening tales from his own personal experiences. Estimé had once related the terrifying story about a particularly cruel *capataz* on one plantation who regularly used a whip called a *"rigoise."* With deliberately sinister design, this whip was made of cowhide and had tiny, sharp hooks at the tip that easily lifted the skin off a worker's back. An individual would be scared for life upon being struck with this diabolical "stimulator." At the dinner table after a day's work, Don Diego Montalvo made a regular point to his sons about the masterful effects of the whip.

"That goddamn *látigo*, I tell you, is what this shiftless bunch needs to keep their miserable black asses on task." He punctuated each word with a hard slam of his fist. There was no doubt about how serious he was in his assessment.

Many an afternoon under the violent heat of the sun, Don Diego would happen upon a group of malingering laborers and could only startle them with offensive verbal assaults or abusive threats of speedy deportation. He had his armed revolver, as usual, but was ordered by central administration to use it only when he found himself in what was considered a life-threatening circumstance or in perceived danger.

"In the olden days this black scum would've had their filthy backs bloodied and raw until they couldn't take it anymore," he mused aloud. "Back then, *coño*, the *látigo* could be counted on to kept these niggers in line. No doubt about it." He was satisfied that he had made his point.

Azúcar had often heard her grandmother tell a group of neighbors about how, during *zafra* many years ago, the work was endless. Doña Fela had told her listeners about the times when the men in the boiler house had their evening meals taken to them on the job. Doña Fela herself at one time had been assigned the task of serving late evening meals in the boiler house. However, what the sometimes elusive old woman did not reveal to the group of listeners, nor to her young granddaughter, was the long-concealed secret that that was how Fela met and fell in love with the only man she ever loved. He would be the man who would father her only child, Azúcar's mother.

"We always knew exactly when we reached the end of the harvest 'cause that was when they gave out the clothes again," Doña Fela remembered having heard her mother say. In this manner of oral tradition, daughter learned from mother, and now granddaughter was learning from grandmother the various stages in the work routines on the plantation. The old matriarch carefully explained these lessons that were never to be erased from the child's memory. Doña Fela continued her narrative.

"Then the slaves cleared the land and planted new fields of cane, weeded the old fields of '*ratooon*' cane -- these was the basal shoots sproutin' from the cut stalks of sugarcane. That meant that things was getting underway for the next harvest. There just was no lettin' up from the already worn out workers -- who just got done with *zafra*. Next, they had to dig trenches on the cleared land for plantin' the new cane. The area was divided up into a lotta small squares and in each square, one man, the 'sower,' would open a furrow, place the cane in the hole the long way before coverin' it up with the loose soil hauled up from the nearby banks. Then when the plants begin growin', another one of the team would come t' weed the fields an' loosen up the soil 'round the young plants. After that, then the whole cycle started over again."

" . . . And that cycle hasn't changed since none," Azúcar reflected silently to herself, noting the conclusion of the lesson. She thought about what she had learned.

But the endless demands and tensions of *zafra* also stole into the Montalvo household. Moreso now than at any other period of the year, this usually very orderly and uneventful household fell into an unrecognizable state of utter franticness. Yet, it was actually a very carefully controlled tenseness. Everybody was reminded almost daily that the very survival of the entire Montalvo clan depended upon a profitable sugarcane harvest for *Esperanza Dulce*. As the very pivotal *capataz*, Diego Montalvo was now operating under enormous pressures, however much he had grown quite accustomed to such tension over the years.

He stormed through the house one evening, pacing out of one room and into another. This was no civil dialogue between mutually attentive conversation partners; certainly his detached wife Cristiana wasn't necessarily listening. He boomed in angry frustration, not directing his concerns to anyone in particular:

"*Maldito sea, coño*! Central administration has set extra high production quotas for us this year and I really don't know how in hell we can meet that! I'm not even certain if they sent us enough goddamn contract laborers to work this year's *zafra*."

The complacent Cristiana had long ago reconciled within herself the fate assigned her. Hers was the traditionally demanding role of the self-denying, passive spouse of a plantation capataz, with its inherent lack of refinement and elegance, even common civility. Sitting alone in her bedroom one morning, long after her husband had left for the fields,

Cristiana confronted her reflection in the mirror and made a remorseful confession, but one that was by no means new. It was one that she had made repeatedly over her many lonely years with her husband.

"*Ay, Dios mío, aquel maldito día!* How I curse that day I made the dreadful decision to marry Diego Montalvo, nothing but an inferior plantation *capataz*. *Qué locura!* What lunacy! What in God's gracious name was I thinking? My entire family warned me that my life would be made dull and unsatisfying, surrounded by lowly Blacks from the *batey* and the pestering, mundane concerns of overseeing the wretched operations of sugarcane." Her soliloquy continued in a tone of deep anguish.

"I was never a part of his world, nor did I ever want to be. My fate was sealed the day I decided to become the wife of the *capataz* at *Esperanza Dulce*. Damn you, Diego Montalvo! *La maldita caña!* Damn sugarcane!"

The intensity of her unbearable frustration led her to throw her hairbrush at the mirror; the brush shattered the mirror in front of her. Cristiana Montalvo had become a strong woman as a result of her fateful decision and thus was always prepared for the onslaught of the tempered madness of the yearly *zafra*. It could be said that a stoic resignation described Cristiana, while the rest of her household became totally consumed by over-taxed production schedules, unrealistic production quotas, dangerously overcrowded conditions in the *batey*, both work crews and managers with hot tempers ready to erupt at any moment. Cristiana's resolve was to make the best of a frustrating and hopeless circumstance in which she found herself permanently trapped.

Therefore, the period of *zafra* for Diego and Cristiana Montalvo was one of more than the semblance of balanced control and domination of the situation. Traditional plantation ethos had not been compromised by human foible or the acknowledged triviality ---at least by Doña Cristiana--- of a poor marriage choice some thirty-odd years ago. Life trudged on with all deliberateness, and most particularly during *zafra*. After all, it was a practical matter of a family's economic survival that there be a bountiful crop yield each year of operation.

Mario and Blanchette's household, on the other hand, was thrown to total abandon and into a state of frightening chaos. Mario was more absent from home now than at any other time— even accounting for his illicit sorties into the batey at night. It was no longer necessary to use the guise of having to "oversee the extended work shifts at the mill" or to "assist his father with supervising the work crews in the fields." This was probably the only time during the whole year that Mario felt discomforting pangs of guilt about being away from the twins Cècile and Chelaine, both of whom he adored more than any other human being, even his mother, and certainly more than he loved his wife.

Blanchette had made it luminously clear some time ago that she no longer desired a conjugal relationship with Mario. For her, their marriage had ended well before it was rumored that Mario had become a scandalous *mujeriego*, a "womanizer" of the lowest sort. Before their marriage had descended into the pit of irreconcilable ruin, Blanchette Origène-Desgraves de Montalvo once during the occasion of an élite social gathering in the elegant manor residence of her parents, overheard the wife of one of the estate managers of a neighboring plantation make a painfully devastating, but truthful remark about Mario's reprehensible behavior.

"*Dios me libre!* May God help me! Did you hear that the no-good *canalla* actually has been seen regularly cavorting with those horrid Black whores down in the batey? That scoundrel."

Some of the other guests who also overheard this gossip didn't wonder in the least if the lack of discretion was deliberate.

"*Pobrecita* Blanchette Poor dear! And to think that she comes from among the finest stock in the entire Island. To have married someone so far beneath her class and pedigree was simply inexplicable."

Poor Blanchette had heard every hurtful word dripping hungrily from the venomous-tongued mouths of these hypocritical gossipmongers with nothing better — or nothing more desirous to talk about. Since that time, Blanchette became increasingly absorbed by the phantoms and demons of her self-styled reality, retreating deeper and deeper --- not into her own psychological misery, but rather into her own secret pleasures and delights. The most striking absorption, perhaps naturally, was her devotion to her beautiful twin girls Cècile and Chelaine. She pushed Mario further away from this reality until it didn't matter at all if this man even existed.

The period of *zafra*, then, meant absolutely nothing to her and her priceless twin treasures. Certainly the anticipated harvest profits were completely meaningless to her in terms of economic survival as it most desperately was for the Montalvos. In all truth, it was no secret that the Origène-Desgraves family was undeniably one of the wealthiest in this primary sugar-producing region of the Island --- if not the entire Island itself. They had been so since before the colony became independent. Although Blanchette's birthright was a direct consequence of sugarcane, she cared nothing whatsoever about sugar and sugar profits. The destructive chaos and undisguised greed and insecurity were all Mario's. It was he who, each year much like his father, became nearly ill with an overpowering terror at the thought of not being able to make the estate's projected annual

99

production quotas. Mario's economic survival, again like that of his pathetically insecure father, did indeed depend on the success or failure of the year's zafra.

"*Coño!* Central administration cannot afford failure, nor will it tolerate as much, goddammit!"

In the meantime, there was another new arrival en route to *Esperanza Dulce* at the height of the *zafra*. But instead of arriving as part of the customary truck caravans, standing upright, tight like packed sardines or squatting in a prized space as though taking a public shit, and at the same time being jostled about at every turn or bump in the long, treacherous, dirt road lealding to the batey, this passenger arrived in enviable style. He traveled snuggled into a posh single seat abroad a luxury jet aircraft. With sophisticated, triple-slotted trailing edge flaps and new leading-edge slats, the sleek Boeing 727 jet, with its spacious interior, could easily have seated perhaps 189 passengers. But instead the Caribbean-bound plane was transporting just twelve individuals, plus the cheerful flight crew. The aircraft seemed to be tailored for the low-speed landing and takeoff performance especially needed for smaller airports and private airstrips such as those found throughout the Caribbean.

The arriving 727 jet was the exclusive property of the Canadian transnational corporation that now owned and administered *Esperanza Dulce* Plantation, as well as sixty-four other currently operating ingenios, out of an existing total of ninety-two across the Island. About fifty *ingenios* were producing sugarcane at a level well below eleven per cent; industry analysts had noted that the proportion of normal sugar production for the Island was generally around eighteen per cent. Something was clearly wrong. So, coming for his first official visit to the problem's epicenter was the chief Canadian research director and energetic head of the field inspection team for global operations in the corporation's agribusiness sector.

He had been sent directly from the Toronto office to investigate and report on the character, degree, and probable cause of the dramatic decline in harvest yields that were beginning to reflect huge profit losses for the corporation. Major stockholders were naturally anxious about these losses. After all, *Esperanza Dulce*, one of the oldest and historically most profitable *ingenios* in the Island, and especially after being made the object of consistent, major improvements in technological advancement by the mid-1920s, had been catapulted to the position of being one of the most efficiently-run plantations in the Caribbean, far outstripping production in the traditionally high-yielding Barbados mills. During that exciting period alone, *Esperanza Dulce* had a capacity for grinding some 4,536 metric tons of cane every twenty-four hours.

With the corporation's aggressive acquisition of nearby *Santa Flor* Plantation shortly afterwards, both mills together had a grinding capacity of nearly 20,000 short tons of sugar per day. This equaled sixty per cent of the total for all the mills owned by the corporation and fully forty-one per cent of the Island's total output. At this current juncture, the total harvest yield was just 3.2 million tons, the absolute lowest in the Island in over fifty years. Therefore, Toronto was desperate to determine and then quickly offset the slump. Stockholders needed to see appreciable profits over recent drops. The Canadian inspector reflected on the situation.

"Profit margins here have been extraordinarily impressive and uninterrupted for the past few years, even doing better than productive estates in Mexico, Brazil, and the Philippines. And now, all of a sudden something has gone wrong? It's not making much sense." He closed the thick report summary of graphs, tables, charts, statement analyses and other verbose bullshit disguising the simple fact that things were obviously changing . . . . and changing fast. It would now be up to this new arrival to resolve the troublesome state of affairs at *Esperanza Dulce.*

"My God, what dazzling beauty!" young Harold Capps proclaimed aloud about the panorama he sighted below from the plane's small, oval window as the 727 landed at the tiny landing strip located just a few miles outside the plantation grounds.

"So this is what Paradise looks like. I've never seen a more spectacular piece of Nature," was how the first-time visitor summed up his immediate impression, even before venturing beyond the landing strip, which seemed to be in the midst of a tropical oasis of botanical splendor. "I can now imagine just how those first arriving Spanish *conquistadores* must have been astonished by such beauty." The excited passenger was truly in awe of his introduction to the tropics.

Dr. Harold Capps, at just twenty-seven years old, was admittedly young for his lofty corporate position with the company. He held a doctorate degree in agronomy. And although with limited field experience, he had made quite a favorable impression among the agribusiness establishment with his published scholarly studies concerning various breakthrough theories in scientific agriculture, with vitally important focus on sugarcane cultivation around the world. He was unmarried, very handsome and considered to be a brilliant young scientist. Dr. Capps was also a painfully restless young man forever seeking new excitement, adventure, and challenge.

"*Bienvenidos a Esperanza Dulce*, Dr. Capps. Welcome. May I take your bags?" This genuinely cheerful greeting directed at the newly arriving young Canadian doctor came from a heavily accented voice, resonating an innocent sensuality.

"Hi, there; I'm Marcelo Montalvo; my father is Diego Montalvo, the *capataz* at the *Esperanza Dulce* Estate. I am the company's temporary regional public relations director and I have been given the pleasure of serving as your local personal assistant during your inspection tour of operations here on the Island." The voice, while clearly that of an educated, impressively cultivated local individual, was at the same time certainly not one to be commonly associated with *Esperanza Dulce.*

"I sincerely hope to make your stay a very enjoyable and productive one," the cultivated voice continued.

The two young men exchanged mutually pleasant, perhaps even noticeably charming smiles in courteous acknowledgment. The exchange was sincere.

"Wow! What a terrific sounding voice," Capps admitted secretly to himself. "Also love that accent of his. Really sexy, too."

Marcelo, at twenty-six years old, was the youngest son of Diego and Cristiana Montalvo. Drastically unlike all his brothers, Marcelo was the polar opposite of his oldest sibling Mario. To begin with, this youngest Montalvo possessed a readily open, honestly inviting smile, not the menacing, scornful look seemingly characteristic of all the Montalvo men. The only one of the four sons to have earned a university degree and the only Montalvo still much sought-after by females in the region ---married or single, the charismatic young Marcelo was widely regarded as quite un premio, "a prize" in terms of eligible and desirable bachelors.

Additionally, Marcelo was undoubtedly the one Montalvo destined to be granted official entry into the inner circle of the social and political élite of the region. His movie star handsomeness was a rather delicate one; although of small frame, he had a beach-resort lifeguard physique. He had short, crisp hair . . . unlike Mario's stereotypical rustic abundance of curly hair hanging loosely into his face; large, round, light brown eyes, not deep-set and dark like Mario's. This youngest Montalvo did have his oldest brother's fleshy lips and was a darker wheat coloring than Mario; Marcelo wasn't the least bit embarrassed by the visible traces of his Haitian Creole ancestry from his mother's lineage. Especially during his two-year residence in Europe did he realize for the first time the seductiveness of his looks; he was extremely popular there. Both sexes found him extremely attractive. He was also tall like the other male members of the clan. Marcelo was different, however, in so many other respects that were he not such a natural part of the plantation environment by circumstances of his birth, he would seem entirely out of place there . . . so refined was he.

"*Ay, santa madre mía.* That *pollito* couldn't be the son of that ugly old goat Don Diego," whispered one admiring female worker upon seeing 'the young chicken' Marcelo on a few occasions upon which he would visit his family during holiday leaves from the university.

"*Pero, sí, eh verda', niña.* True enough, girl. He take his fine looks from his mamá," replied the listener who had also stolen a quick break from her work routine just to gawk at the handsome young Marcelo strut innocently, but in all his glorious sensuality, across the mill yard. It was a fact that Marcelo did not deliberately flaunt his good looks; this was not his character.

Marcelo's far more comfortable ambiance was the cosmopolitan flavor of the university, located in the bustling heart of the Island's capital city. There, life patterns were seen as more non-conformist, often unorthodox and liberal in almost every sense by comparison with the way things flowed here in the rural zones. The thinking here was dangerously archaic, even feudal. The multi-talented, sensitive youngest son of the brutish capataz had traveled to some of the neighboring English-speaking Antillean islands, a few South American capital cities and to the United States. He spoke four languages fluently and had spent two years studying painting and Western philosophy in London, Paris, Florence, and Athens.

While he was growing up, it had been whispered among the domestic help in the Montalvo household that he was definitely Doña Cristiana's favorite child. Despite Marcelo's rugged appearance, he was actually more inclined to tranquil, passive pursuits. It was like oldest brother Mario had often predicted, in the most malicious and hurtful terms, that the "delicate" young Marcelo would grow up to become *"un maricón deprivao.* A depraved faggot."

Young Marcelo took Harold Capp's suitcases and placed them in the back seat of the jeep— the same official vehicle that the two pudgy little White men with the clipboards had used that hot Sunday morning not too long ago to process new arrivals. Harold quickly hopped into the passenger seat alongside the driver, Marcelo.

"The guest cottage near our house has already been prepared for you. That's where I'm taking you," Marcelo informed his cheerful passenger. "You'll love it there."

"Muchas gracias, amigo. Usted es muy amable. Thanks a lot, friend. You're very kind." Harold was anxious to use his excellent Spanish.

"I hope you don't mind if I practice my Spanish on you," Harold said. "Almost every chance I get to speak Spanish, somebody seems to want to practice his English."

"No; está bien. Me parece una excelente idea. No, I don't mind. In fact, it seems like a good idea to me," was Marcelo's response. *"Tú hablas el idioma perfectamente bien.* You speak the language perfectly well."

"So, after working all day, what do you guys do for real excitement around here in this gorgeously enchanting country?" Harold wanted to know.

"Eso depende," Marcelo hesitated with a feeling of discomfort. He nevertheless displayed his instantly winning

smile, which was automatically infectious, for Harold also returned a smile. "It all depends on what you mean by excitement. We are not exactly in the capital, you know. Things out here move a lot slower," Marcelo said half laughing, but guardedly.

"I wonder what this guy has on his mind," Marcelo thought to himself with some minor suspicion about the new arrival from Canada.

"*Sí, mi amigo, yo entiendo,*" Marcelo's engaging passenger hastened to add. "After I get settled in, why don't you show me around? I'd love to see what kinds of surprises lie beyond *Esperanza Dulce.*"

Then completely without warning, a barrage of questions poured forth. "Do you have a wife? Any kids? Or if not a wife, maybe a string of girlfriends? I'm sure the women must flock around you like bees around a honeycomb . . . A handsome stud like yourself. You live alone?"

The young agronomist's casual, yet very quick and candid manner of inquisitiveness disarmed Marcelo altogether.

"*Este tipo está pescando, me parece.* It seems to me like this guy is fishing for something," Marcelo's inner voice told him. The young doctor's questions were beginning to cause some degree of discomfort, if not suspicion, for Marcelo. "But the Canadian's openness with strangers no doubt is peculiar to his culture," or so Marcelo tried to convince himself.

Then, just as Mario's younger brother was about to venture an answer, the jeep swirled sharply to one side, luckily missing a treacherous ditch in the road. The sudden shift of the vehicle easily threw its two occupants off balance; the dislodged passenger found himself nearly in the lap of the driver. When Harold regained his balance, he found his bare, muscular leg still touching Marcelo's hairy leg. By sheer coincidence, both men were wearing thigh-length khaki shorts, thus exposing a great deal of flesh. Neither said anything immediately. As if on rehearsed cue, both stupefied individuals glanced into each other's smiling, receptive eyes. The accidental brushing together of their naked legs now clearly transformed into a kind of sustained rubbing . . . easily sensual, in fact. The mutually understanding glances of both young men confirmed this.

"No; mi amigo. I'm not married; I'm really not interested in getting married. I don't have any kids and no, not even one girlfriend," was Marcelo's response between playful, yet suspicious chuckles. He felt a growing hardness in his groin. Harold could only voice a previous observation.

"What a beautifully seductive country. Y todos son tan amigables como tú? And is everybody as friendly as you are?"

Marcelo couldn't be quite sure if he spied the young Canadian doctor openly gazing at the rather impressive bulge in Marcelo's groin area, steadily growing in size and readily detectable in the khaki shorts. Yes, Harold definitely did notice. In fact, he was almost staring impertinently. Before Marcelo was able to give the matter any further thought, the company jeep was pulling into the driveway of the disarmingly beautiful guest cottage. This was the far-from-rustic facility always made available for arriving company executives. Harold helped his new friend with the suitcases that were now scattered over the back seat and floor of the jeep.

"Oye! Hey, that's our house there behind those tamarind trees," Marcelo said eagerly, pointing in the direction of the shady grove that shielded their spacious house. Then the words just came pouring out, almost non-stop. Marcelo's shyness completely vanished with all the afternoon's excitement. "It would be great if you would come have dinner with our family tonight. It's been some time since my mom has had a guest for dinner. She would love that. Also, you can meet my father, the *capataz,* in a more relaxed setting. Less tense, you know? And our cook Lola has been with us as long as I can remember. She's the best. Por favor. Please say you'll accept my invitation. We eat at eight."

The unwittingly sexy and friendly public relations director winked playfully at the young agronomist from Canada. The idea was exhilarating to the new arrival. It would give Harold a chance to get to know his new friend better and also to learn more about the Esperanza Dulce operations.

"*Está bien, mi nuevo amigo.* You've convinced me. I accept. The flight from Toronto was really exhausting. Right now, what I need is a good a good shower and a quick nap before dinner. *Muchísimas gracias por la invitación.* I'll see you folks at eight, OK? . . . and again, thanks."

ONCE

The sun had dipped abruptly toward the west a few hours ago, tinting everything that surrounded it in the indolent hues and tones so characteristic of seductive tropical evenings. However, it would soon be pitch dark. A chorus of locusts was already beginning to chirr in their harsh, trilling fashion, while a nearby bevy of doves, nestling together and preparing for sleep, began their mournful cooing.

It was almost eight o'clock when Doña Fela and Azúcar sat down together in their cabin for their customary evening meal. Doña Fela had prepared a special dinner for her granddaughter: fish head stew with boiled *yucca* and *plátano*, spiced with *cilantro* and *achiote*. Mamá Lola had salvaged the cast-off fish heads for her old confidant from the over-stocked Montalvo pantry since no one in the capataz's household relished that part of the fish's anatomy. Mamá Lola had also managed to provide the few surprise cassava loaves for the meals. Lately, Doña Fela had been filled with particularly deep remorse most especially because of the convulsive feverishness of her daily work routines during *zafra*, along with everybody else's, of course, meant that those few small, cherished pleasures of life in the *batey* regularly stolen during ordinary times were absent altogether now . . . and Azúcar was Doña Fela's single casualty during the hectic period of the annual *zafra* on the plantation.

"*Por el amor de todo' loh santo*. I know I am not spendin' enough time with Azúcar. I am not fulfillin' my duties as a good *abuela*. How could I neglect *mi azúcar morenita* like I have?"

She questioned her own perturbed conscience. Therefore, preparing the special dinner for Azúcar was a sincere expression of love on the old woman's part. It was one way of genuinely compensating her granddaughter for the treasured moments routinely shared together, but now being robbed by the selfish and insensitive demands of *zafra*.

"*Ay, abuelita*, the stew is delicious; I love it," Azúcar declared in earnest.

"I made it special for you, *mi dulce amor*. And I want you to enjoy yourself eatin' every bit of it." The old woman's eyes were drowning in tears of ecstatic bliss at her granddaughter's expressed pleasure. These were the shared moments Doña Fela delighted in most.

But Azúcar had shamefully lied when she told her tearful grandmother how delicious the fish head stew was. It actually had nothing to do with the stew, which without question had indeed been made to perfection; everybody loved Doña Fela's cooking. Rather, the truth was that the girl simply had no appetite for eating anything that evening . . . She had literally forced herself to eat in order to avoid offending her grandmother, who had clearly gone to great lengths to provide the evening's special treat. Azúcar had been without much of an appetite for some time now . . . and without her grandmother's ever suspecting otherwise . . . so, the child believed.

In fact, for the past few weeks Azúcar had also been experiencing a most unfamiliar nausea, some vomiting and what seemed to be a strange tightening in her stomach when she awoke most mornings. These sensations were totally new to the inexperienced young girl, and so she was genuinely worried, even somewhat frightened. When these sensations would not go away, Azúcar's fears increased as a result of not understanding what was happening to her.

"*Por mi madre*. What is goin' on inside me?" she asked herself with puzzling worry.

110

"Am I sick and don't know it? I have never felt this way before."

It was the overwhelming novelty and fear of these sensations that prevented her from going immediately to her grandmother for an explanation. Until this moment, young Azúcar had always counted on her wise old grandmother to explain anything the girl's unschooled and naïve mind did not understand. "*Abuelita* is so wise; she always gives me answers for everythin'."

Azúcar constantly assured herself. Yet despite her internal puzzlement, for the first time she found herself keeping something hidden from her grandmother. For as long as she could remember, Azúcar always had the uncompromising trust, love, and support of the one human being in this world that she adored most. Therefore, the idea of concealing these unfamiliar, queer sensations now from Doña Fela only caused tremendous anguish for the sensitive girl. Also for the very first time, Azúcar felt a gnawing wave of wrongdoing engulf her. The new sensations, the discomfort, the fear, the remorse— all conspired in unison to render the young girl confused and bewildered. Many a night she cried herself to sleep, her cries carefully muffled in her pillow so as not to awaken her grandmother sleeping a few feet away. All in all, both grandmother and granddaughter managed to finish the meal apparently with mutual satisfaction that evening. Doña Fela confessed to her granddaughter.

"*M'hita*, you bring so much joy to my every day that the saints allow me to live. Seein' you happy make me happy."

Azúcar tried secretly to imagine the consternation she would leave with her grandmother upon revealing the strange sensations presently churning inside her. She smiled in an effort

111

to acknowledge her grandmother's confession.

Long after the dinner hour for nearly everybody in the batey had ended and everybody had returned to their cabins from having been up at The Pit, sleep finally overtook the community. But the idyllic serenity of the night was violently disrupted by the barking of gruff, bellicose voices of two men. There was no mistake that the voices were combative. A serious altercation was underway; these were the familiar sounds that indicated far more than a macho shouting match. The brutal exchange grew louder and harsher, and because of the stillness of the late night the angry shouting could be heard clearly from almost every corner of the sleeping *batey*. Doña Fela and Azúcar, because their cabin was situated so very close to where the booming growls seemed to be emanating, were awakened immediately. They both heard every word . . . and so did everyone else.

"*Maldito negro sucio! Haitiano grosero! Carajo, Quién* crees *que eres tú para hablarme así*? Filthy Haitian! Who the fuck do you think you are talking to me like that?" spewed venomously from the mouth of one of the combatants.

"*Hijueputa vendido! Le cago en la cara de tu madre puta que te parió*! Thrown-away son-of-a-bitch! I shit on the face of your whorish-mother who gave birth to your lousy ass!"

Then the vile insults being hurled back and forth switched in the next second to Kreyòl with parallel force and intent:

" . . . *Jou va , jou vien, m'pa di passé ça.*"

The explosive words were spat out as a direct threat of bitter revenge on the part of the Krèyol speaker to his irate foe. In his often misunderstood and much maligned culture, the phrase implied the speaker's superior grasp of the workings of a world wherein injustice, exploitation and abuses of all kinds occur daily, especially as committed against the powerless by the powerful. The man had shouted the ominous prediction to his enemy that:

" . . . The days may come and go, but just you wait and see; my day is coming."

This was no idle threat . . . to be certain. It was at that precise moment that Estimé, with unstoppable fury and all the while shouting more volatile threats at Mario Montalvo, made a menacing gesture with his seasoned, ever-sharp machete. Since the start of the altercation, Mario already had his revolver drawn, his finger on the trigger; he had the gun pointed at his fearless opponent. The two equally determined men, one armed with a deadly machete, the other with a loaded forty-five caliber pistol, faced each other like two ancient gladiators prepared to fight to the death of his opponent.

Estimé's weapon hovered above Mario's head; one swift blow downward from this expert cane cutter could easily split open his opponent's head like a relenting coconut. Mario certainly had no doubt that standing at such close range to his enemy, a single well-placed shot fired from his revolver would penetrate through the other man's body, splattering Estimé's innards all over the tiny yard situated at the side of the cabin.

The torrid contest was over as quickly as it had ignited. There was just a single shot from Mario's anxious revolver. The powerful hand holding the machete loosened its grip; the weapon fell. Estimé then dropped hard to the black ground. Lolita's loud shrieks were the first ones to be heard; the Haitian's wife had been standing in her nightshirt at the door of the cabin that she shared with her Haitian husband and their three children. All the children, their wide-open eyes filled with terror and disbelief or perhaps confusion, clutched tightly their mother's legs and waist. The children's proud father lay dead on the ground; the capataz's eldest son stood with a still-smoking pistol in his hand over the dead Haitian.

Lolita had witnessed the entire scene unfold before her

unbelieving eyes. Amidst tears, she would later recount for the authorities--- the plantation's own private police agents and prosecuting team--- how she and her husband had been in bed, quietly making love. The three young children were fast asleep on the other side of the makeshift blanket-partition that separated the cabin's sleeping areas. The couple had stopped in the middle of their amorous privacy because of disturbing noises they both had heard outside the window of the cabin.

"The noises," she told the authorities, "they sounded like somebody moanin' or in pain."

Her Haitian husband had gotten out of bed, instinctively grabbed his machete from its resting place in a corner of the cabin, and then slipped outside to investigate the noises. Lolita would remember how both she and Estimé were shamefully embarrassed and at the same time furious (although she was careful enough to omit describing any measure of personal rage to the authorities) to find the *capataz*'s perverted-minded son Mario spying on them under any circumstances. But spying on their lovemaking?!

She would tell the authorities, according to her eyewitness account, how Don Mario drew his revolver on her husband even before Estimé confronted the capataz's son about why he was at their cabin at that time of night. She thought secretly to herself.

"This is the same monster that violated poor, innocent Azúcar. What kind of unnatural beast is he? What did this lunatic bush hog want?"

Estimé's widow never received any answers or explanations. In fact, the prosecutors never even asked Mario about his reasons for being down in the *batey* at night. The brutal, senseless murder of this *"negro sucio,"* this *"haitiano grosero"* would be ruled by an act of self-defense on the part of Don

Mario Montalvo. The entire community in the batey was in a smoldering fury about the ruling from the authorities. The decision was final and there was no appeal. There was nothing anyone could do to change that decision. According to the authorities, "Don Mario Montalvo had acted properly and justifiably in defending himself against the unprovoked machete attack of a crazed sugarcane cutter." Lolita's three small, now-fatherless children were crying senselessly at her side that fateful morning of court deliberations . . . proceedings which took place just under two hours in the familiar squat cinder block administration building at the center of the mill yard. The distraught Lolita let out a shriek and uttered the Kreyòl phrase she had long ago learned from her beautiful Haitian, now dead: *Jou va, jou vien, m' pa di passé ça.* The days may come and go, but just you wait and see; my day is coming.

Most fortunately for her and the children, the plantation authorities decided at the same time not to punish Lolita and her remaining family by deporting them — even though Lolita herself wasn't Haitian; *zafra* was not yet over and so they were safe. In the face of this sudden tragedy and the perpetual state of powerlessness, she seemed unfeeling. She realized the horrible reality of her misery; stored-up desperation and anger seized every portion of her being. Lolita let out a loud scream that was louder than the giant mechanized bellows in the sugar mill.

"When things gonna change?" was her final question before falling into an unrestrained convulsion of crying and screaming.

DOCE

"*Coño*! Here in this *maldito batey*, misery and misfortune don't never seem to wait for a' invitation," Don Anselmo said as he emphasized to the small group of workers gathered outside the widow-Lolita's cabin on their way home from the cane fields that evening.

"Together the two demons they come and make themselves comfortable at your table without asking to be seated."

The young widow had come out of her cabin reluctantly to acknowledge the respect being paid to her dead Haitian. In a gentle, but quivering voice wet with tears, Lolita thanked her friends and neighbors, who were continuing to stop in front of her cabin almost daily for the past two weeks since the cold-blooded, senseless murder of their comrade. She sat down in the doorway, bent over in two as if some giant had placed huge stones on her shoulders. The overwhelming weight of the stones broke her otherwise stoic resignation and poise. Heavy sobs were heard coming from her distorted face.

"*Qué hombrón*! What a man Estimé was!" Tomás said proudly in his tribute to his dead friend. "What a damn good worker too! There wasn't a better one on either side of the Island. But the misfortune of Death made its selection like the blind man at the marketplace who choose the mango: touchin', feelin', pickin' at will 'til he happen upon the right one an' leavin' the bad ones behind."

Someone insisted bitterly, "When will justice decide to visit us?"

Some distance away, but still in closely interconnected time and space, the tense household of Diego and Cristiana Montalvo had once again been visited by the fearful threat of loss and ruin. This latest incident, however, was quite possibly the gravest infraction yet against human decency committed by their wildly capricious and irreverent eldest offspring. Don Diego was burning with rage . . . certainly not due to even the tiniest spark of humanitarian indignation, but more truthfully because of the capataz's innate fear of being evicted from *Esperanza Dulce*. This was a constant terror that loomed heavily over his conscience.

"*Maldito sea ese* Mario! May Mario be damned! Why must Mario always be such a jackass? Why can't he simply stay away from those thick-skulled *cocolos* down in the *batey*?"

Diego made no apologies when using the derogatory term "*cocolos*," even in public, when referring to Blacks from the English-speaking Antillean islands and also to those African-descended individuals from his own Island. It is believed that the term was descriptive of an exceptionally hard outer shell of the coconut.

Doña Cristiana, sitting in her favorite stuffed velour parlor chair, remarked impassively, but knowingly about her first-born.

"*Pobre hombre*. His soul is lost. I suspect that some evil is tormenting him in his discontentment. Look at how everything seems to have gone wrong in his marriage and family life."

"*Pero, coño!* It's his own damn fault," bellowed Mario's father, livid with rage. "How many goddamn times have I warned him about chasing after those big black-assed whores? Do you realize that if the prosecutors had not ruled in our favor, our asses would be facing immediate expulsion from the operations here. The Company would kick all of us out with nothing; there wouldn't be any chance of ever getting another position like this one anywhere on the Island. *Carajo*, woman! We'd be finished. *Entiendes eso?*"

Mario's distraught mother, of course, understood fully. She

lowered her head onto her chest; her frail shoulders bent inward, her hands trembled in her lap. She sighed, "*Ay, Santa Virgen de la Altagracia, Madre de Jesús!* Save my son's soul."

The *capataz's* continuous bellowing and heavy pacing through the front parlor prevented him from hearing his wife's sobs. But then, she had often confused him of being insensitive to human feelings.

In Doña Fela's cabin there was also a very deep sense of freightening loss, anxiety, anger and bitterness . . . all flowing together to coalesce into a state of immense, cavernous dejection that engulfed both grandmother and granddaughter in equal proportions. More so now than ever before, the old woman could be found pacing slowly and aimlessly, almost shuffling across the length of the cabin. All the while she was muttering to herself softly, chanting something that was totally unintelligible to Azúcar. On one occasion, however, young Azúcar did ask her visibly troubled grandmother the meaning of one phrase she had heard several times before while in the cane fields and on the long walk to their cabin from the fields. She had memorized the phrase.

" *Se lè koulèv mouri, ou konn longè li.* Exactly what does that mean, *abuelita*? That's what I used to hear Estimé and some of the other Krèyol-speaking workers say when they seemed really mad," insisted the alert young girl.

Doña Fela had already stopped pacing the floor when her granddaughter distracted her with the question. The old woman, not the slightest perturbed by Azúcar's insistence, offered an immediate translation. "Only when the serpent is dead can you take its measure."

Incessantly curious and at times fidgety, the young girl tried to find a hidden meaning or some nuance in everything that was said to her, especially by her elders in the batey. Her face would make expressive grimaces whenever she truly did not quite understand, never pretending that she had understood perfectly. This time, though, Azúcar smiled a knowing smile.

"*M'hita dulce*, something else has been troublin' my old soul lately," the old woman continued solemnly "You may not have noticed, but I been havin' difficulty gettin' to sleep; a grave forebodin' has swelled in me 'til I think soon my veins will bust open. All kinds of images drift through my mind . . . images that eddy and rip like leaves from the banana tree durin' a hurricane. *Mi dulcecita*, my heart is so heavy. I ask that the ancestors watch over us."

Azúcar remained silent, agitated . . . but listening with full attention to what her wise and seemingly all-knowing grandmother was saying.

"You the only precious thing in this world for me. Next to my loas that protect and guide me daily, you I love more than anyone or anything else in this life. *Mi morenita*, I know you ain't been feelin' good these past months; and I notice you ain't been eatin' right."

Doña Fela frowned and cast a fierce eye at the floor of the cabin, indicating that she was vexed by the presence of that negative thought. She was correct in her observations and her granddaughter knew it. Azúcar felt a sudden impatience that was vague, insinuating, and purposeless; she wished selfishly for the day to hurry and end. She was suddenly humiliated and ashamed of having kept hidden from her abuelita the strange new sensations she had been experiencing. Months had passed and the girl had been unable or unwilling to share her secret feelings . . . the almost daily nausea, the regular vomiting, the sudden loss of appetite . . . with the one person she too loved most in this life. As a result, the girl was unhappy with herself. Nightly, before ultimately falling off to sleep, thinking her secret was still well concealed, she would collapse into a deep despondency and defeat. Now, in the presence of her beloved grandmother, who must have somehow divined her secret, so thought the young girl, Azúcar was sobbing. There simply were no secrets from Doña Fela. The two sat together on the old woman's cot. Sobbing still, Azúcar let her head fall into her grandmother's palms. Doña Fela spoke soothingly to her precious *azúcar morenita*.

"*No te preocupes na', m'hijita dulce*! Don't you worry none, my sweet child! My little brown sugar lump! Your *abuelita* understand and love you with all her old heart. I pray to the ancestors that they protect you from all future demons. *Mi amor*, you all I got in this life. Now you got new life inside you. You carryin' a baby inside you, child. You think I didn't know? What kind of woman I be if I didn't know what was goin' on inside you? And I sure wouldn't be your *abuelita* if I didn't know."

Doña Fela gently stroked the girl's long, coarse hair, then her shoulders and back while continuing her expressive assurance of unconditional love and compassion for her granddaughter.

"You are my beloved. I love you like the sunflower love the sun. You mustn't be afraid of the life growin' inside you. What is happenin' to you now, m'hijita, is what happen naturally to every woman 'bout to give birth." She held her frightened granddaughter tightly to her bosom. Azúcar continued sobbing, more and more distressed. Her face was hidden in her abuela's bosom. The front of her dress and Doña Fela's apron were already soaked with tears of remorse. For some time Azúcar remained like that, not responding to what her caring grandmother was saying. Then suddenly the child suspended her crying, raised her head, and whispered to her abuelita.

"*Te amo mucho, abuelita.* Please forgive me for keepin' secrets from you. Forgive me for not comin' to you sooner. I was afraid and confused. I didn't understand what was happenin' inside me. I didn't want to cause you trouble with us bein' in the middle of *zafra* and all."

Doña Fela reassured her innocent granddaughter.

"There's nothin' to forgive you for. You don't need to be frightened by nothing or nobody no more. Console yourself, child, knowin' that with the protection of the ancestors, you will find true peace and safety. Change also will come one day. And *m'hijita*, don't worry about me. Remember, no matter how heavy a woman's breasts, her chest is always strong enough to carry them. Everythin' goin' be taken care of. You'll see."

Azúcar felt better about her new feelings; she felt happily relieved in knowing what the new sensations were all about. Undeniably though, the mysteries of pregnancy and the prospect of motherhood and what it would all mean for her were overwhelming anxieties for any young girl to face. These new circumstances were certain to change her existence. But Doña Fela's reassurances snuffed out the prior anguish of the girl's bewilderment and fright . . . even though the old woman had not revealed everything to her granddaughter.

Later, when Doña Fela and Don Anselmo discussed the gravity and the ramifications of Azúcar's unanticipated . . . and most definitely unwanted pregnancy, there was voiced fury on the part of both these revered elders of the batey who had witnessed many aspects of life and death among the community residents.

"*Ay, mi hermano* Anselmo, I feel as though I been betrayed again by the powerful evil of the plantation," Doña Fela confessed to her trusted old comrade.

"*Sí, hermana.* I agree. The many years me and you an' the others have sweated an' blistered in these *maldito* cane fields everyday from sunrise to sunset, much like those dark days of slavery in these damn Sugar Islands . . . producin' great riches for the plantation owners. We seen many of our folks die from bein' overworked. Even the little children have suffered.

121

Carajo!" he cursed in disgust and anger. He continued in this spirit.

"Sugarcane ain't never been kind. In no way. The cane fields wear you down 'til you nothin', and no use to nobody no more. From stoopin' and cuttin' all day, the bones in your poor back get all bent up and twisted like the *maldito* corkwood root. Then your hands' soon become fixed like a closed-up claw and you can't use your fingers no more. Your ankles made ugly with machete nicks and scars that remain for the rest of your life . . . bitter reminders of your misery! But, *mi hermana*, there's the one sure thing that keeps you goin'. It makes you keep puttin' up with all the *mierda*. An' you know why?"

Anselmo had no intention of waiting for Doña Fela's answer— even though she most certainly knew the answer to his question. Instead, the old man stretched his arms and closed-fists in the direction of the cool, early evening sky. Then suddenly, in an unrehearsed gesture of rage, he shook his clenched fists angrily at an invisible opponent. Flocks of disturbed scissor tails perched half hidden in a nearby flamboyán tree flew away hurriedly at the old man's loud outburst in a darkened cloud of prolonged, angry cackling.

"It's the naked rage inside --- that's what! Bein' mad an' stayin' mad is our strength to overpower the evil of the cane fields an' the mill an' the heartless capataces an' the greedy plantation masters. It's the centuries of pent-up hatred and indignation we all got inside us for this *maldito* plantation. *Coño!"*

Doña Fela, who had been pinned to every word leaving her old friend's mouth, quickly added with an urgent sense of balance.

"*Sí*, Anselmo, life been hard . . . especially for me and mi dulce Azúcar. I'm a tired old woman now; the plantation has drained me. I have lived for my sweet grandbaby alone," she proclaimed with restraint. "Azúcar is young and innocent, but has new life inside her now. I pray to the spirits that Papa Legba, Master of the Crossroads, will help his child Azúcar find the right road, leavin' behind this road of many sorrows and so much cruelty here in this cesspool of *mierda podrida* [rotten shit]." She had not finished, but now her tone was clearly taking on the vengeance and outrage dictated by the circumstance of the events that were rapidly swallowing up all the residents of the *batey*.

"*Sí, mi hermano, eh verda'*. True, my brother. Being mad keep me goin'. And believe me, so often it's awfully hard tryin' to go on. But that bastard sent from the other side of Hell violated my sweet Azúcar and he will be sorry for what he did. Believe me! And I swear by every santo dwellin' in nan Ginen across the purifying ancestral waters: May the thunder of Changó turn me to useless ashes and my protective mother Ezili Dantò pluck out my tired old eyes if I don't get my revenge! Hear me well, *hermano mío*!"

It had been a very long time since Don Anselmo had seen Doña Fela erupt with such fury. Her face seemed to have metamorphosed into that of a loathsome Harpy. Anselmo recalled witnessing a similar degree of rage on the old woman's part many years ago, upon the occasion of the death of her only daughter, Azúcar' mother, while giving birth to the little girl. And then again when the baby's father was hacked to death by machete. So, a torrent of genuine anger fell over every inch of the old woman's face and was heard in every syllable of the words she uttered.

"That filthy *hijueputa* will curse the day his mother spat him out of her cursed womb and crossed the path of this old black woman."

At this, the supportive ally Don Anselmo, convinced beyond

doubt that his comrade was deadly serious, mused aloud. "Woe to him who laugh just once and get into the habit, for the wickedness of Life don't know no limits. If it give you your heart's desire with one hand, it is only a matter of time before it trample hard on you with both feet and let loose on you that madwoman called "mala suerte", bad luck, who then grab you and hack you into tiny little pieces before scattering your flesh to the hungry sharks in the sea." Don Anselmo then sank into a deep reflection.

About a week later, still at the height of the *zafra*, with every living soul even remotely connected with sugar production working at a nearly non-stop pace and at superhuman speeds, there was still no allowance for any measure or manner of distraction. Nevertheless, there occurred at *Esperanza Dulce* two incidents that jolted everyone to another level of reality. Initially, it seemed that the two occurrences were unrelated, but soon afterwards no one wanted to speak too loudly or openly about the certainty that Azúcar was a key figure in both of these explosive incidents.

The first of the two events was thought to be extremely repulsive and the first of its kind occurring publicly or reported as such. In fact, most people seemed to prefer simply not to talk at length about it ---- that is, of course, the larger community outside the *batey*. As it happened, the advancing stages of Azúcar's pregnancy kept her away from the cane fields altogether. The doctor at the plantation's clinic had to certify the young pregnant girl's official medical condition in order to be excused from any strenuous physical tasks. So, a sufficiently pregnant Azúcar was given the job of baby-sitting all the infants and toddlers whose presence in the fields would be regarded as a "perilous distraction."

One particularly hot afternoon Azúcar and a few of the other youngsters who had been kept away from the fields or the mill house for one reason or another decided to escape the insufferable oven-like temperatures inside the cabins. Instead, they decided to seek refuge under some shade trees in the nearby woods. Specifically, there was welcome coolness under the dense macaw trees. There, a faint breath of wind slipped over and through the leaves in a long refreshing whisper, which succeeded in lulling the infants to sleep immediately.

Then, faintly at first before becoming clearer --- as Azúcar would tell her grandmother without forgetting the minutest detail, from inside the deep shadows of the mangrove, a sensuously melodious voice accompanied by the rich sound of a guitar could be heard. The sweet sounds resonated louder and louder, and seemed to be rather close to where the escapees had taken refuge.

"*Ay, mi madre, qué música más bonita!* What beautiful music!" one of the youngster had sighed.

"Shhhhh! . . . shhhhh!" she whispered to her young companions.

"*Cállate! 'Tate quieto!* Be quiet! Stay still! I want to go see where that music is comin' from."

A few short yards away, camouflaged by the mangrove thicket, was what appeared to be two individuals enjoying an innocent, private picnic. A colorful blanket was spread upon the soft grass. A large wicker basket contained a variety of foods: there were a few bottles of wine and even wine glasses, queso del país ("cheese of the country", or locally-made cheese) bread, fruit, a salami loaf. The lulling sounds of the ballad continued and were now so close that Azúcar herself may well have been sharing the picnic blanket with the romantic duo. Azúcar was able to push aside very quietly a break in the thicket, allowing her to steal an unobstructed view of the scene ahead of her.

What she saw put the naïve young observer in a near catatonic trance; her naturally large eyes managed to stretch even wider in disbelief. But what she saw was at once incredulous and bizarre at the same time. Sitting comfortably on the picnic blanket, the singer of the lovely music was completely naked from head to foot. The seductive music stopped long enough to permit the singer's enraptured listener —also seated on the blanket and also stark naked— to take a folded napkin and lovingly wipe the perspiration from the cheeks and forehead of the naked singer. The appreciative listener then tenderly stroked the singer's cheeks and neck.

"*Dios mío*. You are so gorgeous," one voice uttered slightly above a whisper as Azúcar listened in her confusion of everything that was happening in the mangrove that afternoon.

"*Estoy enamorado de tí. Lo sabes?* I am in love with you. Do you know that? I have dreamt of having a love like yours," replied the other individual in the same soft voice that had earlier been singing the rapturuos ballad.

The concealed observer watched the two naked bodies move closer, now no longer separated by the guitar. They embraced, holding each other for a long time, and then kissed passionately on the mouth, their bodies still in a tight, sensuous embrace. The innocent Azúcar had truthfully never seen two people kiss or embrace in that manner, not even Lolita and her sweet Haitian Estimé or Clementina and Tomás. No one. She couldn't recall seeing anyone in the batey kissing without maybe being slapped or cursed after doing so. It would be quite some time before Azúcar learned the meaning of passion.

Marcelo and Harold, lying there in the mangrove thicket, were mutually enveloped by the naked excitement and pleasure of man-to-man romance and love making, by the joyously innocent sounds of the Nature: the running water, the orchestral sounds of the chirping birds, the gentle rustling of the tree leaves, the tropical afternoon breeze, the aromatic fragrances of the forest--- mixed with the smells of hot sex, the pounding heart beats. The lovers experienced ever so sweet sensations as they whimpered, cried out softly, groaned in ecstasy. Oblivious to anyone possibly spying on them, they were no longer in control of their individually rampant lust. Their two bodies meshed into a non-dissenting oneness, totally lost in the sheer power of masculine libidos.

Just then, a sudden, sharp crackle of crushed twigs startled, maybe even frightened the naked duo; they were like two helpless forest deer whose serenity had been suddenly intruded upon. They instinctively unlocked their impassioned embrace and turned in the direction of the disruptive sound. They saw no one.

"What was that?" asked Harold, who was certain he had heard the sound.

"I heard something. Y *tú*?" he said nervously, looking in the direction of the brook.

"*Sí*, I heard it too. I think someone is out there," replied an equally nervous Marcelo, the singer possessing the mellifluous voice.

"We'd better leave. *Vámonos*, ok?"

So, the two naked men dressed hurriedly, gathered their picnic items and rushed to the parked company jeep. The last thing Azúcar remembered before regaining consciousness back at the cabin was trying to run back to the sleeping infants and the older youngsters watching them. The added weight of her heavy belly didn't allow for a rapid get-away. Her head began to spin; she was trapped in a state of vertigo. The dizziness mounted; she stumbled and fell, then blacked out. The shock and confusion of what she witnessed had overtaken her. Oddly enough though, as Azúcar would recall later, she held no feelings of moral outrage or disgust against the two young men in the mangrove.

Harold and Marcelo, without an instant's thought to inviting personal shame or ridicule — at least not at the moment of their decision to help the expectant mother --- gathered her up, together with all the children as the jeep was forced to accommodate and took them to Doña Fela's cabin. When Azúcar awoke, her grandmother did not have to insist that her granddaughter recount every single detail of what had happened in the mangrove that afternoon. The malicious gossip that immediately embellished the scandal of the two *"perveros,"* the young Canadian agronomist and his constant companion, the *capataz*'s youngest son --- the "delicate" one--- would be whispered about for some time to come, with far reaching repercussions.

The second incident, by far of greater seriousness and with deeper implications for a greater number of individuals, seemed to shake the very foundation stones of *Esperanza Dulce*. As fate would have it, most paradoxically, it would be this tragic incident that would actually save Diego Montalvo and his family from being evicted from the plantation. Just as the whirlwind of activities associated with the *zafra* was coming to its long-awaited end, the entire province received foreboding news of the worse kind. The incident reached the newspapers of the Island's capital city.

As the early morning dawn soared skyward with the crowing of the cocks, in one of the plantation's more remote sugarcane fields, a corpse, — not decomposed, yet charred far beyond recognition and diabolically mutilated--- was discovered among the discarded bagasse cane heaps. As with any dead body anywhere on the plantation, this one too underwent a thorough investigation by the official medical examiner to determine the cause of death. To everyone's astonishment, however, this corpse was not that of some unfortunate cane cutter that had been hacked to death by an enraged opponent embroiled in a fit of drunken fury or in a violent three-way lovers' altercation. Rather, this horribly and deliberately mutilated body was that of Mario Montalvo, the rakish, first-born son of the *capataz* at *Esperanza Dulce!*

TRECE

A small work crew of sugarcane cutters, perhaps ten or so, had piled up a sizable heap of cane in a clearing that had been made for that purpose and was now cutting on the other side of the clearing. Diego Montalvo, of course, could not see them over the tops of the tall sugarcane stalks; but the familiar rustling of the long leaves on the stalks as the swift blows of the machetes whacked low at the roots signaled where the cutters were. The workers, both men and women, bent as low as was humanly possible, were singing vigorously, but bitterly:

> *Caña brava, caña dulce;*
> One is tough, the other sweet.
> Together they make the best sugar,
> the best rum, the best *melaza* for the bosses.
> So, my brothers and sisters,
> chop it all down.
> Whack! Whack! Whack!
> *Caña brava, caña dulce;*
> One is tough, the other sweet.
> Together they make the best *aguardiente*
> for our miserable asses.
> So, my brothers and sisters, chop it all down
> Chop the *maldita caña,* Chop it all down.
> Chop the *maldita caña,* chop it all down.
> Whack! Whack! Whack!

The rhythmic chorus of voices filled the sun-drenched morning, quickly spreading across every inch of the *cañaveral*. The bittersweet song about sugarcane was almost a chant, as indicated by the descriptive theme. The cutters were singing in the traditional antiphonal call-response style characteristic of

African oral lyricism heard across centuries and expressed as work songs. These worksongs can still be heard in the sugarcane or cotton fields throughout the African Diaspora. The lead "caller" skillfully improvised new verses as they were sung; the "chorus" or "gang" of laborers responded accordingly. From the adjacent fields other voices joined in. In the next instant there was an exquisitely crafted symphony of human voices filling the otherwise tortuous air. Even the birds came out of concealment within heavily foliaged trees to listen.

As was his custom, the *capataz*, astride his stallion, loaded revolver inside its holster at his side, lingered half-hidden among the rows of cane just long enough to allow time to overhear random conversations of the cutters--- but also to spy upon individuals idling on the job. Diego could never be quite sure that the workers were aware of or indifferent to his presence. At any rate, often this surreptitious manner of gathering information was an important source of learning about the activities and thoughts of the distrusted workers at *Esperanza Dulce*. Or was it more a traditional pattern of plantation astuteness (trickery?) on the part of the workers to have the capataz hear simply what they wanted him to hear, or thought he might want to hear?

"*Pero qué vaina eh esa*? What is that shit all about?" one man asked with seriousness.

"*Cochon marron*! Wild pig!" said a Krèyol-speaking *bracero* in disgust.

"*Maricónes sucios*! Dirty faggots," was all another cutter blurted out.

Another worker suggested maliciously that the "sugar doctor" really did find the sugar he had come looking for.

"That was one doctor who didn't have to use a machete to get at the sugar."

"*Extrâit caca*! What a shithead!"

"But can you believe it? I heard that both of them didn't

have no clothes on! They were naked like they come into the world! *Qué barbaridad!*"

"*Sinvergüenzas!* Shameless scoundrels! Why you 'spose they was in the mangrove?" was what one woman insisted mockingly, even though she knew the answer, or at least like everybody else, speculated wildly. Everybody laughed hard.

"*Por mi santa madre, no entiendo.* I just don't understand it," Serafina began in her characteristic raunchiness. As cute as he is, that young chicken wouldn't even have to pay me nothin' to try it out," she announced proudly, holding her side from laughing so hard and at the same time pointing to her private parts. She went on.

"Let me tell you one thing: once that *pollito* had some of this delicious *chocha*, believe me, he wouldn't never want to sniff aroun' another man."

Nobody could withhold the eruption of volcanic guffaws and added all sorts of personal taunts and jeers about the "incident" in the mangrove.

What individuals didn't know or weren't entirely certain about, they casually invented or merely embellished with outrageous conjecture. One woman swore, for instance, that "the perverted duo" had even invited the children to share in the picnic that afternoon. The woman's neighbor suggested further that the two deviants had gotten poor Azúcar drunk by giving her so much wine that she had neglected the children in her care. Another totally erroneous account had Azúcar actually witnessing the lovemaking between the young "sugarcane doctor" and "the sweet young Montalvo boy." Of course, what was somehow omitted was the part where the two young men, instead of abandoning the unconscious and pregnant Azúcar in the mangrove and fleeing the scene as quickly as they could, took it upon themselves to carry her back to the cabin.

"*Basta ya, hijos de puta!* Enough now, you sons-of-bitches!

Get your black asses back to work before I get rid of all of you no-good island trash," Diego bullied the workers from his horse. "Move along." He had heard enough, fully aware that he always ran the risk of hearing what he didn't really need to — and perhaps "want" to hear. The idea that one of his sons, a Montalvo, was seen engaged in the unthinkable act of "romancing another man" was monstrous and totally unacceptable to Diego Montalvo. Mario's indiscretions had been considered mild by every comparison with Marcelo's abomination.

"*Caña brava, Caña dulce*. One is tough, the other sweet." The call-response chant resumed, seemingly not having missed a beat. The cutters got back on task.

The titillating gossip and raunchy jokes that greeted the news of the mangrove affair involving handsome Marcelo Montalvo and the young company agronomist from Canada were a far cry from what awaited *Esperanza Dulce* when the thunderbolt of Mario's murder struck. The entire community, from the offices of the central administration to the cabins of the batey — in fact, every segment of the population throughout the region, was transformed immeasurably. The impact of the gruesome murder of the eldest son of the *capataz* at one of the Island's most profitable sugarcane operations sent reverberations all the way back to Toronto, the seat of corporate headquarters.

"Goddammit! What the hell is happening down there? This is really quite sticky, you know," one straightforward executive in Toronto insisted, visibly irritated.

"First that messy business with that little fairy Capps and now we've got a damned murder that actually took place on company property! On our own premises, mine you! How's this possibly going to cut into company profits this quarter?" another infuriated high level executive growled.

"We'd better send down some of our own guys from the

133

New York office," ordered the superior executive.

"Consider it done, chief."

An expert team of New York investment specialists and investigators were on the next morning's company jet to the Caribbean — the same 727 jet that had delivered Dr. Harold Capps to the Island for the first time. The team was ordered to conduct a thoroughly professional investigation into all the possible ramifications of Mario's murder and any probable economic fallout. Further projections of profit losses could be disastrous, especially since Harold's report on the decline in harvest yields had not been completed as yet. The Montalvo family never learned of the company's callousness and indifference on a personal level toward the grieving family. The clear priority for the transnational was the direct effect on its profit margins, stock investments, and reactions of shareholders. With the comforting news from Toronto that the Montalvo family would not be released from their contract nor expelled from *Esperanza Dulce,* Diego would be able to breathe with considerable ease and an appreciable measure of continued security.

Cristiana Montalvo, on the other hand, was never the same with the loss of her first born. Immediately after Mario's funeral and burial, Cristiana went straight to the perceived safety and serenity of her bedroom, her sanctuary, and shut herself up inside to the harsh and unfamiliar sound of the seldom-used lock. This behavior became a daily ritual. She would sit in the darkness of her room for a long time meditating, totally lost in her preoccupations and oblivious of her husband and all else in the household. Nothing else seemed to matter to Cristiana. With an air of unwitting desolation, as if all life had been extinguished from her, this mother in mourning exclaimed impassively:

"*O Satanás!* The devil himself long ago possessed the soul of my son Mario. Mario was powerless and weakened by these satanic forces from Hell. Mario, you are now freed from this torment."

Then she would cry herself to sleep, having eaten nothing all evening. The ritual would repeat itself the very next day and every day after that. Everyone soon realized that Cristiana was becoming spiritually vanquished. Cristiana thought to herself how Mario had feared neither man nor beast – and had scorned God. She recalled how as a young man Mario had always held such unreasonable contempt for the workers in the batey; but whenever he lacked for friends of his own class, he accepted the company of the men of the batey as drinking mates. Well before he married Blanchette, Mario was notorious in his blatant practice of sleeping with several of the older prostitutes of the batey, much to the chagrin of his mother. Blanchette was naturally humiliated upon learning of her future husband's wretched behavior. However, she convinced herself that once married to her, Mario would surely quench his disgusting appetite. Quite sadly, though, he proved her wrong.

But what tormented and pained Mario's mother deeply was the knowledge of the secret that her husband had shared with her about Mario's grandfather, Diego's father. The sordid tale about old abuelo Montalvo went untold for years and most certainly was concealed from his grandsons at great costs to the entire family. For whatever reason, Diego finally decided to reveal his father's secret to Cristiana.

In the tradition of Montalvo men, Diego's father held one of the most important and well respected – and indeed one of the most skilled positions on the plantation, that of *maestro de azúcar*, "boiler-house chief," the vital task of actually making the sugar. One night in the mill house, Diego's father, "the respected sugar master," was caught in the heinous act of brutally raping one of the young girls who worked there; she might have been about fifteen years old. The helpless and terrified girl's screams had brought her young husband running to his wife's rescue. As the story goes, Diego's father, in an outburst of naked rage, pulled out his revolver and shot the distraught husband, then turned the still-smoking gun on the man's horror-stricken, violated wife.

The young couple was killed, and old man Montalvo was never arrested nor ever stood trial for the double murder. Not one of the several eyewitnesses to the abominable crime came forward to testify; all the workers housed in the surrounding cabins were warned at gun point against ever talking to anyone "on the outside" about what anyone had seen that night in the boiler room. It would be years before even Diego would talk about it. It was as if the incident had never occurred. Cristiana was convinced that her first- born son Mario had fallen victim of his grandfather's evil curse. After reflecting on these painful thoughts, Cristiana would then cry herself into oblivion, awakening early the following morning and unlocking her private sanctuary in order to return briefly to the real world around her.

Mario's psychologically tortured wife Blanchette felt at last freed from a nightmarish chamber of horrors upon the demise of her husband. Living with Mario had been barbarously miserable for the delicate princess of Maurice Desgraves and Yvette Origène. Blanchette's only sibling, Pierre-Raymón, was quick to say to his sister, "At last, *ma cher hermanita*, you can breathe freely and get on with your life with the twins."

Of course, Cécile and Chelaine would be fatherless, but not orphaned. Their mother was still very lovely and quite vibrant to be able to rebound wholesomely from any imagined sting of her loss. And there were any number of very worthy suitors anxious to share Blanchette's pillow— and the hefty portion of an inheritance awaiting her. Blanchette's mother would at last be vindicated by her daughter's marriage to "one of our own," as the class-conscious, but obstinately honest Yvette remarked aloud, especially whenever referring to the Montalvos. It was no oversight that all sympathies rested with the long-suffering Blanchette and the twins. Mario's surviving brothers Miguel and Manolo, but not the youngest Marcelo--- who was himself trying to deal with recent scandal and rebuke by family and friends--- pledged nothing short of the bloodiest revenge. Mario had been a kind of champion and hero to both Miguel and Manolo.

"*Coño*. The cowardly black dogs who did this horrible thing to our brother Mario will fuckin' pay with their own shitty lives," Miguel swore with solemn rage.

"Whoever committed this goddamn act," Manolo growled with a surly tone of determined fury, "is going to suffer a worse fate than our dear brother Mario. By every fuckin' thing that is holy, I say we find the bastard and cut off his black *cojónes* and boil 'em in hot oil. That'll teach all the black bastards one good lesson they'll never forget."

Reactions throughout the batey to Mario's terrible murder were more somber. There was certainly no jubilation. Upon hearing the dreadful news, nearly all the residents felt the threat of immediate and inevitable suspicion and subsequent harsh reprisals. The community was not mistaken nor were they unjustified in their fears, which were quite real. It was no secret outside the batey that Mario had been extremely abusive, physically and otherwise, against the powerless residents there.

"Would any of those monkeys down in that scum hole actually be so stupid to think they could get away with murdering the capataz's son?" expressed many outsiders.

"*Coño*. They may just as well have committed suicide," was a common reply.

"*Malè pa gin klaksonn*. Disasters always arrive without warning," was how Césaire voiced his reaction to his comrades in the men's barracks one night after work.

"We better not let down our guard. You know they gonna take it out on all us."

"*Se lè koulèv mouri, ou konn longè li.* Only after the serpent is dead can you take its measure," Vincent, sitting on the cot next to his friend, replied thoughtfully as he considered Mario's sadistic behavior.

"Would all this hell ever end? An' when?" asked so many people, still wondering.

Mario's prearranged acquittal in the cold-blooded murder of their countryman Estimé escaped no one as they each reflected on Mario's subsequent fate.

"*Sé pa vouazin ka va ranjé sa pou nou.*" Césaire translated for longneck Teresa's brother, Ramón. "*No es el vecino el que va a arreglar esto por nosotros.* It's not our neighbor who is gonna fix things for us."

The message struck Ramón with immediate clarity. "That *hijueputa vendido* Mario got what he deserved, *carajo*," replied Ramón in anger, banging hard with his fists on the table. "I just wish I'd a had the *cojónes* to do it my damn self. What that filthy *puto* did to little Azúcar ain't got no words, *Carajo!*"

Everybody sitting around the barracks agreed without a single dissent. Such sentiment, though not necessarily voiced, was widespread throughout the community of cane workers.

"*Bay kou bliye, pote mak sonje,*" Vincent said, shaking his head as if to add his own "Amen" at the same time.

"What does that mean?" Ramón asked.

"It's an old proverb I used to hear my grandfather say," answered Césaire, the translator.

"Those who give out the blows forget, while those who bear the scars remember."

Not many people understood why Mario's badly mutilated body, gruesome as that was, presented an even more macabre aspect since the man's face had been literally peeled from ear to ear with a keenly honed machete. It was Don Anselmo who explained with utmost discretion and in patient detail that particularly bloody, secret ritual to a carefully hand-picked group of comrades.

"It was a traditional way to torture people even in the afterlife," he practically whispered. "Since before ancient times the elders have believed that such ritual would prevent a proper burial for a person who had done so much evil in life by trappin' the spirit of that person in a state of eternal sufferin'."

Without hesitation, the authorities classified Mario's sadistic murderer as "a crazed savage," and to avoid mass hysteria and panic throughout communities outside the batey, they released reports that omitted altogether the description of Mario's faceless body.

Mamá Lola, because, of course, she worked directly in the elder Montalvo household and was exceptionally vigilant during the recent misfortunes to strike at Don Diego's door, reported regularly to her friends and comrades in the batey what she had learned.

"Doña Cristiana is almost lost her mind. Won't hardly eat nothin'. Right after a little lunch she lock herself in her bedroom. Won't come out till the next mornin'."

"What about the *capataz*?" somebody more than merely curious wanted to know. Mamá Lola continued her report.

"He can't control hisself. He and the two middle sons plannin' some real hard revenge. They can't hardly wait to find Don Mario's murderer, I heard'm say. They ready to take revenge at any minute. We all gotta be real careful. Everybody a walkin' suspect."

Doña Fela took special care in calling upon her protective loa Ezili Dantò. But this time she wanted her protectoress to watch not just over herself and her granddaughter, but also collectively over her entire community. She was justifiably and genuinely concerned for the physical safety of everyone. There were clear indications that the normally ruthless capataz would be relentless in the pursuit and capture of his son's killer or killers and absolutely merciless in his revenge. The entire batey had now become a suspect and thus a ready target of the indiscriminate release of Diego's potent venom.

The old woman, her arms and eyes upraised, fell to her knees and, with clenched teeth, exclaimed solemnly:

"Oh compassionate guardian Ezili Dantò. I also call upon the fearless Mayanèt to walk alongside Dantò. Together in your combined powers, cast your benevolent, protective eyes upon this sufferin' community. Take pity on our oppressed souls and protect us from our cruel tormentors. Don't permit these devils to overpower us."

Doña Fela, with deliberation, explained carefully to her very pregnant granddaughter that the capataz and his sons, with the single exception of the youngest and very decent Marcelo, were seeking uncompromising vengeance at whatever costs.

"They are obsessed with findin' and punishin' whoever was responsible for Mario's killin'," she pointed out to Azúcar.

Everybody was certain, also, that the punishment would be as equally grotesque as was Mario's murder. Don Anselmo was worried . . . and had been so for several days since the revelations of the two incidents that had rocked the stability, order, and predictability of *Esperanza Dulce*. He was very circumspect as he assembled a select group of men in council late one night in his own cabin.

"We all gotta be extra cautious and alert. *Coño!* Don't nobody do nothin' to aggravate the wrath of the capataz . . . 'specially now. *Zafra* is over, and now come *tiempo muerto*, 'dead time,' — no activity, *nada*; but in ways we never seen before. We all in serious danger," warned a very worried Anselmo.

He was deeply concerned about the welfare of all the *batey*'s powerless residents. He was particularly worried about the fate of soon-to-be-mother, little Azúcar. It had all visited him in recurrent dreams that each time awoke him in the middle of the night, bathed in heavy sweat. In the dream sequence, there appeared not the beautiful, sweet Yemayá, protectoress of the sea and of maternity, but rather her evil opposite from mpemba, land of the dead. One of the mistresses of Baron Samdi, Grann Oyá, would appear at midnight, standing in the middle of a stream, innocently combing her long, flowing hair while singing such erotic lyrics that even raunchy Serafina couldn't match in boldness. The lyrics were intended for solitary listeners; the lyrics became more erotic as the listener drew nearer the stream —not really believing what he was hearing. In a flash, according to Anselmo's vivid dream, Grann Oyá's enchantment overpowers the listener, now standing dangerously close, like a skilled fisherman's net snarls the careless fish. Grann Oyá's enticing smile and voice lure the listener into the middle of the stream, so that he is standing alongside the seductress. He follows her beneath the surface of the waters -- down, down, down they go together to such unknown depths that the seduced listener never returns. Grann Oyá rises to the surface only to begin her seduction for the next unwitting listener. The dream, for Don Anselmo, was a harbinger that real trouble was not far behind.

For his part, the capataz made certain that extra caution was the order of the day. Now that *Esperanza Dulce* would be entering the phase of operations traditionally known as *tiempo muerto*, when most of the contracted workers would either be returned to their "sender" islands, or be sub-contracted out to other plantations prior to being transported back to their point of origin, and the labor assignments lessened, idle time would subsequently be in excess. Real problems could — and generally did occur if those in charge carelessly lowered their guard.

Don Diego himself also called a meeting of sorts. Just as *zafra* ended, the *capataz* assembled the entire work force of *Esperanza Dulce*. The workers were herded into the mill yard one afternoon as the final oxcarts were loaded with sugarcane stalks and driven off to the mill house. The day was nearing dusk . . . the sky not quite dark . . . shadows not yet giving chase. Huddled together on this final day of *zafra*, the workers –with their over-taxed bodies glistening with profuse sweat, their machetes safely sheathed in brown rawhide coverings dangling against a tired leg--- stood listening to what a vengeful Diego Montalvo had to say. He informed them of . . . "precautionary measures to be enforced immediately." He was deliberate in his announcement.

"We are imposing a strict curfew for the entire *batey*. Front gates will be locked from eight o'clock at night until four o'clock the next morning. Violators will be dealt with severely. You will be deprived of your accumulated earnings and sent back to wherever the fuck you came from. We are restricting the sale of *aguardiente* and *kleren* at the bodegas . . . weekend sales only, none during the week. We are banning all visitor permits to *Esperanaza Dulce* from neighboring estates. And finally, this year there will be no celebration for the *Reino de Ga-Ga* Fiesta."

Of all the new measures to be imposed on the community, the cancellation of this year's traditional, anxiously awaited festival of *Reino de Ga-Ga* undoubtedly was considered the most cruel and disappointing to the listeners. This act alone struck a cord of deep resentment with everybody assembled in the mill yard. There was muted anger. All eyes were centered on the vindictive *capataz*.

"Can that old fool feel the boiling anger targeting him?" Don Anselmo wondered.

The colorful, African-derived, quasi-religious festival of *Reino de Ga-Ga* was transported from Haití and has a long tradition in nearly all the *bateys* of the Island. Since shortly after abolition, sugarcane workers began setting aside four special days following the end of *zafra;* these exuberant days were devoted to unrestrained dancing and calling up the ancestral spirits, all in celebration of the end of the harvest. The festivities usually coincided with the Catholic tradition of Holy Week, *Semana Santa.* In one segment of the ceremony, a group of very skillful men dance with rapidly twirling machetes in a kind of mock combat. A group of women don wedding veils and perform an unmistakably seductive, sexually explicit dance to arouse the men present. The uninhibited merriment is unrivaled in intensity --- relieving months of unbearable toil and degradation in the sugarcane fields and mill houses . . . to say little of cushioning the repressed tension and rage.

Doña Fela also was very angry. *"Pero todo' loh santo.* There always been a celebration for us to honor *Reino de Ga-Ga.* I just can't never remember the time there wasn't none," she had said to Azúcar, her voice choked up with controlled rage. When anger flared in the old woman, she would tighten her whole body and appear taller than she actually was. Her voice, rather than become louder or shrill, remained steady and deliberate, but the words cut like carefully aimed machete blows.

"This is the naked vengeance of that hateful old devil Diego Montalvo; he really mean to punish all of us. This is a very bad sign." Doña Fela repeated the phrase with the same calmness. "A bad sign." As the assembled workers listened to the capataz, some of them scowled and muttered under their breath. Spanish, Kreyòl, pidgin, patois ---- it was a grumbling babel of registered discontent. After hearing enough of the *capataz's* sinister pronouncements, most individuals just lowered their head or looked away from the visibly hostile speaker, shuffling their bare feet with carefully concealed anger.

Some time after an uneasy calm was restored to the *batey*, after extremely harsh and unjust measures of further control and intimidation of the residents were enacted and zealously enforced, after most everybody managed to reconcile himself to the hard reality of Don Diego's obsession to avenge the murder of his son Mario – months had passed and still not one individual had been arrested and convicted of the crime, there was one event that did inspire a modicum of joy in most folks. Azúcar gave birth to a set of adorable twin girls. Upon receiving the news that Doña Fela's once virgin granddaughter, azúcar morenita, was now a mother, someone remarked,

"*Eso no augura nada bueno.* That's a bad sign."

But almost daily, Estimé's widow Lolita, still oblivious to events taking place around her, would sit in the doorway of her cabin, rocking her shrunken body and muttering to no one in particular.

"*Jou van, jou vien – m'pa di passé ça.* The days may come and go, but just you wait and see; my day is coming."

CATORCE

Against tremendous sorrow and the frailty of life's circumstances, they say, there is most likely and will probably always be an amalgamation of human fantasy and vanity. Change does eventually come. It may well have been thanks to the fantasy of an unlikely couple in love, young Marcelo Montalvo and "the sugar doctor" from Canada, Harold Capps, that Azúcar succeeded in becoming a mother of adorable twin girls. That hot afternoon in the mangrove when she lay unconscious, had it not been for the unselfish and humane behavior of the two decent, sensitive human beings, the girl might not have lived to experience motherhood.

"*Óyeme*! Listen to me, we can't just leave her here, Harold; she may not regain consciousness and will die alone out here," the genuinely compassionate Marcelo had said to his lover.

"*Tú tienes razón, querido.* You're right, babe. We've got to get her back to her cabin . . . and immediately, or she'll suffer dehydration and die for sure."

The two young daring lovers would worry later about what people would say about their reported depraved behavior in the mangrove.

Now at nearly fourteen years old, Azúcar was a mother. What did she know about the frightening responsibilities of motherhood? Her grandmother had been the only mother she ever knew.

"*Tengo miedo.* I am afraid," she used to cry herself to sleep many a night thinking about what it all meant. "I'm pregnant. I'm gonna have a baby. How am I suppose' to feel? Will the baby be a girl or a boy? Who will it look like?"

Delivery had been difficult and especially painful, given the young mother's tender age and the dire lack of adequate prenatal care and proper nutrition, plus any number of other normally favorable conditions that would automatically guarantee a safe and healthy birth. Such was the ugly and distasteful reality of life in the *batey*. Obstetrician? Gynecologist? Pediatrician? Absolutely not. Azúcar had only the services of the compound's general clinic the day she delivered. Her attending physician was the plantation's veterinarian ---since the general practitioner was never available on weekends. Of course, Doña Fela and most of the other older woman remembered well, in times past on the plantation, when a *partera*, a "midwife," was the only "experienced medical personnel" whose services were regularly provided for expectant mothers in the batey. So, Azúcar had been quite fortunate that day.

Even though the twins were unquestionably identical in every physical aspect, what was unusual about their birth, according to the older women present, was the fact that the babies were delivered from their frightened mother's young, untested womb a full thirty minutes apart!

"*Ay, por todo loh santo*. That's a bad sign," said one of the old women in attendance.

"*Sí, eh verda'*. That's true. Nothin' good gonna come from this, Créeme.

Trust me," replied another, looking sorrowfully.

"*Rivyè debòde. Rivyè debòde*. The river overflowed. The river overflowed." That was all that one old Krèyol-speaking *partera* uttered in whispers as she saw the twins being delivered thirty minutes apart. Mamá Lola knew immediately what this cryptic phrase meant.

"*Ay, por el amor de lo' santo'*. Azúcar gonna meet with some kind of calamity an' much sadness involvin' water," she said mournfully, but with a firm certainty." She most likely was referring to the stream in the forest. The old midwife then hurried away . . . not wishing to be blamed for the inevitable misfortune she knew would visit the young mother.

The mother gave her twin girls the names Felicidad and

Caridad. Quite thoughtfully, Azúcar wanted to honor first her devoted grandmother, who tried to teach the importance of trying to find a measure of happiness, *"felicidad,"* amidst overwhelming sadness and misery. The girl also wanted to show her gratitude to the friends and neighbors who, over the years living among them, had extended such sincere charity, *"caridad,"* and benevolence toward her.

"*Abuelita*, you are my greatest love in this world," the girl had said to her grandmother.

"More than anything, I just want to treasure always my deep love for you by namin' the first of the twins after you."

"*Ay, mi azúcar dulce.* For such a tender young child, your thoughts weigh so heavy," Doña Fela replied with tears filling her eyes.

Azúcar was pleased that her grandmother seemed pleased and accepting. While everybody else who paid visits to the new mother and found the occasion joyous and the newborn twins adorable, Azúcar's grandmother, quite to the contrary, was not at all weighed down with any amount of exuberance. Doña Fela displayed no exhilaration --- nor was she doting on her identical great granddaughters. Only the ever-observant old eyes of Don Anselmo noticed this, but said nothing.

The tiny Felicidad and Caridad were beautiful babies with their big, round, deep-set, marmoset-like eyes, jet black baby-fine hair, and exotically lustrous, light-colored wheat complexion -- *"trigueño"* the color was called. The puffy little lips of both infants, rather large for their minuscule, cherubic face, seemingly curved upwards in a permanent smile. Their little noses were identically pudgy. Azúcar was indeed a new mother, but wasn't certain what she was expected to do. But learning would come automatically, instinctively. With absolute certainty, however, she knew that both Felicidad and Caridad had been the bitter results of a monstrously unforgettable attack one blistering hot afternoon nine months ago when she found herself alone in the cabin. The new mother felt an instantly strange mixture of fear and anger. She held the babies protectively tight to her bosom.

"*Me preocupo muchísimo*. I am very troubled by this birth, " Doña Fela admitted to her old confidant Mamá Lola. "You know, the twins didn't come out one right behind the other?"

"*Kalfou danjere*. Very dangerous crossroads," Mamá Lola replied pensively upon hearing this revelation from Doña Fela.

"Then the twins emerged with weakened powers than normal because they didn't come at the crossroads. This ain' good. *Éh mal. Mal*. No good," Dona Fela said, this time barely audible .

Mamá Lola felt an obligation to recall another ancient lesson for her old friend. "*Pero, mi vieja amiga*. But my dear friend, the petal of the frangipani tree that falls into the pond won't rot the same day." She thought about what the old Kreyòl-speaking midwife had said before hurrying off after Azúcar's delivery.

"In the old days we always had the *partera* attendin'," Doña Fela reflected in sadness. She alone was the one who read all the important signs of the delivery and then passed this information on to the parents." Doña Fela reflected long and hard about what was unfolding. The knowledgeable old woman quite naturally was reminded of the ancient tradition of "magique marasa," the Sacred twins, Marasa, and so respected their magical power— along with their accompanying element of danger. So strong were their powers that the twins, Marasa, were said to join Papa Legba at times as the guardians of the crossroads. This is where the world of the living intersects with the world of the dead. Doña Fela was mindful of the predictions regarding the birth of twins to her granddaughter, a granddaughter who had been brutally violated, deflowered --- and as it would be later discovered, permanently damaged during Mario Montalvo's savage attack on the young virgin. Profoundly worsening the tragic circumstance of this ritual cosmos of Marasa for both Doña Fela and Azúcar was the visible fact that the actual father of the twins, who normally would have the power to open the spiritual world, was not "one of their kind."

Thus, the twins' father represented a gross abnormality; he was a cold-blooded, murdering snake. Estimé's widow, for one, would never forget that sickening reality. It was precisely because of the horrid circumstances of the birth of the twins, a circumstance that the elders concluded was a bad omen, that no one dared enact the honored tradition of placing the mother's afterbirth in a hole behind her cabin, nor of planting a banana tree over that hole to ensure long life for the new arrivals. The baby's father traditionally performed this ancient ritual. But, in Azúcar's case, everybody just remained silent about this honored tradition that would now be ignored. It was thanks also to the fantasy of the same two honestly decent young men — although perceived as reprehensible by nearly everyone outside the batey— that Azúcar began the tedious, yet frightening journey on the road to important self-discovery and personal transformation. It would be no accident, for instance, that the young pariahs Marcelo and Harold would begin taking a very special interest in Azúcar and in the welfare of her twin infants.

Almost no one was terribly surprised to see the two young "outsiders" visiting at Doña Fela's cabin one early afternoon shortly after Azúcar had given birth to Felicidad and Caridad. Since the jeep that the young men were driving had to pass along the length of the main road running parallel to the batey's central trough, those residents living closest to the entry gate naturally were the first ones to see the company vehicle arriving. Most people stopped what they were doing in order to watch this novelty— since nobody from the "outside" actually visited the *batey*. The smaller children, many of whom were naked, ran alongside the slow-moving jeep, open hands extended, screaming for cheli and chicle, " pennies" and "chewing gum."

"*Mihter, dáme un cheli; dáme chicle*. Mister, give me a penny; give me some gum."

Well before the advancing afternoon shadows began their descent, the roadway leading down to Doña Fela's, a small, very excited crowd began gathering by the jeep parked in front of her cabin. The crowd had come to get a better view of the visitas desde afuera, "visitors from the outside"--- but equally important, to find out the nature of their visit. Two emaciated little puppies hobbled around to the jeep, sniffing at the strange, round, black things on each side of the vehicle. Swarms of uninvited mosquitoes, hungry gnats and other flying insects also invaded the animated scene in front of the cabin.

"Santa Altagracia. You not gonna believe who just stepped up in front of Doña Fela's! Come here and see for yourself," one-eyed Clementina called to her husband Tomás. But Tomás was less in awe than a kind of satisfied hope when he saw the two young visitors.

"*Qué bueno*! Those the same two *muchachos* that saved little Azúcar in the woods that day! I guess they come to see the twins." Unlike almost everybody else, Tomás was rather nonchalant about the arrival of the visitors. In fact, it was as if he had actually been expecting them.

Marcelo handed the old woman a magnificent bouquet of flowers.

"*Para usted, señora*. For you, madame."

Doña Fela hesitated slightly before taking the bouquet, not certain if she should.

"*Gracias*," she replied courteously, nevertheless. She received the two young men with genuine politeness. "*Bienvenidos, señores. Mi casa es su casa*. Welcome, sirs. Please come inside; my house is your house. And again, I thank you a thousand times for rescuin' my grandbaby that afternoon in the mangrove."

It was quite true that, at this sincere offering of her hospitality, the thought never entered Doña Fela's mind the scandalous reason these two young men were in the mangrove in the first place. Harold and Marcelo had brought all kinds of wonderful gifts for the new mother and her twin babies. Never before had Azúcar and her bewildered grandmother, nor any of the curious neighbors standing around outside seen such a shower of unusual and pretty things made especially for infants: brightly colored baby's sleep wear, dainty dresses, bibs, intricately knitted bootees, patterned blankets, sun bonnets with long teasing ribbons, frilly shawls, baby powders, oils, creams, an ample supply of baby's diapers. Perhaps the most spectacular of all the presents was a beautiful oblong wicker basket-like bed, large enough to hold two infants comfortably inside.

The visiting Canadian informed the suspicious Doña Fela that this was called a "bassinet" and "it was where new-born babies usually sleep." The skeptical old woman frowned at the French-sounding word only because she could not begin to imagine her granddaughter's twin babies sleeping apart, separated from their mother's instinctive protection, in a "big vegetable basket."

"*Qué ridículo*! How ridiculous!" she thought to herself, not wishing to offend the generous visitors and rescuers of her precious granddaughter. She again smiled graciously in silence.

Lying comfortably in her cot, a twin snuggled under each arm, a wide smile on her face, Azúcar presented a striking antithesis of motherhood. She was herself still a child, still not yet fifteen years old. Both Felicidad and Caridad were asleep in their mother's arms. The two visitors bearing gifts greeted Azúcar and bent over to get a closer look at the twin girls.

151

"*Qué lindas*. How beautiful they are," said Marcelo, grinning broadly.

"We brought these things for you and the babies," Harold added with equal delight. He presented each gift with a descriptive explanation of what each item was. The young mother's eyes sparked with delight

"*Muchísimas gracias. Muy agradecida*. I appreciate very much your kindness."

Azúcar accepted the gifts with naïve excitement and a degree of puzzlement, given her lack of exposure outside the batey. The two young men did not stay long. It was not necessary to prolong their visit; moreover, the expanding afternoon shadows were announcing the rapidly approaching darkness.

"*Bueno, hombre*, we'd better get going, don't you think?" Harold directed to Marcelo.

"*Sí*, it's getting dark and the roads are terrible enough during daylight hours," Marcelo responded. But he was actually thinking along other lines about why they should leave so soon after a short visit of just a few minutes.

It was Marcelo who sensed that their presence in the batey was an oddity in itself and was perhaps causing a slight degree of tension and discomfort, not only for the old woman, but for the neighbors as well. There was still a prevailing tone of mutually deepening mistrust and an irascible layer of antagonism — which rested slightly below the surface— between the residents of the batey and the larger community beyond the entry gate. It was certainly no secret to anyone that Diego Montalvo's blind and obsessive vengeance was targeted at every living soul in the batey.

"You want to know something? It does my soul good to know that the workers here have never stood me alongside my brother Mario," said Marcelo with heart-felt assurance. "They always saw us as two totally different individuals, even when we were young boys."

He was extremely pleased at the level of sophistication on the part of most of the batey's residents in their willingness to distinguish clearly the characters of the youngest and oldest Montalvo brothers. Some workers found it difficult to believe that the two were, in fact, blood brothers.

"*M pa konpran.* I don't understand," said one worker upon being told that the youngest Montalvo and the eldest were brothers.

"How can it be that they so different, but from the same mother's womb?"

"The truth from what I heard," replied the worker's companion, "is that the mother had a *baka,* bad spirit, inside her womb when she was carrying the first born. That's what I heard."

Particularly now that tiempo muerto had arrived and there was a reduced presence of contracted laborers, with a less hectic schedule of work assignments, there was by contrast much more time to think about many more things besides sugarcane. With the birth of Azúcar's twin girls, almost everyone's thoughts raced back to the violent and obscene circumstances surrounding the innocent girl's pregnancy. Mario's reprehensible acts had offended deeply all the residents of the community.

There was a growing climate of suspicion now targeting all the male residents of the *batey,* young and old, since no one had yet been apprehended for the assassination of the *capataz's* eldest son. However, outside the *batey* the horrible fate of "one of those crazed sugarcane cutters" had all but faded from recollection. The *batey,* on the other hand, would never allow Estimé's vicious murder by that same son of the *capataz* to be erased from the collective memory.

"Ezili Mapyan, the pitiless avenger, has performed well for

153

you," whispered one of Estimé's comrades one evening to the slain man's widow as she sat –in her customary form --in the doorway of her cabin. Lolita's smiling quietly to herself said everything that needed to be said.

Doña Fela showed no disrespect for the unexpected visit by the two young men who had been completely unselfish and honorable with regard to Azúcar. Besides Mamá Lola, who had long been intimately familiar with every conceivable aspect of the Montalvo household, Doña Fela was the first person in the batey to recognize and acknowledge the essential differences in the perverted Mario and the sensitive youngest Montalvo boy.

"Ese jovencito tiene mucho azúcar. That young fellow got a lot of sugar in him," she had always said about Marcelo's delicate, almost feminine mannerisms and simple kindness – referred to as "sugar". This was in stark contradiction to the brutish, foul-tempered beast that was Mario.

The old woman meant not the least bit of malice, since this youngest Montalvo was always genuinely pleasant and respectful toward all the residents of the *batey.* Everybody noticed, for example, how Marcelo always used "Don" or "Doña" before the first name of any elder person, without regard to the individual's social rank. Doña Fela never managed to overlook the personal insult whenever plantation managers and other individuals who were scores younger than she automatically addressed her by her first name only, never bringing themselves to the point of saying "Doña Fela."

Everybody said their "goodbyes" and the crowd outside dispersed as quickly as it had gathered. All curiosity had been satisfied.

"Muchas gracias de nuevo. Thanks again for everything," Doña Fela said to the departing couple. "Come back whenever you feel like visitin'. You both are always welcome here."

"We were hoping that we would be able to check on

Azúcar and the twins from time to time. *Muchas gracias,*" Marcelo expressed gratefully. What a welcome contrast between Doña Fela's unaffected reaction and his family's to the unfortunate disclosure of "the mangrove incident". He thought back to the moment of the profound hurt and the humiliation he was forced to endure upon the raw, unleased rebuke by his characteristically macho, unapologetically homophobic father and brothers.

"*Coño. Maricón sucio!* Goddammit! Dirty faggot! I didn't raise any of my sons to be faggots. *Qué asqueroso!* Fucking disgusting! Pack your goddamn things and get the hell outta my house," was Diego's singularly crude way of not dealing with the circumstance of his youngest offspring.

Marcelo's mother, on the other hand, still traumatized by lingering grief and filled with more than a headful of sedatives, continued to languish in a kind of self-induced malaise. So, she expressed empty indifference. Her love for Marcelo was more a product of her deep-seated feelings of guilt, coupled with the feeling that she had to protect her 'delicate son' from her husband's total irrationality and embarrassing stupidity, than merely loving the young man for who he was . . . her son.

"*Pero, Dios mío,* Diego, is that really necessary? Where will he go?" she had said in trying to counter her husband's brutally unreasonable reaction.

When Marcelo was cast out of the only home he had known, he went with his few personal belongings to Harold's cottage nearby. He explained through a flow of hurtful tears his father's tyrannical behavior; Harold responded with instinctive tenderness and compassion.

"*No te preocupes, mi querido.* Don't worry, babe. We'll work this mess out together. You and I will survive this hell," young Capps promised. They kissed on the lips while holding each other tightly. Both men sobbed real manly tears.

They didn't care who might have been spying on them. Of course, the *Esperanza Dulce* administration office was abuzz with the wildest gossip about the young Canadian scientist and his male, island paramour. Yet, perhaps because the staff there was mainly North American, not local, the affair was handled with a more noticeable degree of sensible discretion than it would have been otherwise. And the Toronto headquarters was extremely quick to remind everybody that . . .

"Our primary focus must never be circumvented nor compromised under any circumstances. That focus must consistently and exclusively be on sugarcane profits! Sugar is our only warranted preoccupation and as such, these are the only legitimate concerns that actually matter to us."

This was the clearly understood, single message that reached the Island. But the corporation's highly respected agronomist, the young Dr. Harold Capps, was reading a different message as a result of findings from his intensive research. Thus, he found himself possibly in a different kind of difficulty. As it turned out, this year's harvest yield fell short of about 400,000 tons below last year's yield. Two of the Island's provinces, Villa Clara and Céspedes, the latter being the one where Esperanza Dulce was located, produced what equated to just half their expected goals. Among corporate executives there was real concern that investment stocks would fall as a consequence. Instead of Harold's being handsomely rewarded for his successful efforts in improving the productive yield and essentially the overall quality strain of the Island's sugarcane crop, the young "sugar doctor" was summarily ordered to explain precisely what had happened.

A few years prior to his fateful arrival to the Island, Harold had confined himself to the Toronto research laboratories, testing an ambitious hybrid strain of the cane plant. After much diligent persistence and with elaborate, high-tech protocols involving DNA samples of several diverse cane species from around the world, the self-denying, dedicated agronomist finally developed what he believed to be a genetically superior variety of sugarcane that would literally revolutionize the industry and make billions of dollars for the transnational corporation.

How he had terribly miscalculated. All the sophisticated scientific testing and analyzing couldn't begin to explain what had gone wrong. For all his brilliance, Harold was baffled by the results of his exhaustive research.

"I'm convinced there's definitely some totally unknown chemical imbalance here," was how he explained it to himself. "There's something I'm just not able to see. I don't understand what's gone wrong."

Don Anselmo, and Doña Fela as well, were reading the signs altogether differently, but perhaps more accurately than the young doctor. Both elders agreed that their respective feelings were revealing to them that the change was coming at an even quicker pace than previously imagined.

At the same time, Harold was beginning to devote more serious thought to the future of his personal life. Since arriving to the Island, his priorities were beginning to shift. Even though he kept his position with the corporation, and absolutely nobody in Canada or New York expended one iota of energy about with whom the talented scientist was sharing his Caribbean mosquito net, all truly important matters turned toward the corporation's apparent losses in economic terms. Ever so slowly, questionable notions were beginning to stir concerning Toronto's future investments in the Island. There were also concerns about personal investments of a different kind.

"Realistically," Harold pointed out to Marcelo, "I think it would be much wiser and more practical for us to find a place of our own, away from your lunatic father. It's going to be hard enough as it is trying to sustain our love for each other under the narrow constraints of life out here in the country. The dangerously archaic views of your family could only make our lives a hellish nightmare. *Qué piensas*? What do you think?"

"*No hay duda. Estoy de acuerdo contigo, mi amor.* No doubt about it. I agree with you, my love," Marcelo admitted without reservation. "I also thought about that. *Escúchame.* Let's begin looking for some place else to live. True. I know it would be better for everybody if we were some distance from here. My father is completely nuts right now with all that's happened."

Harold and Marcelo had no difficulty in finding just the kind of safe haven the couple desired; they waited no time in acquiring it. Capps' handsome salary allowed him to lease a conveniently secluded and semi-luxurious bungalow located almost an hour's drive away from *Esperanza Dulce*. The recently vacated, but tastefully furnished, spacious and airy house was a well maintained country villa belonging to a prominent Island banker whose family now lived permanently in the capital and also kept a house abroad. Marcelo could not help taking note that the ample, fully equipped horse stable on the premises, without exaggeration, was in shamefully superior condition compared with the substandard living quarters in the batey where Azúcar lived with her grandmother. The anxious couple set up housekeeping immediately; the new residence became their sanctuary.

If for Marcelo the idea of openly establishing a household with Harold was the start of a new, exciting and most daring adventure, the journey for Marcelo's mother, by contrast, was coming to its tragic end. Doña Cristiana Montalvo was slipping rapidly into darker depression. She frantically desired the arrival of each new morning in order to try forgetting the previous night and freeing herself as quickly as possible from the torturous cycle of remembering her painful losses--- her first born and now the youngest son. She reached her lowest spiritual ebb parallel with the point at which time young Marcelo was beginning his scandalous act of beginning *"una relación doméstica,"* a domestic relationship, as people began whispering aloud in describing the affairs of the young couple.

"That scandalous young Canadian doctor has brought nothing but chaos and calamity here since his arrival," someone from Cristiana Montalvo's social circle had remarked. And again the rumors flew about in all directions as if caught in the tailspin of one of the dreaded seasonal hurricanes.

"Ay, pobrecita Doña Cristiana. Young Marcelo's latest act was a travesty of all decency and has really caused his dear mother great personal shame. Just imagine! Living like a married couple, I hear, " commented one close family-friend of the Montalvos.

"*Claro.* Certainly. The boy's moving into the villa with that foreign scientist was what sent the poor woman over the edge," affirmed another of Cristiana's longtime friends.

"*O Dios mío, José y María, Santa Madre de Jesús.* You know she was simply devastated by what happened to that wicked oldest boy of hers," agreed another.

"Under heavy sedation every day, they tell me." The woman quickly and solemnly made the sign of the Holy cross.

"*Pues, sí.* Cristiana, *pobrecita,* finally suffered a debilitating mental breakdown and Don Diego had her placed in a sanatorium," volunteered another female friend, dabbing here eyes with an embroidered lace handkerchief. "Poor Don Diego. He certainly doesn't deserve this pain. How much more can the dear man endure?" In synchronization, all three of the women nodded in agreement.

The Montalvo household fell into a slow, irreparable deterioration with the prolonged absence of Doña Cristiana, who, in former times, was ritualistic in her attention and fastidiousness to her beautiful home. Her inevitable hospitalization created an unexpected void of another sort in the surprisingly secret world of her daughter-in-law Blanchette. Before marrying Mario Montalvo, the very sheltered Blanchette had never known debauchery or wickedness of any kind; she had never dreamed of violating her God's laws or the Holy Convent of the Church. It was her husband's escalating lasciviousness and moral bankruptcy that in the end managed to betray the young bride's trust altogether. This betrayal armed her, not so much with vengeance as with a blanketing and dangerous indifference.

"*Por mi santa madre,* there's not a decent household in the whole fuckin' province that hasn't heard tell of all the God-awful evil that those Montalvo men have committed over the years," a neighboring plantation capataz had remarked. "I've known the Montalvo clan for many years. Real trashy family background; all 'slavers,' you know."

The man, with intended malice, was clearlyl referring to the Montalvo clan's traditional occupational involvement with the various aspects of plantation slavery and sugar production, which were parallel developments throughout the Caribbean. The observation seemed to take on a certain edge of tragic reality in terms of the Montalvo personality. "Bad stock, that's all."

In the face of Mario's increasingly shameless indiscretions, it wasn't at all strange when Doña Cristiana convinced Blanchette that . . . "while love was the most precious of God's gifts, it was also the most delicate -- often lasting just a few short moments." The older, very astute woman was attempting genuinely to console the disenchanted younger woman. With that seed safely planted, Doña Cristiana next convinced Blanchette to become her active, full partner in the ongoing, very lucrative business venture that brought to the *capataz's* wife carefully-concealed profits on a regular basis. So well hidden were Doña Cristiana's profits over a few years, that not even the normal scrutiny of the shrewd *capataz* had uncovered the existence of his wife's rapidly mounting private savings   . . and certainly not the remotest suggestion of the despicable source of those accumulated funds.

"*Que Dios me proteja.* May God protect me. There's so much money to be made down in that filthy *batey, mi hija,*" the older woman said in guarded confidence to her more-than-curious daughter-in-law, keenly watching and waiting for the younger woman's reaction to everything being said.

"And it's all based upon an individual's need for just a moment's   worth   of love. Man's life is nourished by the continual hope that he will be loved. Don't you agree, *querida*?"

The innocent, young Blanchette, whose privileged, sheltered life prior to marrying into the obscure Montalvo family had been extremely bland and without excitement, never had to think about such puzzling matters. This new terrain was murky and uncharted. After hesitating a few long seconds, the inexperienced explorer ventured a thoughtful answer to her mother-in-law, who was eying unflinchingly the younger woman, still waiting for a sign.

"But, Doña Cristiana, is that really love? I mean, aren't you exploiting the weaknesses of those already miserable souls down there? How do you justify that?" She honestly wanted to know.

"My dear child, those wretched creatures in the *batey*, just like everybody else,   need   the warmth and glow of uncomplicated human love. What we're doing . . . all that we're doing is facilitating that warmth . . . but at a price, of course. *Me comprendes*?"

Blanchette was at first too petrified and confused to be shocked by her mother-in-law's raw directness. But as the recent

161

bride was being increasingly humiliated by her new husband's publicized philandering down in the batey, Blanchette's attitude was beginning to acquire a hardening nonchalance that easily turned to concrete once the twins Cécile and Chelaine were born. So, yes, she understood perfectly what her mother-in-law was saying. But still she offered no sign.

"Believe me, *querida*, you have no earthly idea of the small fortune I've made in this business; and that's precisely what it is, dear, . . . a business," Cristiana emphasized adamantly.

"Especially during the Christmas Season and immediately following *zafra*, both very important to the business," –she again emphasized— "since those are the times the workers receive their bonuses." The *capataz*'s wife used her fingers on both hands to meticulously enclose the word "business" inside quotation marks.

And she was quite correct. During *zafra* particularly, literally hundreds of contract *braceros* were swarming about like gnats in heat with hefty bonuses, eager to reward themselves by spending their money on instant gratification. Anything left over would be remitted back home. Finally, Blanchette's mouth widened into a recognizable and approving smile. This was the sign that her mother-in-law had waited for. The two women were now on an equal footing of comfort.

Thus, the pristine character of the highbred Blanchette was dangerously compromised when she joined in secret partnership with her persuasive mother-in-law to operate the "ownerless" prostitution ring that serviced the *batey*. The two unlikely partners, over time, displayed sharp entrepreneurial skills that rivaled those at central administration offices. The stable of rainbow-hued, multilingual, ethnically diverse *putas*, *bouzen*, or *dame-gabrielle* --- just "whores" in any language --–

was transported from all across the Island. They arrived by truck caravan under the dark cover of midnight and housed in unsuspecting barracks located on the opposite far end of the batey, just beyond the largest of the three *bodegas* scattered throughout the community. On several occasions when she was a younger child, Azúcar had accompanied her grandmother to that particular bodega for provisions.

"*Abuelita, no entiendo*. Why I only see pretty women sittin' out in front of the barracks there? And why I never see them in the cane fields workin' with us?" The young girl was persistent, but still naïve in her curiosity when she asked such questions of her grandmother. The child was referring to the very gaudy manner in which the *putas* usually applied their facial make up and had coifed their hair. And their dresses always seemed so uncomfortably tight!

"They be workin', *m'hita*. They just be assigned different work from us, that's all," was how Doña Fela simply replied with an angry grimace.

Azúcar remained innocently confused until much time later on when she knew better. She also found out that there was absolutely no truth to the rumors about big-bosomed Nadine's willingness to "spend the night with a man for a mere plate of food containing a piece of meat." As it turned out, the child learned, every man in the batey who "visited the pretty women in the tight dresses" had to pay; "*na' eh grati aquí*, nothing is free here" was the rule of the day . . . or night.

Cristiana explained to her novice partner that the women traditionally were required to pay a certain percentage of their "earned wages" from each customer — these were charges for housing and general maintenance --- to the co-partners. No one ever discovered who was actually at the helm of this successful, clandestine operation, nor did any other silent partner ever replace the tragic departure of Doña Cristiana Montalvo when her husband finally committed her to the institution. For how long, no one was certain. Blanchette grew extremely competent in running *el negocio*, "the business," and remained the sole proprietress of this "love-for-sale" enterprise without the slightest remorse or detection. Any amount of earlier, nagging remorse was quickly superseded by steadily rising profits. Blanchette added considerably to her already-secure Origène-Desgraves inheritance. Before long, she was operating a tight network of "*casas*" associated with sugarcane plantations that stretched across the Island.

QUINCE

After twisting and turning in his ancient cot for what seemed like the entire night, a frustrated Don Anselmo conceded that it was impossible to sleep. So, he got up drowsy and fatigued, grabbed his pipe and went to sit in the doorway of his cabin. As he lit the pipe, zooming in from nowhere, a bat on the curve of its swift flight grazed the old man's face with the tip of its grotesque wing.

"*Carajo*! Another bad sign," he thought to himself. "When will this *vaina* be over?"

With his tired old eyes, he gazed out across the nearby forest, heavily shaded in subdued tones from the horizon. The silence was dominant, but he could nevertheless hear the rippling waters of the stream in the dark forest. Sitting there alone in his doorway, puffing slowly on his pipe, Don Anselmo immersed himself one again in thinking about the mysterious uneasiness that had afflicted him lately. It was the very reason he had not been able to sleep throughout the night.

"*Por mi madre, coño*! It's that same dream! It just won't go away," he said in a tone of annoyance to the cool night air. It was the dream that clearly was another sign of impending trouble, according to all he knew about the spirit world. "I feel much trouble nearby."

Once again in the dream, Grann Oyá from the land of the dead, mpemba, was standing in the middle of a stream, combing her long hair while singing. That was usually how the dream began. Again, as each time before, Grann Oyá's entrancing voice lured the listener, who had been standing immobile on shore, into the middle of the stream. The one important difference this time, however, was the identity of the listener— who now followed the enchantress deep down beneath the waters. For the first time, it became clear that the bewitched listener was none other than Don Anselmo himself!

And this time, as the two, Grann Oyá and Don Anselmo, together sank deeper into the blackness beneath the water's surface, they raised their voices jointly in a prolonged and melancholy song:

M' domi, m' reve sou lan m'te ye
Zetoiles leve grand jou
M' domi, m' reve nan pays-m m'te ye
Soleil claire lan nuite.

Ous va di yo: malade la gueri o
Potez nouvelle la: mo yo pa' ler o
L'Afrique a camper: coutez ca l'ap di
Ginen lever: tendez ca par' alle di
L'heu-a rive.

I slept, I dreamed that I was below the sea
Stars rose with the dawning day.
I slept, I dreamed that I was in my homeland
The sun shone in the dark of night to say:
The ill have been cured; take the news back with
You: The words speak; Africa stands: listen to
what she has to say --
Ginen under the sea rises: listen to what she is
about to say --
The time has arrived.

The song ended abruptly in subtle moans or perhaps imperceptible mumbling; Don Anselmo couldn't be certain. But, as he recalled, the lyrics of the song were perfectly intelligible. "The time has arrived for what?" the old man wanted to know with great impatience and puzzlement. Each time in the dream there was never a clear answer since the song ended in the manner that it did. And it was usually at this point that Don Anselmo was awakened from the tortuous dream. Each time he had this dream, his perplexity increased.

The rain came crashing down hard late that evening. Lightning and thunder followed. Three darkened figures were huddled together in one of the sheltered corners of the one-room cabin where the roofing did not leak the intrusive water. Lightning sporadically lit up the darkened room, displaying glimpses of an ancient cot against one wall, a huge machete in its rawhide sheath standing at attention next to the cot, some few items of clothing dangling lazily from sturdy, rusty nails driven into the wall, the suggestion of solemn faces on the three figures. The thunder roared again, this time so furiously that the occupants in the dark room could feel the tremors making their way up from the cabin floor and into the old bones of the trio seated around the empty, wooden *bagasse* barrel that served as their table. There was no fear that the lightning would strike the three figures, and the thunder rumbling through in the background was harmless as well. Had one of the seated figures not gotten up to go to the door of the cabin for a quick breath of fresh night air, none of them would have been aware that it was raining so hard outside, so totally absorbed and consumed were they in their secret purpose for having come together.

"The Marasa can't be honored with the traditional ritual feast," said Doña Fela. "I knew it was a bad sign when the twins came out of my child's womb thirty minutes apart."

"And for them to be born of the seed of *baka*, the evil spirit, only made matters worse," Mamá Lola added glumly. Again, she thought about the old Kreyòl-speaking midwife who had been present at the moment of Azúcar's delivery; it was she who had whispered *"Rivyè debòde. The river overflowed."*

"That evil Montalvo boy was the one what brung all this misfortune on all us. We must think hard about our next step. It won't be easy on nobody. Remember that because of the *baka*, the twins came with weakened powers . . . and they wasn't at the crossroads."

The final member of the trio huddled around the table spoke next.

"*Kalfou danjere!* Dangerous crossroads," Don Anselmo mused aloud, recalling all that he had been taught long ago. The hard rain continued falling. The concentration inside Don Anselmo's cabin was so heavy that all three elders ignored the piercing sound of the thunder and the intermittent flashes of lightning. The solemn trio was focused singularly upon the heavy dilemma confronting them. Don Anselmo was trying to piece together all the elements of his agonizing dream. With aged wisdom and experiences in such matters that both Doña Fela and Mamá Lola possessed, it was possible to make the necessary connection between the dream and the troublesome birth of the twins. The trio indeed understood the sacred importance of water.

"*An ba dlo.* Underneath the water," Mamá Lola offered with tightly closed eyes. "That sacred place where the spirits live." She was thinking about where human souls go for exactly one year and a day after those souls die.

"*Anonse, o zanj nan dlo!* Announcing, Oh angels in the water!"

Don Anselmo's thoughts carried him immediately to his dream and especially that hypnotic song that he and Grann Oyá sang together:

> *M'domi, m'reve sou lan m'te ye . . . M'reve nan pays-*
> *m m'te ye.*

Very carefully, piece by piece, things were falling into place and beginning to make sense to him. It was Doña Fela who deciphered the various loose elements and finally made the seemingly disparate connections lucid.

"The dream is about the other side . . . the passage between life and death. That's the importance of the water; life and death signify water. Death is the new beginnin' . . . representin' a passage into the sacred spirit world."

Don Anselmo nodded to indicate that he at last understood. Mamá Lola continued with the interpretation.

"*Oui. L'heu-a rive.* The time has arrived. The initiated should and will go *an ba dlo* -- underneath the water -- or to the other side. Stars rose with the dawnin' day . . . and the sun shone in the dark of night," Don Anselmo said, reciting the mystical lyrics of the song that had been sung in the dream. "*An ba dlo.* Underneath the water."

Suddenly, there was a noticeable stillness inside the cabin. Outside it seemed to be raining even harder than before; the hammering of the rain on the corrugated zinc roof was almost deafening. All three darkened figures in the room stared at one another, then up at the ceiling, where they heard actually for the first time the heavy, steady pounding of the night rain. The resultant effect was measured rhythm.

"*Ou a di-m sa pou m fè.* Tell me how I must do it," Doña Fela wanted to know. She looked first at Mamá Lola and then at Don Anselmo . . . she waited for her instructions.

"*Mi hermana.* My sister, we know the task set before you is a very difficult and painful one," Mamá Lola replied in an honest attempt to console her friend. "You must consider it in the deeper sense . . . We know also that it will torment your heart for a long time. But you must remember one thing, mi hermana: the deepest form of knowing is through doing. Know that Ezili Dantó will guide you."

Don Anselmo now had all the pieces he needed. Finally, everything was in place. He was clear about the recurrent dream sequence and his role in it. He also knew what he had to do in the scheme of things. The storm had passed. It had stopped raining and the air was fresh as the trio joined hands and recited in hushed unison:

"*O zanj nan dlo, m'a sembler moune nous lòt bo*. Oh angels in the water, I will assemble our people on the other side."

It was well after midnight when they embraced one another and said "*adieu*" before departing, the two old women leaving their old friend Don Anselmo standing alone in the doorway of his dark cabin.

Just a few days following that stormy night when the three elders of the *batey* held their clandestine meeting in Don Anselmo's cabin, the community would again be shaken by a quick succession of horrific events. Almost nobody expected what happened . . . nobody, that is, except the three individuals who had huddled together a few rainy nights ago. Upon hearing the grim news, everyone was aghast; those closest to Azúcar were paralyzed with shock.

Each player in the predestined drama knew exactly the role to be executed. There were no second thoughts about what had to be done; all the signs had been declared and confirmed. All the interpretations had been clearly studied. There was no remorse on anyone's part. It was decided that the act would unfold as ordained. On the designated mid-afternoon, with Doña Fela away from the cabin and Azúcar left alone with the twins Felicidad and Caridad, Don Anselmo arrived with a jar of his homemade guanábana juice which he had prepared especially for Azúcar.

"*Buen día, m'hijita. Cómo estás?* Just thought I'd pass by here to pay my respects to you and the twins. I also brung you your favorite fruit juice . . . *jugo de guanábana*."

"*Muy buen día a usted*, Don Anselmo. It's always so good seein' you," Azúcar expressed with maximum delight.

170

"*Perdóneme,* but since the birth of the twins, I haven't had time for much else. Haven't had no time to see much of nobody lately. *Ay, mi madre.* Your special guanábana juice! You know I love it more than anything. You make the very best! *Muchas Gracias,* Don Anselmo."

Little Felicidad and her twin sister Caridad were fast asleep in the bassinet, the much talked-about gift from Harold and Marcelo. Don Anselmo feigned genuine excitement about wanting merely to steal a peep at the slumbering infants.

"*Qué bonitas son!*" How beautiful they are, "he said to their mother, as he touched each one of the tiny twins lovingly on her tiny cheek. Azúcar finished her guanábana juice and was not prepared for the heavy drowsiness that overtook her a few minutes later. Her head drooped onto her chest; then her body wavered on her legs. In anticipation, Don Anselmo had positioned himself alongside Azúcar to catch her once she finally buckled. In preparing the fruit juice that Azúcar loved so much, the old man, according to the plan, had stirred into the mixture a special powdered form of a local, but hard-to-find herb so potent that it could sedate an ox for a few hours before the animal ever thought about awakening.

Once in the thick, colorless heart of the forest, where even the cruel sun's blistering mid-day rays could not manage to penetrate, three dark figures once again found themselves together, this time standing on the embankment of the pond. Two small burlap sacks were at their feet. Faint, muffled cries came from the sacks, as well as pulsating jerks and what seemed like attempted kicks and punches. In the daytime darkness of the forest, Doña Fela ---who had already been waiting for her two companions to arrive with the sacks--- lowered her eyes in solemnity. She seemed to be praying. Her lips and her nostrils quivered; her bosom was heaving beneath her dress. She was anxious to begin and conclude this most secret of secret ceremonies as quickly as possible. Her two accomplices were breathing heavily in the coolness of the forest's dark center. In front of the trio, a not-so-deep pit containing a small oblong box --but wide enough for two small burlap sacks-- was also waiting . . . to be filled.

"*L' heu-a rive. O zanj nan dlo.* The time has arrived.
Oh angels in the water."

Doña Fela ceremoniously initiated the ancient chant; she half-whispered, half-sang ... as though in a lullaby. Both Mamá Lola and Don Anselmo quickly joined in repeating it. "*L'heu-a rive. O zanje nan dlo.*"

It was also Azúcar's beloved grandmother who had placed the two sacks, from which something inside both seemed to be struggling to escape, in the oblong box resting at the bottom of the open pit near the embankment. Small mounds of fresh dirt waited to be shoveled hurriedly into the pit. This final task remained for Don Anselmo.

"*Kalfou danjere. O Marasa Bwa , potez nouvelle la,*" whispered Doña Fela a final time, ending the sacred ritual only when the last shovel-full of dirt had been thrown into the pit to cover it up completely. The three dark figures had concluded their secret drama in the forest and departed without delay . . . without a word said to anyone.

Very few people in the batey these days could remember ever hearing about the ancient ritual of the Marasa Bwa, "Twins of the Forest." Perhaps fewer still could vaguely remember the last time such a ritual had been performed; it was believed that it had been abandoned a long time ago. But most people, however, were aware of the tradition that twins, even when young, were at the same time powerful and dangerous. Everyone was of the opinion that Azúcar's twin girls, Felicidad and Caridad, symbolized an exceptionally bad omen because they had been produced by the *baka,* the evil seed of the capataz's eldest son Mario. Most people also felt certain that that particular circumstance was the reason why the mother's afterbirth was never placed in a hole and the banana tree planted over it, according to respected tradition. Everyone also understood fully that with Mario's violent death and that of the twins, the unforgivable violation of the young virgin, who of course later became the mother of the twins, was finally avenged. Her spirit would become purified and, as a result, would be able to pass safely "to the other side," *nan dlo*, without fear when the time came.

But as much as her grandmother tried explaining everything to Azúcar, the now childless-mother understood nothing.

"*Por qué*? she screamed. *Abuelita, por qué? Díme cómo lo pudiste hacer una cosa tan bárbara*? Why, *abuelita*? Tell me how you could actually do such a terrible thing?" Azúcar was delirious with mixed rage and confusion. Explanations from everybody -- close friends and neighbors alike — from Mamá Lola, one-eyed Clementina, longneck Teresa, the widow Lolita, and especially from the wise old Don Anselmo, who had given the girl that fateful guanábana juice --- were of no avail. But still Doña Fela harbored no regrets.

"*M' hijita dulce*. I did what I had to do to save you," insisted the old woman. "It was all accordin' to the loas that we traditionally obey. To disobey would be a frightful mistake. Raisin' those twins would have meant your doom . . . and theirs, too. Someday you will understand all this. *Mi azúcar morenita*, know that I truly love you so dearly. My duty was to have the powerful spirits of our ancestors protect you."

Azúcar tried hard to make sense of all that had happened. Confusion, torment, and fear gripped her. While the brutal rape she had suffered still psychologically wounded her irreparably, she was also agonizing over the gift of motherhood that had been suddenly snatched from her . . . all without explanation. Just before giving birth to the twins, Azúcar had begun a conscious wondering about the path toward which she was headed. She was beginning the perilous journey toward selfhood and early womanhood. A very observant and instinctively intelligent youngster, she sensed quite early her own powerlessness and that of her grandmother and of all the others in the batey, against the uncaring, cruel plantation system at *Esperanza Dulce*. Without any question, they were all helpless prisoners in the same giant cell. She experienced the realities of the injustices and abuses in the system that exploited her and the others connected with sugarcane. Her major complaints, even as a young girl, were not so much the hardships of work or even the deprivation of practically every conceivable material comfort, but more so the naked assault and violation of all sense of common personhood. Everything about the batey troubled her enormously. Azúcar began to realize her deeply agonizing hatred for the batey . . . . and ultimately for sugar itself!

When both Harold and Marcelo, two genuinely concerned "outsiders," finally heard about the barbarous act that had taken place deep within the forest, they were furious and completely mystified . . . and equally enraged by the senseless explanations accompanying the facts.

"*Por Dios*! What kind of goddamn superstition and lunatic behavior are they practicing down there?" Harold asked in anxious disbelief and horror. "This is the twentieth century, for God's sake! This is all insane!"

"*Cálmate, mi querido.* Calm down, love. Believe me when I tell you . . . you will never arrive at a true understanding of the strange ways and thinking of the batey," Marcelo replied in genuine efforts to not allow the affairs of the batey to consume the well-meaning, scientific-minded Canadian. "There's much I myself don't even understand ." Marcelo was truthful about his not understanding much that goes on in the *batey*.

"*Es un mundo aparte.* It's a different world altogether.

But right now our single worry now must be Azúcar. What will become of her? What will be her future in that world?"

After calming himself, Harold was in perfect accord with his mate. Both he and Marcelo, as unapologetic humanitarians, had frequently wondered aloud about the fate of this extremely bright, sensitive, inquisitive, and innocent young girl who was developing into young womanhood. What does she dream about? What does she wish for herself? What thoughts and feelings race through her? Upon reflection, both Harold and Marcelo expressed fear that the monstrous death of Azucar's twins was indicative of the degree of retrograde thinking that provided the very solid and uncompromising foundation for the amalgam of beliefs and practices at *Esperanza Dulce*. And the idea that the authorities would do absolutely nothing regarding the perpetrators of the heinous act of infanticide was equally reprehensible. The official account, without a shred of concrete evidence, was that "death was due to accidental drowning." Besides, who on the "outside" would dare acknowledge the Marasa Bwa ritual anyway?

The next phases of the saga moved exceedingly fast. Harold and Marcelo felt totally justified in approaching Doña Fela about the idea of allowing Azúcar to come work at their villa as general housekeeper ---or such was the pretext under which to get the young woman away from her misguided, though well intentioned *abuelita* and the corrosive influences of superstition and ignorance so rampant in the *batey*. The grandmother, along with the other elders, saw convincing merit in affording Azúcar the chance, as housekeeper, to earn twice the wages she would in the sugarcane fields. Even the characteristically circumspect Don Anselmo had no objections, and in fact thought Azúcar would gain a great deal from being away from the decay of the *maldito batey*.

175

Even well after Azúcar was settled at the villa, and in the judgment of her new benefactors, she had become satisfactorily acclimated to the strange new surroundings and routines, there was still a great deal of ambivalence about being away from her *abuelita* and the *batey*. There was also a certain amount of gnawing anger and confusion about what had happened to her twin babies; she was visibly unnerved, and so her hosts felt it was now time to execute their carefully tailored agenda. The new arrival from the *batey* was not assigned general housekeeping tasks as she herself had initially thought was the reason for her being at the villa; an experienced local woman would handle these mundane chores.

Rather, the plan called for preceding immediately with intensive, almost around-the-clock academic remediation and tutoring, beginning with basic literacy and simple arithmetic computing. This became Marcelo's exclusive domain. Before long, two additional professional teachers became a permanent part of the villa's tutorial team. After she learned to read with ease and progressed not at all surprisingly to impressive levels of proficiency, Azúcar was taught penmanship and public oratory, literature of the Island, local geography and history, biology, and art. Later would follow chemistry, geometry, economics, philosophy, and world history. Her grasp of all this new material was astonishing

After several months of living at the villa, Azúcar may well have been on the other side of the globe— so far removed was she from her former circumstances. The separation was a complex psychological and physical distancing, from both her *abuelita* and the *batey*, along with all that this place symbolized in the life and soul of Azúcar. The separation was also difficult and painful for her. After all, she had been born at *Esperanza Dulce* and had never once set foot outside its limits before now. The young woman knew nothing of the world beyond the restrictive and repressive plantation. This had been her only space all these years since her birth. It was the existence and development of an unrestrained imagination that served as catalyst for Azúcar's aggressive inquisitiveness. Nevertheless, she had often consciously wondered, even dreamed what awaited her some day on the other side of *Esperanza Dulce*. So, in large measure, there remained little doubt that the adjustment to her new world was facilitated by her own insatiable hunger to know, to learn, to inquire further about new things--- *"para saber lo que hay al otro lado del monte,"* --- to know what is on the other side of the mountain. The climb would be arduous.

DIECISÉIS

A rapid two and a half years had fled by since the tender Azúcar, then thirteen and a half years old, lost her motherhood status in a strange traditional ritual deep inside the forest. The virtual whirlwind of events and circumstances engulfed everyone standing in its path or within close proximity, so powerful was its suction force. Azúcar's personal and academic progress had been phenomenal in every sense, quickly out-pacing the most ambitious expectations of her two sincerest champions and mentors, Harold and Marcelo. They had monitored feverishly every phase of her advancement, making certain that no area had been overlooked or short-changed. As characteristically unselfish as they both were, they particularly made certain that their special pupil and new personal responsibility had not severed contact altogether with her grandmother. Doña Fela, after all, was still a very real factor to be dealt with in the girl's much altered life since leaving the *batey* and becoming part of Harold's and Marcelo's supportive, although rather unique household. In all probability, Azúcar did not necessarily care to think about it — or actually did not have to. It was nevertheless an issue to be confronted . . . and that confrontation would indeed come.

Marcelo, for instance, could not convince himself fully that he had attached so much significance to the granddaughter-grandmother relationship and even attempted to persuade himself, as well as Harold, that the former had intended that relationship as a kind of compassionate indulgence toward Azúcar. Yet, Marcelo's very soul rebelled against the thought of failing to arrange that Azúcar return to the batey in order to visit her grandmother. That first visit had been disastrous for Azúcar, who genuinely did not wish to go under any circumstances.

Was it perhaps still too soon after the unbelievably horrible Marasa Bwa ritual? The replicas of unconscious memories, from which Azúcar still suffered, raveled her in the worst manner.

"Marcelo, *por mi madre*, do I honestly have to go?" she pleaded, wiping away heavy tears.

"Azúcar, *escúchame bien*. Listen to me; I know it has not been easy for you, love. But she's still your grandmother despite everything that has happened; you told us once that she even taught you how to find a little piece of happiness there. Remember?" Marcelo said respectfully, agonizing secretly about the thought of having to return to the batey, however briefly. But he was quite unyielding in believing that the decision to have Azúcar visit her *abuelita* after being absent for a few months was a responsible one . . . and the correct one.

Only after listening patiently to the persuasive arguments from her two trusted mentors did Azucar agree to go. They finally convinced her that such a visit would be a genuinely honorable thing to do. But the girl was unable to conceal her reluctance and deep apprehensions about the pending visit. She did not dare share with her two benefactors, for instance, having sighted on the night prior to the anticipated visit the bird of ill omen, the legendary and mysterious *chotacabras*, the tropical nighthawk that stalked the Caribbean and inspired fear even in adults.

It had been early evening, well before nightfall, with its refreshingly cool breezes ruffling the leaves of sweet jasmine and flamboyán trees. The air was saturated with delicious sensualness when Azúcar suddenly heard the distinctly uncanny trilling of the dreaded *chotacabras*, a sound that was as monotonous and as eerie as was the bird itself hideous. She recalled instantly the terrifying stories her *abuelita* had told her about how this flying nocturnal scavenger had the detestable trait of *cantar a los muertos*, "singing to the dead."

"*Ten cuidado, m'hijita*. Be careful, child," Doña Fela would warn her attentive granddaughter after relating another of the old woman's foreboding tales.

"The *chotocabras* is worse than the daytime vulture that just sit aroun' and wait for its prey to die. His evil singin' before eatin' an already dead meal is a bad sign that tell your heart that some misfortune gonna come."

And the old woman would grimace, clicking her tongue. Azúcar never forgot these frightful tales. And now she had seen with her own eyes this unsightly bird, its crooked beak ajar, emitting its harsh cries as if announcing the arrival of death. Were Doña Fela's tales another element of batey folklore, superstition and ignorance that compensated for Azúcar's lack of scientific reasoning? She did not wish to risk compromising the trust of her mentors in her advancing formal education; therefore, she said nothing to them about the omen of the *chotocabras*.

The return visit succeeded in conjuring up certain trepidation. Azúcar had not stepped foot back inside the sordid world of the batey since she left some months ago with Marcelo and Harold. The journey was a psychologically difficult one, filled with a variety of conflicting emotions and thoughts. The rapidly maturing young woman tried to gauge the depth of her sincere love for her grandmother. Azúcar's efforts were futile mainly because she was thrown and obstructed by one confusing revelation after another, surprised by what she was slowly uncovering inside her. But she was also frightened by her own secret thoughts as if some malicious, unknown person seeking to do her harm was exposing such thoughts in their nakedness. A multiplicity of feelings surfaced regarding seeing her abuelita after such lengthy absence. It was still a fact that grandmother and granddaughter had never been separated from each other for more than a couple of hours --- and only then about four or five times that Azúcar could remember. Her spirit fumbled about clumsily as though she were lost deep inside the dark forest where the sun is not allowed.

"*Ay, por mi madre que nunca conocí,* how must I react?" she soliloquized. "Ain't my anger justified from the unspeakable horror against my innocent babies? Will I ever allow myself to forgive *mi abuelita?* Should I? For my mother who I never knew, may all the protective spirits help me understand why!"

Not only was attempted reunion between grandmother and granddaughter unfulfilling for the two, but it was also much too brief, awkward, and almost hostile. The visit in the end accomplished nothing very positive in terms of mutual reconciliation and an open expression of understanding.

"*Ay, m'hijita dulce, mi azucar morenita.* How I have missed you," the old woman began.

"*Cómo te ehtán tratando?* How they treatin' you, child?"

Doña Fela moved instinctively to hug her long-absent granddaughter, but Azúcar's initial response was marked by a frozen stillness that did not reciprocate the well-meaning and sincere embrace. The young girl's mouth dropped open, but no words poured out; just the stillness. It was as if Doña Fela were embracing death itself; she could not hold back the flow of sorrowful tears. Azúcar's grandmother felt dispirited and hurt, almost doubtful about any degree of remaining love her granddaughter might still have for her.

"*Ehtá bien, mi dulce. Yo entiendo.* It's all right. I understand. You still holdin' against me what the ancient spirits directed us to do. *Yo entiendo,*" the wise old woman continued.

"You will one day understand that what we did was only to protect you forever from certain misfortunes that would be placed in your path because of the Marasa. I know you don't understand nothin' of this right now. In time, you will, *mi Azúcar dulce.* You will."

"*Abuelita, créeme!* Believe me, I have honestly tried to

181

understand all that happened, but I am still very tormented that I don't understand any of it," Azúcar finally relented and began answering. "I know that deep inside me, in my heart, I do love you; but I just can't forgive you for what you did. What kind of protective spirits would let something like that happen?"

She was now almost shouting angrily at her grandmother. This released anger surprised Azúcar much more so than it did Doña Fela. It was also now the wounded granddaughter's turn to cry complex tears. However, hers were easily tainted with a noticeable mixture of anger, disbelief, frustration, and love.

"You have caused me much grief and anger," she snapped as she brusquely forced herself out of her grandmother's tight, but loving embrace.

Rather than the expected reaffirmation of love, warmth, and understanding, what resulted instead was a further emotional distancing between the two . . . who really did love each other. Grandmother and granddaughtyer both remained silent for what seemed like an hour, but was really only a few minutes. There was an unsurprising unspoken remorse on the part of both tormented individuals. Azúcar felt a frightening desire to cry out, but could not. Doña Fela sensed her granddaughter's anguish, but resisted any hope of consolation. The confrontation was quickening in its intensity.

By this time, everybody living in relatively close proximity to Doña Fela's cabin--- and that included the households of close friends and neighbors like one-eyed Clementina and her always jovial husband Tomás, the widow Lolita, longneck Teresa and her husband Cirilo, Teresa's talkative brother Ramón, and of course, Don Anselmo, and the seemingly countless children in these households. Out of sheer curiosity and an undisguised, honest desire to see their beloved Azúcar they came. It was at first difficult to recognize the sweet, naïve, young Azúcar who had left the batey months ago with two *mariquitas*, "faggots."

Returning now was a mature, visibly self-confident young woman devoid of any trace of a former girlish shyness. This returning, new Azúcar was even wearing shoes! Also, she was outfitted in one of those fashionable academy uniforms customarily worn by the school-aged "*riquitos*," children of the upper classes.

"*Hola! Azúcar.* Welcome back!"

"*Sa ou fè ?* Hi! How you doin'?"

"Bienvenida, Azúcar querida. Welcome, dear Azúcar."

"*Adieu, oui.* You come back home."

"Azúcar, how you been, *chica*?"

"*Qué preciosa! Qué guapa!* How precious you look! How beautiful!"

"How beautiful and grown up she has become!"

"*Kan ou ale voue avèg femen je w*! When you go to the land of the blind, you must close your eyes, or as you would say: When you in Rome, do like the Romans do!" Teresa's talkative brother Ramón jokingly reminded their returning star.

The greetings were all very enthusiastic and not in the least bit false. Everyone was eager not just to see their Azúcar *preciosa y dulce*, but also to inquire about her new life beyond the front gates of the *batey* and away from the familiar pulse and pace of daily activity at *Esperanza Dulce*. There erupted an explosion of questions of all sorts. "Did she miss the ever-renewed frenzy of zafra? What kind of food was she eating now? Is there much work to do in the 'sugar doctor's' house? Does she sleep on a cot or a straw pallet on the floor? . . . And what about those shoes she's wearing?"

To everyone she appeared instantly different; she talked differently; she walked differently; thanks to the fragrance of the talcum she had earlier dusted all over her body after showering in preparation for the visit, she certainly smelled differently; nobody here smelled like that! Not even the pretty ladies in the

183

really tight dresses who never seemed to work like us. The overall transformation, at this point of her first return trip, was in stark contrast to the Azúcar they had known prior. And instead of evoking any possible jealously, however minimally, what was displayed by all those individuals who dearly loved and cared about Azúcar was a very unique sense of pride, *"orgullo,"* that "one of their own" had managed to escape the *batey*! In this hellish place, as time passes unnoticed, so grows the dire wretchedness of the occupants there. Unknowingly, they sink deeper and deeper into cowardice and become resigned to their circumstance. Mere daily survival easily becomes their refuge, their consolation, consuming them entirely, body and soul. So then, in having experienced life in the batey, with its systemic misery and inherent exploitation, Azúcar, along with all the residents of this captive circumstance, had learned early the brutal realities of that peculiar institution and its environment. She recalled how the now-deceased Estimé, Lolita's beautiful Haitian, frequently used to say:

"Once you do leave, you can honestly say: *Kaka pa pikan, men kan ou pile-l fo' k ou bwete!* Shit never stings, but you nevertheless tiptoe when you do walk through it."

Estimé's observation now made much more sense to the transformed Azucar. Something else happened during Azúcar's first return visit to her old world of the *batey* . . . claiming a second disaster for her. Ever since that unforgettable and terrifying afternoon long ago in the cabin with the savagely violent son of the dreaded *capataz*, Mario, Azúcar had unknowingly developed an instinctive fear of men. At the same time, though, she had an agonizing curiosity about them. In no small way, not having known a father also contributed to these conflicting feelings regarding these strange beings –men.

Then, of course, the more recent circumstance of living as part of Marcelo's and Harold's genteel and exquisitely serene setting at the villa added yet another significant element to Azúcar's confusing perceptions.

One-eyed Clementina and her seemingly always-jubilant husband Tomás had a brood of six amicable children, four boys and two girls. It was as though the children had each been born exactly one year apart, in six consecutive years. When placed one alongside the other, the children presented a perfect stepladder formation; the oldest, Tomás, Jr., stood on the top rung. These had been the neighborhood youngsters with whom Azúcar had played and squabbled before they were old enough to work together in the sugarcane fields. These were among the children who had formed the regular audience whenever Doña Fela told her famous *"Cric? Crak!"* tales and riddles. Tomás, Jr. was the same age as Azúcar. As younger children they were inseparable companions, whether as playmates or cane workers. They had laughed together and shared countless secrets between each other. Now they were, of course, older. When Tomás, Jr. saw his childhood pal return as a mature young woman, and with noticeable breasts, he quivered in disbelief . . . and she was wearing shoes!

"Pero cómo eh posible? How is it possible? Is this is the same shy little brown sugar lump -- *la azúcar morenita* -- I used to call a lizard and throw stones at?" the young man asked himself. How beautiful she has become. *Qué guapita."* He felt a shudder of nervous excitement inside his moist loins. Rather than approach Azúcar, he stood awkwardly at a safe distance from her. There was no doubt that Azúcar had claimed the day; she radiated a wholesomeness and grace that was alien to *Esperanza Dulce* . . . and everything even remotely associated with sugar! For Tomás, Jr. the newly transformed azúcar morenita was the brilliant tropical sun, the refreshingly cool sea breezes, and the deliciously scented flamboyán and guanábana trees. The young man stood mesmerized by the sight and smell

of her. The amazingly new Azúcar remained unperturbed and dispassioned ---or so she seemed outwardly. But internally there were privately annoying pangs to talk with Tomás, Jr.

"But why am I feeling this way?" she asked herself in pretended anger. "Am I supposed to have these feelings?"

Tomás, Jr. had grown to be quite a handsome young man: smooth, dark chocolate skin; tight curly black hair; solidly sculptured body with bulging muscles seemingly on every portion of his solid, lean body ---a result no doubt of the hard physical labor since a very early age; limpid eyes that missed nothing. And he had his father's ready joviality. He was shameful opposite in attire to Azúcar: ragged khaki pants held up just across his firmly round butt-cheeks by a thin piece of sisal. He was wearing no underwear, but Azúcar thought she detected perhaps a big stick of some kind in the pocket of his pants, which, strangely, as she further thought, he made efforts to conceal. He was completely shirtless and shoeless, and emitted a quite strong, oddly sensuous and pungent sweat and had crusty feet. It didn't matter; Azúcar's heart was nevertheless racing fast and she wouldn't dare speculate why. She was actually afraid to do so.

"*Por mi madre*. Why doesn't he come over here to me and at least ask how I'm doing in my new job?" she asked herself impatiently.

"*Coño*. Why can't I just go over to her and start up a conversation?" Tomás, Jr. tortured himself secretly.

Instead, much like Azúcar, he stood motionless at first, simply gazing at each other in mutual silence, separated unnecessarily by just a few silly yards. His stomach was churning. He began to fidget, shifting one crusty foot on top of the other. Both friends managed to exchange nervous smiles. Finally, but only after summoning the courage from some unknown source inside himself, Tomás, Jr., crusty feet and all, approached his friend and stood directly in front of her.

"*Hóla! Azúcar. Cómo ehtás?* You been all right? You like where you live? How you like your new job? How they treat you out there?" he blurted out all at once. He waited anxiously for her reply to his steady stream of questions. There was no embrace, no handshake, and no physical contact of any kind --- only the uneasy, childlike gawking.

"*Hóla!* Tomás, Jr., *Estoy bien, gracias.*" she answered just as quickly. "Everything is going well, thank you. It's really different being away from the *batey.*"

She suddenly hoped that the noticeable correctness of grammar she now was accustomed to using in her new circumstance did not intimidate her childhood pal.

Before there had been the chance possibly to expand the dialogue between then, it was time to leave and begin the trip back to the villa; it was nearing dusk and the roads could be hazardous once nighttime fell. It was Harold rather than Marcelo who had driven the jeep to the plantation that day, since Marcelo had chosen to continue avoiding any encounter with his still irate family, most especially the *capataz.* His mother was still hospitalized and so there was really no need to go to *Esperanza Dulce.* Moreover, Harold used the occasion to turn the visit into a necessary research-related trip. Azúcar said her appropriate "*Adios*" to everybody. She didn't get to see Don Anselmo or Mamá Lola on this first trip, but wasn't particularly annoyed about not being able to do so. Her urgent concern, however, was the disastrous encounter with Tomás, Jr. and the strange sensations she felt in his presence.

DIECISIÉTE

The curfew had long ago been lifted and as a result the laborers enjoyed greater freedom of movement and social interaction between the neighboring plantations. Also, the *Reino de Ga Ga* Festival customarily following *zafra* enjoyed an exhilarating rebirth. Don Diego was particularly distressed, though, that these newly reenacted measures, in his opinion "spelled impending disorder and ruinous abuses by the irresponsible workers." For instance, he had always favored keeping the front entry gates of the batey closed and bolted after a certain hour every night, remaining locked until early the following morning. In that way, according to the capataz, there would be more restrictive controls in place. But after repeated attempts to persuade the local administrators, he was unsuccessful in winning approval for his personally vindictive controls.

Such were the circumstances that accounted for the three workers from *Esperanza Dulce* being outside the *batey* early one Sunday morning, well before dawn broke, as everyone else was still asleep. The horizon had begun to be dabbed slightly with crimson for its joyful, daily resuscitation . . . that is, of course, before turning sinister with its later, usual unbearableness. The eagerly waiting sun was preparing to make its dazzling appearance high in the sky. In a wink of the eye, a swirl of flame would rip through the dawn, bathing everything below in bright, warm tropical morning light.

"*Qué amanecer más bello, no?*" Ain't it a beautiful mornin'? How beautiful!" Ramón exclaimed to his traveling companions. The beauty of the morning escaped none of the three revelers on their way back to the batey.

"O Saints of Ginen! *Mais oui, c'est délicieux.* It sure it," Césaire agreed. Through hazy eyes and despite the heavy drinking all night, he was nevertheless able to appreciate Nature's gift. The third traveler was lagging some distance behind his fellow partygoers. Jérôme was Césaire's younger brother, still a youngster at fourteen, but performing admirably an adult's job in the cane fields. It had not been quite a year since he joined his older brother; he had arrived at *Esperanza Dulce* as part of a truckload of recruited *braceros* for the most recent *zafra*. Jérôme, who had not as yet accustomed himself to all-night revelries, was practically asleep as he struggled to keep up the pace with his companions. He slackened so gradually that before the others realized it, he was out of sight altogether.

"*Coño*. I remember a shortcut through the forest. Let's take it and we'll soon be at the front gates," suggested Ramón.

Césaire grunted his sluggish consent and without resistance followed his Panamanian comrade off the main road and into the dark forest. Neither of the two noticed that little Jérôme had lagged so far behind them that the newcomer was now no longer a part of the trio. A small, unidentified and frightened forest animal ran out from its concealment, darting across the path of the sleepy intruders. Ramón and Césaire were also quite unaware that, aside from little Jérôme, they were not the only human beings in the forest that beautiful morning. Had they been more alert— as they normally were when cutting sugarcane, they would undoubtedly have sensed that two other unseen individuals were present . . . were actually stalking them like stealth predators. The two armed hunters had been tracking their helpless prey for quite some distance without being noticed in the least.

Neither Ramón nor Césaire stopped to turn around when they must surely have heard the loud, sharp snapping of broken tree limbs or twigs. Even if they had, it would have been too late to dodge the on-coming bullets, one each intended for the two premeditated targets. First the Panamanian, then the Kreyòl-speaking Haitian: they were each shot in the back at close range by the two carefully-aimed bullets. Almost simultaneously they both staggered before falling. They were unaware of what had hit them and never regained consciousness. Now, the two satisfied predators stood over their fallen prey, still-smoking rifles pointed at the two limp bodies on the dark forest floor.

"*Malditos negros asquerosos!* Damn filthy-assed niggers," one of the hunters directed at the limp carcass on the ground. "Thought you stinkin' shitheads could get away with murder, did you?" At this, what seemed like an entire round of ammunition was then emptied into one of the already dead men lying there.

"*Hijos de puta sucia!* Did you dumb *cocolos* really think we wouldn't track down your black asses even if it took years to find you?" the other killer-stalker shouted, also at the ground where the bodies lay. Then it was this tracker's turn to empty his rifle . . . riveting the second fallen corpse with any remaining bullets. The ground became littered with spent shells.

"*Carajo.* That's for Mario, you filthy bastard," he said as he continued firing until there were no more bullets left in the rifle chamber.

Miguel and Manolo Montalvo had been relentless in their vengeful pursuit to find the culprits responsible for their older brother Mario's assassination and savage mutilation a few years ago. They had thoroughly convinced themselves that, through their own investigation efforts, helpful tips from supposedly reliable *chivos*, or "paid informants," and lucrative monetary incentives, the trail would end at the doorstep of Mario's killers. To the satisfaction of the obsessed Montalvo brothers, the trail led to the speedy conviction of the two cane workers Ramón and Césaire . . . even though the Panamanian and his Haitian companion were completely innocent and had been falsely accused of the crime.

Césaire's little brother Jérôme, at a considerable and ironically safe distance far behind and therefore completely out of sight of the tracking predators, was immediately revived from his walking-slumber by the booming rifle blasts, sounding as they did more like canon fire in the bowels of the otherwise silent forest. The Montalvo brothers never learned that there had been a third person – a living witness— tagging along with the targeted duo. A petrified Jérôme, now fully-awakened, sat on the blood-soaked ground next to the two bullet-riddled corpses, crying until he was empty of tears. He sat there for an entire day before he miraculously found his way out of the maze-like thick forest. It was Jérôme who reported the shooting deaths of his brother Césaire and Césaire's friend Ramón, but it didn't make any difference. The authorities did absolutely nothing . . . as always before. No one thought they would.

"*No creo en la justicia; no creo en nada . . .Ni en mi sombra.* I don't believe in justice; I don't believe in nothin' . . . not even in my own shadow," Ramón's bereaved sister, long-necked Teresa screamed after the plantation authorities displayed no signs of trying, or even desiring to solve the heinously vengeful murders of the two defenseless *braceros*. Someone reported that in recent days the *capataz* seemed to have an uplifted spirit of late. The entire work crew noticed that Don Diego did indeed appear to be going about his routines with more of an obvious hint of a broad smile of satisfaction on his face almost daily since the reported killings. No one in the batey expressed surprise at the outcome.

"*Kon sa bagay la yé.* That's the way it is here in the *batey*," Don Anselmo said to a still-grieving young Jérôme in attempts to explain to the boy the senseless reality that existed in the circumstance of the batey.

"*Bastardos podridos.* Rotten bastards!" the normally jovial Tomás said angrily in describing the plantation authorities and their traditional pattern of injustice.

"*Coñazo.* They don't respect us here; nobody does; never

191

did," Don Anselmo continued calmly, addressing Césaire's surviving younger brother. "The only goddamn thin' these greedy pigs respect is the profits from sugar. *Maldito azúcar!* Goddamn sugar! To them we ain't even human beings . . . look how they just kill us off daily . . . in one way or another, and then replace our black asses just as quick. So, the cycle is endless. It starts up again, just like that."

He snapped his strong fingers together loudly to emphasize the point. Young Jérôme, despite his youthfulness, was completely absorbed in what the older, wiser adults were saying. Whether the message was clear would remain to be tested. He was consumed by grief for his brother.

Although it wasn't immediately realized by everybody, the disclosure of the recent murders of Ramón and Césaire— a hideous act said to be revenge killings for the assassination a few years earlier of the capataz's eldest son— had surprising repercussions. What became resolutely clear to both Harold and Marcelo, for instance, was that they definitely no longer wanted to be part of this repressive, intellectually insipid and inferior, unjust, and truly violent island environment.

"Es la gota que desborda el vaso. It's the last straw that broke the camel's back!" Harold was livid with rage about the killings. "Those wretched souls don't have a chance; they lose at every conceivable turn. Everything is stacked against them: the administration, the managers, the laws, the batey . . . every goddamn thing. Where is the fuckin' justice in that?" His sense of personal integrity and human decency had been assaulted. He was indignant.

"Estoy contigo, mi amor. No hay justicia. I'm with you, my love," Marcelo agreed. "There's no justice here for anybody. *De ninguna manera.* Not in any form. The really sad part is that everybody becomes a hapless victim— everybody is imprisoned in one sense or another . . . and without even realizing it. This is

the story of this miserable Island. This is what this fuckin' sugar does!"

"Please go on," Harold insisted, desirous of having Marcelo be more lucid.

"*Mira.* Look. The Island's entire goddamn economy evolves around sugar exports, *verdad*?" Marcelo reflected. "*Bueno.* Well, sugar cultivation in these modern times is determined by that pseudo-governmental agency known as something ridiculously called the State Sugar Council. Imagine! This is simply the modern version of the historical Slave Trader, directly responsible for bringing in contract laborers, *la mano de obra*, actually cheap labor— from Haiti and from other economically depressed areas around the Caribbean. Marcelo was now pacing the floor in the living room of their villa. He continued his pronouncements in his careful, very deliberate manner.

"These workers, as you've come to witness, are treated worse than a lump of shit; they are abused, exploited, discriminated against; their very presence among us is resented, even while they sustain this damn economy. Their children, despite being born here, are denied citizenship status. . They don't have any status, in fact. Without these poor souls, the relative wealth enjoyed by this Island— especially, of course, those few at the top of the food chain— would not be! Period! This Island is sugar; sugar is this Island. Shamefully, though, the relationship is parasitic: the Island exploits the sugarcane worker without making any honest and just return to the worker who makes it all possible. Where's the fuckin' justice in that arrangement?"

He paused and looked firmly at the Canadian "sugar doctor" to see if the message was registering. It was, so Marcelo continued.

"You can't know what it's like. Do you suppose it's easy

being a Montalvo here? Do you think I am proud of what my father is? What he does? *Un condenado capataz!* A fuckin' plantation overseer! A modern-day slave overseer is what he is, damn his soul! It goes against everything I stand for. You think I don't realize that my mother is institutionalized this very day because of my father's bankrupt tyranny and Mario's sadistic abusiveness? Harold, *mi amor,* my whole family is pathological. They're fuckin' sick. Look at those murderers Miguel and Manolo! They are my own brothers, for God's sake! *Son unos casos mentales.* They're both mental cases! The Montalvos and their locura . . . their "lunacy" is this goddamn Island itself!"

"*Querido,* I've thought about this for some time now," Harold directed to his partner calmly. "I want you to consider carefully what I'm saying." Marcelo was more than anxious to share Harold's thoughts.

"My work here is completed. There's no earthly reason to continue being here. And quite frankly, I think it's time to move on . . . to move out. I know definitely that my life, my future. . . is with you, Marcelo; and our life together is not here on this Island. No way! It would be further lunacy. This latest atrocity is only the beginning. Believe me!"

"No, Harold," countered Marcelo. "It actually began a long time ago... centuries ago with that first primitive sugar mill, a *trapiche* they called it. It began with those first sugar exports and the abominable plague of the slave trade. All that ugly, shamefully haunting history was my primary reason for leaving this putrid cesspool . . . to get as far away as possible from this corrupt, violent, retrograde society. *Te digo la verdad.* I'll tell you the truth; I'm ready to leave whenever you are."

"*Vaya.* Good. What do you think about the idea of living in Toronto?" Harold asked excitedly. "*Qué te parece la idea?* Life would be so much better for us there. Please say you'll come with me." Slowly, he moved closer toward the man he wanted to take with him toToronto and grabbed him gently by the shoulders and caressed him soothingly. The two men looked directly into each other's eyes. The "sugar doctor" began crying softly.

"*Todo va a estar bien, querido,*" Marcelo assured him. "Everything is going to be okay."

"I know it will," Harold answered.

The open, breezy and elegant, L-shaped, three-bedroom bungalow, with its easy flowing access to a central courtyard and swimming pool, well-tended lawns and lush tropical gardens at every angle, had become the perfect sanctuary for Azúcar. Of course, she had never seen living quarters so sumptuous in all her life. Adjustment to such astonishing surroundings had been painstakingly difficult for the young girl from the tradional squalor of the *batey*. Since first arriving, she marveled each day at the prevailing serenity that epitomized the villa's entire ambiance. The color scheme and prevalent tones in furnishings throughout the house were varying shades of brown, blue, and green— cool, earthy tones that were restful and relaxing.

To her initial amazement, Azúcar was given her own bedroom! She couldn't believe it. Imagine! Her very own bedroom with private bath ... indoor plumbing and electricity, among other wonders! The theme of cool colors and airy furnishings continued here in her bedroom. Green hues predominated, with white and beige as well. An Indonesian wood armoire with latticework, harmonized with side tables of woven wicker and native mahogany. Hanging over the head of the bed was a linen mosquito net with strips of green to complement the color of the curtains and bed linen. This had been her private refuge since leaving the world of the *batey*, her *abuelita*; Don Anselmo, Mamá Lola, one-eyed Clementina and her husband Tomás and their six children, including Tomás, Jr., the widow Lolita and her three youngsters, long-neck Teresa and her husband Cirilo . . . and of course sugarcane, *el maldito azúcar!*

Now, she was seated comfortably in the spacious dining room that featured a solid, oval antique mocha-washed island pine table with seating for eight. The chairs had woven fan-shaped backs, and soft seat cushions of beige-and-taupe striped silk. She was waiting anxiously for her mentors Harold and Marcelo, who had mentioned earlier that day that they had something of extreme importance to discuss with her and they would do so over dinner later that evening. Amid the inquiring glances of the attentive and intelligent young woman, first Marcelo, then Harold presented their deliberations on why they had made the joint decision to leave the Island. Their reasons would prove to be profound and would have an equally deep impact on Azúcar's ultimate decision to act.

"*Hierba mala nunca muere.* Weeds never die, Azúcar." Marcelo began carefully, but also quite puzzling. "Have you noticed how no matter how hard you try to eradicate these ugly pests of Nature, they manage in time to reappear? Weeds just seem impossible to kill. Well, Azúcar, that's how I see the sickness of this *maldita Isla.* So deeply rooted in the psyche is this sickness that complete eradication becomes a deceptive lie. And no degree of reform seems to help. Attempts at reform are also a well-promoted myth. By the way, that's also how I describe the entire Montalvo clan — *mi maldita familia* -- nothing but a well-promoted myth."

"You see, Azúcar, *mi querida,*" Harold emphasized carefully, "there is definitely the appearance of eradication; but in absolute truth, it's all just an illusion."

"Think of *la hierba mala* in terms of sugar!" Marcelo continued with what was clearly becoming a mini-lesson in the political-economic history of the region. "Think about what sugar — or *la hierba mala*— has done not just in this Island, but to a larger or lesser extent in all of these Sugar Islands. Since the advent and evolution of the sugar industry, there has been a parallel development of monstrously brutal forms of oppression that have eventually led to physical, social, and psychological death. And all because of sugar! Look at what it has done to us: slavery, latifundism, sharecropping, inhuman living conditions, below-poverty, fixed wages, excessive capitalism, absentee landlords, foreign ownership, transnational corporate control, imperialism— all the most grotesque manifestations of human exploitation."

"And the violence . . . in one form or another affecting all of us whether directly or remotely associated with *la hierba mala*," Harold was quick to continue.

"This culture of sugar, as I call it, is a perverse, evil culture of oppression, racism, violence and injustice. I am ashamed that I blindly chose to become part of all this . . . through my work. I had absolutely no idea of the associated violence. As long as I was confined to the safe, protective environment of the research labs far away in Toronto, I saw nothing. I knew nothing of the terrible nightmares of the culture of sugar. Maybe I didn't really want to know. Now, however, at close range I see differently. I see that sugarcane inevitably engenders brutality and inhumanity toward the powerless. I shudder every time I think about those souls out there, condemned to the batey . . . Azúcar, when I think how that was once your life . . . how it could have been your future . . . the disgraceful cheapening and ultimate waste of human life. Azúcar, you can't ever again be a part of that world. *Nunca jamás!* Never!"

"*Qué barbaridad!*" Marcelo joined in registering his disgust. "It is a system that denies all human dignity... all human rights to human beings whom it has subdued by violence, and keeps them by force in a state of eternal misery and ignorance and superstition... as I quote my readings of Jean-Paul Sartre, of course," Marcelo boasted. He was proud to be able to recall much of his philosophical readings while studying in Europe. These readings produced a great impression upon young Marcelo's thinking about himself, his circumstance, and his life as a Montalvo, traditionally connected with plantation sugarcane.

Azúcar, persistently inquisitive from a very early existence in the *batey* with her beloved *abuelita*, and now possessing a more sophisticated and discerning mind after intensive, disciplined study and guidance at the villa, was totally absorbed in what Marcelo and Harold were saying. She thought about everything with a certain sadness that could be best described as heavy, limitless and profound. There was no question that everything made sense to her; she readily identified with the ideas and theories being presented. She made immediate connections to her own circumstance, past and current. She remained motionless, seated at the elegant dining room table.

"Azúcar," Harold interrupted her silent thought, "Please forgive us, but Marcelo and I have considered very seriously your future; we've thought about what becomes of Azúcar ... about the world that awaits her beyond this living Hell here on this Island."

"And what, *favor de decírmelo*, please tell me, have you two concluded?" she asked respectfully, at the same time anxious to know. She sat erect and poised, as she had learned at the elegant villa with the two caring, sensitive young men. Then, without wasted prefacing came the jolting invitation.

"We are inviting you to come live with us in Canada, where you would have the opportunity for a brilliant new life, a life of enlightenment, of progress and refinement," was Harold's calculated response.

"Are you asking me to abandon my Island?"

"We're asking you to abandon the morbid illusion of existence here. El maldito azúcar . . . *la hierba mala que nunca muere* has been the destruction of life here. Come with us to Toronto! We'll arrange everything . . . a safe and comfortable home, preparatory school, university, a career . . . a future . . . a life! Azúcar, you must say 'yes'!"

Azúcar said nothing immediately, again, as she had learned to do: think first and reflect; be circumspect before answering in reckless haste. She considered heavily all that she had heard that evening. *La hierba mala* . . . abandoning the Island . . . a bold, new life in faraway Canada , with challenging opportunities to learn new things, to grow. But what about *mi abuelita* and all the people I have loved so dearly throughout my life? . . . the undeniable horrors of the *batey* . . . the sadistic *capataz* . . . his monstrous son . . . the brutal murder of poor Estimé, Lolita's beautiful Haitian . . . the bizarre, unforgettable Marasa Bwa ritual in the forest . . . the cold-blood murders of innocent Ramón and Césaire, and their known murderers going unpunished . . . and of course the most tyrannical and destructive force of all . . . Sugar! *El maldito azúcar!* All these painful thoughts raced through her subconscious, haunting her in the fiercest way.

She closed her eyes tightly and immersed herself once again in the whirlpool of conjecture and doubt. Once again this intelligent, introspective young woman, not at all frightened, overwhelmed or surprised by her thoughts, reached deeply within her young soul for meanings.

"What does all this mean? How am I supposed to interpret all this? Have the ancestors deliberately selected me for some special purpose I just don't know about yet? Is this what abuelita meant when she said the sacred spirits would forever protect me? *Ay, por todos los santos, dáme respuestas.* Give me answers. Why isn't *mi abuelita* here with me right now to help me find answers?"

Rather imperceptibly, Azúcar had grown accustomed to regarding her grandmother as her true source of strength and wisdom. Little by little, even while absent from the batey and Doña Fela, and without realizing it, Azúcar had been linking her dear grandmother to all the secret aspirations of her own life. When all the voices inside her fell silent, Azúcar heard one clear word alone soar easily above all the others: "leave." And that single word grew louder and louder, expanding itself, transforming itself into one massive, haunting cloud that shrouded the young woman's entire miserable past . . . blocking out completely all other thoughts.

DIECIOCHO

It might otherwise have been a typically beautiful tropical morning that greeted everyone in the batey, the first early rays of a gloriously welcomed morning sun having already dried up the previous night's profuse and uncomfortable humidity. But this morning was different. Don Anselmo felt a heavy sorrow as he slowly approached Doña Fela's cabin. Nevertheless, it was there that he headed feeling uneasy and admittedly oppressed.

"*Kité mwin sél, mwin ginyin la pèn.* She is leavin' me alone and I am in a lot of pain. How it hurts my soul! I am finally loosin' my one true comrade from difficult times past that few of us still remember," he muttered to himself mournfully as he reached the door of the cabin.

Inside the cabin, the atmosphere was extremely doleful. There was a terrifying silence all around the old woman lying motionless on her narrow cot. Already assembled were Azúcar, who had been there for a few days now, Mamá Lola, the widow Lolita, one-eyed Clementina, and longneck Teresa. All the women present were in quiet torment upon witnessing a no-longer strong, independent, indomitable spirit like their Doña Fela who now lay helpless and defeated.

For the first time in her very long life, Doña Fela herself was aware that things were being done to her or for her. Someone else, for the first time, was giving her spoonfuls of special herbal potions . . . a full array of colored liquids. Someone else was feeding her, washing her, caring for her in every regard. She had grown too old or perhaps too tired to do for herself. The ferocious toil over the many years in the *maldito* sugarcane fields had been the single culprit that cheapened and wasted her life: robbed her of all normal encounters with life; deprived her own family of her potentially abundant, unconditional love . . . denying her very personhood.

La maldita caña had wrecked her life. The painful reality struck Don Anselmo. "My old friend is ready to cross over," he was forced to admit himself. A strong desire loomed over him to cry out loud, but he didn't.

Azúcar sat silently on the floor next to her grandmother's cot, resting her mournful head across the old woman's spent body. Doña Fela reached for Azúcar's cheek and stroked it gently. She then whispered to her granddaughter.

"*M'hijita, mi azúcar morenita*, come closer, child, and listen carefully. What I tell you now will help you understand everything. I want you to gather together all the broken, scattered and mixed-up pieces of the kanari jar and restore that sacred vessel with painful care and much love. This act will free you of the shattered memories of a haunted past."

It didn't matter in the least that there were other people crowded around the room, thereby affording grandmother and granddaughter no true measure of privacy; but it really didn't matter to Doña Fela at this point. Azúcar lifted her head and gave her attention fully to her moribund *abuelita*.

"Leave this filthy pit of human misery, *m'hijita*! Leave, I tell you! It will destroy you just as sure as it done destroyed all of us, if you stay. *La maldita caña* is the only true enemy that, in all its cursed sweetness, will bring all of us down. *Sálte ahora, mi querida*, before it's too late."

Suddenly, Azúcar heard the phrase that she had heard at the dinner table some nights ago at the villa . . . the very phrase that now brought new illumination to everything that might still have been in darkness.

"*La hierba mala nunca muere*," she heard the words from her grandmother's feeble, dry lips.

"Weeds never die." And then, with a sudden, miraculous resurgence of strength, Doña Fela began to narrate a series of startling revelations to her granddaughter that would jolt the young woman initially, but would nevertheless be etched indelibly in her conscious. The endless range of her future thoughts and actions would forever be determined by what her wise old grandmother revealed to her that doleful morning. Her voice quivering slightly, nevertheless managing to utter clearly every detail, Doña Fela began by putting everything in perspective.

First, she unraveled for her puzzled granddaughter the mystery that had surrounded the long relationship between old Mamá Lola and Yvette Origène-Desgraves. The two women had known each other intimately well before Yvette Origène married the rich old Maurice Desgraves. It seems that Yvette had engaged in an illicit love affair with Lola's only son, a robustly sensual, captivating mulatto sugarcane worker named Felipe. Their steamy romance produced a son; but the infant was immediately whisked away to live with a mulatto couple on the other side of the Island. Considerable sums of money were sent regularly for the child's maintenance and the couple's silence.

This concealed arrangement continued for years until finally Lola heard no further word about her grandson. When Yvette's family negotiated a marriage of convenience with the wealthy, elderly bachelor, Maurice Desgraves, Yvette insisted that Lola become part of the new housekeeping staff. No one questioned her request. Both Yvette and Lola, the boy's mother and grandmother, respectively, never again broached the subject of the little boy on the other side of the Island. It was learned that Yvette's handsome lover Felipe drowned in the shark-infested waters of the Mona Passage, along with everyone else crowded aboard a poorly-constructed "yola", as people called those rickety, wooden rafts bound for Puerto Rico. Lola never quite forgave herself for feeling that she had abandoned both her son and grandson, whose name she never learned.

Mamá Lola herself, it turned out, had also been married . . . the man's name was Alix and this Alix was a distant cousin to Felicidad, Azúcar's *abuelita*. It was Alix who introduced Fela to her future husband, Justín, who worked in the boiler house. Fela used to carry him late evening meals. Fela and Justín gave birth to a baby girl, Azúcar's mother, whom the young newly-weds named Solange. Together, Lola, her husband Alix, Fela and her new husband Justín, then somewhat later, a younger brother of Justín's named Anselmo, all found themselves working together on the same plantation named *Esperanza Dulce*. This was where Azúcar's mother grew up and remained until she herself died while giving birth to her only child . . . named Azúcar.

Unforeseen horror struck hard and swiftly when a diabolical scheme almost decimated the entire population of Blacks in the Island, especially those that had come from the other side of the river. The sinister plan had been executed by the ruthless dictator at the time, the maniacal Rafael Leónidas Trujillo, who had long expressed openly his bitter distaste for — and his actual fear of the growing numbers of Black people on his side of the river . . . even though his maternal grandmother was clearly "one of them," and "he wasn't exactly White himself "--- as almost everybody knew, but merely whispered this truth. When the idea of an imposed quota on the percentage of non-native sugarcane workers that a plantation could employ failed, Trujillo took more draconian measures. Doña Fela recalled the nightmare as if it had occurred the previous night. Her eyes became saturated with painful tears. She narrated the events with surprising clarity . . . . . .

"I'll never ever forget it. It was at a dance given in the dictator's honor at a town near the border, the night of October 2, 1937, that *El Jefe*, ' The Chief,' — that's what everybody called him-- declared how he was gonna' solve the problem:

*"Está ordenado que todos los haitianos que hubiera
en el país fuesen extermindados."*
It is ordered that all Haitians that are in the country be
exterminated.

"These were *El Jefe*'s orders. *M'hijita,* during the next week,
'*El Corte*' or 'The Cutting' as it was called, swept 'cross the
whole Island, brutally killin' Haitians on sight . . . men, women,
children. It didn't matter. *'Operación perijíl,'* or 'The Parsley
Test,' was the way the death squads determined just who was
and who wasn't Haitian. When one of the soldiers held up in
front of you a twig of parsley, *perejíl,* an' then asked you what it
was, the way you pronounced the word *'perejíl'* in Spanish told
the soldier whether you lived or died. For a lotta folks on the
other side of the river, the letters ' *j* ' and ' *r* ' was always very
hard to say like they 'sposed to be. So, that's what told Trujillo's
militia if a person was Haitian or not."

Doña Fela, her voice saturated with grief, also told how the
blood-thirsty squads did not target those Haitians living on
plantations that were owned by *"los gringos"*, but rather all of
those *braceros* found outside the cane fields. She continued
painfully.

"Even those Haitians and Domínico-Haitians who been
livin' in the territory for many years or who was really citizens
by birth was just rounded up and killed. The slaughterin' was
en masse; the troops used machetes to hack people to death,
people said, so they wouldn't waste no bullets. Thousands of
people was forced to jump off piers or cliffs, drowning or
either bein' eaten by the sharks waitin' down in the sea below. .
. Many tiny babies an' small children was dashed against rocks
or tree trunks, or tossed into the air, only to be speared by the
soldiers' waitin' bayonets as the helpless little angels came
fallin' down." Truthful history, of course, now acknowledges
that between 30,000 to 40,000 Black people who Trujillo

regarded as "an undesirable menace" were massacred in this campaign of genocide.

Only because they happened to be caught at one of the unprotected plantations, *Esperanza Dulce*, Alix, Justín, two of Anselmo's brothers and both their parents were among the defenseless, innocent souls who did not manage to escape "*El Corte*." There had been a profoundly special bond among the three elders of the batey --- Doña Fela, Don Anselmo, and Mamá Lola --- ever since that unpardonable and nefarious campaign of genocide of the Island's Blacks.

The sickening narrative produced a singular effect upon Azúcar's very soul. The tale was at once hypnotic and sobering, provoking angry tears in the young woman's eyes. In fact, everybody in the room, having also listened to what Doña Fela had just revealed to her granddaughter, remained transfixed by the old woman's gripping account. Such a chilling silence ensued that even Mamá Lola and Don Anselmo, easily the oldest individuals present --- along with Doña Fela, of course, were filled with torturous memories. For these survivors, hearing the ghoulish saga was like reliving it. Azúcar could do nothing more than slowly lower her eyelids. A profound feeling of horror inside her overtook her emotions. She burst into a heavy cry.

"Those dogs!" one anonymous voice sounded.

"Remember well all you heard here this mornin'," another unidentified voice added.

Don Anselmo reached down to Azúcar; she stood up to face him and fell into his tender caress, still crying aloud. "No, don't torment yourself, *m'hijita*. You must take from life what life offers. Always remember: "*Labou glise men solèy seche li*. Mud is slippery, but the sun soon dry it all out."

The ever-alert young girl understood this perfectly. Content with knowing that she had finally told Azúcar all that the dying old woman wanted her granddaughter to know, Doña Fela let out a heavy sigh of relief and then said in a gentle voice, *"Adieu, mi preciosa azúcar morenita. Te amo."* . . .

Doña Fela's cabin remained vacant seemingly forever following the series of elaborate, traditional social activities and religious rituals performed in preparation for her journey back into the community of ancestral spirits in Ginen. Azúcar remembered once, as a curious small child, asking her grandmother, *"Abuelita,* where is Ginen?" Eager to have the child appreciate all the honored traditions she herself had learned from her own elders, Doña Fela had said patiently,

"Ancient Ginen is deep under the sea . . . and this faraway sea is deep underneath the earth."

"Under the sea . . . underneath the earth?" little Azúcar repeated aloud, puzzled.

"Sí, mi preciosa azúcar morenita. You will understand in time."

At the funeral ceremonies of her now deceased grandmother, a much more reflective Azúcar thought about all she had learned over the years from this wise old woman. Azúcar realized, probably more than anyone else present in the cabin— and in a most ironic sense— the significance of her grandmother's death and the accompanying rituals. They symbolized Azúcar's pending journey toward her future; this journey would be the birth of an entirely new dimension of life. Like Doña Fela's spirit – now free --, the young woman's new life would symbolize a new state of freedom . . . freedom from limitations and restrictions of the *batey,* of Esperanza Dulce . . . ultimately of the Island itself! Free!

Part of the ceremonies centered on the complex ritual of passage, the *'desounen,'* that, according to ancient belief, separated the soul from the body.

"*Desousen* will preserve Doña Fela's divine heritage," affirmed Don Anselmo, who officiated at the intricate, multi-layered ritual for his departed sister-in-law, friend and comrade of many, many years. "The divine essence of your dear grandmother's life will now become a long functionin' force in your own household no matter how far away you are," he informed Azúcar in a most solemn tone.

Another important part of the celebration included a ritual bathing of the corpse with secret herbal concoctions prepared by Mamá Lola to render her long-time confidante acceptable to the spirits, which Doña Fela would soon join "on the other side." For this special cleansing, enough floorboards inside the cabin had been removed so that a trench could be dug. There the corpse was placed in order to collect the spilled, defiled water. In that way, the water "of the dead" would not drain out of the cabin, thereby polluting the community "of the living." Azúcar had to admit to herself that this was rather ironic, since the sewage trough was just out front— and a more threatening pollutant to the community there certainly wasn't.

There was a special wake during which friends came to visit from neighboring plantations; there was also the spewing of *kleren* in the formation of a cross to the four corners of the universe. Still in his official capacity, Don Anselmo also spewed out kleren over the corpse. He closed the ceremony by rubbing this same raw cane liquor upon a tall earthen jar — the sacred *kanari* jar that Azúcar remembered hearing about from her grandmother — before breaking it into hundreds of tiny pieces and saying the final prayers. It was through the personal efforts of the Canadian "sugar doctor," who intervened directly on behalf of the workers, that central administration granted a rare, one-day work moratorium for individuals who wanted to participate in the ceremonies for Doña Fela.

"The bastards!" someone said with righteous disgust. "*Coño.* Just one day for our Santa Madre. That's all. The oldest livin' worker on this *maldita plantación* and they give us just one fuckin' day!"

"*Sí, señores,*" another person added. "And we still gotta work on Sunday to make up for the lost time. So, the greedy pigs really didn't give us a damn thing!" *Mierda. Somo' todavía jodío.* Shit. We still gettin' fucked over."

"I'm so weary of the dirty games they keep playin' on us," one woman said, realizing that she had been deceived once again . . . like so many times before. "But still, *Bondye bon.* God is good."

Once significant element of Doña Fela's living legacy remained in the form of her cherished *conuco* growing at the side of the now-vacant cabin. Had it not been for one-eyed Clementina's loving reverence held for her neighbor and friend, weeds would have over-run the vegetable garden.

"Doña Fela wouldn't of wanted her *conuco* to go unattended," Clementina had said to her husband Tomás. An' Azúcar ain't here to look after it."

"*Tieneh razón.* You right. And besides, it sure put out more vegetables than anybody else's 'round here. It would be a big waste to let the weeds destroy it," Tomás said. "I'll tell Tomás, Jr. to begin takin' care of Doña Fela's garden."

Therefore, it was a result of the special care and attention given to the old woman's *conuco* that her spirit remained a living memory within the community. Without fail everyday after leaving the sugarcane fields, and despite how physically drained he was from his tasks there under the sun's unsympathetic rays, Tomás, Jr. went directly to the waiting garden to see what needed to be done there. The chore became a welcomed ritual with the young man. As if as a reward from Doña Fela herself, the well-tended conuco continued providing Clementina's family with an abundant supply of víveres, "vegetables," for their dinner table: maíz, yucca, yautía, batata, mapuey, frijól, perejíl. Besides, by tending the rejuvenated conuco, Tomás, Jr. reasoned, in his private fashion, that he was establishing a kind of spiritual connection with Azúcar, for whom he had definitely begun to feel something very special. And although they would be separated physically by thousands of miles, at least in his mind the *conuco* would bind the two.

As for Marcelo, this would be his final *"adios"* to what remained of his family. Any manner of connection had been severed some time ago. He knew in his heart and soul that nothing could conceivably draw him back to the Island once he left. The separation would be permanent. The last altercation with his father had ended in severely bitter recriminations and rejection by his father. Miguel and Manolo had also refused to accept what, in their view, was their younger brother's intolerable actions and scandalous thinking. Thus, the resolve of the family was to distance themselves as much as possible from Marcelo's "perverted character " at whatever cost.

"*Carajo, hombre.* No fuckin' brother of mine would even think about setting up house with another man," Miguel ranted furiously. "Everybody's already talking about those two maricones."

"*Pero qué es esa vaina*? What kind of fuckin' bullshit is that? They're not even real men. *No son machos de verdad.*" Manolo declared angrily. "I wish the two of 'um would just leave here for good. Go as far away from here as possible.

"What a fuckin' embarrassment. *Coño,*" Don Diego had bellowed. He also wished the "problem" would just disappear forever.

Doña Cristiana, on the other hand, who was still hospitalized and heavily sedated constantly, offered no judgment on her youngest son's actions primarily because she had not been kept abreast of events. She had absolutely no idea what was going on around her. Her dementia, according to the doctors, was worsening and placed her well outside the realm of reality. She could recognize her son when he made his final visit, but an enormous time lapse had set in to disorient her altogether.

"*Querido hijo mío*, remember to eat well so that you'll have energy to study your lessons and don't stay up too late at night. You need your rest, *m'hijo*," she said, thinking that Marcelo was preparing to leave for university study abroad. She had drifted easily and completely back to a long-gone, but more trouble-free past life, remembering those events that brought her joy.

"Also remember to send me lovely picture post cards regularly, dear." Marcelo simply bent down to kiss his pathetic mother on the forehead; the tears draining from his large eyes soaked his cheeks. He knew that he would never again see his mother alive.

Without doubt, the departing visit that Azúcar made to the Origène-Desgraves Manor was the most unanticipated, the most dramatic, and also the most surreal. Azúcar was bewildered by the notion that Madame Yvette Origène-Desgraves, the mother of Blanchette Desgraves Montalvo, who, of course, was Mario's widow, had sent word through Marcelo that Madame --- as almost everybody called her --- had invited Azúcar for tea at the manor before the young woman was scheduled to leave the Island for Canada. The urgently requested *tête-à-tête* would prove to be a private meeting that was to change Azúcar's life forever. Her characteristic inquisitiveness was more than peeked; it was burning with impatience and conjecture that became bewitching.

"*Por mi madre*, why would she invite me, of all people, to have tea with?" Azúcar asked not only herself, but also Marcelo and Harold. "I don't even know the lady and we certainly have nothing in common." The remark was not intended maliciously because Azúcar was genuinely mystified.

"*No te preocupes.* Not to worry, Azúcar," Marcelo replied, assuring his young friend that indeed if Madame had requested someone for tea, then it must surely involve something extremely important. "Madame has never been known to be trivial; she has always taken everything quite seriously. And without question that she has been the single most outspoken liberal in this region for decades— of course always being overpowered by the reactionary forces here. Hers has been the voice of sanity and reason. You know, from the very beginning she was bitterly opposed to the marriage between her daughter Blanchette and my brother Mario because she always knew that Mario was un monstruo and that my father was a bigoted conservative and racist. She suspected that such a union would be a catastrophic failure . . . doomed from the start!"

"I understand she has been petitioning the government for years to require that the sugar industry improve the working conditions of the *braceros* and also to do something about improving the deplorable living conditions in the bateys . . . like providing running water, indoor plumbing, sewage system, electricity . . . basic human necessities," Harold added. "I'm convinced that the lady is quite a decent human being."

"*Sí, es verdad.* I too have heard the stories about her personal human rights campaign," Azúcar finally admitted. "Still, though, I'd like to know why she's invited me to the manor." It was true; the motives underlying the purpose of the eleventh-hour rendezvous escaped Azúcar.

Azúcar arrived at the resplendent and superbly maintained Origène-Desgraves Manor house in the early afternoon, just past mid-day. The visit produced a mixed sensation of hot chills and palpitating anxiety. She had never met Yvette Origène-Desgraves and had only heard positive tales about her legendary benevolence. A very confident Azúcar silently crossed the wide veranda that was tastefully flanked with luscious, potted tropical plants--- mainly ferns of all varieties. Caged birds — two chattering, green cotica parrots, a rare quetzal, a pair of tropical thrushes, a whiter-than-white cockatoo with its long, erect crest, all sang with unified, forlorn cries as they greeted visitors — hoping as if Madame's already liberated, sympathetic guests would release their feathered brethren from the gilded prisons. Azúcar did not miss this noticeably blatant contradiction in Madame's otherwise noble persona.

A uniformed mulatto steward, who immediately escorted her in silence to Madame's quarters on the second floor of the magnificent residence, met Azúcar at the main entrance. Madame herself was waiting at the door of her private sitting room.

"*Bonjour, ma cherie.* We finally meet. Do come inside. I've heard so many wonderful things about your personal and academic development," Yvette said with a genuinely warm smile, leaning forward and planting a light kiss on the delicate cheek of her guest. "I am happy that you were able to come."

"*Encantada.* I am delighted to meet you, Madame. It was very kind of you to invite me."

Yvette closed the door after showing Azúcar inside the stately room and offering her one of the two comfortable highback armchairs in front of the panoramic window overlooking the lush patio gardens below. A sterling silver tray of carefully prepared croissant sandwiches and an assortment of sugar sweets rested on a small table, a classic Victorian teapoy, placed between the two women; the matching silver teapot shared the tray. Once the formal exchanges and pleasantries were concluded and the two teacups were filled, the no-nonsense *gran dame* wasted no time in moving directly to the real purpose of their discreet meeting.

Deliberately without sharing with her special guest any pertinent, never-before disclosed episodes of an earlier, otherwise orderly and privileged life prior to marrying Maurice Desgraves, Yvette did produce for her special guest a certain piece of vital information. There was a particular individual living in Canada to whom Azúcar was being asked to hand-deliver an important letter. Absolutely no one was to know the nature of the meeting that day between the two women and especially nothing about the extraordinary request to act as secret courier to a stranger somewhere in Canada.

"Ma cherie, you must promise me that under no circumstances will you tell a living soul about this special favor I am asking of you," Madame practically whispered to her young guest, as if there were someone secretly positioned to eavesdrop from outside the door of the sitting room. "It is of extreme importance that secrecy be maintained at all costs," she added. *"Entiendes?"*

"Sí, entiendo. You have my word," Azúcar promised. *"Pero*, Madame, how will I find this person in such a big place as Canada? I will need help, don't you think?"

"There's no cause for alarm. I have carefully arranged everything for you, my dear," Madame said very judiciously, allaying whatever anxieties Azúcar might have had. The older woman had anticipated any probably concerns on the part of the young, inexperienced, but keenly intelligent courier. Without being made aware of all the details --- or at least so felt Azúcar--- she was delivering some manner of very important communication to a gentleman named Lucien St. Jacques, who was living and working in the city of Montreal in Canada. This Lucien was a young corporate attorney, twenty-five years old and a bachelor. He had been educated in an exclusive private academy somewhere and had gone to Montreal to study law at a rather prestigious university there, from which he graduated with high honors.

Azúcar learned further that this Lucien, upon being awarded his law degree at quite a young age, was offered a lucrative entry-level position at one of Montreal's most respected corporate law firms. So stellar was the caliber of this young barrister's performance that he was promptly transferred to the firm's biggest client to handle the legal affairs of that company's international accounts. Much to Azúcar's surprise, this was the same multinational conglomerate that owned sugarcane plantations and monopolized the sugar industry in the Island that she had just abandoned! It was the very same parent company, with an important branch office and research laboratories in Toronto, where her mentor and friend, Dr. Harold Capps, conducted his research! But still, certain questions plagued Azúcar: Who was this mysterious Lucien St. Jacques? How did Madame Yvette Origène-Desgraves know him? What connected them? What was in this letter that seemed so important? Azúcar was ablaze with curiosity to learn the answers to these pressing questions.

The stately hostess saw no need to prolong the meeting and was thoroughly satisfied that her instructions had been clear. Once Azúcar had agreed to honor the request, Yvette opened a small, handsome brown Morrocan leather case trimmed around the edges with tiny silver studs. She took from the cigar-box sized case a thick envelope that was bound by a tightly drawn red ribbon. Written on the front of the envelope was the name "Lucien St. Jacques," including the name and address of his work site in Montreal. "Confidential" was printed in large red block letters across the bottom of the tightly sealed envelope.

"Azúcar, *ma cherie*, guard with every discretion this letter and deliver it personally to the individual whose name appears on the envelope," Yvette said as part of her final instructions. "You must not leave it with anyone else, not even with his personal secretary. Only Monsieur Lucien himself. This letter is very, very important. *Entiendes*, child?"

Azúcar understood perfectly, but she insisted in knowing, "How will I know this Monsieur Lucien if I have never seen him before?"

"Once you've settled in Toronto and have found your way about, you must then proceed directly to Montreal. You'll be provided a recent photo of him so that you'll have no problem in recognizing him. It is important that this matter be concluded within exactly sixty days."

Azúcar focused on Yvette's every word.

"*Et maintenant*," Yvette pointed out, "This other envelope is for you, my dear. The amount inside should be more than enough to take care of your expenses plus the cost of any inconvenience encountered on your part in honoring my request," she said, handing Azúcar the other thick envelope with her name written on it: "Azúcar" . . . nothing more.

"Now, you must go quickly before Monsieur Desgraves and the other members of the household return," Yvette said as she rose from her chair, gesturing that her guest do the same. "Truly, my dear, it has been extremely important for me to meet you. How I've waited for this moment. You are a very intelligent young girl. I have no doubt that you will be very successful in Canada. I wish you nothing short of good fortune. *Merci beaucoup* for coming and thank you very much for your help, Azúcar. *Vaya con Dios*." The two women said their farewells with a mutual embrace and exchanging a grateful kiss on the cheek.

"In all honesty, Madame, I have always wanted to meet you. *El placer ha sido mío*. The pleasure has been mine. And please be assured that I myself will personally deliver this letter to Monsieur Lucien. *Adios*, Madame."

The meeting lasted exactly one hour, as Yvette had meticulously planned that it would. Marcelo, who had driven Azúcar by jeep to the Origène-Desgraves Estate, was punctual in returning for her in order to avoid anyone's suspicion or speculation about this unlikely encounter between two unlikely individuals, Azúcar and Madame Yvette Origène-Desgraves. But as fate would ordain it, just as the jeep was pulling away from the front veranda, another car was approaching from the opposite direction. The driver of the sedan was Marcelo's sister-in-law, Blanchette Montalvo, with two small passengers in the rear seat, the twins Cécile and Chelaine, who were chattering like two magpies and playing clap-hands-together. The two vehicles passed each other slowly, as do two domesticated animals--- circling, sniffing, unfamiliar with each other, but curious nevertheless because of their belonging to the same breed. Both drivers politely nodded at each other in acknowledgment and continued driving pass. Marcelo and Blanchette had never actually been what one might call friends . . . for no other concrete reason than the fact that they shared no mutual interests or ideologies. The two were merely civil toward each other.

Blanchette tried desperately, but failed to catch more than a fleeting glimpse of her brother-in-law's female traveling companion. Since Azúcar was now considerably older and more sophisticated in appearance than before and Blanchette had never really known the young woman, Mario's widow would not have recognized Azúcar under the most ordinary of circumstances. Nevertheless, the curiosity strained Blanchette's resolve to remind herself to inquire of her mother who was the stranger with Marcelo. And why was Marcelo visiting? Perhaps to say farewell? The forever cautious Madame would undoubtedly invent a plausible distraction of some kind in order to avoid having to reveal Azúcar's identity and equally important, of course, the true nature of the visit.

After all preparations had been completed and everything readied, with nothing left unattended, Marcelo, Harold, and Azúcar, without ceremony or fanfare, boarded the waiting Boeing 727 jet that would transport the trio to their new life together in far-off Canada. As the plane climbed higher and higher into the tropical skies, Azúcar looked out the small, circular window in awe; this was, after all, her first experience aboard an airplane! If somehow by the magic of some gigantic magnifying glass, Azúcar had been able to see the people on the ground below, as the aircraft flew over the batey, she would have gotten a close-up view of two poignantly sorrowful sights: first, the widow Lolita, her head bent over so that her chin lowered onto her sunken bosom, tears having dried on her cheeks, was sitting in the doorway of her cabin, still waiting for her beautiful Haitian Estimé to return from the sugarcane fields; and second, the restless dreamer, young Tomás, Jr., standing with crusty feet, in secret behind his family's cabin, a puzzled look on his handsome face; he was glancing down in frustration at the letter he held with both hands . . . a letter written by Azúcar, who had obviously forgotten that the young man had never gone to school and had never learned to read! But alas! From the dizzying height at which she now sat, Azúcar saw only the reality of acres and acres, and then many more acres of the maldita caña down below.

DIECINUEVE

It was almost midway during her third month living in Toronto when Azúcar received the photograph of Monsieur Lucien as Madame Yvette Origène-Desgraves had promised. Now with the necessary photo in hand, Azúcar would be aided considerably in the task ahead of her. A great deal of mystery had been removed as a result of receiving this photo. She also felt more comfortable now that she was able to put a human face on the former phantom to whom an important communication was to be delivered.

"*Ay, mi madre. Qué guapito*! What an attractive man," she thought to herself as she held the snapshot up to the natural light of the bright afternoon Canadian sun entering the wide living room windows of the townhouse. "His eyes are penetrating, but also a little melancholic. And he certainly doesn't look native-born Canadian to me." Although she didn't admit it at first, there definitely was "something" about the man's face that immediately called Azúcar back to the Island she had recently abandoned. She couldn't identify exactly what that "something" was.

"*Qué raro*! How strange!" Marcelo gasped as he looked at the face in the photo. It was as if he suddenly recognized the face staring back at him . . . as if he had seen the face somewhere before. "Do I know this guy?" Marcelo asked himself aloud.

"Well, let's just hope he wasn't some dude from the gym who slipped you his phone number," Harold quipped teasingly. All three accepted the tease with a round of light-hearted laughter.

Like Azúcar, Marcelo was instantly drawn to the distinct "Island-ness" in the man's handsome face. "This marvelous face has *Esperanza Dulce* branded across it," Marcelo affirmed seriously before passing the photo to Harold. "And there's really something about his eyes," Marcelo added. Not simply was Lucien "gorgeous," agreed Harold, but the stranger in the photo was exotically seductive. Showing the photo of Monsieur Lucien St. Jacques to her two friends wasn't the only thing that Azúcar shared with them --- even though she knew that Madame would not have approved. After all, the entire matter was one of the strictest confidentiality. But Azúcar felt no breech of trust by informing Marcelo and Harold of the intrigue surrounding the delivery of the letter to the young attorney in Montreal. In fact, Azúcar knew she could count on her two resourceful friends for any manner of assistance in complying with Madame's request. Azúcar didn't have to be reminded that Harold and Monsieur Lucien worked for the same company; therefore, she would have immediate access to any number of offices and various departments. She was convinced that it wouldn't be difficult locating Mr. St. Jacques with Harold's help. Harold made immediate preparations for the shuttle flight to Montreal.

Back in her own room, under the comforting shelter of her secret thoughts, with the intimate stillness of the room softly illuminated by the ebbing Canadian sunset, Azúcar had time to reflect upon much that had happened since coming to Canada a month ago. She thought about her initial arrival and how terrified she was. She had been terrified about leaving the Island, terrified about coming to Canada. Toronto intimidated her at first.

Toronto! Canada's largest city and premier inland port. It is home to more than two million residents; dynamically cosmopolitan and maintaining this distinction by consistently wisely refurbishing itself, staving off the urban deterioration that traditionally eroded the foundations of so many other North American cities. Toronto, possessing a resplendent flair for blending old and new, but also with a deliberate vision of the future, was frightening to this young, guileless immigrant from the distant, sugarcane-infested Caribbean. The question of Azúcar's naïveté was quickly resolved by the well-planned blueprint designed by the two ambitious, but compassionate architects who were committed to ringing about a complete and lasting metamorphosis in the new arrival.

Harold and Marcelo truly felt that they had done everything to prepare Azúcar, who literally had never ventured more than an hour's drive beyond *Esperanza Dulce*, for the strange, but potentially vivorous and challenging new life that she would begin in Toronto.

"*No te preocupes*, Azúcar," Harold had said to her. Don't worry. There's nothing to be afraid of. You'll soon feel totally at home here. Toronto truly is Canada's immigrant center; one in every four immigrants living in Canada lives right here in Toronto. Just imagine! Nearly half of this city's population are immigrants like yourself and Marcelo."

"*Sí, mi amor*," Marcelo said, also trying to make Azúcar feel at ease with her new setting. "I understand that over thirty percent of all recent immigrants to Canada are here in Toronto. And Asia has now totally replaced Europe as the main source of immigrants . . . with the highest numbers coming from places like Sri Lanka, China, Hong Kong, the Philippines, and India. As you can tell, I've done my homework." He chuckled.

"It's true alright," Harold emphasized. "Immigrants help this city tremendously to constantly renew itself."

There was little question in anyone's mind that every imaginable effort had been made to assure Azúcar's smooth and trauma-free acclimation to the drastically new environment of Toronto. Harold, for example, was especially sensitive to the possible cultural issues that might result in serious difficulties in the young arrival's adjustment. But his fears proved groundless. The transition, surprisingly, created no major or noticeable concerns. The unconventionally compatible trio moved into

Harold's elegant, spacious, three-story townhouse in the trendy King Street Theater District of the city. Harold wasted no time in enrolling Azúcar in the Faculty of Arts and Science at Victoria College, one of the seven colleges on the downtown campus of the world-renowned university with its ethnically and culturally diverse population. Harold and Marcelo were desirous of having Azúcar experience the richness of an educational setting that faithfully mirrored not only the region's demographics . . . but more importantly, they felt, the world's.

Marcello shared with Azúcar much pertinent background information he had gathered about the site of their new adventure. Azucar learned that . . . "Toronto lies on the shore of Lake Ontario, the easternmost of the Great Lakes, a factor that helps to dispel the stereotypes of severe Canadian weather; the city is the cultural, entertainment, and financial capital of the country. ...It also abounds in investment and employment opportunities; it has a thriving arts community; there are fourteen beach locations across the city; one-third of Canada is located within a ninety-nine mile-radius of Toronto and one-half of the entire population of the United States is within one day's drive of Toronto. The city has five daily newspapers; and after New York and Chicago, Toronto is the third largest financial services sector in North America." All this was absolutely astonishing for Azúcar; yet she absorbed every piece of new information with joyful eagerness.

In a span of three months, Harold had made certain that Azúcar saw practically all there was to see and experience in this marvelous city. Aboard a classic turn-of-the-century trolley and then an official London-style open-top double decker sightseeing bus, the trio had visited Toronto's major attractions: most of the important museums, including the breathtaking Royal Ontario Museum, Canada's largest; the Art Gallery of Ontario and the Grange, one of North America's largest art museums with fifty galleries, and one of the oldest brick houses in Toronto, respectively; Spadina Historic House and Gardens; the Bata Shoe Museum, showcasing the evolution of footwear around the globe; the Botanical Gardens with its huge collection of tropical and exotic flowering plants, which at once reminded her of her Island; several cultural and performing arts centers; the spectacular Ontario Place waterfront entertainment complex that resembles a city within a city with its winding canals, lakes, lagoons, smart boutiques, theaters, amusement rides, and exhibit pavilions, and chic restaurants. But undoubtedly the most awesome site they visited was the celebrated Canadian National Tower in the heart of the entertainment district.

"An impressive monument to the strength of Canadian industry," Harold boasted not at all with any sense of national chauvinism, but more genuinely to point out to Azúcar and Marcelo that the CN Tower, at 1,815 feet was the world's tallest freestanding structure. Azúcar knew that if one day she were to tell Tomás, Jr. or perhaps the wise old Don Anselmo that she had dined at a restaurant "located so high in the sky that the people on the ground below looked like tiny ants; or a restaurant whose floor rotated once every seventy-two minutes so that you get a complete 360-degree panoramic view of the city stretched out below you." --- No one would believe her *embustes*, 'lies!'

Although it was quite probable that there remained any number of unforeseen, additional steps to be mastered in the overall process of reaching a comfortable level of socio-psychological adjustment, Azúcar nevertheless felt certain that she had achieved--- in a remarkably short time--- a realistic level of confidence in coming to grips with her new, mind-boggling circumstance. She was honest with herself in admitting her personal satisfaction with the manner in which she was confronting the multitude of odds of this circumstance that daily challenged her intelligence and resilience. "*Abuelita* would truly be pleased," she said to herself, smiling confidently.

Meeting the mysterious, "gorgeous" Lucien St. Jacques was a profoundly transforming experience for Azúcar. It was one that would permanently alter the way she navigated her energies toward the goal of responding faithfully to the spirits, knowing that the spirits would not betray her . . . much like Doña Fela and Mamá Lola had done in committing all their energies to obeying and respecting the ancient loas. Her heart beat fast as she waited for the receptionist to say, "Mr. St. Jacques will see you now. You may go in." The words seemed never to come. Despite how hard she tried, Azúcar couldn't keep her mouth from dropping open or her legs from collapsing under the weight of considerable nervousness. She was still almost in a state of disbelief that she was in this place called Canada!

Harold was seated patiently alongside her in the attractive reception area, skimming leisurely through a magazine he had instinctively grabbed from the mound that had been stacked randomly on the table next to the posh leather sofa. But Azúcar preferred not disrupting her private thoughts by engaging Harold in nervous chatter. Instead, she tried secretly and persistently to recall the handsome face in the photograph. It was an ardent, tropical face, she remembered. The large, melancholy, but powerful eyes affected her in a strange way. The magic words from the stoic, blond receptionist finally came: "Mr. St. Jacques will see you now." The door to his magestic office opened and his personal assistant directed Azúcar inside . . . leaving the two strangers together.

"How do you do? Lucien St. Jacques at your service. I'm so sorry that I had to keep you waiting. Forgive me and please make yourself comfortable," he said with debonair aplomb. He displayed a broad, friendly smile and bowed slightly. Harold, of course, had telephoned about a week ahead for the fixed appointment, and so Lucien had been anticipating Azúcar's arrival as much as she was anxious about making the visit. Azúcar was dazzled by Lucien's striking physical appearance in person--- a handsomeness that far exceeded his photo. Lucien's very expressive look was what could easily be called exotic, suggesting the distant and mystical tropics. His skin complexion was difficult to classify: a hybrid coloring somewhere between the commonly- seen medium-hued *trigueño* of the Caribbean and a kind of subtle-to-dark Mediterranean tone. Lucien was unmistakably of mixed-race parentage. Large, black, wide-set eyes bordered unusually long black eyelashes for a man; high-cheek bones --- only Destine, the always-laughing, very black Domínico-Haitian woman married to Noél, back in the batey, had more pronounced cheekbones; black hair, neither shiny nor silky, but kinky or perhaps tightly curled like Don Anselmo's; the familiar fleshy, sensual lips and wide mouth revealing sparkling white teeth.

There was something odd, however, about the man's face. Azúcar felt a bewildering sensation about what she saw as a contrast between Lucien's somewhat rigorous countenance and the seemingly contradictory sadness in his large, expressive eyes. Or was it really more of a longing than anything else?

"*Sin duda*. Yes, no doubt," she decided, "there was a discernible melancholy in Lucien St. Jacques's eyes. But why?"

At the same time, she also recognized in Lucien's "Island-ness" a particular force, a certain supremacy or mastery of self so common of Caribbean peoples . . She had admired greatly this unique quality in only one other human being, her *abuelita*. But the more she thought about it, the more she definitely found this Lucien St. Jacques a very unique and indescribably exciting individual. Extending her hand, Azúcar honestly appreciated Lucien's gracious welcome.

"It is my sincere pleasure, sir. I am delighted that you

were able to see me so soon. I can only imagine how terribly busy you must be. So, you apparently understand the urgency of my visit?"

And indeed he did, for when Azúcar attempted to recall for Lucien the circumstances of the meeting on the Island with Madame Yvette Origène-Desgraves, the young attorney indicated politely that he knew every detail of the event and its carefully orchestrated secrecy. In fact, he was more thoroughly informed than his enchanting visitor. It was therefore not necessary to belabor the point of urgency. Once Azúcar had handed Lucien the envelope from Madame --- because after all, the primary motive for the trip to Montreal--- there was then no reason for him to detain her.

But Azúcar was not mistaken in her feeling that Lucien appeared to be interested in learning more about the Island . . . her Island. And he was especially curious about who she was. Then quite unexpectedly, he expressed a strange curiosity about Madame herself.

"But please, you must tell me . . . what kind of person is Yvette Origène-Desgraves? What do the local people there think of her? Did you, Azúcar, have any personal dealings with her prior to your meeting together?"

Azúcar became lost in the labyrinth of conjecture on her part regarding the motives behind Lucien's questions. The trip to Montreal would prove to be the first of many for Azúcar. Equally, Lucien would have his personal assistant book many-a-shuttle flight between Montreal and Toronto . . . and elsewhere with this intelligent, attractive, young new arrival from the Caribbean.

Several days after returning from the meeting in Montreal, it was Marcelo who first noticed a perplexing silence in Azúcar . . . whether she was seated at the dinner table or out on the sundeck at the rear of the townhouse. The half evasions when

226

asked the most innocuous question, the reticence with which she spoke to her housemates about Lucien made Marcelo even more suspicious about Azúcar's spirit since the encounter in Montreal with Lucien St. Jacques.

"*Pero, por Dios*, Azúcar. You seem terribly quiet lately. What on earth happened in Montreal with our exotic Islander?" Marcelo was anxious to know.

"*No estoy segura*, Marcelo. I'm not sure," she responded hesitantly. "But Lucien seems to hold a strangely magnetic pull, an irresistible and dangerously mysterious charm."

"Ah! But dangerous for whom, *querida*?" Marcelo interrupted playfully. "Am I hearing a possible hint of romantic fascination with this St. Jacques person?"

"Honestly, Marcelo, this man produces in my mind the effect of a potent, almost intoxicating wine . . . sweet, yes, but mysteriously unique at the same time. *Me entiendes?*"
Marcelo understood what his young friend was saying. Both of them together speculated about Lucien. Those questions he had asked Azúcar about Yvette Origène-Desgraves were particularly strange . . . as if seeming to arise from nowhere . . . unprovoked. In all, they both felt, there were still many blank spaces left concerning Lucien's background. For Marcelo and Azúcar, all the veils within which they had enveloped Lucien made him all the more magnetically alluring to Azúcar . . . even with the melancholic shadow his large eyes could not camouflage.

As for Lucien, his reflections after meeting Azúcar a month ago were faithful to his spirit. It had been many years since he had first dared admit to himself this notion of "placing his confidence in the spirits, believing that they, in turn, would have confidence in his never betraying or distrusting these spirits." Lucien couldn't recall exactly when or where he had been introduced to this "strange kind of thinking ". . . it was such a long time ago. Now as an adult, he certainly never risked sharing such private and "strange thoughts" with his closest friends and pals in Montreal. Despite being a skillfully alert and brilliant attorney with one of Canada's most influential multinational corporations, Lucien nevertheless, on many occasions, secretly followed (obeyed and respected, perhaps?) his inner spirits ... rather than any degree of scientific reasoning.

Now, alone in the study of his luxuriously comfortable Montreal apartment, Lucien poured himself a glass of cognac and then sat down heavily on the sumptuous sofa in front of the gaping fireplace. He had already stacked enough logs that would burn most of the chilly, late autumn evening. A repressed desire was consuming him--- and had been since first meeting Azucar: to find her and reveal everything about himself, about his past, about who he was . . . about the contents of that enigmatic letter she had brought with her from the Caribbean.

Azúcar's sophisticated and graceful manner intrigued him--- actually enraptured him. True, he was exposed routinely to Montreal's most charming, glamorous, and intelligent young women, many of whom were also stunningly beautiful and urbane. His world, both social and professional, comprised such women in ample supply. But there was something spiritually captivating . . . maybe "other worldly" about this alluring creature from the sugar-producing Caribbean, even though Lucien found himself in the hub of this throbbing global milieu with its myriad cultures and exoticisms. Amidst such vast array of differences, Azúcar alone drew Lucien's attention like nothing he had experienced before. He was struck by what his keenly perceptive eyes saw as a kind of regal bearing mixed capriciously with the raw honesty of tropical sugarcane ... *Caña brava*, "wild, but sweet cane," would describe this quality. The tenderness of his heart experienced an instant, tantalizing sweetness. He could not erase the thought of this wild sweetness from his sensibilities.

The meal, at once sumptuous and elegant, inspired by international cuisine, yet was prepared with a natural talent and sincere love of the craft. There was fresh pumpkin soup, broiled dolphin in white wine and garlic mushroom sauce, creamed parsley potatoes, coconut soufflé, baked granny apples in cinnamon syrup served with pistachio sorbet topped with rum sauce. The wine was a vintage Chardonnay. Indeed, Harold felt victorious; he prided himself on his passion for cooking and his highly applauded culinary mastery. He sparkled in delight in planning and executing an elegant dinner party for very special friends. It was all a matter of conscious with Harold to appeal to a sense of aesthetics in whatever he did.

The occasion for such meticulous preparation and fuss was Lucien St. Jacques. He had finally been able to accept Azúcar's dinner invitation at the Toronto townhouse, where Harold and Marcelo also extended the hospitality to include a weekend stay. Because of a hectic business schedule during the past few months, Lucien was prevented from honoring previous invitations to come to dinner. Even so, both he and Azúcar had been exchanging several one-day shuttle trips to Toronto and Montreal, respectively.

Azúcar experienced considerable difficulty in falling asleep almost nightly; she was anticipating her marvelous role as hostess to Lucien's stay with all kinds of unknown excitement. She knew perfectly well that her feelings were certainly not deceiving her; she simply would not allow her spirit to be tormented by folly or fantasy of any kind. Magnificent images of Lucien paraded boldly across the young woman's conscious mind, veritable rays of joy and sunshine. Her spirit became newly endowed with a fresh source of energy and exuberance;

such was the powerful spell that Lucian had upon her. Harold and Marcelo were equally excited about the obvious change in Azúcar's spirit from an earlier, recalcitrant uneasiness afflicting her to the currently jubilant one.

"Harold, I don't think what's happening between our sweet Azúcar and Lucien is mere fantasy," Marcelo confessed. "I'm not sure that a special fate isn't somehow drawing those two together, trying to eventually link them to a common destiny."

Harold understood the profound implications of Marcelo's observation. "You may be right. I think little by little and without fully realizing it, both of them will begin linking each other to practically all the aspirations of their own individuals lives," Harold ventured to say.

Marcelo could not contain himself before blurting out: "*Es muy claro*. It's very clear. They're in love! No doubt about it. The drama is over." So, at the appointed hour of the long-awaited dinner party, Harold, seated at the head of the resplendent table set for eight, raised his crystal wine goblet as high as his head in offering the first toast of the evening. "A toast to Azúcar, whose uncompromisingly fresh example serves to restore confidence in the human spirit."

"*Salud!*" All eight of the dinner guests shouted in chorus. Lucien, seated directly across from his hostess, was prompted to continue the accolade. "To my new friends. I also raise my glass to Azúcar, whose untainted charm and overflowing Caribbean glow, her unusual intelligence, her sparkling beauty--- both inner and outer, have conspired to captivate our hearts. *Muchas gracias*, Azúcar, for inviting me not only to tonight's dinner, but into your pure heart."

The melancholic shadow that normally hung over Lucien's large eyes began to dissipate slowly, uncovering eyes that were dancing brilliantly and playfully. His eyes, now very alive, gazed without fear across the table into those of Azúcar. She did not turn her eyes away, but instead smiled acceptingly. Her eyes seemed to be moist. "*Salud!*" rang out unanimously for the evening's second toast.

The camaraderie among the special friends that had gathered for the evening's intimate dinner party was more than congenial. Although Marcelo, Azúcar, and of course, Lucien had not been a part of Harold's social world for as long as the other individuals at the table, a distinct feeling of trust and confidentiality nevertheless emerged almost instantly. Yannis Kotrinis and Tina Sarabalis were noted stage actors with the Canadian National Repertory Theater Company. They migrated to Toronto from Greece some years ago during that country's civil strife and had become enormously popular with theater audiences throughout Canada; they were long-standing intimate friends with Harold. Carlos Peña and Tony Rivera, a domestic partnership sharing fifteen years together and who were owners of a successful Toronto advertising firm, were Harold's closest friends. In fact, Harold and Carlos had been confidants since their days together as undergraduate roommates at the University of Toronto.

Everybody, especially Carlos and Tony, was ecstatic at the news that their friend Harold had at last found a compatible mate and that the two were returning together to live in Toronto. There had been fear among all his pals that Harold, "the boy genius" would become so absorbed in his endless laboratory research and scientific experiments that he would miss out on the really meaningful discoveries of life in the here and now. When it was clear that meeting Marcelo had changed completely Harold's perspective on life and his spirit, Harold's friends welcomed Marcelo Montalvo most genuinely.

"What a fantastic change in you since you returned from that *Infierno Verde*, "Green Hell," Carlos had said to his scientist-

231

friend, referring to what he, Carlos, had always regarded as the disagreeably humid and hot tropics. "But, my dear *amigo,* going down there was really the best thing that could've happened to you . . . from the looks of what you packed in your luggage. How'd you ever get through customs with that hunk?"

Everyone at the table laughed raucously and long at Carlos's impressively sharp wit and skill at verbal jousting; he was, of course, referring directly to Marcelo's unexaggerated physical beauty and charm. The good-natured teasing continued with Tony's unsolicited approval.

"Yeah. All those months of dedicated research and solitary work must have been somber ones," he added. "It's just the discovery you needed, *mi querido.*"

There were more hearty laughs. Were Marcelo lighter in complexion, he would have been able to blush at the amount of complimentary attention being directed at him.

"Honestly, though, my friends, we're all very happy for the both of you," Yannis finally remarked. "I offer *Salud* to new beginnings!" Everyone echoed the sentiment.

The riveting conversation at the dinner table was comfortably intelligent, at times provocative and penetrating . . . but never threatening, insensitive or inane. The topics were eclectic, covering a wide range of humanistic inquiry. There was ample opportunity also for the evening's hostess to update quite proudly her progress with her university studies. After thoughtful discussions with Harold and Marcelo and thorough investigation and career counseling, she had decided that professional hotel management sparked her interests.

"With your tremendous talent and refreshingly open, hospitable spirit, Azúcar, your career options in the fledging tourist industry would be limitless," her academic advisor at the university had assured her in earnest. "You would be in on the ground floor of this exciting new industry."

Yannis and Tina found the moment to share their personal

thoughts on the state of contemporary theater worldwide. Carlos presented insightful comments on the negative side of current trends in media advertising. But undoubtedly, there was one subject that most intrigued everyone at the table, opening up the unanticipated discussion of broad socio-political and economic implications: the question of the distastefully exploitative character of the profitable sugar industry in the Caribbean. It wasn't difficult to see the interconnecting thread reeling its way through the lives of the majority of the individuals seated comfortably around the dinner table. With the exception of the two Greek émigrés, who nevertheless were personally and painfully familiar with political upheaval and repression, the primary motivation for forsaking their Hellenic homeland, everyone else was prepared to share the most gruesome of horror stories associated with sugar.

Harold began by confessing openly that he would no longer allow his conscious to be betrayed nor his intellectual talents be prostituted in the service of earning enormous sugar profits from the exploitation and misery of thousand of powerless sugarcane workers.

"What I saw first-hand in the inhumane conditions of the *bateyes* of that marvelously beautiful Island will never permit me to sleep comfortably, knowing that I am directly contributing to the suffering of those workers down there," he testified.

Yannis, admittedly unfamiliar with the peculiarly Caribbean term and its hideous implications, asked for and received a vivid description of the batey. Marcelo continued the denunciation by revealing that, by circumstance, he had been born into a family closely linked to sugar production. His was a family victimized for generations by the vicious entrapment of this traditional island mono-crop culture — sugar.

"I have long been ashamed of the fact that my own father is a plantation capataz . . . which in former times was the dreaded slave overseer. My father is inhumanly cruel, sadistic, and bigoted in the worst sense. The thought that he despises me for who I am and how I accept myself is sadly ludicrous and hypocritical. The entire line of Montalvo men . . . my brothers, my uncles, and my grandfathers, both paternal and maternal . . . together they symbolize a long, ugly tradition of repression. The notion still gnaws at my conscious that, by blood, I am linked to this tradition of modern-day slavery. You can't begin to imagine how I hate that!"

Carlos, originally from the island of Cuba, and Tony, whose birthplace was also an island nation in the region, Trinidad, but had also lived in Barbados, took their turns in offering their respective histories and personal views. "I can remember that the wages of the contract workers were always so awfully low -- -- determined by the weight of the cane. The scales were always rigged so that they reflected a weight that was decided by the plantation officials operating the scales. The poor guys never escaped being cheated," he recalled.

Tony added, "In most cases around the region, sugarcane cutters are still being paid with vouchers, instead of real money. These vouchers are not accepted outside the plantation; they can be used only at the company bodegas located throughout the *bateyes*."

However, it proved to be Azúcar's poignant narrative, that, while not eclipsing altogether the other nightmarish tales of horror, did succeed in evoking tearful empathy from Tina and, most unexpectedly, an audible rage from Lucien. Yannis was also noticeably shaken by Azúcar's personal account. She volunteered her experience of growing up and living daily in the unimaginable misery of the *batey* . . . and working slavishly since the tender age of eight or nine alongside her seemingly

234

tireless and ageless grandmother in the oppressive sugarcane fields.

"In the *batey* there still are no schools for the children, no medical facilities, none of the common amenities most people elsewhere take for granted --- and are so very basic for human beings to live decently . . . to like human beings. I never experienced the excitement of living with electricity or indoor plumbing until Harold and Marcelo, my dearest and most beautiful friends, in their unbelievable generosity, invited me to come live with them. *Que todos los santos los protejan siempre.* May all the saints protect them always."

Azúcar's level of sophistication and acute sensitivity at this stage in her remarkable personal development guided her in terms of not speaking uncharitably and publicly about the tyrannical practices and reactionary thinking of Don Diego. It was enough that Marcelo had already served to indict this cruel individual. But far more than her learned finesse, it was her unconditional love for Marcelo, and of course Harold, that clearly had restrained her from retelling . . . or indeed reliving the excruciating terror of that sweltering afternoon so long ago in the secrecy of the cabin with Marcelo's monster of a brother. She purposely omitted all this. Nor did she share with her assembled group of eager listeners the macabre episode of the ancient Masara Bwa ritual deep in the forest. Harold and Marcelo understood perfectly that Azúcar didn't wish to be reminded that at one time in the past she had been the unwilling mother of beautiful twin baby girls, Felicidad and Caridad. For Azúcar at this moment, however, it all seemed so very long ago and far removed from this present reality of beauty, serenity, and hope.

Lucien, after listening to what everybody had said, finally offered his own thought-provoking observations. "I've recently come to realize that the traditional boundaries conveniently

235

separating economics, politics, culture, ecology, and progress and development are rapidly fading . . . until disappearing altogether. You really can't explain or deal with one without necessarily referring to the others. Harold, I look at the corporation we are linked with as an example, and I'm sure you realize this also; the single driving force behind the corporation's fierce globalization efforts is free-market capitalism and astronomical profits . . . meaning the undisrupted spread of free-market capitalism to every corner of the world . . . with its own set of economic rules. Shamefully, I think, the human element is not a part of this formula . . . not even a fraction of concern for the suffering and exploitation of powerless groups everywhere. In trying to come to realistic grips with this new, brutal system of globalization and bring it into clear focus, I'm having to retrain myself and develop entirely new lenses to see it. I don't know if I like what I see as I listen to these horror stories tonight. These aren't just myths you read about in books somewhere."

Marcelo next presented strongly supportive evidence for Lucien's point about the brutalizing effects of globalization. "I have personally discussed the question of what is commonly called illegal or unacceptable official residency with immigration officials and have actually seen confidential reports on the subject. All estimates – official estimates, mind you -- quite easily suggest that roughly from 500,000 to 700,000 Haitians, for instance, reside in Dominican territory . . . but only about ten percent of these individuals are ever granted official identification documents. *Imagínate!* Just imagine. Some of these persons have lived in the Island for twenty, thirty years or more and still have been refused legal status . . . that is, national citizenship or permanent residency status. The children born in the labor camps or the batey are also usually denied citizenship status. How cruel and inhumane!"

"It's quite true, added Azúcar. "Documentation is hard to obtain, even if the children are born in nearby hospitals or clinics; many hospital officials are very sadistic in not issuing a proper birth certificate."

"And the parents are classified as 'seasonal contract worker' or 'foreigner in transit' despite having lived for years on the other side of the Artibonito River," concluded Marcelo.

"So, tell us what you possibly see as a realistic escape from the criminal brutality of these nightmares?" Tina asked provocatively, visibly disturbed.

"For one thing," Harold responded thoughtfully, "I see transnational corporations like ours trying to figure out ways to manage unselfishly, humanely, several global strategic alliances that, while filling the company's coffers, they are also benefiting people who traditionally have been the most marginalized, left out and disaffected by globalization. You have only to take a look at those tropical sugarcane workers living in the *bateyes*. I think how dangerously resentful and on the edge they must be. Very dangerous, indeed."

"I don't see any promise of peace, or stability or universal progress toward equalization for anybody if the terrible specter of exploitation and racism is allowed to flourish . . . all in the name of spreading ruthless capitalist values and networks with the ultimate and singular goal of earning huge profits," lamented an angry Lucien.

" . . . And as for the future of sugar on the Island?" Yannis planted the question dramatically as though everybody had been waiting for it all evening, but didn't want to push it.

Again, it was left for the evening's exceptionally keen, intelligent hostess --- perhaps most fittingly positioned among all the dinner guests to do so --- who, with an uncomplicated reply, lashed out mercilessly at globalization and, as far as Azúcar was concerned, its immediately-felt manifestation --- *la maldita caña*. Undeniably, in her view, sugar was the culprit! She offered not the slightest economic alternative. "This abominable evil must end completely. It can't continue like it has . . . for centuries destroying lives. In wave after wave, thousands of ignorant, desperately poor, hopeless *braceros* from every port of call around the Caribbean have come to cut sugarcane, only to be ultimately claimed by the hypnotic power of sugar. This power has claimed so many, many disillusioned victims."

Azúcar's eyes more than suggested tears at this point. Her listeners were clearly moved by her unrehearsed diatribe. With no intention of patronizing Azúcar, of course, Lucien was the first to feel compelled to offer literally a comforting shoulder of support to a now tearful Azúcar. The gesture, however, wasn't necessary. Her tears were more of blistering anger and fiery rebellion than any indication of a helpless damsel in the throes of romanticized distress.

On that note, the evening's penetrating discourse came to a close. It was well past midnight when everybody began saying their final "Good Nights" and " Thank You's."All agreed that the evening had been shared most splendidly, with genuine promises that "this wouldn't be the last, but rather the beginning of many similar, future moments together in such glorious company." Lucien, in silence, agreed as he looked toward Azúcar. She thought she saw him wink.

"It truthfully gave me something besides the theater to think quite profoundly about," Yannis had confessed. Tina reminded Azúcar –who still needed to complete her new wardrobe -- of their scheduled date to spend the next few days engaged in some serious shopping at Toronto's exquisite boutiques. Yannis bid everyone *Kalinichta*. Goodnight.

VEINTE

"Good night, Azúcar," Lucien said reluctantly to his truly enchanting hostess, obviously not wanting to bring the evening to its unavoidable end, despite the lateness of the hour. "And a millions thanks again for inviting me and allowing me to share in this evening's splendor."

"I'm just happy that you enjoyed yourself and found everything so wonderful," Azúcar replied in gracious acknowledgment. Lucien's compliment was well deserved and without an ounce of hyperbole. Everyone agreed that the dinner, from start to finish, had been scrumptiously delicious and the assembled camaraderie equally wonderful and stimulating. The whole evening had been one of unpretentious success.

The guest quarters where Lucien would lodge and Azúcar's suite, separated strategically by an almost empty hobby room, were both located on the third floor of the townhouse. The two new friends accompanied each other up the long flight of stairs that, to Azúcar when she first saw the massive staircase, seemed to reach up to the sky. The two jittery individuals, who really showed no sign of fatigue after a really full evening of feasting and provocative conversation, arrived first at Azúcar's door and stopped. Lucien, still nervous, reached for Azúcar's hand, held it to his full, sensuous lips, then placed a delicate kiss on the back of her small, soft and luxuriously manicured hand . . . A hand that, hideously calloused, once -- thousands of miles away (and seeming like an equally lengthy number of years ago) held a savage machete to cut stubborn sugarcane stalks on an ancient tropical plantation.

The two uneasy, but eager individuals moved even closer together until finally surrendering first to a tender caress, then to an intimately tight, passionate embrace. They said nothing initially; words between them didn't seem necessary. Then Lucien spoke; he said her name softly, "Azúcar." Nothing more. By now, she was using her one free hand to reach behind her and open the door to her suite. The only word she could manage to utter was his name. "Lucien," she said. By now she had become a willing victim of this man's sweet seduction. Their youthful, hot and anxious bodies, almost melting together into one, pushed their way into the pitch-dark room. Azúcar made no effort to switch on the lights. Then it was her turn to speak. "*Ay*, Lucien, hold me and never let me go!" It startled her that these words seemed to pour freely from her mouth. "Lucien, how many more secret treasures of gentleness and love are concealed behind those glorious eyes of yours?" She really wanted to know. In her pounding heart, she did not want Lucien to release her. It dizzied her to think of herself being held in the strong arms of this truly beautiful man. She allowed herself to be pleasantly and slowly overcome by the gentle force of his seductive grip. Like a cool tropical breeze at night, Lucien blew tender words of desire into her receptive ear.

"Azúcar, don't be afraid of your heart; let me be the only one to compliment the sweetness of your spirit . . . tonight and every night hereafter." He drew her tighter still to his hot body. Her blood hurried through every artery of her body. The house was completely silent and impregnated with the sweet aroma of smoldering jasmine and orange blossoms that had been burning throughout the evening. Lucien and Azúcar kissed passionately, slowly undressing at the same time. He kissed her smooth neck and shoulders, nibbled her firm, inviting breasts, licked across her chest. The two easily complemented each other. Lucien satisfied Azúcar spiritually and physically and she, him. They both knew it because they both had felt it. They responded mutually, in synchronic harmony to the inner rhythms of their individual spirit. His large, yet tender hands began massaging her round buttocks; his sensuous lips planting soft, sweet kisses on her breasts. With the skill of an experienced surgeon, his hands moved delicately downward to Azúcar's moist, waiting private aperture. Standing there in the middle of the room, in the dark, in total nakedness, the young lovers were enraptured. She instinctively reached down, exploring, searching, before discovering by touch that Lucien had quite an appreciable erection . . . bone hard . . . stiff . . . waiting to be invited inside her. She was ready, and so, assisted the entry by gently grabbing Lucien's sizeable penis and guiding it gently towards its target. This tender love act was the beginning of many a joyous night still to come for the duo.

Except for a fleeting instant, Azúcar did not permit this delectably sweet moment to be usurped by bitterly intrusive thoughts and ugly images from a remote past, far away . . . in a plantation shack . . . alone with a fiendish monster on the attack. During that brief moment, as if having been kidnapped and trapped in time and space, she almost reflected back to that long-ago tropical afternoon. Since that nightmare, no other man had touched her before tonight. For the longest time imaginable she had feared and suspected that the nearly-forgotten pain would still be alive inside her, for the ugly wounds of childhood do not heal easily, if ever at all.

However, to her astonishment, owing to the collective powers of her guardian loas, there would be no obstacle blocking her path to true joy awaiting her this night. This was part of what Doña Fela had promised her granddaughter. Azúcar knew that Mayanèt and Anaïs, but more so Ezili Freda, the spirit of love herself, were now smiling approvingly, protectively. The night belonged singularly to Azúcar's joy. The newly initiated couple spent the night together in uninterrupted ecstacy. Lucien and Azúcar made love until the early hours of dawn. Azúcar had never before tonight tasted sweet passion. It proved far sweeter than the memorable, rich black cane juice she had first tasted as a child in the batey so long ago, so far away. She told herself that she would never forget this glorious night with Lucien St. Jacques.

Before long, the special relationship that developed between Azúcar and Lucien had become the single focus of conversation at nearly every evening meal the household shared together. And it wasn't a matter of random chatter, nor any manner of good-natured joking, and certainly not the unsolicited casting of value judgments that often comes from one's elders. Quite to the contrary, Harold and Marcelo relished in the notion that their precious azúcar morenita, very clearly, was now in an adult love relationship. And so the conversations took a decided turn toward serious commentary about the substance and development of relationships. Harold voiced his exuberance first.

"The metamorphosis is nearly complete," he said. "I can hardly wait to see the day when you emerge a whole individual, fully healed of those ugly wounds from that hurtful past."

"*Mi preciosa*, you can't imagine the excitement Harold and I have felt seeing you grow and blossom into the radiantly intelligent and talented butterfly you are now," Marcelo added. "We've waited with guarded patience for this inevitable transformation. We're both so extremely proud of you, Azúcar. It was all true enough and Azúcar herself realized it. She reflected thoughtfully upon how she had miraculously survived all the hurt and torment of that hellish existence in the batey . . . upon what, for her, was the unsheathed brutality of the deceptive tropics, where sugarcane alone often dominated and dictated an individual's fate. She smiled lovingly . . . knowingly, whenever she thought back upon that precise moment when Harold and Marcelo made that risky decision to engineer her escape. They had carefully plotted, navigated, and monitored that dangerous course . . . a treacherous one in every regard that boldly defied all kinds of personal risks to themselves. So, Azúcar was quite mindful that her truest friends were genuinely caring in their deep personal concern for her well-being. The exciting relationship between herself and Lucien, as everyone felt confident was far more than a transitory adventure; it was an important part of the necessary healing that had to occur before Azúcar's metamorphosis could be considered total. A very introspective Yannis, sharing his own personal experiences, observed the unique sparkle between the romantic couple.

"What Azúcar and Lucien have together is what I'd describe as an eternal illumination of the spirits . . . a sensation I have experienced only at the Acropolis against the magnificent reflection of glimmering stars at night," he had said.

"There's no question. Their relationship seems deeply spiritual and permanent," Tony remarked on one occasion when commenting about this young couple in their special love for each other.

"A wholly positive spirit and much encouragement, as well," affirmed Lucien. He could not disguise the anxiety his words provoked in him whenever he tried to describe his special feelings about Azúcar to his closest friends.

"Lucien, it's clear that you are delirious with love for Azúcar; act on those feelings now or you'll never know true love," urged one of his friends.

Lucien was definitiely feeling what Azúcar was feeling genuine desire to love and be loved uncompromisingly. And perhaps without even realizing it, Lucien was, at the same time, piecing together the entire troublesome and elusive puzzle of childhood reminiscences. "Why is it that when I'm with Azúcar,

I feel that something is pulling me back toward where I was born?" he asked himself constantly. There still remained certain unsolved mysteries and secrets about his birth. With Azúcar and her gentle honesty, Lucien grew more absorbed in irresistible speculations about his disconnection from his past. Both Lucien and Azúcar felt that the element of tenderness and truth, which they shared somehow, connected them to a common, although not as yet comprehensible past. They both felt the need to surrender the collective spirit between them. But surrender to whom? Of course, for Azúcar, her *abuelita* continued to exist in spirit.

For Lucien, on the other hand, there was still the pressing urgency to uncover those long-unresolved questions about exactly who he was . . . and the exact circumstances that had brought about his existence. Little did he suspect at the time that his most powerful talisman would be his new love --Azúcar herself. She was the one who would unlock the door guarding a wealth of mystery . . . and that door lay hidden beneath the protective canopy of tropical intrigue and deception. After years of being enmeshed in doubt, speculation, and puzzlement about his past, Lucien finally had the murky shadows of this uncertainty lifted. Azúcar unlocked the ponderous door, first, with the delivery of the letter from Yvette Origène-Desgraves. Once Lucien had gained completely Azúcar's confidence and trust, he disclosed to her the full contents of that letter.

"Among many other urgent matters discussed, that letter indicated that I am named one of three primary beneficiaries — actually inheriting the largest portion of the estate of Yvette Origène-Desgraves," Lucien revealed. "But the biggest blow came when I learned that both my mother and my paternal grandmother are still living. They're both there still on the Island. I even learned the name of my natural father, a certain Felipe St. Jacques!"

Lucien stared blankly out the window of his apartment in Montreal, where Azúcar was now spending the Canadian Thanksgiving Day holiday. The same crowd from Toronto had been invited, plus one additional couple that lived in the same apartment complex as Lucien. Lucien and Azúcar were alone in the apartment, since Harold and Marcelo and Carlos and Tony had chosen a nearby hotel for accommodations, thus allowing the host couple some desired privacy.

"Lucien, *mi amor*, did you learn the full name of your grandmother?" Azúcar asked. "Or your mother's full name, for that matter?"

"No. Just that one name. Felipe St. Jacques; nothing more."

There were many, many priceless lessons Azúcar, the diligent and intelligently gifted student, would never learn in the university lecture halls. Instead, the truly important lessons were those learned while living with her abuelita and the other elders in the batey at Esperanza Dulce Plantation. The one that undoubtedly left the deepest impact was the lesson about listening quietly, carefully, and fully before trying to reconstruct and link together the dispersed fragments of incomplete and seemingly unconnected recollections from the past.

"*La hierba mala nunca muere*," Doña Fela had taught her granddaughter. "Someday – if you stay here long enough -- you gonna' understand just what *Esperanza Dulce* is all about," Azúcar recalled *abuelita* saying by way of summarizing that particularly memorable lesson . . . ' weeds never die.'

Azúcar thought about all this, reflecting on the legendary, multi-layered intrigue of the relationship between old Mamá Lola and Madame Yvette -- the secret tale that her *abuelita* had whispered to her about the clandestine love affair between Yvette Origène and the handsome mulatto sugarcane cutter named Felipe before Yvette married the elderly, rich planter Maurice Desgraves; the birth of a beautiful baby boy and then the newborn's sudden disappearance to the other side of the Island; the drowning of poor Felipe while attempting to escape the Island for a better life elsewhere. Azúcar carefully connected all the fragments. The earlier, persistently suffocating intrigue of *Esperanza Dulce* dissolved . . . just as the wise old teacher, before she died, had promised it would.

A sharply perceptive Azúcar would uncover later more important details about her own grandparents, Felicidad and Justín Bustamante; their only child, a girl they named Solange, would marry a certain sugarcane worker, a contracted *bracero* named José Ferrand. Solange and José would produce an adorable baby girl whose most unusual complexion was that of coarse, unrefined brown sugar— *"azúcar moreno."* This peculiar coloring of the infant would stay with her throughout her young childhood and adolescence. As an adult in faraway Canada, she displayed this same unique coloring she had carried since birth, only now slightly richer in texture and capturing the attention of practically everybody at Victoria College . . . even given the dynamic multiethnic exoticism on the Toronto campus.

Again, it was Azúcar who unlocked the unanticipated second and final door when she made yet another vital connection. Lola's husband, Alix St. Jacques, was a first cousin to Felicidad, Azúcar's maternal grandmother Doña Fela. In that instant, all the complex pieces of the confusing puzzle suddenly fell magically into place for Azúcar. Everything had been linked. She looked directly into Lucien's large, attentive eyes. "Lucien, I know who your mother and your grandmother are," she said

246

calmly, but with the firm voice of certainty. For the very first time, Lucien's usually penetrating, black, wide-set eyes seemed void of all expression. His long black eyelashes were still. The young attorney was struck with disbelief . . . however much he honored Azúcar's unwavering truthfulness. It was Azúcar who thus revealed to her lover the undeniable truth about his mysterious origins.

VEINTIÚNO

It all seemed so miraculous that here in this magnificent, vibrant metropolis on the shores of Lake Ontario, an unlikely young woman whose past knew only the inhumane perversity of sugarcane culture thousands of miles away in the tropics, was now graduating with honors from the country's illustrious Victoria College. Miss Azúcar Ferrand, bright, talented and stunningly beautiful, was a recently naturalized Canadian citizen and was now prepared to take her rightfully earned place alongside her fellow graduates. They all were accepting the bold challenge to embark upon exciting new careers in a fast-changing, even frightening and often complex modern world. Seemingly so improbable a few short years ago when this timid young woman with the coloring of natural brown sugar had no inkling of a city with the name that sounded like a tropical fruit— "Toronto" . . . to say even less of receiving a university degree.

It seemed improbable also that Miss Azúcar Ferrand, even before the concluding graduation ceremonies, would be the highest achieving fourth-year undergraduate student in the School of Hospitality and Hotel Management. She would be the sole recipient of the coveted internship award with Canada's most prestigious transnational corporation. Miss Ferrand won the opportunity to participate in an exciting, innovative project with high-level company market researchers: conducting feasibility studies to determine the profitability of tourism for corporate investment in the Caribbean. When she learned that the targeted island under study would be the very Island where she was born, and that the company was the same international octopus that employed both Harold and Lucien, Azúcar was in euphoric disbelief. Another miracle or the protective powers of

248

intervention of Mayanèt? *Abuelita* would know even if no one else did. But Azúcar knew to light candles in every niche and corner of her suite of rooms that night after the graduation dinner in her honor. She thanked her loas.

Everyone felt genuinely proud and jubilant about Azúcar's phenomenal triumph, most especially of course, Harold and Marcelo, her two consistently loyal friends and trusted mentors. They had both recognized something truly special in the young and bright Azúcar morenita since the beginning of their chance acquaintance together in the batey.

"You've accomplished the near impossible, Azúcar," Harold said with tears running down his cheeks. "What you've done would certainly fill your dear abuelita's heart with joy if she were alive and with us right now."

"*Pobrecito.* Poor thing . . . little does he realize," Azúcar thought to herself, "that *mi abuelita* is very much with us at this and every moment. She never ever leaves me. My loas are also always present."

"*Mi querida,* you are the undeniable envy of everybody ...and I do mean everybody... on campus at Victoria College," Marcelo remarked gleefully. "Everybody is happy for you. Nobody else could possibly have had to jump higher hurdles than you did, my dear." Marcelo, then Harold, planted a loving kiss on either side of their protégée's cheeks.

All the guests present at the intimate celebration at the townhouse saluted Azúcar in a round of champagne toasts. The toasts sparked an extra special tone of elation when a prideful Lucien, with dear Azúcar at his side, formally announced their marriage engagement in the presence of a supportive circle of very intimate friends. There wasn't the slightest register of surprise on the faces of anyone, only the unrestrained outburst of delight. Everybody had been solidly convinced before this afternoon of the solid intensity of the love between the couple.

249

"Well, it's about time," one voice cried out.

"Tell us what took you so long, Lucien?" another friend wanted to know, but almost in jest and again readily sharing the sentiment of everyone present. *Qu'est-ce qu'il y a ?* What's the matter ? So, what were you hesitating for?" Without exception, everyone regarded the marriage as inevitable. The room erupted spontaneously into doubly congratulatory toasts, cheers, and well wishes for the beaming couple. Azúcar felt even more convinced than ever that powerful forces genuinely committed to her happiness now and in the future were protecting her. No date had been set for the wedding, and so, for the moment, Azúcar could concentrate on the task immediately ahead of her. Returning to the Island of her birth, but a return trip marked by a set of dramatically unique circumstances, produced mixed emotions.

On the one hand, an irritating sense of reluctance clouded her hopes; but on the other hand, an enchanting surge of excitement within her memory teased her. An array of opposing recollections about her formative years spent in the Island bounced about in her mind. While it was true that Harold was totally happy for Azúcar's stellar achievement in winning the much sought-after internship, he was quite uneasy about the assignment with his former employer. Harold carefully outlined his position.

" Listen to me carefully; the main reason that I decided to resign from the company was due precisely to my sincere opposition to the company's blatant abuse of human rights and their arrogant violation of international environmental policies which, in my opinion, still reflect a decadent colonial mentality of operations strategy. Wherever I was assigned, from the Philippines to Brazil to the Caribbean, I saw this overbearing arrogance that deliberately placed less developed countries in an increasingly dependent, subservient relationship with the developed countries which led to large-scale, gross interference in their economic, social and political lives and a consequent loss of actual sovereignty." Harold eagerly continued his thoughtful, heart-felt polemic. "I continued witnessing how the company, in its very slick, sophisticated and steady take-over of the Island's old *ingenios*, conducts itself no differently from the traditional slave-plantation mentality. The absentee ownership, the barbarity of the capataz system, the ruthless exploitation of the hundreds upon hundreds of helpless contract *braceros* and the expatriation of profits; the whole scenario is quite humiliating and despicable."

At this point, Marcelo joined the discussion. "So, Harold, are you suggesting that the company will also dominate the growth of the tourist industry once the feasibility studies show that there is indeed significant market potential for tourism in the Island?"

"Absolutely, by all means," replied Harold. He felt certain that once tourism proved profitable, the company would have firm, dominant control of the new industry's vital arteries. "Management, marketing, and transportation . . . all these related operations . . . total control by the greedy tentacles of the far-reaching transnational corporation," Harold said angrily, spreading his fingers, extending them outward and grasping at some imaginary prey— much as an octopus would do.

"I personally see tourism as a possible future benefit or, at worst, a necessary evil," Azúcar interrupted in her own defense. "Carlos and Tony both obviously agree, too. They're equally excited about my assignment. I've arranged for their agency to get the contract for the ad campaign. They stand to make a fortune."

"But enough of this tiresome rhetoric," Lucien interjected. "Let's just all be happy for Azúcar's golden opportunity to gain invaluable first-hand field experience and to broaden her career

251

options. Becoming involved in this project will be great for her."
Although he chose not to reveal his honest thoughts on the
subject, Lucien was completely sold on the idea of the
desperately needed transformation of the Island. He saw change
as vitally necessary.

"The Island simply has got to move from an isolated
relic of barbaric feudalism to an open, modern, and hopefully
profitable commodity tailored for a smart, international crowd
of pleasure seekers. Just imagine! The Island would be a perfect
haven for fun and frolic."

Secretly, Lucien envisioned the potential for a booming tourist
industry, and in short measure easily becoming the single most
important source of revenue not just for the Island, but also for
the entire region. He also saw a handsome opportunity and a
secure spot for both Azúcar and himself in the larger scheme of
economic development relative to the corporation's future, very
pivotal role in the Island. But he had yet to share his vision with
Azúcar.

It was during this stolen moment of contemplated bliss and
explosive excitement that an important, unexpected letter for
Lucien arrived . . . it was from the Island. The contents of the
letter left a strange and sudden sadness pressed upon his heart.
This time the sender of the letter identified a respected law firm
in one of the Island's regional capitals, located about two hours
from the vicinity of *Esperanza Dulce*. The letter announced the
death of Lucien's mother, Madame Yvette Origène-Desgraves.
Lucien felt an immediately disheartening grief and the sense of
heavy loss; the words themselves had a strange ring for him . . .
"the death of your mother." At the same time, he felt an odd
yearning for a native Island almost as unknown to him as the
secretly-guarded circumstance of his birth. With equal force
there was the unknown strangeness throughout all these years

of a mother who had just died. . . in a faraway island. There was a frantic rush of questions without yielding any answers "Exactly what was my mother like? What did she look like? Why didn't I have a picture of her? Was she a beautiful lady? A beautiful spirit? What things made her laugh or cry? What were her dreams? Did she ever think about me? Why did she abandon me?" Lucien feared a tremendous anguish, even disillusionment . . . of some unanticipated dread that could possibly devastate his suddenly frail spirit. "Why am I afraid of some painful, perhaps merciless truth about my mother . . . a truth that might conceivably shatter my sense of who I am? Why hadn't anyone in all these years told me about my mother? Where was the sense in all this? And my father? Who was Felipe St. Jacques? And what about my grandmother, Lola St. Jacques, still living in that Island? Why has the truth remained so mysteriously hidden?" These questions prompted an agonizing churning in the pit of Lucien's stomach. Lucien did not like these feelings.

He sat silently in the chair at the desk in his study, immune to the disturbance of normally heavy traffic outside in the street below at this hour. The letter, which he read several times over for verification of its actual existence, was almost soaked with his own wet tears, profuse and steady. He tried wiping them away, but they remained stubbornly in evidence. He remained motionless, in near disbelief that he was holding in his nervous hands a letter telling him that his mother had died in her sleep thousands of miles away in a stately mansion in the sugar-producing tropics.

Both he and his fiancée were deeply affected by the letter. It was difficult for them to talk about the many implications of the sorrowful event. Lucien's spirit was heavily tormented. Azúcar tried searching for explanations; she wished hard that her *abuelita* would guide the young, inexperienced couple toward the light. Groping about in agonizing darkness was tortuous. Perhaps Doña Fela did appear to her granddaughter, offering to the young university graduate a piece of illuminating wisdom that agelessness possesses exclusively, and certainly not found in classroom text books.

"*M'hijita*, remember that death is a new beginnin' and it is the journey into the sacred world of the spirits," whispered the voice that seemed to come through the walls of Azúcar's bedroom suite. "Life is a gift of givin' and you must accept it as it is given; you now know what you must do." The voice concluded in the same hushed tones in which it began. The walls then fell silent; enough had been said and Azúcar had heard clearly and without error every utterance. "*Mi abuelita* has given me the explanation I was looking for to stop Lucien's torment," she thought.

After the necessary arrangements were made, Harold drove Azúcar, Lucien, and Marcelo to the airport from which the departing trio would travel together back to the Island. Azúcar and Lucien would attend the funeral of Madame Origène-Desgraves. Lucien would also see his grandmother. Azúcar, by coincidence, would also begin her internship assignment with the company's important project. Marcelo would see his institutionalized mother for what he knew would be for the last time.

Funeral services for Yvette were not the extravagantly pompous social event that would ordinarily have befitted a member of her anachronous breed. As especially those individuals belonging to this class were made to realize, Yvette was not one for senseless ostentation on any level. Her devoted husband for many years, Maurice Desgraves, had died a few years prior, so the funeral arrangements had been made by the executors of her estate. It was the very same law firm that had contacted Lucien in Toronto to notify him of his mother's passing. Yvette's wishes were honored in every detail for an unceremonious memorial tribute at the local chapel. A traditional Requiem Mass was eliminated altogether, causing a muffled stir among the region's social élite. But again, Yvette herself had stipulated beforehand this omission. Even her children Blanchette and Pierre-Raymón were impotent in their protests.

"I simply won't allow it while grave social and economic injustices persist," she had said in anticipation of this moment. "The sad truth is that many of the people I care about deeply wouldn't be permitted to attend. So, why should I encourage the hypocrisy?"

During the service at the chapel, nobody recognized Lucien and Azúcar . . . at least, nobody from the upper social echelon. Blancette and her twin girls Cécile and Chelaine, now teenage girls at the lyceum, sat in the family pews located at the front of the century-old, elegant sandstone, colonial chapel. Blanchette's gambling-addictive brother Pierre-Raymón, now with his fourth wife, sat alongside other surviving Origène-Desgraves family members: Yvette's spinster, but rakish sister Nanette, who had been living a hedonistic existence for the past few years on the Italian Riviera with an endless stream of young, international gigolos; a number of cousins, widowed aunts, and a few of the blank-eyed offspring from Pierre-Raymón's previous, failed marriages. Glaringly absent were all the Montalvos except Miguel and Manolo with their respective families.

"*Mami, por Dios,* who on earth is that beautiful, stunningly dressed lady sitting there next to that really handsome man? I don't think they're from around here." Chelaine whispered with undisguised excitement to her solemn mother. Blanchette had also noticed slyly the striking couple.

"I haven't the slightest idea, *preciosa*," Blanchette replied disappointedly, also in a whisper. "I've never seen them before either." She tried hard to appear nonchalant, but failed. She was burning with curiosity to learn the identity of this exquisitely strange couple that had come to her mother's funeral service. She soon found out.

But it was Mamá Lola, before anyone else, who first recognized and knew rather instinctively who the couple was. She began to stare with concentrated intensity at the tiny flames of the votive candles arranged neatly on the altar. Her heart seemed to prepare to leap through her chest and into the flames of the candles. Seeing the handsome Lucien sitting there, tall and distinguished in the chapel, for Mamá Lola, was like seeing life itself reawaken. Seeing him was like a violent burst of light produced by a flint struck sharply inside a pitch-black tomb. Before now, since Doña Fela's death, Azúcar's departure, and Madame Yvette's death, old Mamá Lola had been battling merely to exist between the night and the night. She didn't even know how she recognized her grandson, Lucien St. Jacques . . . she just knew. She also knew that the elegant young lady seated at his side was Azúcar Ferrand, always inquisitive, always attentive little granddaughter of her friend Felicidad . . . Azúcar *morenita*.

The funeral was held at about mid-morning, after most everyone except sugarcane workers had had their leisurely breakfast. But by mid-afternoon, just after the blistering rays of the tropical sun announced its indomitable presence, news of Azúcar's surprise return to the area had spread like ravaging flames in an abandoned mangrove thicket. One might easily have thought that even the birds and winged insects had an additional role besides their usually supportive one in pollination efforts.

"*Por loh santo*," how you know it's really her for sure?" asked one curious soul from *Esperanza Dulce*. "She been gone so long, it be hard to recognize her."

"*Coño*. It was her eyes, I tell you; they never lie," replied the listener, who swore on his mother's grave that he had been an eyewitness to Azúcar's arrival at the chapel. "She had them same big round eyes and that same funny color skin." Although the description was accurate, the commentary in itself had, of course, not been true.

All the sugarcane workers were restricted to their usually assigned tasks in the fields or in the mill house at the scheduled hour of the funeral services. And besides, the estate managers had not sanctioned any leave day away from the fields to commemorate Yvette's passing. The name Yvette Origène-Desgraves had long become an anathema to all the region's sugarcane plantation administrators because of her unyielding campaigns against the sugar industry's human rights abuses and exploitation of the *braceros*.

By late afternoon when the news finally reached the ancient ears of Don Anselmo, Miss Azúcar Ferrand had already arrived by car, which she herself drove, at the front gates of the batey. Crowds of adults and children alike gathered, with individuals wondering aloud if the rumors they had heard were true. Yes, Azúcar had indeed returned, but few people in the mounting crowd recognized her; she had been so totally transformed beyond anything anyone remotely imagined. And who was the handsome stranger seated beside her in the car? The anxiety and intrigue heightened to dramatic proportions as the car inched its way down the central artery of the batey, running parallel to the open trough, moving slowly in the direction of Don Anselmo's cabin. Lucien had accompanied Azúcar for many reasons; there was really no doubt that his most prominent motive was to reconnect with his grandmother, Mamá Lola — but in truth, to attempt a spiritual and emotional reconnection with everything he regarded as his stolen . . . and nearly forgotten past.

"Azúcar, my dearest, you have been tremendously helpful in preparing me for this moment," he proclaimed to his fiancée as she parked the jeep as close as possible to the cabin. "I'm also filled with a lot of heavy emotion," she confessed. "Don't think for a second, Lucien, that coming back to this place hasn't been difficult for me. All the horrible memories. All the awful nightmares. I've tried very hard to erase it all. Mostly, I've been able to do just that . . . thanks to you, Lucien, my love."

"But, Azúcar, according to what you've told me, there were some pleasant, even beautiful moments you spent here," Lucien said, interrupting her negative portrait. "You can't altogether forget about that."

The crowd had swollen to quite a sizable one, with over-zealous individuals pressing against one another to get a better glimpse of the 'celebrity couple' that had come to the batey, and more particularly, as it was rumored, to visit old Don Anselmo. Rumors also circulated that the young woman with the "strange coloring" was none other than Azúcar, Doña Fela's little *azúcar morenita*, who had left some years ago. Slowly, Azúcar began recognizing ever so many familiar faces from her childhood days . . . one after another . . . faces that had matured rapidly with time and circumstance . . . faces that were no longer the scrawny, innocent baby faces of years long faded . . . faces that slowly brought back memories of all sorts. But Azúcar also saw that these were the many faces of a youthful hardness --- all contemporaries of Azúcar, to be sure, but faces made unjustly old and leathery by hour upon hour of unbelievably tortuous labor among the unsympathetic sugarcane stalks . . . and under an always scorching sun. She also remembered how unrelenting the heat was here now that she was living in Canada.

She recognized five of the six strapping, grown children of one-eyed Clementina and Tomás . . . Tomás, Jr. was not among them. Clementina and Tomás were much older now, but still formed part of the work crew in the fields. The same was also true for longneck Teresa and her husband Cirio; their grown children were at their parents' side, yelling Azúcar's name. More than one young woman, head wrapped in colorful bandanas, were holding infants in their cuddled arms. All three of the widow Lolita's handsome sons, now with families of their own, stood among the crowd outside Don Anselmo's cabin.

"I wonder if their poor mother still sits slumped over in the doorway of her cabin, waiting for her proud Haitian to return from the fields?" Azúcar thought to herself. The thought was agonizing. "Pobre mujer. Pitiful woman."

Mamá Lola was the first to approach the visiting couple. With streaks of tears falling upon her puffy old cheeks, she embraced Azúcar, whispered the young woman's name, and held her tightly to her sagging bosoms. The older woman then moved away and just stood there with a broad smile on her illuminating, wet face. She stretched open her beckoning arms.

"Mon petit-fils. My grandson," was all she said.

Lucien, also crying heavy tears of joy, replied with a simple, "Ma grand-mère." Their tight embrace was overwhelmingly emotional for the reunited couple.

Supported by a naturally twisted, caoba wood walking stick, an ancient figure was standing assertively in the darkened doorway of the tiny cabin. His old skin still glistened with the same piercing blackness he had worn years ago. His short, unruly beard was now white like bleached sugar. Totally bald and much thinner now, but with the same sharp, all-seeing, all-knowing, close-set eyes, he was unmistakable. He glared out at the excited crowd. It seemed as if all the residents of the batey had assembled for some special event. A quick smile emerged from behind a near toothless mouth. The beautiful, young female visitor, whose skin had the strange, rich coloring of unrefined, raw sugar walked proudly towards the welcoming village elder. They embraced respectfully.

"My dear Don Anselmo, have you been well?" the young woman asked. "How very often I have thought about you." The sincerity in her voice lingered heavily on everyone's ears.

"*Ay, mi azúcar morenita,* you grown into a beautiful young woman," Anselmo replied. "I just know your intelligence match your radiant beauty many times over. After all, *m'hijita,* you Felicidad's granddaughter." The old man was visibly filled with overwhelming pride.

Mamá Lola, thanks to the benevolence of the deceased Yvette Origène-Desgraves, was now living in the abandoned bungalow once scandalously occupied by the young Canadian "sugar doctor" and the capataz's oddball youngest son. That was where the party of four spent the duration of their visit together. The property was one of many that had belonged to Yvette, who, well before her death, decided to indicate in her will that the bungalow would be left to her secret friend of many years, Mamá Lola. For the first time in his life, Lucien was able to sample his grandmother's unrivaled island cuisine, along with long-concealed family secrets and intrigues. Mamá Lola remembered everything and revealed even more during the course of her grandson's visit. No remaining doors remained locked for Lucien regarding his birth and related circumstances, events and individuals associated with his early existence.

"It was Madame who took care of everything," Mamá Lola disclosed in detail to her anxious grandson. "Your early years on the other side of the Island . . . those nice folks who took care of you . . . that fine lyceum you went to . . . even your college education in Canada; Madame was responsible for it all. She always said it was the least she could do. Her conscience tormented her over all these years . . . not being able to see and love you like she wanted to. I prayed to the sacred ancestors every night for them to protect you. And, *mon petit-fils*, look how you turned out. You do us all proud; you have brought me special joy." She planted a delicate kiss on her grandson's forehead. I love you, boy." They embraced tightly while tears flowed freely down Lucien's very masculine cheeks.

After eating a truly unforgettably delicious island meal --- prepared by the capable hands of Mamá Lola -- everyone then listened to Azúcar as she shared the nature of the investigations that the intelligent, eager young university graduate would be conducting on the Island. Don Anselmo sat listening pensively. He simply stared at the floor for a long while, saying nothing immediately . . . just staring. He pounded the floor softly with his twisted walking stick. He finally spoke; his close-set eyes narrowed into two long and piercing slits.

"*Coño*. For too many years I dare to count, one *zafra* after another, I saw the overloaded oxcarts wobble alone the path on the way to the mill. I knew that I would live to see those old oxcarts come to a final halt. *Coño*. No more stinkin' back-breakin' cuttin' *maldito* cane stalks under the hungry sun . . . or suffocatin' in the boiler house . . . No more paper-thin, razor-sharp leaves slashin' ugly welts across your legs . . . or the misplaced whacks of the vicious machete . . . instead of the swift low blows to the tough stalks, the blows accident'lly gashin' the ankles an' shins or heels of the stooped-over cutters. No more brutal *capataz* hollerin' senseless orders for us workers to speed up our pace . . . snapping' his *maldito látigo* over our heads as he rode by on his evil-eyed horse." With his alert eyes wide open, Don Anselmo continued offering his vision of things to come. "But I see the end of sugar announcin' somethin' newer for the greedy bosses, but not necessarily sweeter for the poor, already miserable, exploited souls who remain here enslaved in this shit-hole."

Little doubt remained that Don Anselmo's keen perceptions held everyone's attention, especially that of Lucien, who of course really did not know this mystical old man. Mamá Lola's newly reconnected grandson, while now possessing much needed answers and explanations about his past and present, was nevertheless legitimately captivated by the visions of this ancient plantation relic. The trance was broken by a sudden loud and unexpected knock on the front door of the bungalow. Mamá Lola went to see who was there.

"*Por todo loh santo.* Look who's here!" she announced in disbelief, but with genuine cheerfulness. "What a real pleasure to see you, *m'hijo.* Come in an' join us."

"Tomás, Jr!" Azúcar almost shouted, losing all composure as she saw her childhood friend come into the room. She practically leaped from her chair in excitement.

"*Buen día,* Azúcar!" Tomás, Jr. said, exchanging the exuberant greeting. Only Don Anselmo and Mamá Lola recognized Tomás, Jr.'s female companion. Azúcar had left the Island well before knowing even casually the young woman standing at the side of her childhood pal. Both her slender arms were locked protectively into his, suggesting immediately a certain level of mutual intimacy. But it was highly unlikely that the two young women would even have met under any previous circumstances.

Tomás, Jr., the eldest son of Clementina and Tomás, Sr., had evolved into an intelligent, maturely alert, and handsome young man who was strongly determined not to remain among the miserable souls trapped at *Esperanza Dulce*. Driven by a cancerous restlessness that was eating away inside him since a long time ago, the young man had decided boldly to embark upon a meaningful life for himself far from the shit-infested batey and brutalizing sugarcane. From an early age he had never permitted himself to be seduced by the sweetness of sugarcane; he somehow realized that there was something more to life . . . something better waiting for him. Tomás, Jr. also never forgot what he had heard Estimé, Lolita's beautiful Haitian, say many times.

"*Dèyè mon gen mon* ... "Beyond the mountain, there are also other people (another world)." He politely introduced his shy companion to Azúcar and Lucien. Azúcar in turn introduced her fiancé to Tomás, Jr. Everybody waited to meet the young woman with him.

"Azúcar, please meet the woman who's goin' to be my wife, Cécile Montalvo," Tomás, Jr. declared firmly like a man who knew well ahead precisely what he wanted to say at any given moment.

"Azúcar Ferrand. I'm truly delighted to make your acquaintance," a poised Azúcar offered with an instant smile, extending her hand graciously to Cécile Montalvo, who had definitely inherited her father's dark, attractive features: deep-set, large dark eyes, long, flashy, almost flirtatious eyelashes;

shiny, curly black hair that had to be constantly swept off her lovely face and tucked behind her ears. Her complexion was trigueño, unlike her twin sister's golden wheat coloring and light features — which clearly were traces of their mother. Cécile had her maternal grandmother's graceful Origène-Desgraves bearing, but wore it with reluctance or perhaps shyness . . . much like her uncle Marcelo.

"Cécile Montalvo; I'm so thrilled to finally meet you, Azúcar. Tomás has talked about you so often and with such fondness that I feel that you and I have already met." Tomás, Jr. had insisted that she not refer to him in the juvenile manner with "Junior" attached to his name – and this was not intended as any disrespect for his father, whom Tomás, Jr. loved dearly. Cécile, although somewhat shy, but with an open face, was genuine— also immediately likeable, not offering the slightest trace of a social standing that, on the Island, would normally be characterized by a traditional and immediate or automatic disdain for individuals perceived as "below her class ranking." Rather, her smile was large and conveyed warmth. Everyone present felt this genuineness.

If Azúcar was completely stunned, no one noticed. She had thoroughly learned that sophisticated tactic of convincing dissimulation. Harold and Marcelo would be extremely proud of their stellar pupil who navigated expertly this truly awkward moment. Azúcar Ferrand was well versed in the art of disguising or concealing her true feelings, and she found nothing deceitful about this art. In fact, the acquired skill actually proved helpful on a number of occasions. This was certainly one such occasion upon which concealment was the more prudent response. Azúcar thought to herself, "What would be the point of raising the ugly and unwanted monster of anger and indignation at the innocent Tomás, Jr. for the audacity to introduce her to the daughter of the monster who had brutally raped her so many years ago?" No, it would prove nothing and, really, such a display of crassness would be well out of character for Azúcar. She had most assuredly moved beyond such level of destructive small- mindedness.

Although Azúcar was unaware of the fact, Tomás, Jr. had never shared with his intended wife the horrible experiences that his childhood friend Azúcar *morenita* had suffered at the hands of his would-have-been father-in-law. In reality, much of the fiendish behavior of Cécile's long-deceased father, Mario Montalvo, had been very carefully concealed from the twins Cécile and Chelaine. Their mother, Blanchette, along with every other member of both sides of the family--- the Montalvos and the Origène-Desgraves--- had been successful in protecting the twins from the potentially damaging truth of their father's life. Even the precise circumstances of his death had been twisted and reinvented to satisfy the personal motives of Blanchette Montalvo. The persuasiveness and power of money and status reigned supreme in determining what would be regarded as truth.

"I can truthfully say that I am only vaguely aware of who your dear mother is. Doña Blanchette Montalvo?" volunteered Azúcar in a tone of feigned uncertainly. She blatantly lied, of course. "And I believe you also have a sister?" Azúcar did not dare disclose the additional fact of knowing who the young woman's paternal grandfather was, the sadistic and much hated capataz at *Esperanza Dulce,* Diego Montalvo. Nor did she mention knowing most intimately Cècile's Uncle Marcelo. The twins had also been thoroughly shielded from the scandal and thus had not the slightest notion that it was this very same Azúcar who had fled to Canada with their *"tío maricón."*

"Yes, that's quite correct," responded the shy Cécile. "I have a twin sister . . . Chelaine. "And yes, it's perfectly true; Tomás, Jr. and I are going to be married . . . but also without the blessing of the Montalvos, I might add. And believe me, we don't care and we certainly don't need their blessings. We love each other so much and that's all that matters to us."

Although she was amicable, Cécile was slowly uncovering her guarded personal thoughts to the long-time friends of her future husband. Tomás, Jr. supplied the awaited explanation for the startled listeners, but rather as though they were not present.

"Cécile and I are elopin' to Cuba, where we hope to start a new life together. She is the true love of my life; I love her more than life itself." The testimony was strong and deliberate. Cécile, still clinging tightly onto his powerful arm, learned toward him and kissed him fully on his sensual lips. Tomás, Jr. continued his proud monologue.

"Azúcar, like everybody else, I too heard that you had returned. I wanted to see you before we left. I also wanted you to know how much your bold departure inspired me. You were always my hope . . . my hope and determination to also leave this unbearable place that has caused so much sorrow. There's no future for any of us here. You, Azúcar, proved that for me. But even long before that, when Lolita's sweetly innocent and proud Haitian, Estimé, was viciously murdered by unknown killers, I realized as a very young boy how totally meaningless and doomed life here was."

More intentional concealment. Tomás, Jr. again had decided very judiciously to hide from Cécile the painfully difficult fact that he, along with every other soul in the batey, knew exactly who the beast was that had murdered his Haitian neighbor many years ago . . . Cécile's wicked father, Mario.

"Azúcar, please take these; they are for you."

Tomás, Jr. then handed his friend two folded envelopes, one much yellowed with age. This one contained the crumbled, handwritten note that Azúcar had written to Tomás, Jr. years ago, just prior to her departure from the Island. It was the same note he had held in his hands as he stood behind his mother's cabin . . . crying in shameful frustration and bitter anger because at the time he had never learned how to read. He had watched the plane flying high in the sky that day . . . watching through tearful eyes. The other envelope contained a fresher-looking letter, also handwritten, but one he himself had written in reply to Azúcar's outdated note. Tomás, Jr. stood proudly, appearing almost taller, more erect in a strange sense. Much had happened in his circumstance since Azúcar's departure; one very important change had been his learning to read and write. Azúcar would read the notes later, once in the sanctity of her private thoughts.

"Azúcar, like you, I am a totally changed human bein'. From your spirit and also from Doña Fela's spirit has come a whole new meanin' of life that both Cécile and I see as continuin' to exist beyond and in spite of the senseless cruelty, the ugliness, the misery and exploitation we all been flounderin' in here in this hogshit emptiness. Cécile and I have decided this is no place to raise our baby that we goin' to have."

Smiling broadly and with fatherly pride, he leaned forward and gently caressed Cécile's unnoticeably pregnant stomach. All the listeners remained without words, merely staring at the young, seemingly mismatched couple. In actuality, though, they were exceedingly compatible in every regard . . . and perhaps most importantly, very much in love. Joy radiated from both their faces. It was true; Azúcar realized the transformation in Tomás, Jr. She was moved to joyfully sweet tears. She approached him and gently kissed her friend on his cheek; she then kissed Cécile on her soft cheek as well.

"Sincerely, I wish the three of you all the happiness you so richly deserve. I hope life for you will be more meaningful in a completely new society, far away from here. And Cécile, please know that I am especially happy about your baby. You two obviously share so much love for each other that your baby is guaranteed to come into a love-filled and safe home. *Qué se vayan bien y qué todos los santos les acompañen y protejan siempre.* May you go in peace and may all the saints accompany and protect you always."

No question remained; the afternoon had been filled with boundless joy and unrivaled surprise and discovery for everybody.

VEINTIDÓS

Lucien, by now, was saturated with a vast array of transforming images –some of which were rather confusion-- and information about this strange place of his birth, as well as about the many different characters in the drama that would subsequently unfold during his stay in the Island. He no longer felt the frantic desire to inquire about his origins; the torment of all his unanswered questions finally disappeared. The only unfinished item was the potential intrigue surrounding the reading of the last will and testament of Yvette Origène-Desgraves. Would there be more discoveries?

"I will have to return to Montreal immediately after the reading of my mother's will," he announced to Azúcar. "There's nothing more for me to do here. Besides, I've got to get back to what I'm certain is a stockpile of waiting assignments. My sweet, will you be all right with that?"

"Of course, Lucien, *mi amor*," Azúcar assured him. "My investigations should take maybe two months at the most. After that, I'm out of here, too. So, I'll join you soon enough. I can do the summary reports from Toronto. *No hay problema.*"

The appointed day of the reading of the will arrived amidst surprising rumors, conjectures, and anxieties . . . at least for the curiosity-seekers, of which there was an abundance. The largest surprise came from the mysterious appearance of the refined, stunningly exotic couple rumored to have traveled all the way from Canada. However, to everyone's astonishment, the pair, despite their obvious cosmopolitan air, gave off a "tropical-ness" upon closer inspection. There was something about their coloring: a familiar, recognizable "something " that could not be easily concealed. Everybody noticed this. "*Es la mancha del plátano*" . . . "the stamp of the plantain," someone explained quite simply. In other words, as it was said: no matter how far a person strays from the Island, or regardless for how long, that individual still carries an indeligible stamp, *"la mancha,"* that forever identifies and reveals one's Island roots. It was true.

"*Mami, pero mira.* Look! That's the same strange lady who came to *abuela's* funeral at the chapel! Who is she?" Chelaine nearly shouted to Blanchette when both mother and daughter saw Azúcar and Lucien, arm-in-arm, entering the reception area of the attorney's office where Yvette's will was to be read. Blanchette's brother Pierre-Raymón also turned in the direction of the reception area and spied the arriving pair. But quite frankly, Blanchette and Pierre-Raymón could not be counted among the number of bewildered spectators. Rather, they formed part of the cast of principal characters in the drama since they were named two of the primary benefactors of their mother's estate. If there was any question of lingering mystery, at least for these two anxious siblings, it was about the probable size of their respective shares of the inheritance.

Moreover, for brother and sister alike there was little doubt about the actual identities of the two strangers who had appeared at the chapel. Blanchette had learned much sooner than her brother; her information sources always proved most reliable and she seemed never to have the occasion to question the accuracy of such information. It therefore remained for this last elusive piece of the haunting puzzle to fit neatly and convincingly into its proper slot.

"*Mi hermano,* you do realize who they are, don't you?" Blanchette inquired of her brother, whispering in his ear so that Chelaine would not overhear. "That's the little *puta* from the *batey* Mario was accused of brutalizing," Mario's widow said scornfully. "Of course, everybody knew what really happened that day. It's been so long ago, I hardly recognized the black whore . . . she's quite grown now, as you can see, and is apparently living the high life from the way she's dressed."

"The girl is truly a beauty, I must admit," Pierre-Raymón added with a rakish smirk. "I understand she left for Canada? That young stud with her couldn't be who I think it is, could he?"

"Yes, he most certainly is. There's just no doubt about it . . . her handsome companion is our real concern, *hermano*," Blanchette finally admitted in a now agitated tone to her brother. "For your information, that's the bastard child our dear mother gave shameful birth to before she married *papá.*"

Over the years, Blanchette —most advantageously for her own personal aims— had managed with measured skillfulness to siphon from a variety of unlikely sources otherwise concealed information, bases of rumor or gossip, and fragments of local history not intended in the least for public consumption. Blanchette's clandestine enterprise with her mother-in-law Cristiana Montalvo had long been a natural conduit for such titillating trivia and, in a most secret fashion, served as Blanchette's main source of entertainment as well.

The formality of proper introductions completed, the legal proceedings got underway at once. There was a thick layer of tension oozing from every crevice of the large, ornate room, located on the second floor of the restored, fortress-like structure, preserved from the Island's colonial period. The presiding probate judge sat at the center position of a long, Spanish colonial-styled table placed at the front of the room. A huge circulating ceiling fan provided the necessary cooling for the stuffy, museum-like room. On either side of the solemn-looking judge was an attorney representing the principal parties in attendance— the named beneficiaries. A double row of high-backed chairs, also Spanish colonial-styled, separated by an aisle, faced the ominously long table. It was as though the chief officer of the historically intimidating Spanish Inquisition were about to begin his dreadful sentencing. Seated together on one side of the aisle were Lucien, his grandmother Mamá Lola, and his fiancée Azúcar, leaving the second row empty.

Seated directly across the aisle from them seemed to be a small tribe of assorted members: Blanchette; one of her twin daughters Chelaine . . . a pregnant Cécile was already en route with her sweetheart Tomás, Jr. to Cuba, perhaps there by now; Pierre-Raymón and his current wife; Yvette Origène-Desgrave's only sister Nanette, with an unknown, handsome young male escort who didn't seem to understand nor care about the intrigue presently developing; several cousins and distant relatives from the Origène-Degraves clan; and a few top local administrators from the *Esperanza Dulce* operation; these last non-relatives had received special notices requesting their presence for some undisclosed reason. (The requests were more than courtesy invitations.) The mere fact of their being present seemed to perturb the *Esperanza Dulce* administrators in the worst way; total boredom had registered on their faces since arriving.

The judge read Yvette's will with the same degree of solemnity that characterized his whole presence. The reading was deliberate and precise . . . no areas were left overlooked or glossed over hurriedly. The entire session ended before anyone on either side of the aisle had a chance to become comfortable in the stiff, high-backed wooden chairs without padding or cushions of any kind. But what truly left everybody's mouth gaping open like the mouths of an entire school of snarled sea bass was the manner in which a shrewd Yvette Origène-Desgraves had bequeathed her earthly possessions. Moreover, there were intricately woven clauses that laced her shocking will with the legal impossibility for anyone to contest it or tamper with her final wishes in any fashion. She had triumphed even from the tomb! Another one of Life's many ironies!

"Being of unquestionably fit mind and lucid reason, I, Yvette Origène-Desgraves . . . " was the carefully crafted manner in which Yvette introduced her plan. Then she moved swiftly to the core of the matter. Her reckless and irresponsible son Pierre-Raymón received a considerable sum to allow for the repayment of his rather embarrassing, accumulated debts and for the costs of the education of his cluster of blank-eyed, seemingly unhappy children. He also received the clear title and deed to one of the smaller properties, including the comfortably large house where he now lived with his brood. Yvette herself had successfully managed to have all her grandchildren live with her son, despite his three failed marriages. But in all, it seemed certain that Pierre-Raymón would finally be forced to use his own ingenuity in finding gainful employment, rather than continue his existence as a pathetically hopeless sycophant.

Yvette's daughter Blanchette, whom Yvette considered a cautious, conservative type, received a larger cash amount in redeemable certificates and stocks, along with the manor house, stables, livestock and grounds. Yvette's twin granddaughters, her acknowledged favorites since their celebrated birth, each received appreciable amounts of cash. Cécile's share would eventually reach her in Cuba several months later, in time to greet the joyous arrival of the new baby boy, whom the parents named Estimé --- the bitter irony of honoring the memory of the murdered Haitian cane cutter was not lost on Tomás, Jr.

"Lolita, the spirit of your proud Haitian has at last been avenged," he whispered inaudibly to no one but himself.

The estate executors had conducted an extensive search to locate Cécile's whereabouts. It was learned that Chelaine's twin sister had married a certain Tomás Polanco, Jr., who had once been a sugarcane cutter at *Esperanza Dulce* Plantation and was now a naturalized Cuban citizen. He was employed with the new revolutionary government's communications bureau. Mamá Lola's right of ownership to the bungalow she presently occupied was made official by a stipulation in her secret friend's will. Yvette's sister Nanette received a fair quantity of valued house furnishings and jewelry, as did several cousins, nieces, and nephews, although on a much more modest scale.

Then the first bomb exploded . . . without warning.

"To my long-abandoned, first-born, rightful heir, my son Lucien St. Jacques, I do bequeath all my real estate holdings, consisting of four manor houses and grounds located on the other side of the Island, across the Artibonito River. I also do bequeath to my beloved son Lucien my entire portfolio of Canadian investment holdings . . . "

As mouths of the other stunned listeners flopped open, only Lucien sat stoically, immobile, revealing his honest and unblemished gratitude by a lone tear that not even Azúcar seated immediately next to him saw swell up and lodge in the corner of one eye. Lucien was overpowered by what was his rightful inheritance, although he did not perceive it as such and certainly wasn't expecting the lion's share of his deceased mother's estate. His grandmother, smiling victoriously but without uttering a word nor even looking in his direction, clasped his smooth hand in hers and patted it softly with her free hand. He held onto the wrinkled, tired old hand as tightly as he could.

"*En nombre de todo loh santo*, I thank you, Mayanèt," was all that Mamá Lola could managed to say to herself – between exuberant tears. She then closed her eyes. Azúcar, like the others across the aisle from her, merely sat in total numbness . . . although she wanted impulsively to scream out loud for sheer joy.

"*Pero, por Dios, mamá,* how could you do such a cruel and idiotic thing?" Blanchette thought almost aloud. Pierre-Raymón heard his sister's thoughts exactly and with the same sense of disbelief.

"*Coño.* Can you believe what the sly old bitch did?" he yelled loudly with naked bitterness. He didn't care who among his assembled tribal members had heard his invective hurled angrily against his deceased mother. He felt certain that they all shared the same sentiment, but simply chose to conceal it. Only Yvette's worldly sister Nanette revealed a different response. Hers was a delayed outburst of laughter muddied with revulsion and irony simultaneously. Everyone present looked in the direction of the uncanny laughter.

"Has she completely lost her mind?" her relatives all wondered.

"Cac-cac-cac-ca-ca," Nanette cackled loud like a satisfied old crow. "*C'est délicieux vraiment, ma cher soeur.* It's truly delicious, my dear sister. Indeed, you fucked everybody royally. We all got exactly what we deserved . . . exactly what you intended us to have. Delicious! *Merci,* my dear Yvette. Cac-cac-ca-ca-ca!"

Nanette's handsome young gigolo was now altogether baffled and didn't quite know what to make of his elderly, but extremely generous playmate. Nanette had deliberately brought him along to the reading to taunt the other judgmental clan members, who, for years, had never ceased ridiculing her behavior, which they regarded as scandalous and obscene, but which Nanette herself considered the ultimate relish of hedonism. She was truly savoring this moment.

A second bomb exploded. The unanticipated explosion threw Azúcar into a colossal tailspin of confusion. She tried to maintain her appearance of calmness. She did not succeed. Disbelief placed the first stain on the genuineness of her poise. The solemn-face Inquisitor from a decadent past read from the document with the emptiness of a pontiff.

. . . . "To Azúcar Solange Ferrand, whose bold spirit and strength of character symbolize the collective pain and long-suffering of an entire exploited community condemned to the toil of sugarcane cultivation, I do bequeath my stock portfolio in the *Esperanza Dulce Central* . . ."

Blanchette Origène-Desgraves y Montalvo was dangerously close to a loud shriek, so heavy was her outrage and shock. Her brother Pierre-Raymón had been so thoroughly humiliated and wounded earlier during the day's proceedings, he felt in all earnest, that he decided not to bear any further torture. A rising fury bore its way through his entire body. He jumped up, knocking over the heavy, wooden Spanish colonial chair, and bolted out of the room, but not before yelling at the top of his lungs:

"*Coño*! Fuck all this! Fuck all of you! Especially fuck you Yvette Origène-Desgraves! Fuck you straight to hell, *mamá*!"

Everyone was suddenly in a dilemma: being torn between looking at an irate Pierre-Raymón who had just cursed his dead mother's soul or remaining transfixed by what they had heard the judge read from Yvette's will . . . "my stock portfolio in the *Esperanza Dulce Central*." The words resonated a striking chorus of echoes in the ears of the stunned listeners seated in the high-backed Spanish colonial chairs in the restored museum. However, absolutely no one was prepared for this thunderous bombshell. The entire story about *Esperanza Dulce* remained shrouded in carefully crafted mystique and intrigue . . . lies, myth, half-truths, ingenious concealment at its best. A Canadian transnational corporation, very quietly and very gradually had bought out the powerful, local family consortium-owned sugar company holdings in the Island. *Esperanza Dulce* Plantation, in more modern times referred to as a *"Central"* because of the self-contained inclusion of all the related components in the operations, was the largest estate and thus a crucial key player in the sugar consortium. During that period of transition, the beginnings of a radical union linked to one of the Island's most potentially threatening revolutionary political parties was crushed by the reactionary government; all the union's top leaders were murdered. The quiet, seemingly mild-mannered, but truly Machiavellian-cunning of Maurice Desgraves played a major role in the scheme to sell the *ingenio* to the Canadian corporation and also was directly linked to the murders. But over the years, there was nothing that could ever be substantiated with solid evidence. Significant increases in the United States sugar quota granted to the Island helped the corporation's profits — as well as real power-- in tremendous fashion. Desgraves himself became extremely rich and powerful.

Although *Esperanza Dulce* had passed from the hands of a prominent Island family of sugarcane planters and into the octopus-like tentacles of the international conglomerate based in Canada, a handsome portion of corporate stock remained silently in the iron-clad grip of the planter-family with deeply anchored roots dating back to pre-independence days: the Origène-Desgraves. Yvette and her sister Nanette were the last immediate survivors of that family. Yvette's late husband Maurice Desgraves had been a distant cousin. So, Nanette's sardonic laughing reflected the reality of this long, effectively concealed historical irony.

Undoubtedly more than anyone else present, Azúcar was not able at first to grasp the fullest measure of this unimaginable bequeath. As she sat passively, trying somehow to replay in her mind what she had heard the executor read, she clutched Lucien's strong arm as if bracing herself against a potentially injurious fall, even though she was seated. She felt her head whirling with dizziness. But before she could recover, the third and final bomb rounded out the already splintering afternoon of bombardment. The overhead ceiling fan, offering no relief from the mounting heat, now seemed like another mere ornate fixture in this restored colonial fortress.

"*Por el amor de todos los espíritus.* For the love of all the ancestral spirits," Azúcar trembled and cried in silence, but motionlessly and tearlessly. "I know with all my heart, *abuelita,* that you continue to guide me as Mayanèt continues to protect me." She felt the immediate warmth and power of Doña Fela sitting alongside her in the room. Such was the second stain on Azúcar's otherwise unflappable composure.

The suspense engulfing the presence of the adminstrators from *Esperanza Dulce* ended when the judge concluded the reading of the will with the next and final section. It was directed specifically to the impatient officials, tortured mercilessly by the sweltering heat as the hours wore on. The headlines in all the leading newspapers across the Island, including those on the other side of the river, the next morning revealed the phenomenal enormity of Yvette's wealth and influence.

"*El Gobierno construirá acueductos en los bateyes del país para beneficiar a miles de familias que carecen del servicio de agua potable.*" The Government will build aqueducts in the *batays* throughout the country, benefiting thousands of families that lack the service of drinkable water.

"*Qué carajo ehta pasando por acá*? What the hell's goin' on here?" Don Anselmo muttered when he heard the startling news. "This is pure revolution! Seem like the power of old Yvette's money struck terror in the mountain like a burst of dynamite. That sly ol' fox Yvette fixed 'em real good!" He chuckled heartily, smoking on his pipe, pondering the irony of the one individual who had become a powerful, secret ally after all. Unbeknownst to him, Yvette, of course, had been so for a long time.

It was true. In time, it became apparent that with death, and accompanied by the enormously persuasive powers of her money, Yvette finally was able to bring about the almost total eradication of major wrongs in the Island's sugar industry. Especially noticeable was the gradual disappearance of many of the more blatant exploitative practices of the industry against the powerless *braceros*. Also, there was the slow demise of the substandard living conditions of sugarcane laborers. All the indignations and injustices against which Yvette had long battled until the moment of her death began to crumble. Perhaps in secret pain and misery, she too had suffered her own guilt, as well as that of the horrendous wrongdoing committed by her husband-cousin Maurice in the name of profit. Perhaps that was part of the reason she had fought so adamantly to correct the defective scales of her circumstance.

Since the reading of the will and its shocking stipulations, Azúcar had a great amount of work to accomplish — both business-related and personal—well   before leaving the Island for Toronto. Lucien had already left and so she was quick to realize the return of the normal rhythms and routines of Island monotony. Thus, she dedicated herself almost around the clock to non-stop involvement in her important company assignment, the tourism feasibility studies. Fortunately for her, Marcelo was still there with her; his earnest companionship would be a veritable lifesaver since Lucien's necessary departure. Being with Mamá Lola and Marcelo in the comfortable bungalow, Azúcar recalled pleasantly sweet memories of an earlier period wherein she had spent there with her compassionate mentors.

As for Marcelo, he had visited his mother at the sanatorium on several occasions now. He admitted sadly, but quite honestly to himself that these would be the last few times he would be with her. Cristiana Montalvo had been diagnosed with a kind of seriously incapacitating senile dementia.

"*Pobre mamá*," Marcelo sighed heavily, explaining to his friend Azúcar his most recent and deeply painful visit with his mother, who in all honesty did not even recognize her youngest and gentlest offspring. "There's not much hope left for her. The doctors now say her overall condition is progressive and incurable. Her mind is gradually ceasing to function even normally. And the mental deterioration can be expected to advance more rapidly in a very short time."

"*Ay*, Marcelo, *Lo siento*. I'm so sorry. Your suffering has been long, but now will come to an end," Azúcar offered in efforts to console her already-grieving companion.

The intoxicating aroma of sweet island jasmine and fragrant tamarind permeated the seductive evening air. The skies were empty of clouds, signaling that the tropical rains would soon come. Those evening birds still awake flaunted their stamina like flamboyant jewels as they each made their way from the lure of one delicately perfumed blossom to the very next, just before total darkness obliterated everything. Seated together on the veranda of Mamá Lola's impeccably tidy bungalow, Azúcar and Marcelo were sharing precious final moments on the Island before they both had to return to the bustle of Toronto. During the few days remaining before her departure, Azúcar indulged herself with thoughts about her future happiness and success. Although she was somewhat apprehensive, she was still radiant with satisfaction. Brimming with an excited impatience, she revealed her concerns to her trusted friend.

"*Querido Marcelo*, I am really worried," she began. "There's no escaping the inevitable. Tourism is definitely coming to the Island. My analyses are conclusive even at this point in the investigations. Tourism is going to change everything here."

"No need to worry yourself," Marcelo replied. "Change is deceptive; often no real change occurs, only the cleverly disguised appearance of change. That's really what I believe your tourism is going to be . . . Believe me, Azúcar, just the appearance of change. I'm thinking about the question of the continuous need for cheap labor, for example."

"I'm not quite sure I understand what you mean, Marcelo. Don't you think it really is market potential rather than available, cheap labor that is the primary reason for investing in overseas markets?" asked Azúcar.

"Absolutely not!" answered her friend. "I don't believe for one minute that tourism is going to be the panacea for most of the economic and social ills here. An unavoidable necessity, perhaps. But who will gain the greatest share of the profits? . . . As if I had to ask."

"That's also what's troubling to Don Anselmo," Azúcar confessed. She had had several lengthy discussions with the wise old Anselmo about this very topic. "He is warning that the Island, in the name of this new potential giant of an industry, is selling itself into a new slavery. He also says that it's going to be worse than sugarcane ever was! *Ay, mi santa abuelita*, Marcelo, am I doing the correct thing with these studies? Is it a good thing I'm doing for the company? . . . For the Island?"

It was at this dramatic climax in the provocative dialogue between the two friends that Marcelo reached back to the days of his formative university studies, in philosophy class, to provide Azúcar with a needed response to the agonizing question she had posed. "In his classic work, *Beyond Good and*

Evil, Friedrich Nietzsche, I remember, talks about the social dynamic as being that of Nature. In Nietzsche's vision, a view which I share —and Harold is fully aware of my thinking on this point— life is essentially appropriation: suppression, severity, injury, conquest of the strange, among other elements. And if I recall correctly, exploitation for Nietzsche does not belong to a depraved, imperfect or primitive society. No, *señor!* It belongs to the nature of the living being as a primary organic function. Exploitation is a consequence of the intrinsic will to power, which is precisely the will to life itself. Therefore, *mi querida* Azúcar, the relation between the two opposing groups is practically symbiotic." Marcelo continued his dramatic delivery to an alert friend.

"Oh, Dear God, how I've seen this relationship all my life! *Esperanza Dulce*, my sadistic father, *el capataz*, my monster of a brother Mario, my other pathetic, murdering brothers Miguel and Manolo . . . *la maldita caña*, the whole fuckin' sugarcane industry are all perfectly valid examples of this very exploitation that Nietzsche talks about. And that, *querida*, is how I see your tourism ultimately overwhelming our Island."

Azúcar listened thoughtfully, reflecting as heavily as the tropical noonday sun upon what Marcelo had said with such total commitment and passion. She couldn't remember the last time when she had acted as catalyst to ignite Marcelo's explosion of profound thought. Perhaps the last such thorny issue had arisen years ago with the decision to leave the Island altogether and resettle in Canada with Harold and Marcelo. Now, Azúcar found herself uncannily thrust into the midst of monumental decisions that were destined to transform forever her native Island . . . Don Anselmo's Island . . . her *abuelita's* Island . . . Estimé's Island . . . Felipe St. Jacques's Island . . . the

Island's entire population. She knew beyond doubt that the results of her investigations and analyses of the feasibility of her corporation's taking important initiatives to market tourism in the Island would determine the future course of a nation, perhaps the whole region. Azúcar pleaded silently to Doña Fela for guidance. "*Mi querida abuelita*, I beg you in the name of all the sacred and ancient spirits to place my unknowing and unsteady feet on the certain path of wisdom and truth."

The Canadian-bound jet was filled currently with business class passengers eager to return to their corporate offices, but a consistently alert Azúcar easily envisioned future commercial flights that would be filled with tourists. Her Montreal-based company would be aggressive in its campaign, in its most seductive forms imaginable, to attract international pleasure-seekers to this region of frolic and fun . . . a veritable tourist paradise. She felt confident that as a result of her meticulous investigations, the company could definitely spearhead the movement of transnational corporations to dominate the new, untested industry. The bulk of the tourism plants in the Island such as hotels, casinos, airlines, cruise ships, and travel agencies would be under the exclusive control of corporations like hers. The possibilities and profits seemed endless. But Azúcar, not surprisingly, did not display a smile of any personal satisfaction that, under other circumstances, might readily have accompanied such a magnificent victory. Rather, she had a certain look of sadness, or perhaps more correctly, foreboding, on her face as she sat pensively in the first class seat next to a sleeping Marcelo.

As the jet carrying the two expatriates back to their new home soared overhead, down below sat a sorrowful Don Anselmo. He cocked his ancient head skyward as he heard the jet's roaring engines, thinking about Azúcar and the youngest

Montalvo boy . . . little Azúcar *morenita* from the batey and Marcelo, the genteel, 'odd' son of the brutish plantation capataz.

"What a pair those two! *Agua pasada no mueve molina,"* Anselmo directed to the skies. "Water gone by don't move the mill." He had known all along since Azúcar's return to the Island that she would be permanently transformed. Returning would not be the same for her or for anyone else as when she left initially. Like an ancient soothsayer, this wise village elder, in his own inimitable way, had said it all before to his comrade Mamá Lola. He had seen it coming . . . this new industry that would replace sugarcane!

"*Ay carajo*! Yet still another form of *maldita* exploitation! Sugarcane and African slavery come hand-'n- hand at the same time to these islands . . . both of 'um comin' from somewhere else far away. Now, it's the same ol' wicked thing repeatin' itself . . . only this time with a totally new name, that's all. Restructurin' the whole goddamn society is the true solution, not jus' reformin' it." He instinctively looked toward his long-time companion, waiting for her to say something. Mamá Lola was prepared with her response.

"But Mayanèt is a very tough lady . . . very tough indeed. Now is her time to come and protect us all again. *Ou ka konprann mwen*? You can understand me, no?"

EPÍLOGO

Mayanèt in all her toughness truly dealt the supreme vengeance. A heavy dosage of irony, as well, accompanied her planned actions. Don Anselmo lived to witness some rather startling transformations. He could not say with absolute certainty that Mayanèt had nothing to do with mounting global constraints and increased world financial opportunities. Or that the Island's United States sugar quota, which for quite a long time allowed for most of its sugar to be sold at higher-than-world market prices, plummeted so sharply. Who could say for sure that Mayanèt's vengeance didn't cause the production of European sugar beets (of all things!), provoking in turn a sudden shift from importing to exporting sugar by European producers? Did Mayanèt have a scheming hand in the creation of corn syrup and other artificial sweeteners, and in sinister fashion, ultimately replacing *la maldita caña*? Don Anselmo suspected that Mayanèt was probably smiling with special satisfaction at these turns of events.

Don Anselmo saw sweeping changes that were absolutely mind-boggling: broad acres of sugarcane fields being converted into luxurious tourist enclaves with spacious hotels and casinos, golf courses, horse racing tracks; *bateyes* becoming the official residences for the multitudes of the cheap labor supply for the resorts and related trades; hordes of international travelers seeking hedonistic pleasures, often at the expense of victimizing the local populace, including even under-aged children; the Government leasing airplanes and high-speed, air-conditioned buses to provide rapid transit service for significant increases in arriving tourists; the newly-constructed hotels dumping their sewage and other gross disposables into the nearby rivers and streams; the local ecosystems becoming severely threatened by gradual deterioration; more and more "outsiders" investing

285

heavily in various local enterprises, thereby hastening the erosion of autonomous economic development.

There was not the slightest measure of doubt on the part of anyone: *Esperanza Dulce,* with all its now- revealed, agonizing secrets from a turbulent past, experienced an unbelievable transformation in every sense. The century-old, exceedingly profitable sugarcane plantation became an exclusively luxurious, modern resort complex, renamed "Canaveral Resort," which in the Anglicization of the word -- rather ironically-- means "sugarcane fields." It was a completely walled community (or fortress?) with its own armed 24-hour operating security force. The complex featured a private airport; two olympic-sized swimming pools; several five-star gourmet restaurants and cafés; a European-styled health spa; up-scale duty-free gift shops, two glitzy nightclubs, and an impressive assortment of state-of-the art recreational facilities. A regional resort management office, a subsidiary of a globally powerful and highly respected transnational corporation that was based in Canada, administered Canaveral.

The management team was under the skillfull directorship of the talented, ambitious and young Mrs. Azúcar Ferrand St. Jacques, who operated out of her Montreal office headquarters. Under her aggressive marketing strategies, annual profits for the corporation soared to record levels. Overall exchange earnings from the Island's tourism revenues grew steadily from about $220 million in one year to over $800 million in just a three-year period, with net corporate earnings of more than half that amount. By the end of a five-year period, because of tourism's dazzling success and sugar's miserable decline, net foreign exchange earning from tourism easily surpassed those from any remaining sugar exports. Mrs. Ferrand St. Jacques was credited singularly for this spectacular performance of the corporation's stock. She was rewarded quite handsomely, including a handful of lucrative company perks.

Chelaine Montalvo went to New York to study journalism and stayed there to become a noted free lance writer for several of the city's prominent magazines; Blanchette Montalvo was rumored to be the "Madame" behind a lucrative, call-girl/boy escort service associated with several of the Island's more fashionabe hotels; two of Clementina's and Tomás's sons each worked their way up to the prized position of croupier at the casino tables at Canaveral; the unbelievably cruel, sadistic capataz, Diego Montalvo --- to nobody's surprise – became a miserable and embittered old drunkard, having been severely injured in a mill accident. Nobody expressed any pity. But most workers doubted whether it really was an accident when a huge boiler kettle broke loose from its ancient frame, falling on the capataz's leg, crushing it and causing the leg to be amputated. Also, one entire side of Diego's body was horribly disfigured by the scalding sugar liquid . . . *la maldita caña!*

Sarafina, much older of course, but still the big-bosomed, saucy-tongued, irreverent character, became Diego's willing concubine . . . "to escape the damn fields," she shrewdly calculated. She literally took care of old Diego in every sense: bathing him, feeding him, administering his medications, changing his prosthetic, and of course, servicing his sexual appetite, which was never curbed by his unfortunate "accident."

"Our Mayanèt is truly a tough lady!" Don Anselmo reminded himself.

It had been one of those typically sultry, oppressive days of unrelenting tropical heat so familiar to everyone; guests at Canaveral were satisfactorily ensconced in the pampered protection of air-conditioned lounges and recreation areas or under the shielded comfort of enormous umbrellas, sun-screens, sunglasses and extraordinarily wide, floppy straw hats favored by tourists. Don Anselmo was standing at the rear entry door for deliveries to the kitchen of one of the gourmet restaurants where all three of the widow Lolita's now-grown children worked. The oldest son, named Toussaint, was head chef and consistently provided succulent daily meals to the long-time friend of his deceased father Estimé. To Don Anselmo, these meals were always a culinary treat, the likes of which the old former cane cutter had never before known, but truly delighted in discoverying.

Don Anselmo's excited attention to the prepared meal was cut short when one of the kitchen crew suddenly yelled, "A new load arrivin'. Wonder where they comin' from this time?" Don Anselmo's curiosity led him, along with several others of the kitchen workers, to the kitchen door in order to see this "new load." What he and the others saw took the old man back many, many years to the first time he had witnessed this familiar, but tragic sight. A huge, canvas-covered, government issue infantry transport truck pulled up behind a squat, boxed-shaped, red brick building that was located just a few yards from the hotel's massive kitchen. Two chubby, pasty-faced White men, both dressed in standard khaki uniforms, each holding a clipboard, stood at the back of the truck; they were directing the slow, careful descent of the truck's cargo. From behind closed flaps emerged one individual after another, men and women, slowly climbing down out of the sinking, dark bowels that was the truck's holding pen for dozens of newly recruited workers at Canaveral. Only this time, the arrivals weren't destined for the resort's namesake. Instead, this new load was bound for the miscellaneous tasks comprising the mammoth tourist complex.

As with previous eras of sugarcane production, the current period of tourism development required successive waves of staggering numbers of cheap labor to fuel the industry, assuring an efficiently running and maintained operation. The labor supply, again as in the plantation era, routinely came from throughout the Caribbean and arrived in cycles; the crews were regularly shifted and rotated from one resort locale to another as needed around the region. Don Anselmo stood alone, motionless, almost mesmerized by the illusive feeling of *déjà vu* as he watched the expressionless souls climb out of the back of the truck. This new load had been transported from across the Island or from across the river and beyond to furnish the vitally needed manual labor and upon landing were parceled out to every conceivable work area of the resort operation. Each worker displayed prominently, attached to his or her uniform's lapel, a sizable metal tag that had, not the name, but instead, a special number that identified the exact point of origin or previous resort where the individual had last worked. The admittedly callous system proved quite efficient
. . . as it had always been.

"Okay now, step lively. Hurry along!" barked impatiently one of the chubby White men holding a clipboard. His companion, wearing thick glasses that constantly slipped from his sweaty nose, checked the large identification number against the columns of numbers on the papers clamped to his clipboard. There was a brown-complexioned local official, also dressed in standard khaki, who served as translator when needed, since many of the "new arrivals" spoke other regional languages and dialects heard around the Caribbean. Don Anselmo was unable to control the open rush of tears cascading down his wrinkled old cheeks; the tears were mixed with rage and sorrow.

"*Coño*. The bastards won't even call out the names of those poor souls; they're just numbers on a fuckin' clipboard. Oh, *mi* Azúcar, *m'hita morenita*, if you only realized what you done! *Maldita caña*! . . . "